SHADOWS OF BUTTERFLIES

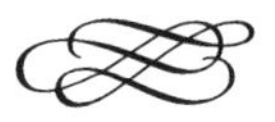

M S TALBOT

Shadows of Butterflies

This is a work of fiction. Names, characters, places, and incidents are products of the author's imagination or are used fictitiously. Any resemblance to actual events, locales, organizations, or persons, living or dead, is entirely coincidental.

ISBN: 9781099605819

ACKNOWLEDGMENTS

To Dawn McMahon, a fellow author for her patience, support, and invaluable advice. To my editor, Brian Schell, for his expertise and calm advice when I was floundering.

With best wishes.
M. Talbot.

For my children and grandchildren, for their unswerving support and unconditional love. Love you all to the moon and back.

CONTENTS

PROLOGUE

Shorehill, a small estate village of mill workers, shopkeepers, and farmers, nestles deep within the folds of the gently sloping green hills of the Darenth Valley and beside the clear, spring-fed waters of the River Darent. Old Mill Lane, a shady country lane, winds down into the village through fragrant bluebell woods and hedgerows awash with wild garlic and cowslip. The soft, mossy banks have fallen away in places, exposing the thickly knotted roots of tall trees whose topmost branches entwine to form a leafy bower high above the lane.

In winter, when the countryside glistens with frost, and the black rooks swoop and caw high in the bare trees, small boys on crudely made sledges hurtle down the snowy lane, screaming in delight. But when the snow drifts begin to thaw, and the river roars and swells, the residents of the village stack sandbags against the front doors and watch the rising levels fearfully. The children hold their breath in hopeful anticipation. If the water inches toward the red mark on the post by the bridge, then the school will be closed until the danger from flooding has passed.

At the bottom of the hill, the rush of the river grows louder, the trees begin to thin, and Shorehill's medieval, humpback bridge comes into view. Old Mill Lane continues down beside the bridge and follows the path of the riverbank to the Maycroft Paper Mill and Riverside, home to the Maycroft family. Across the bridge lies Shorehill Village, where shops and neat cottages mingle comfortably together along the narrow, winding High Street. For generations, the village children have scrambled up onto the ancient bridge that spans the swift-flowing river. They sit together on the sun-warmed stones, dangling grubby, bruised knees over the parapet and lean over to fish with rods of sticks and twine. When farmer Pat O'Donnell leads his giant shires to splash their feathered hooves through the pebbled shallows by the bridge, the children rush to the bridge and lean over to watch the gentle giants. The shires stand quietly resplendent, with faultlessly plaited tails and manes, droplets of water glistening on their velvet flanks. They toss their huge heads and snort water through wide nostrils, and the children squeal with delight.

The old men of the village, the Ancients, meet on the bridge to smoke their pipes, leaning with bony elbows on the pitted and hollowed parapet, gazing with rheumy eyes into the timeless river as it rushes down to the weir. Perhaps they are remembering their far-off youth of never-ending summers and careless childhood games played by the same river. Hazy memories of when they, too, lay under the willows, the sun flickering on upturned faces as they dangled their feet in the cool rushing water.

The tiny village school, with its walled playground, is in the middle of the High Street, and Grace Dove is the much-loved and gentle school-mistress. Willy Dales's butcher's shop is next to Tom Wood the baker, and the general store on the corner of the High Street and Farrow Lane is run by Vera and Jack Barton together with their two spinster daughters. Fern Cottage tea rooms and the village sweet shop are run by the sharp-eyed and watchful Lovett sisters. Jacob Brown, the blacksmith, has his forge and cottage at the end of Farrow Lane. George Dace, the coalman, delivers the coal to the village along with paraffin oil, candles, and lamps. Mick Carey is the landlord of the village pub, the Hop Vine, where he lives with his wife Sylvia and daughter Moira. The village Post Office and newsagents is proudly run with meticulous care by Grace Peabody, the shy, rotund postmistress who lives in two tiny rooms above the post office. At daybreak every morning, Pat O'Donnell, the dairy farmer, delivers the milk to the village, the clank of the churns on the milk float keeping time with the clip-clop of the horses' hooves on the cobbles.

Dr Bill Winter holds a surgery twice a week from his home on the top road and is a familiar figure in his pony and trap trotting through the village to make house calls and visit the remote farms. When money is short, his patients pay in fresh eggs, vegetables from the allotments, meat from the farms, and the occasional bloody partridge or rabbit smuggled in under a coat, much to the consternation of his young wife and the horrified delight of his two small children.

By the bridge where the river runs low on shingled shallows, three neat, whitewashed, thatched cottages sit sedately behind low picket fences. They lean and huddle together, like three old friends in close conversation, the diamond-paned windows glinting under beetling thatched eyebrows that look across the sparkling river to the wooded bank beyond. Grace Dove and her mother Blanche, a retired headmistress, live in Nut Cottage. William Hunter, the Maycroft estate manager and gamekeeper, his wife, Dorothy, and son, Billy, live in Poacher's Cottage. Dorothy and her sister run the village laundry from the back of their mother's cottage, and Billy helps the beaters in the shooting season and patrols the woodland for illegal snares. The third cottage, Meadow Cottage, was home to Ezra and Becky Dawes and their daughter Polly. When Ezra, a mill worker, died of consumption in 1898, Polly went into service with the Maycroft family at Riverside, and her mother, Becky, a lace maker, left the village and went to live with her sister in Sevenoaks.

The acres of meadows around the cottages are a meandering haven of whispering, tall, purple-tipped silver grasses, creamy meadowsweet, lacy cow parsley, and scarlet poppies. In early spring, Pat O'Donnell brings his tractor down to Lower Meadow and cuts the grass back in readiness for the summer fetes, the visiting fun fairs, and family picnics. At the bottom of Lower Meadow, stands an old, disused hay barn, its great doors hanging open on enormous iron hinges. Thin shafts of light quiver through the splintered wood and flicker onto a floor, dusty with corn husks. Thick twists of rope hang from the massive cross beam above the hay loft. A roughly hewn wood ladder is propped up against the hay loft, and broken bales of sweet-smelling hay are stacked in the dim corners of the barn. Once used by the farmer to store his winter feed, it now stands empty, but not unused, because this is where the village children come to play, summer, winter, spring, and autumn, on school holidays, at weekends, and after school, the freedom of the barn and meadow is theirs. In the crystal-cold water of the river, the boys learn to swim and fish for the swift brown trout and slippery eels that dart in and out of the bull rushes and hide among the smooth pebbles on the riverbed. Sometimes, they enlist the girls to make dams using fallen branches and mud from the riverbed. When the sun sets over the ripening cornfield beyond the meadow, and all the jam sandwiches have been eaten, it's time to go home. It is time to reluctantly find hastily abandoned shoes, unroll hitched-up skirts and trousers, shoulder the makeshift fishing rods, and make for home and tea.

As November approaches, the village prepares for the much-awaited annual Guy Fawkes Night bonfire. In a fenced-off corner of the meadow by the river, the excited village children watch in anticipation as the pile of wood and branches grows higher and higher as the night draws closer. Finally, it's November 5th, Guy Fawkes night, and time to run shouting and whooping through the village and into the silvery, mystical meadow, so familiar during the day, but mysterious and shadowy at night. The bonfire is lit, and the flames shoot high into the night sky, lighting the faces of the exited children as they point and shout in delight. It's a night to stay up past bedtime, to toss mouth-watering, hot, roasted chestnuts from hand to hand, and to play tag and ghosts in the dark.

When Irish Tip, the tiny groom from Riverside, sits down by the fire, the children gather round cross-legged and wide-eyed and listen to his cautionary tales. Most have heard Tip's stories before, but when he begins, they are captured by the magic of his soft voice as the flames from the bonfire flicker across his wrinkled face. When an older boy dares to mock, there is a gasp as Tip fixes him with his brilliant dark eyes, wags a bony finger, and, in a soft Irish lilt, warns the culprit that "Pooka" is watching and listening, and the wide-eyed boy is silenced.

In a hushed voice, Tip warns them again of the fairies, watching and waiting in the shadows to cast a spell on the child who wanders into a ring of bluebells. He tells of the May Tree that guards the entrance to the fairy realm, where no child must ever tread, and of the blackthorn, the sacred tree of witches and devils. Lowering his voice even further, so the children lean forward to hear, he whispers, "Remember that November is the month when spirits have the most power. Remember what Tip tells you. Never dance to the sweet music you hear on a faraway hill, for the pipes will call you away from your home and your family, like the golden-haired girl who could not stop dancing until a prince stopped the music and saved her." There is a dramatic pause, and Tip stares into the faces of his mesmerized audience. Then he shakes his head sadly, "But there are many who are not saved, and if you hear the music of the pipes, you may see the poor souls forever dancing and skipping and twirling their endless dance in the moonlight." The children blink, and their parents wait. A collective sigh sweeps through the group as Tip jumps lithely to his feet and with a wave and a flourish, the diminutive Irishman bows low to his audience, tucks his hands into his pockets, and saunters off into the night whistling under his breath. It is time for the cold and weary parents to gather up the over-excited, chattering children and trudge home across the bridge. The smallest sleepy child is carried high on father's shoulders, and the parents hope that Tip's tales will not give the little ones nightmares.

When winter arrives and frost silvers the grass and nips at fingertips, the boys make splintery rafts from fallen branches to skim across the frozen fields. The grass is icy, the mud frozen and hard, but there are girls watching, so when they fall off, the boys rub their bruised elbows and knees but never cry. When the nights are too dark and cold to venture into the meadow or the barn, the children's thoughts turn towards Christmas. Sitting by the fire, and with fingers fervently crossed, they write their letters to Father Christmas, asking for a new book, or a spinning top, maybe a baby doll, and for the boys, a new hoop, a cap gun, or catapult.

In the week before Christmas, Miss Dove gathers the excited children together and marches them across the bridge to St Dominic's to practice carol-singing for the Christmas concert to be attended by proud parents. That week, lessons are abandoned, and the children, with sticky fingers and faces creased in concentration, happily set about making brightly coloured paper chains to decorate the school hall and classroom. A few days before the end of term, the school hall is cleared, ready for the much-awaited Christmas party. The nativity play is rehearsed over and over again, and the major roles of Mary and Joseph are much coveted. Once the three kings have been cast, Miss Dove calls for the sheep to come forward. Being cast as a sheep is far better than being just part of the crowd, even if you have to crawl through the hall on all fours, and so the reluctant sheep hold up their hands. It has been a long-held tradition that the owners of the paper mill, the Maycroft family, donate the finest Christmas tree for the school hall. The tree is grandly decorated with holly, ivy, and mistletoe, green and red ribbons, waxy white candles, and spicy fir cones. The little glass angels and stars which have been treasured and lovingly wrapped away in boxes are gently taken out and unwrapped, eliciting a sigh of pleasure from the lucky child entrusted with the duty of revealing them.

Every year, the tree is hung with brightly coloured paper chains, carefully glued end-to-end by the children. The Misses Lovett make twists of barley sugar for each child. Mr Wood, the baker, brings deliciously-hot mince pies and iced buns, thick with raisins and orange peel. Willy Dales marches in with a tray of his succulent homemade pork pies and another tray of thick, pink ham. Jacob Brown, a gentle giant of a man, makes iron hoops for the boys, and Jack and Vera Barton bring bags of broken biscuits, oranges, and silk hair ribbons for the girls. Beautifully decorated parcels, gifts from the Maycroft family, arrive from Brooms, the big Sevenoaks toy and bookshop, and the excitement is palpable as the familiar red-and-white van trundles over the bridge. Each boy and girl receives a special gift, carefully chosen from the list of wishes written by hopeful children, and placed reverently in the wish box in the school hall. On Christmas Eve, the children gather together in the school hall to receive their special presents, and for the younger children, there is a lucky dip full of small toys and painting books.

Set back from the old bridge and facing out to the river sits a rambling old Vicarage, its flint walls hidden underneath a tangle of blue wisteria. In the pretty gardens, an old cherry tree scatters its blossom like confetti in the wind. Red roses and purple lavender fill the garden, and the sweet fragrance of lavender drifts through the open windows of the Vicarage.

Beside the Vicarage lies St Dominic's, the little 16th century village church, the crenelated bell tower just visible through the ancient yew trees. A thatched lynch-gate shelters beneath the branches of a giant oak tree, and an inscription carved into the gnarled timber beam reads "Deus in Nobis." The slate floor has been swept clear of twigs and dead leaves. Notices of village events, the dates and times of church services, and bell-ringing practice times are written in Annie Wellbeloved's careful hand and pinned neatly around the old timber frame.

A narrow, cobbled path leads from the lynch-gate through the pretty churchyard to St. Dominic's. In the peaceful old graveyard, pitted and lichen-covered gravestones lean wearily to one side, the barely legible inscriptions a reminder of the families who, for generations, have lived and worked in the village. In contrast, with freshly turned earth and posies of bright flowers laid beneath clean white gravestones, the graves of the recently departed are smaller, closer together, and less imposing than their grander neighbours.

Inside the church porch, it is dim and cool, the cracked grey-and-white tessellated floor dips in the centre, worn down over hundreds of years by the steady passage of the faithful. A corbelled stone arch spans the church entrance, and the studded door is heavy and wide with spearhead door hinges and a solid, iron-ring handle. By the side of the porch, a worn flagstone path leads up to a small gate set in a low, mossy wall. The brass plate on the gate simply reads "Maycroft." This is the entrance to the private cemetery for the Maycroft family, mill owners and landowners in Shorehill since the 17th century. Generations of the Maycroft family rest here, small graves marked by a simple, white, stone cross, others by a granite headstone, and some by a recumbent stone effigy.

All rest peacefully under a blanket of daisy-covered grass, some sheltered under the sweeping branches of giant oaks and others under white-blossomed wild cherry trees, but all safe within the old drystone walls.

The only sound to accompany them in their endless sleep is birdsong and the distant gentle music of the rushing river. Set deep in the wall on the north side of the church is a low, arched door with a rusted metal crucifix hammered into the wood. In medieval time, the door on the north wall was known as the "Devil's Door," and it was said to prevent the devil from re-entering the church.

The Rev. Andrew Wellbeloved, on arriving in Shorehill in the summer of 1912, discovered the hidden doorway behind an old cupboard in the vestry. Intrigued, he enlisted the help of Ernie Brown, the verger, and together they pulled the boarding off, revealing the ancient door and the hidden path outside. This little-used path led through a wooded copse and into the back garden of the vicarage, and despite the fact he had to bend almost double to get through the door, Andrew loved his peaceful stroll home through the woods. It was a good time for Andrew to reflect on a busy day, and if he was late for his evening meal, Annie Wellbeloved knew where to find him, leaning up against a tree with his eyes closed; a peaceful smile on his face. It was Andrew's claim that he composed his best sermons in his leafy hideaway.

On the west wall, beneath a lovely stained-glass window depicting St Francis of Assisi nursing a newborn lamb, an old wooden bench faces the setting sun. The seat is hollowed and smooth, the curled arm rests are worn and shiny, and the simple inscription carved on the backrest reads "Rest in the Arms of the Angels." Opposite the bench, set apart from the family graves and almost hidden under the low-hanging branches of a wild cherry tree, is a single memorial encircled by a delicate metal filigree fence. Artfully crafted within the finely worked metal, tiny birds appear to flutter, and a golden butterfly, breathtakingly beautiful, glitters in the centre of the latched gate. Sweet-smelling chamomile grass carpets the ground, and in the centre stands a simple two-tier white marble plinth.

On the top plinth is an exquisite bronze statuette of a girl child, her two plump arms balancing a small bowl on the tips of her fingers, whilst a hovering butterfly trembles on the brim. The tiny girl, captured in a moment in time, is no more than five or six years old, her thick, bronze curls are piled in a cluster on top of her head and caught in a daisy chain around her delicate ears. Her head is turned, and she is looking down, entranced at a butterfly that has settled on her elbow. The sculptor has caught the very essence of her childlike innocence in her delighted smile and the sweep of her lashes on rounded dimpled cheeks. Her dress falls away in soft folds down to where two tiny feet peep out from under the hem, and she is standing barefoot in a circle of daisies. The misty sunbeams that slant through the blossom-heavy branches touch lightly on the girl's bronze curls and glance on the brass plaques highlighting their sombre dedication:

IN SACRED MEMORY OF
ESTELLE MAYCROFT - NEE GRIEVES-CROFT
AUGUST 4TH 1877 - APRIL 15TH 1912 -
TRAGICALLY LOST ON THE TITANIC
BELOVED WIFE OF HENRY MAYCROFT
LOVING MOTHER TO JAMES MAYCROFT

IN SACRED MEMORY OF
HENRY MAYCROFT
OCTOBER 10TH 1870 - APRIL 15TH 1912
TRAGICALLY LOST ON THE TITANIC
CHERISHED HUSBAND OF ESTELLE MAYCROFT
DEVOTED FATHER TO JAMES MAYCROFT

Hidden away and sheltered within this verdant valley, Shorehill is a world away from the crime, the teeming, filthy streets, the disease, and the grinding poverty of the overcrowded towns and cities. But like all communities, Shorehill has endured heartbreak and sorrow, as well as joy, hope, and laughter.

In April 1912, an unthinkable tragedy rocked the village. In its wake, it was to reveal carefully concealed secrets known only to a few and shared by none, and some secrets remained untold for decades, but a far greater tragedy was waiting in the wings, and this way of life, unchanged for generations, was about to end. 1913 was to be the last summer of peace for four terrible years, not just for sleepy Shorehill, but for the rest of Great Britain and beyond.

THE MAYCROFT FAMILY

Bernard and Henry Maycroft inherited the Maycroft Paper Mill and the Maycroft Estate in the spring of 1889. Their parents, Edward and Mabel Maycroft, on an ill-fated trip to visit relatives in Bradford, were caught up in a sudden smallpox epidemic. The alarmed couple, who were hastily planning to return home without delay, sadly succumbed to the virulent disease and died within days of each other. Edward and Mabel Maycroft had been rather dull and somewhat narrow-minded parents, but they were hard-working, conscientious individuals, and both were unswerving in their commitment to the village and to the welfare of their employees and tenant farmers. Like his ancestors before him, Edward Maycroft was always aware that the life of the village depended not just on the Maycroft Paper Mill, but on the sprawling estate farms, and he considered it his duty to ensure that both the mill and the farms prospered.

At the time of Edward and Mabel's sudden departure from this world, Henry Maycroft was just nineteen, and Bernard, ten years his senior. Henry, their younger son, was exceptionally handsome, just over six feet in height, broad shouldered, with an unruly mop of fair hair and thick-lashed, piercing, ice-blue eyes and was also possessed of a devastating charm.

Coming to his dour parents late in life, Henry was both a bewildering surprise and a complete mystery to them both. After leaving his boarding school, Henry idled through a couple of terms at Eton, suddenly appearing one Christmas announcing airily that, "Eton College is not for me after all, Pa."

Edward Maycroft, after a short and heated discussion with the Principle at Eton College, accepted that Henry had been sacked, together with another student, and from that day forward, Edward refused to discuss the mysterious circumstances of Henry's sudden dismissal, even with his confused and distressed wife.

Bernard Maycroft was two inches shorter than his younger brother, dark haired and slender, with soft, brown eyes and a gentle smile, and in times of stress, like their late father, he had inherited a slight stammer that surfaced when he was nervous. From an early age, Bernard had been fascinated by the workings of the mill and the entire process of paper-making. He listened avidly to his father as he repeatedly told the boys about their ancestors and the history of the mill and the village and how Shorehill had prospered when the railway came to the village in 1860.

With Edward's approval and secret delight, Bernard, although a good scholar, had also decided that Eton was not for him, stating that he would prefer to spend his time in the mill working side-by-side with his father. Bernard's enthusiasm and commitment to his chosen path even earned grudging praise from Cedric, the surly mill foreman.

Bernard, after recovering from the shock of his parent's sudden death, decided not to employ a general manager to run the mill as the family solicitor had advised. Bernard was confident that with Cedric's help and guidance, together with the ever-loyal work force, he would be able to take over the management and running of the mill. The outlying tenanted farms, however, presented more of a problem. Silas Brook, the elderly Maycroft estate manager, was already reaching retirement age when he heard the news that Edward Maycroft had died and took the opportunity to announce his own retirement.

Bernard was clearly worried, and knowing that he himself had little experience of estate management, decided that, as Henry was both an excellent shot and huntsman, he should step into Silas's shoes. Henry, however, had recoiled in horror when Bernard broached the subject, and despite Bernard promising hopefully that Silas would be willing to stay on for a while, Henry was adamant in his refusal.

A disappointed Bernard paid a visit to Poacher's Cottage to seek Silas's advice on where to find an experienced manager to replace him. Whilst sitting peacefully in the old countryman's garden enjoying a cider and listening to the honeybees busy in the tree above Silas's precious hives, Bernard explained his dilemma. When he reached the point in the conversation about approaching Henry about the estate manager's job, old Silas took his pipe from his mouth, threw back his grizzled grey head, and gave a great guffaw of laughter. "Master Henry!" he spluttered. "He be no good, Mr Bernard," and shook his head. "Sorry, sir, but that young dandy might look strong, but he be as weak as a kitten and lazy with it."

Bernard looked astonished and slightly affronted, but before he could reply, Silas carried on. "Now don't you worry about all that, Mr Bernard. My nephew, young William, will fit the bill just right. You wait and see!"

After a long and serious talk with Bernard about his family duties, Henry made a half-hearted attempt to take more of an interest in the busy paper mill, but after watching Henry stroll around looking bored and generally annoying the short-tempered Cedric, Bernard realised that he had to reach a compromise.

Henry, he decided, would be better served using his considerable charm visiting their existing London customers and securing more orders for Maycroft's fine hand-crafted paper. Putting forward his idea to Henry over dinner, Bernard was not at all surprised that a delighted Henry, with eyes shining, agreed wholeheartedly.

Henry immediately set about contacting a distant cousin who had recently inherited a town house in Park Crescent overlooking Regents Park. As it so happened, the cousin, Reginald, spent most of his time in Europe as an importer of fine wines and was more than happy for Henry to keep an eye on the house in his absence. In the autumn of 1887, Henry, with bags packed and standing ready in the cavernous, damp, dark hall of Riverside, the family home, had looked the benevolent Bernard straight in the eye, given him a bear hug and a dazzling smile, and left for the bright lights of London. He paused just once at the door and patted Bernard on the back, "Just you wait Bernie old boy, I will return with a whole packet of new orders, I promise."

Bernard had never resented Henry's obvious lack of interest in the family business, and to Henry's delight, and against the family solicitor's stern warning, Bernard agreed that Henry could draw a monthly allowance whilst he settled in London. It was only when Henry admitted to overspending and had to ask for an advance on the next month's allowance, that Bernard took him to task, telling him sternly to get on with finding new customers. Henry, taking these warnings in good humour, used his London connections and his effortless charm to secure appointments with several London paper merchants and stationers.

Despite Henry's scant knowledge of the intricate art of paper making and the complex workings of the mill, by using his easy confidence and ready wit, he regularly secured new orders. So, when Henry journeyed back to Shorehill, triumphantly flourishing a batch of new orders, Bernard was delighted and satisfied that his instincts about Henry had been right.

This arrangement appeared to suit both brothers, as neither Henry nor Bernard seemed in a rush to secure a wife. Bernard was quite content to live a bachelor life at Riverside and oversee the running of the mill and the estate. When asked by a hopeful spinster sister of a family friend, he had replied, laughingly, "I am far too busy to look for a wife, and anyway, I would make a dreadful husband."

Henry, with no intention to wed, was thoroughly enjoying his busy life in London, and was a regular visitor in the clubs and theatres and was an oft-invited guest to all the numerous London parties. When he did return to Shorehill for the annual shoots and the Boxing Day Hunt, he was always accompanied by a group of carelessly elegant young men and beautiful but vacuous girls. For the next ten years, little changed. Henry continued his life in London with the occasional duty visit to Riverside, whilst Bernard remained as committed as ever to the running of the mill and the Maycroft estate.

However, in the summer of 1897, the year of Queen Victoria's Diamond Jubilee, a forthcoming visit to Royal Ascot was about to alter the pattern of both brothers' lives forever. For this was the summer when Estelle Grieves-Croft danced and sang her way into Henry Maycroft's life.

ESTELLE GRIEVES-CROFT

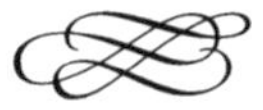

Early on the morning of June 15th, 1897, Henry Maycroft was standing on the platform at Paddington Station with a group of excited friends, eagerly waiting to board the train to transport them down to Windsor for their annual pilgrimage to Royal Ascot. Royal Ascot was a racing event eagerly awaited every year by Henry and his friends, but this year was different to any other, for Queen Victoria was celebrating her Diamond Jubilee, sixty years on the English throne, and England was caught up in a fever of excitement and patriotism. Towns, cities, and villages planned to celebrate the occasion with street parties, processions, fetes, bonfires, and fireworks.

George Grieves-Croft, Henry's closest and oldest friend, had, through his father's influence, secured entrance to the Royal Enclosure at Ascot for a small group of close friends, of which Henry was one. Lord Archibald Grieves-Croft, director of an elite firm of naval architects, and his wife, Lady Rose Grieves-Croft, were in Paris on holiday with their daughter, Estelle, and George's wife, Jenny.

Giving in to his son's pleas and assurance that "I will make sure that everyone behaves themselves, Pa, I promise," Lord Archie reluctantly agreed to allow George and a group of his friends to stay at Grieves Manor for Royal Ascot meetings.

Lord Archie and Lady Rose, handsome, well connected, and wealthy, travelled extensively throughout Europe for most of the summer months, staying for some weeks in their Paris home. In their absence, Grieves Manor, nestling in the tiny Berkshire hamlet of Hope Green, was run with military efficiency by their devoted butler, Brent, and Mrs Brent, the ever present and efficient housekeeper. Patrick, the head groom and coachman, tended the stables with the help of several grooms. His brother, the water bailiff, ensured that the lakes were kept well stocked for the fishing parties. The head gardener and his apprentices tended the beautiful gardens, and the estate manager supervised the regular, well-organised shoots held in the acres of private woodland.

Henry looked thoughtfully at the excited group of friends milling around the platform and noticed with some regret that their numbers had diminished even more since last year. So many of his chums had married and settled down, and now George Grieves-Croft, who had always been a willing ally, was also a family man.

A little over two years ago, George had married his childhood sweetheart, Lady Jenny Fitzwilliam, and shortly afterwards, Jenny had presented an astonished George with large and lusty twin boys. When an exhausted Jenny had been advised to rest, she heeded the doctor's advice and accompanied her in-laws to their Paris apartment and reluctantly passed her twins over to the very competent Nanny Ryan. Nanny Ryan briskly enlisted the help of two underhousemaids and set about arranging to take her energetic charges down to stay in the Grieves-Croft Farmhouse in Dawlish together with Sadie Grieves-Croft, Lord Archibald's young niece, and her Nanny Florrie.

George, finding himself surprisingly free of responsibility for a short time, reverted briefly to the bachelor life, and much to Henry's delight, agreed to stay at the London town house whilst the family was absent. Although he would never admit it to his friend, Henry had begun to envy George and his family life, because, despite many brief romantic liaisons, some rather more promising affairs, and regretfully, a few broken female hearts, Henry had remained a free man.

After ten years, life in London had lost some of its appeal for Henry and his losses at the gaming tables were concerning, even to him. Henry's somewhat lavish lifestyle had attracted the attention of the family accountant, and just recently, he had managed to avoid the terse and frequent requests to contact the accountant's office. Perhaps, Henry thought ruefully as he ran his fingers through his unruly blond locks, he should consider lowering his sights a little in his search for the perfect wife. Frowning, he touched his hair again. It felt thinner, and George had teased him about it only the night before. Glumly, Henry renewed his options. Perhaps he should settle for one of the wealthy-but-dull young ladies he was continually being introduced to by gimlet-eyed mothers anxious to offload a plain, if wealthy, daughter.

Henry Maycroft, unattached, of private means, was considered to be quite a catch, and as such was pursued hotly every season by a bevy of determined matrons. Henry was still entertaining this unattractive option, when a loud shout from his fellow travellers signalled the approach of the train. The headache that had woken him that morning from an alcohol-induced slumber was still lurking behind his eyes, but, taking a deep breath, he moved forward, grabbed his bag, and joined the rowdy crowd of friends. Pushing each other good-naturedly and waving their straw boaters above their heads in high good humour, they tumbled each other into the first-class carriages with a rousing cheer, hauling various pieces of luggage with them. Slumping down next to Henry, George looked at his friend keenly. "You're very quiet, old chum, what's up?"

"Oh, nothing really," Henry replied brightly. "Perhaps too much champagne at the party last evening. A good luncheon will do the trick." He looked around him and nodded with approval. "I say, this carriage looks brand new. Let's hope those ruffians don't ruin it. I rather think they are still drunk." Henry pointed across to the group of friends on the opposite seat who were gamely attempting to open a bottle of pink champagne.

George, glancing around the elegant carriage, the plush, dark-blue velvet seats, embroidered with a gold Fleur de Lille pattern, the snowy-white cotton head pads, the polished walnut interior, and the gleaming windows, replied wryly. "Yes, very nice, but seriously, Henry, is anything up? Business still good is it, or has a member of the fair sex broken your heart for a change? You are looking somewhat jaded."

Henry shook his head, wincing ruefully as his head thudded at the sudden movement, but before he could think of a response, Peregrine Porter, an old school friend, lurched across the carriage, waving a bottle of champagne at them. "Come on you two, stop gossiping and join in, let's get the betting going."

George and Henry were drawn into the heated group discussion about the merits of the runners in the Royal Ascot Gold Cup. The most fancied was Persimmon, the beautiful, high-spirited bay colt owned by Edward, the Prince of Wales.

George argued the case for Limasol, and Peregrine loyally spoke up for his uncle's runner, Winkfield's Pride. However, by the time the train arrived at Windsor Station, and after several bottles of champagne had been consumed, most of the friends had changed their minds about their favourite runners or forgotten their choices entirely and were singing a selection of lewd rugby ditties at the top of their voices.

A piercing whistle announced their arrival at Windsor, and as the train puffed and screeched its way into the station, George stood up, and grasping the leather strap, he opened the window and leant out, searching through the crowded platform for his valet, John. The train slowed to a stop, and all along the length of the train, carriage doors were flung open, and descending from the carriages, a bevy of lovely, laughing beauties gaily waving their parasols were gallantly helped down onto the platform by elegant young men in boaters and top hats.

On the edge of the platform, an elderly man, immaculately attired in a dark suit with a striped waistcoat, had seen George immediately, and he lifted his bowler hat high in the air to attract his young master's attention.

"This way, Master George, if you will," John called, and ushered forward three porters, who, having received a handsome tip, were waiting patiently with their trolleys. One by one, the party jumped from the train and followed George as he led the way along the packed platform towards the elderly man. Grinning broadly, George patted the man on the back.

"John," he exclaimed, "on time as usual. Are you ready for these hooligans?" He waved his hand toward his waiting friends.

John smiled gravely at George, nodded to the group of young men, and with barely concealed affection replied, "We are indeed, sir, and greatly looking forward to having the house full again. It has been very quiet without the family, and Cook is especially missing the babies and young Sadie."

Turning to the excited group of young men, John pointed to the exit and urged them firmly toward the open doors, calling out loudly, "Come along now, gentlemen, this way if you please, no dawdling now."

The group, who had stopped to admire a party of giggling girls, looked a little startled at the sharp order, and apart from Peregrine, who scowled at the impatient valet, meekly trooped out of the station. Henry was a regular guest at Grieves Manor and was very familiar with the rather dour Scotsman, and he laughed. "Trust John to have everything organised, but just look at Perry's face, George!"

Two smart, dark, green-and-cream horse-drawn carriages, each displaying the distinctive gold Grieves-Croft family crest, were standing in the shade of the trees outside the station. Four horses, ebony black with thick-plaited tails and manes, had been waiting at the station for some time and were now arching their proud necks and pawing the ground impatiently. With a few quiet words and very little fuss, John divided the group, four in each carriage, and waited until all the luggage had been loaded on before climbing nimbly up on the lead carriage next to the driver.

"Ready to go, Master George?" he called down, and receiving an answering wave from inside the carriage, nodded to the driver. With a light flick on the reigns, they were off. The sound of the horse's hooves clip-clopping through quiet, leafy lanes dappled with June sunlight was soothing after the noise and clatter of the train, and Henry settled back in his seat. He closed his eyes and sighed with sheer pleasure,

"This is absolutely perfect, George," he said. "I do love coming back to Grieves Manor."

George eyed his friend and replied, "So do I, Henry."

George had enjoyed his stay in London, meeting up with old friends, dining out in the best restaurants, visiting the music halls, even chancing his luck at the gaming tables, but after two weeks, he was ready to come home. On waking that morning, he had felt a stir of excitement and anticipation at the thought of going home to Jenny and the boys. Since the birth of his sons, George, who had always been the first to party and the last to go home, had settled down to the family business, spending less and less time in London and found surprisingly that he did not miss the glitz and glitter of London at all. Now, he looked across at his sleeping friend and wondered what time Henry had arrived home that morning, but guessed it was the early hours, probably forgetting about the early start today. Henry's head rolled with the movement of the carriage, and he moaned softly in his sleep. He looked pale, George reflected ruefully, not surprising considering the hectic social life that Henry led and was glad that he had declined to accompany the group of friends back to London after the races.

For months now, London society, in a frenzy of excitement, had been preparing for an endless round of parties and elaborate balls to celebrate Queen Victoria's Golden Jubilee, each prominent hostess determined to outdo her rivals and attract the cream of society to favour her event above all others.

The air of excitement in London was palpable, and thickly embossed gilt-edged invitation cards had been arriving daily, many lined up on Henry's mantelpiece as the available eligible bachelors were more sought after than ever. Henry secretly favoured the

Duchess of Devonshire's much-vaulted lavish and exclusive fancy dress ball to be held at Devonshire House in Piccadilly. It was widely rumoured that the Prince of Wales had been invited to attend together with his wealthy and aristocratic friends. When Henry's invitation to attend the ball had arrived just the day before, Henry had opened it with a studied nonchalance. George hid a smile, aware that Henry had been more than a little worried when, a week previously, Peregrine had waved his invitation triumphantly above his head when they had met for lunch at Boodles.

As was usual, the eligible bachelors were invited to bring a guest, and it was an unwritten rule that a carefully-selected male guest would also be acceptable to their hostess. After reading the simply worded invitation out loud twice to George, Henry had looked at his close friend expectedly.

George shook his head firmly, "No, Henry. I've had my fun in London, and now I want to see my wife and boys, and before you say anything else, I won't change my mind. Take Foxy as your guest. The dear boy will jump at the chance."

The Honourable Basil Foxborough, sturdy with thinning fair hair and an irrepressible sense of fun, was known to all as Foxy. The Hon. Basil was an impossibly wealthy, incredibly generous, and flirtatious young man whose latest romance had been with the much-older wife of an American diplomat. The diplomat had been summoned back to Washington at short notice, and for a while, Foxy had been cold-shouldered by even the most liberal of London's hostesses. But Foxy's time as a social outcast in the wilderness was coming to an end, however, as he was an engaging, good-humoured, and entertaining friend and a highly amusing weekend guest. As such, he was much missed on the social circuit. Henry, at first disbelieving that George would choose to miss the most talked-about social event of the season, sulked for a few hours and then, accepting that George would not change his mind, agreed to enquire discreetly whether Foxy would be a suitable "other guest."

After a peaceful half-hour drive, during which even the ever-ebullient Foxy had been lulled into silence, the carriages turned into an avenue of ancient lime trees, and the tall, black-and-gold imposing gates of Grieves Manor came into view. As the carriages drew close, a small figure in a flat cap, riding boots, and chequered jacket emerged from a flint stone gatehouse. With a salute to the drivers, he strode over and unlocked both gates, and they swung open silently on well-oiled hinges. The man dropped the bolts into the ground and stood back to wave the carriages by.

John called out a greeting to the man by the gates, and George leant out of the carriage window. "Thank you, Finn. How are you?"

The man responded with a wide smile and touched the rim of his cap, "Very well, thank you, Master George," and turned back to close the gates behind them.

As they turned into the drive, Henry yawned and stretched, woken by the cheerful exchange of greetings. The sun was hot now, beating down on the manicured lawns. The carriage wheels crunched over the gravelled drive and mingled with the sound of trickling water and bird song. At the centre of the long drive was an imposing two-tiered circular marble fountain, each tier separated by a pair of stone unicorns, and from the top tier, clear sparkling water spouted enticingly down into a pool of darting goldfish.

Grieves Manor was a stylish and elegant house of mellow stone with rows of distinctive Palladian triple windows which looked out imperiously at visitors as they approached the house. Glittering marble steps curved in two sweeping semi-circles to meet in front of a soaring gabled portico supported on four ornate columns.

In the June sunshine, the lovely old Manor House sat gracefully in a tranquil setting of twenty acres of private parkland and formal gardens, surrounded by ancient woodland and fragrant meadows awash with grasses, wild thyme, and orchids. With just twelve bedrooms, Grieves Manor was considered small in comparison with the many-bedroomed country houses dotted around the affluent surrounding Berkshire countryside, but it suited the Grieves-Croft family perfectly.

A red-roofed stable block lay to the left of the Manor House, and on this hot summer day, the horses were grazing on the tender grasses in the shady paddocks behind the stables. To the right of the house, a vast, gravel lake shimmered in the sun, and the tall trees lining the banks were mirrored in the still water. Beneath the wooden boathouse, three blue-and-white rowing boats bobbed gently on their moorings, and a family of ducks drifted around in the shade of the jetty.

When the carriages neared the Manor, two footmen, smartly attired in green-and-cream livery, stepped forward to open the carriage doors, and the excited friends tumbled out chattering and laughing. George ran eagerly up the steps and into the cool, marbled entrance hall, where Brent and Mrs Brent were waiting with the household staff.

"My goodness, Brent, it is jolly good to be home again," George grinned. "Mrs Brent, I do hope this noisy bunch won't cause too much work for you."

"Good afternoon, Master George." Brent bowed gravely, "It is very good to have you home, sir, and I can assure you that Mrs Brent has everything organized for your guests."

The tall, thin housekeeper's normally stern face broke into a smile. "No trouble at all, Master George. Perhaps the gentlemen would like to wait in the drawing room whilst their luggage is taken up and unpacked." Then, turning to the maids, who were waiting with arms full of snowy linen, she gestured toward the stairs and said sharply, "Two front bedrooms, quick as you like, then back down for the rest." The girls nodded respectfully and scurried up the stairs.

Brent addressed the friends as they followed George into the house. "We have drinks waiting in the drawing room, gentlemen, and Cook has prepared a light lunch in the dining room." At the mention of drinks, there was a general murmur of approval, and Brent led the way into the drawing room. Henry turned back to look at Foxy, who was staring around him in awe.

"What's up Foxy? I thought you said you were hungry."

Foxy shook his head, "I am old boy, but I say, what a place, I mean just look at those ceilings!"

Henry looked up in surprise, forgetting that Foxy, who rarely ventured out of London, was used only to the dark fussiness of the Victorian house and the opulence of the nouveau riche.

"Come on, Foxy. You can admire the architecture later. I need a drink." Henry was hot, and he still had a nagging headache. He marched into the drawing room, leaving Foxy still staring around him in wonder.

Grieves Manor, designed in the Palladian style, was cool and stylish, with pure white walls, moulded arches, and soaring ceilings with intricately painted and gilded cornices. In the centre of the hall, an elegant cantilevered marble staircase spiralled up through the centre of the house. A polished ebony handrail topped the sweeping black-and-gold curlicue banisters, and at each level there was a circular landing with ornate arches leading off to individually designed bedrooms. High above the stairs, a stained-glass cupola threw rainbow-coloured splinters of light dancing down into the stairwell and onto the black-and-white tessellated hall floor below. Whilst there were obvious trappings of immense wealth, there was no opulence; Grieves Manor was simply classically beautiful.

An hour or so later, duly refreshed and fortified by a delicious lunch of poached salmon and salad washed down with a quantity of excellent wine, the group were ready for some fun and growing restless. George innocently suggested a little wager and led his friends through to the snooker room. Despite the warmth of the day, a fire had been laid in the grand fireplace. The snooker room, like the music room, was positioned at the back of the house and only received the sun in the late afternoon. George and Henry, after losing the draw to begin the match, lit their cigars and waited their turn at the table, shouting encouragement to the players whilst booing and cheering in turn. John appeared with the drinks trolley assisted by a pert and pretty maid. A rousing roar of approval greeted her, and she ducked her head, placed a tray of glasses nervously on the table, and blushing shyly, she fled the room.

George looked surprised to see his manservant serving the drinks. "Is everything alright, John? Where's Brent?"

"Yes, indeed, Master George, but I wanted a quiet word, sir. Lord

Archibald wanted you to know that Miss Estelle is on her way home with Mrs Grieves-Croft."

George looked at him in astonishment. "What! from Paris you say? Estelle and Jenny travelling on their own, without the parents, I thought everyone was arriving tomorrow?"

"No, sir. The ladies are travelling back with the Royal party on the Osborne but left earlier than planned, as Prince Edward wanted to see Persimmon and be back in plenty of time for the races. Lord Archibald and Lady Rose are visiting in town first and said that they would meet you at Ascot."

"Ahh, I see. Thank you, John. Yes, very exciting about Persimmon. I think we all fancy a wager on the favourite, or at least some of us do, eh Perry?"

Peregrine Porter raised his eyebrows and sniffed through his long, aristocratic nose. "One has to be seen to be loyal, old chap, and after all, I am the heir apparent, so its Winkfield's Pride for me I fear."

There was a hoot of derisive laughter from the Persimmon supporters, including George, who grinned and remarked to Henry, who was listening with interest. "Henry, do you remember my little sister, Estelle?"

Henry frowned and drew on his cigar. "Yes, I think I do, skinny little thing, same awful red hair as yours, and very annoying as I recall, although I haven't seen her for a few years."

John chuckled quietly as he turned to leave the room, "Well, Miss Estelle has changed a bit, Master Henry, as you will see for yourself when she arrives."

"Do we know when they are due, John?" George called out after him, elated at the thought of seeing Jenny again.

"Later tonight, I do believe, sir."

George nodded. "I just hope that Estelle has behaved herself. Jenny needed a rest, and Estelle is lively company and can be headstrong."

Henry did not reply, concentrating as he was on the game going on between Foxy and Perry, apart from which, he found George's obsession with his wife vaguely irritating. However, the imminent arrival of Estelle and Jenny was soon forgotten as the room filled with cigar smoke and whisky-fueled shouts of laughter as the group of friends played each other in fiercely fought matches before retiring to their rooms to dress for dinner.

Mrs Barker, the cook, an honorary title as the good lady had never been married, was bored with cooking for a diminished household, was delighted at the return of the family. Knowing George's favourite dinner, she served up an enormous platter of rare roast beef and Yorkshire pudding with a mountain of vegetables, followed by sherry trifle topped with thick Devon cream, and a steaming, fragrant apple pie with custard. After the cheese and port, some of the guests declared themselves ready for bed. George, however, alert for any sign of the returning ladies, suggested a game of cards. There was a loud protest from the weary, but persuaded by Foxy, they trailed into the music room. The fire had been lit in the music room, and the yawning friends slumped down into the deep leather chairs. Replete and relaxed, but also not ready for an early bed, Henry suggested a sing song and was instantly shouted down, but undaunted, Henry lifted the lid of the piano, pulled the stool out, and sat down, flexing his fingers.

As a regular visitor to both the Oxford and The Eagle Music Hall, Henry was a fan of the infamous Marie Lloyd, and taking a deep breath, playing with vigour and style, he began with a rousing *A Little Bit of What You Fancy Does You Good*. Drawn by the naughty popular song, the friends, one by one, abandoned their comfortable chairs and gathered around the piano, shouting out their favourite songs. George, egged on by the group, was loudest of all, singing lustily to his favourite Katie Lawrence song, *Daisy Bell*.

Brent was summoned for more drinks and on entering the music room, was persuaded to put the tray down and sing along with *Oh Mr Porter*, which he did with a grave bow, adding a very passable baritone to the warbling renderings from the now slightly drunk choristers.

Jenny Grieves-Croft and Estelle Grieves-Croft, meanwhile, were travelling through the late evening sunshine and making good time crossing the country from the docks at Dover.

HMY Osborne, carrying the Prince of Wales party across the

English Channel, had docked early, much to the satisfaction of both ladies, who were eager to reach Grieves Manor before dark. When the carriage turned into the drive at Grieves Manor, Jenny, leaning out of the window to catch a glimpse of her beloved home, burst out laughing. "Look Estelle, I think George and the boys have arrived before us."

Lights blazed out like beacons in the soft dusk, and as the carriage drew closer, the girls could hear singing and laughter drifting through the open windows, and Estelle's face lit up. "Now that sounds like a party to me, Jenny, and we have arrived just in time to join in," and her eyes sparkled with fun and laughter.

Brent, alert for the arrival of the ladies and hearing the carriage wheels crunching on the gravel, hurried out to greet them. The waiting footman opened the doors and handed the ladies out, as the butler stepped forward and bowed slightly to Jenny.

"Master George and his party are in the music room, madam. Cook has left supper in the dining room if you are hungry."

"Thank you so much, Brent, we are earlier than expected," Jenny replied, smiling. "The luggage should be following on soon."

Brent nodded. "Very well, madam," and turning to Estelle, he bowed again,

"It's very good to have you home, Miss Estelle, I will have your luggage taken up to your bedroom. Mrs Brent has it all prepared for you."

Estelle Grieves-Croft, unlike her contemporaries, had firmly refused to attend finishing school in Switzerland, or indeed to do "The London Season," pleading, "Dearest Ma, please do not present me like a prize cow at a farmer's market." Lady Rose, after consultation with Estelle's doting father, agreed that, instead, their wayward daughter, accompanied by a suitable companion, could explore Europe's cities, museums, and art galleries. At the end of the tour, she was to meet her parents and Jenny in their Paris apartment.

Now, Estelle turned and grinned at the butler and leant forward giving him a quick hug. "It is jolly good to be home again. I have missed everyone, Brent, but you most of all," she teased.

Brent nodded and raised his eyebrows. "That is very kind of you to say so, Miss Estelle," he replied, hiding a smile. "Come along inside now, you must both be very tired."

Estelle linked her arm through Jenny's and whispered, "So, you're a madam, now are you? How very grown up, I must say, Jenny Wren," but in truth, nobody had been happier than Estelle when her big brother George had declared that he was totally smitten with her best friend, Lady Jenny Fitzwilliam, and had set out to win her heart.

Once inside the hall, the footman took their cloaks and hats, and Brent said, "I shall inform Master George that you have arrived safely, madam. I will let him know that you are having supper and will join him later."

Jenny nodded. "Thank you, Brent, although by the sound of the party in the music room, I doubt if he has given us a second thought."

Brent turned to leave, and Estelle, struck by a sudden idea, put her hand on his arm. "Not yet, Brent. We want to surprise George, don't we, Jenny?"

Jenny shook her head. "Estelle, what are you plotting now? I am rather tired, and I need my supper."

"Please, Jenny," Estelle begged. "It's just a little joke. I'll tell you my idea whilst we have supper. I promise you it's only a little fun."

Jenny sighed and nodded to Brent, "All right, Brent, we shall find the gentlemen after supper. Don't bother with a maid, we shall serve ourselves."

Brent frowned and hesitated before replying a little stiffly, "Very well, madam, if you are sure."

When they were both seated at the table, Jenny looked over inquiringly to her sister-in-law, observing the familiar, naughty smile on Estelle's lovely face. "Well then, what are you plotting, Estelle?"

"As I said, it's just a bit of fun with the boys, Jenny Wren, honestly."

Jenny listened carefully to her sister-in-law's little plot and agreed reluctantly that it sounded harmless and could be a lot of fun.

"Now can we get on with supper, please, Estelle, because I am very hungry even if you are not, so please be patient."

Estelle, not known for her patience, picked at her supper whilst sighing and fidgeting around in her chair. The second that Jenny laid down her knife and fork and folded her napkin, Estelle was instantly up on her feet.

"Right, Jen, I've worked it out, and the quickest way into the garden is through the kitchen, because from there we can creep around the back to the music room." Before Jenny could protest, Estelle had ushered her out of the dining room and into the hall. The music and shouts of laughter still resonated from the music room, and they tiptoed lightly across the hall and down the stairs into the kitchen. Cook, John, and Brent were seated at the table eating supper, whilst Mrs Brent was organising a rota for the two patiently waiting maids. John looked astonished, stopped eating, and went to stand up, but Jenny stopped him and held up her hand.

"I am so sorry, John, we've interrupted your meal. Please don't get up." Jenny was contrite and embarrassed and pinched Estelle's arm.

Estelle flashed the astonished staff a cheeky grin, nodding to the two maids who were staring at the pair open-mouthed, before grabbing Jenny's hand and fleeing out the kitchen door into the shadowed garden. Before Jenny could admonish her, Estelle had picked up her skirts and was creeping around to the side of the house. Jenny peered into the dusk. "Estelle, wait, where are you?" she hissed.

Estelle was crouched down under the music room window. "Hush, Jenny. I am over here. Look, we can hide under the bushes. The window is open, and we can peek in."

Inside the music room, the singing had stopped, but Jenny and Estelle could hear the light-hearted arguments about the choice of the next song. The evening was warm, and a slight breeze lifted the flimsy curtain away from the open window, bringing a sweet scent of roses into the smoky room. Henry, taking a break from the piano, lit a cigarette and strolled over to the open window with his whisky. Leaning both elbows on the window ledge, he peered into the darkness. A sliver of eyelash moon hung in the clear night sky, and somewhere in the woods, an owl hooted mournfully, the only sound to disturb the still and peaceful dusk. Henry sipped his whisky then jumped as something rustled the bushes under the window. He leant out further and stared down into the darkness. "Is there anyone out there?" He waited, then feeling a little foolish, muttered, "Probably a fox." He turned away from the window to take his turn at the piano.

Pressed up against the ivy-clad wall under the open window, Estelle and Jenny clung to each other, stifling their giggles, moving only when Henry had disappeared back into the room. Brushing the twigs and leaves off their gowns, they stood up on tiptoe and cautiously peeked into the smoky room. Jenny Grieves-Croft, spotting her red-headed husband with his head thrown back, singing lustily out of tune, clapped both hands over her mouth and bobbed down again, giggling. Estelle looked thoughtfully over at the handsome, fair-haired man pounding on the piano and then sank down next to Jenny. "Who is the pianist, Jenny?" she whispered.

Jenny stood up and peeked over the window ledge. "That's Henry Maycroft, philanderer, heartbreaker, and single. You must remember him, Estelle. Henry has been George's friend forever. I have always thought that he rather resented me for marrying George," she added ruefully.

The loud singing stopped, and there was the chink of glasses being refilled. Estelle stood up and looked through the open window and over to where Henry, still seated at the piano, was lifting a large malt whisky to his lips. She frowned and stared for a minute before recalling a tall, skinny schoolboy who used to visit in the school holidays. She also recalled that he had rudely ignored her and, worst of all, encouraged her beloved George to do the same.

"Come on Henry, let's have another," a shout came from inside the room, and Estelle recognised her brother's voice.

"And it's *Burlington Bertie* next, by popular vote," George announced.

"Oh, no it's not," giggled Estelle. "Come on, Jen, we shall give them our rendering of *The Boy I Love*."

Jenny, now caught up in the spirit of fun, nodded nervously, and they stood up close to the open window. Henry was seated back at the piano, and so was hidden from the girls' view as the group of friends crowded around, but they heard him say loudly, "Ready now, gentlemen, as loud as you can, let's raise the roof." The group around the piano nodded eagerly, and there was much clearing of throats. As Henry's hands hovered over the piano keys, a low, throaty giggle floated across the room from the open window, followed by a melodious duet, one voice low and husky, the other clear and bell-like, but both singing with gusto. "The boy I love is up in the gallery."

The group in the room, startled into silence, turned as one. Henry stood up and got a clear view of the two girls framed in the window. With linked arms and swaying to the rhythm, they lifted their heads and sang at the tops of their voices.

"Estelle," groaned George, and walking across to the window, he added in a resigned tone "and, of course, my Jenny," smiling into the sweet, upturned face of his wife.

Recovering from their surprise, the rest of the friends cheered and clapped the serenading girls, joining in with the chorus. That is, all except Henry, who, following George across the room found himself looking into the lovely, laughing face of Estelle Grieves-Croft and was instantly captivated. Estelle Grieves-Croft was not a beauty in the traditional sense. Her wild, dark-red curls bounced around a tiny elfin face as she sang with enthusiasm, all the time staring directly at him. Henry, for once, found himself lost for words as he gazed into a pair of slanting, green eyes framed with long, dark lashes. The pert little nose was covered in freckles, and below that, her wide mouth was curved with laughter. Estelle, in turn, faltered slightly under the intense stare from Henry's ice-blue eyes, but remembering Jenny's words, recovered herself and tossed her head proudly at the last chorus. The song was over, and there were plenty of eager hands to help the two girls climb up through the window into the room.

George tenderly scolded his laughing wife. "Jenny! What on Earth would our boys think of their mother scrambling through a window?"

Jenny Grieves-Croft was tiny and birdlike with dark, brown eyes below winged brows. With her shining cap of brown hair and upturned nose, she did indeed resemble a little wren. George, short, red-headed, with a tendency to put on weight, adored her and was inordinately proud of his red-headed sons. Picking his wife up in an enormous bear hug, he kissed her roundly.

"I have missed you, my Jenny Wren, and the terrible two. In fact, Henry has accused me of being a total bore," and he turned to look at Henry for confirmation. But Henry was busy, and ignoring the hoots of laughter from his friends, he had taken Estelle gently by the hand and was leading her out of the room into the sweet-scented evening air. That was the last the friends saw of Henry until breakfast the following morning.

Eager to get to the races, the friends were up early and had gathered in the dining room for breakfast. Henry, helping himself to kippers and bacon from the sideboard, sat down, unfolded his napkin, and waited until Brent had poured the tea before asking casually, "Are the ladies not joining us for breakfast, Brent?"

Brent walked around the table pouring the tea and said gravely with a hint of a smile, "I fear not, Sir. As they are not going to the races today, they said that they will take breakfast a little later, after the gentlemen."

"Not going to the races? Why on Earth not, for Heaven's sake?"

At Henry's exasperated tone, George looked up and grinned over to Henry, who was looking decidedly put out. "Estelle has agreed to help Jenny to get the nurseries ready for the twins and little Sadie. The nannies are bringing them all back later today. Never fear, Henry, Estelle and Jenny will not miss the Gold Cup tomorrow."

Around the breakfast table, the lively chatter among the rest of the group was all about the racing day ahead, but Henry was unusually silent, and George, still grinning smugly, slowly buttered his toast. There was a clatter of hooves and the sound of wheels on the drive outside the dining room, and John appeared in the doorway.

"The carriage is here, sir, if the gentlemen are ready? Cook has prepared the luncheon, and the hampers are being loaded on."

"We certainly are ready, John." George stated, and after one last bite, abandoned his toast and turned to his friends, most of whom were already standing, all eager to make the most of the fine day.

"Gentlemen, if you would follow me?" and with a bow and a sweep of his arm, George led the group ceremoniously into the hall, where several footmen were waiting with dress coats and top hats at the ready. Peregrine Porter, however, paused and turned to Henry, who was still seated at the table, his breakfast largely untouched.

Raising his eyebrows, Perry sardonically addressed his friend, "Are you coming Henry, or will you be joining the ladies preparing the nursery?"

Foxy gave a snort of laughter, at which, Henry pushed his chair back and stood up. "Of course, I'm coming. Don't be so bloody Perry," he snapped and marched stiffly out into the hall.

Peregrine shrugged himself into his coat, adjusted his top hat, picked up his cane, and drawled. "And don't you be a bloody bore and sulk all day, old man. I am sure that the delectable Estelle will be waiting for you on our return."

George, who, in the meantime had been up to the nursery to bid the ladies goodbye, came running down the stairs, taking two at a time, and joined the party as they made their way out to the waiting carriage. The champagne and the hampers of food had been carefully strapped on to the back of the carriage, and the group of friends climbed aboard. With a clatter of hooves and a great deal of good-humoured shouting, they were off thundering down the drive.

Looking down from the nursery window at the top of the house, Estelle and Jenny watched as the loaded carriage with its excited group of passengers disappeared down the drive in a shower of gravel. Jenny beckoned Estelle out onto the landing. The two nursery maids were busily making up the tiny cots with clean sheets, whilst another maid prepared the small bed in Sadie's room.

"George thinks that the invincible Henry has fallen under your spell. George says that he has never seen him like that before, and he has forbidden you to break his heart." Jenny widened her eyes innocently.

Estelle, totally unfazed, replied airily. "My big brother can just mind his own business, Jenny, and you can tell him that from me."

"Yes, I will, but you have to tell me. You do like Henry too, don't you? I can tell. What were you two talking about in the garden last night? You were gone for ages. I heard you creep in, and I knocked on your bedroom door, but you wouldn't open it."

"That was because I knew it was you, Jenny." Estelle laughed, then turned to her friend with shining eyes and added. "Actually, I admit it. I do like Henry Maycroft; I do Jenny, oh so much."

"Aha, I knew it. I want to know more." Jenny put her head around the twin's bedroom door and addressed the maids, "Thank you girls, we will be downstairs if you need anything." Then she grabbed Estelle's arm. "Come on, let's go down to breakfast, and you can tell me all about what happened before the little ones arrive home."

But by three-thirty, there was still no sign of the twins or their nanny, and Jenny was becoming increasingly restless. "What on Earth can be keeping them, Estelle? Nanny said they would catch the early train."

Estelle watched her sister-in-law pacing up and down the drawing room. "Let us take a turn around the garden, Jenny. We shall walk down to the lake and then have some tea. I am sure everything is alright. Nanny Ryan will take good care of the children, never fear." Jenny nodded, her face pinched with worry.

It was another two hours before the hansom cab clattered up the drive with the two exhausted-looking nannies, together with the irritable and snivelling twins and a pale-faced Sadie. "We have had a terrible journey, madam. Sadie was sick this morning, and we nearly missed the train. Then I mixed up the timetable, and we had to sit in the station for ages." Nanny Ryan admitted, looking distressed.

Nanny Florrie nodded. "And those boys have been holy terrors," she grumbled, cuddling Sadie. Nanny Ryan frowned at her, but Jenny was too relieved to see her precious boys again to pay much attention.

"Have they been naughty? Poor Nanny, but I have missed them so much," she said, trying to cuddle her grizzling, red-faced sons.

"We should take them inside and settle them down, they are hungry and tired." Nanny Ryan was firm as she beckoned to the waiting nursemaid to take the twins before leading the way up the steps and into the house.

Jenny took Sadie's thin hand, "I have missed you as well, little Sadie. Were the twins very naughty?"

Sadie smiled and shook her head. "Just a little bit" she whispered, "I was sick, but I am all right now."

A short time later, a riot of cheers heralded the triumphant race-goer's return. Jenny was upstairs helping nanny to bathe the twins, and Estelle was in the library reading quietly to a sleepy Sadie. Henry ran up the steps, and striding through the hall, he thrust his coat and hat impatiently at the waiting footman. The group followed, loudly congratulating each other on their winnings as they crowded into the music room calling for drinks. But Henry turned to Brent, who had been waiting in the hall for the returning party.

"Miss Grieves-Croft?" he asked. Brent inclined his head toward the library and walked over to open the door.

"Mr Maycroft, Miss Estelle," he announced to the slight figure curled up in the armchair by the fire.

"Thank you, Brent," Estelle whispered and held a finger to her lips. "I wonder, could you send Nanny down for Sadie? Poor little thing is exhausted."

"Of course, Miss Estelle," Brent said, smoothly closing the door.

Henry felt a frisson of annoyance as he looked at the sleeping child on Estelle's lap, but forced a smile when Estelle said softly, "Do sit down, Henry, but please don't wake Sadie."

"But I wanted to tell you..." His voice tailed off when Estelle frowned.

"Shh! Later, Henry, please. When Nanny has taken Sadie, we can walk around the garden."

Henry nodded and sank gloomily into the opposite armchair and stared into the fire.

That evening, the group of friends enjoyed a sumptuous and noisy five-course dinner, during which Henry barely took his eyes off a blushing and radiant Estelle. The talk was all of the Gold Cup the next day and the forthcoming celebrations for Queen Victoria's Diamond Jubilee. It was late when the group broke up and went their separate ways. Foxy suggested a game of snooker to Perry, whilst the others chose to relax in the drawing room with cigars and brandy and discuss the day's outing yet again. George and Jenny went upstairs to check on the twins before retiring early themselves.

Henry and Estelle, once again, slipped away into the soft summer night, watched by a scowling Peregrine Porter and a thoughtful Foxy.

It was June 17th, 1897, Royal Ascot Gold Cup Day, and breakfast was served early at Grieves Manor. The friends, all well rested, helped themselves to the impressive breakfast laid out for them in the silver platters on the sideboard. There was an air of barely contained excitement and anticipation as they sat down to eat. Despite the fact that they were a wealthy and privileged group of young men, few had ever been invited into the Royal Enclosure.

George, remembering his father's instructions, warned them again that everyone must display their badges and be in the Royal Enclosure before the Queen's carriage arrived for the Royal Drive around the course. Watching his over-excited friends and recalling how many magnums of champagne were currently being brought up from the cellar to be consumed at the races, George issued a further good-humoured warning.

"And please behave like the gentlemen I know you all to be," he called down the table, and his final warning was met with roars of approval.

It had been arranged that the brake carrying the men to Ascot would collect the party at eleven o'clock sharp whilst Jenny and Estelle would follow on in Lord Grieves-Croft's newly acquired brougham. Peregrine, unusually silent, had seated himself opposite Henry at the table and was now watching through narrowed eyes the gentle flirting and little smiles that passed between his close friend and Estelle. He finished his meagre breakfast, laid his knife and fork on the table, and dabbed his moustache delicately with his napkin. Drumming his immaculate fingernails lightly on the table, he leant across and, in a soft voice just loud enough to be heard, he addressed Henry. "Will you be travelling in the ladies' carriage today, dear boy, or will you be travelling with the great unwashed?"

Henry, who had been speaking in a low voice to Estelle, flushed and glared at Peregrine, but before Henry could respond, Estelle laid a cool hand over his.

"Perry, don't be spiteful, sweet boy, why on Earth would Henry travel with us? If you are very nice, Henry will sit next to you at the races," and pouting prettily, she blew him a kiss.

Peregrine, who was known for his cutting and sometimes cruel ripostes, flushed and smiled back grudgingly, knowing that on this occasion, he had been bested. George, seated next to Peregrine, gave a shout of laughter and slapped him on the back. "Don't mind too much, Perry. I have never won an argument with Estelle yet have I, eh little pigeon?"

Estelle smiled sweetly in agreement, Henry glowered and Peregrine discomforted, nodded and inclined his head toward Henry. Henry returned the nod, acknowledging this was the only apology he was going to illicit from his complex and sometimes difficult friend. The tension at the breakfast table eased, and the general chatter returned to the forthcoming races. Jenny, who hated arguments relaxed, and George shot her a reassuring and loving smile.

The ornate onyx-and-gilded mantle clock chimed the hour, and Jenny leant over to Estelle. "We really should go and get ready now, Estelle. It's ten o'clock already." She reminded her friend, who, head tilted to one side, was once again listening intently to Henry.

"Oh, my goodness. I'd forgotten the time," Estelle laughed, and ignoring Peregrine's raised eyebrows, she stood up and, addressing the assembled company, said, "Gentlemen, we shall meet at the races," and with a swish of skirts, both ladies were gone, giggling and running out of the dining room and up the stairs.

George stood up. "We should do the same, gentlemen, and please do not forget the badges. If we get separated, you will need them to get into the Royal Enclosure."

Henry, impatient as always, was dressed early and stood on the top of the steps enjoying a cigarette whilst idly swishing his cane backwards and forward. From the direction of the stables, a smart black-and-gold brougham appeared, drawn by a pretty, piebald pony and came to a halt in front of the house. The coachman, immaculate in green-and-cream livery, high riding boots, and top hat, tied the reigns around the brake and jumped down onto the drive. The piebald snorted and tossed her head, a front hoof pawing impatiently at the gravel. The coachman reached out and stroked her nose gently, all the time speaking to her softly. Henry frowned and ran lightly down the steps and addressed the groom. His tone was sharp.

"That filly is a little lively for the lady's carriage, is she not? Is she used to being in harness? It's going to be noisy at the races, you know, and she's already a bit skittish."

The man holding the horse's head held Henry's stare before nodding politely. "Pepper is Miss Estelle's favourite, sir, she is a young filly, and the brougham is nice and light for her. She'll settle down once we are off," he advised calmly, watching as Henry, still frowning, walked slowly around the carriage, lightly tapping his cane against his boots.

One by one, the race-goers came noisily down the steps, headed by George, who greeted the groom. "Good Morning, Patrick. What a fine day. The ladies won't keep you waiting for too long, I hope."

The coachman touched his forehead. "Good morning, sir. We have plenty of time." At the sound of George's voice, Henry appeared from behind the carriage, and George looked at him in amusement.

"What on Earth are you doing back there, Henry?"

Before Henry could reply, the coachman, in a soft, southern Irish drawl, said smoothly, "The gentleman was a little concerned that Pepper seems a little racy this morning, sir. I said she is Miss Estelle's pony, and that she will settle."

"Of course, she will, Henry. Heavens above, do stop fussing." George was clearly irritated. "Move her along a bit though, Patrick, I hear the wagon."

Sure enough, a large four-horse brake came rattling down the drive, a driver and a coachman on the dickey seat next to him. Patrick clicked his tongue, and taking Pepper by the halter, quietly led her to the side of the house out of the way of the brake. As the wagon drew up, Brent signalled to the waiting footmen, who came forward with hampers crammed with food and strapped them to the wagon before returning to the kitchen to collect the crates of champagne. George, the first to board, looked around him, counting, as one-by-one, the friends hauled each other up into the back of the open-topped carriage. "Who are we missing?" he called out.

Peregrine waved his cane lazily in the direction of the house. Foxy emerged, last as always, hopping down the steps, clutching his top hat in his hand and laughing good-naturedly as his fellow passengers jeered loudly. "Shut up, you lot. I'm here now," and he clambered clumsily up onto the empty seat next to George.

"Ready driver," shouted George, and the wagon moved off, the passengers cheering loudly and waving their top hats in the air.

Patrick looked after the departing wagon thoughtfully. "Now, we don't like that fella, do we, my Pepper," he mused, and reaching inside his coat, he pulled his cigarette case from the inside pocket. Pepper was quiet now, standing in the shade of an old oak tree. She snickered and shifted patiently from foot to foot. Brent appeared from the front of the house, tugging at his waistcoat and smoothing down his coat.

"Do you want to bring her round the front again, Patrick, although the ladies will be a while yet."

Patrick, leaning back against the brougham, shook his head and blew a thin trail of smoke in the air. "No, we'll stay awhile in the shade, eh Pepper?"

"Good idea. The sun is hot." Brent wiped his perspiring face with a large handkerchief.

The coachman offered the cigarette case to Brent, who hesitated, took a hasty look around, and moved into the shade of the trees before taking the proffered cigarette. Patrick was aware of how many times the butler, escaping his wife's gimlet eye, sneaked off to the stable yard for a stolen cigarette, and he chuckled. "Sure now, Mr Brent, relax. Your missus won't be able to see you round here."

It was peaceful after the departure of the noisy guests, just the sound of water trickling from the fountain and the hum of bees on a lazy summer afternoon. From the open kitchen windows at the back of the house, there was the sound of muted laughter, the clash of pots, and then footsteps in the kitchen yard, followed by singing as the downstairs maid pegged the washing out to dry in the sunshine. The two men stood for a while in companionable silence, each enjoying a quiet moment in what was going to be a hectic day. Patrick straightened up with a regretful sigh. "Come on Pepper, sweet girl, let's go and collect our lovely ladies." He shook his gloves from his pocket, replaced his top hat, and together, the two men walked to the front of the house. "Sir Archie and Lady Rose back today as well, Mr Brent?"

Brent nodded, "Yes, full house later. They went straight from Dover to the London house. You having a flutter today, Patrick?"

Patrick grinned broadly, "Well, you know what they say about the luck of the Irish."

Brent laughed and made his way up the steps, "Good luck to you then," he called over his shoulder.

A few minutes later, accompanied by two maids holding aloft lacy white parasols, Estelle and Jenny emerged into the warm June sunshine.

Estelle was stunningly beautiful in a brilliant emerald green gown caught in at the waist and falling away in soft ruffles down to her pretty laced boots. The wild red curls were pinned firmly under a wide-brimmed green hat adorned with layers of lace and finished with curling white feathers. In contrast, coolly elegant, Jenny's gown was a simple soft peach sheath trimmed with creamy lace at the collar and around the cuffs. Her simple boater-style hat was set at a jaunty angle on her cap of shining, nut-brown hair, and linking arms, the friends stepped daintily down the steps.

Two footmen, gravely formal, stood by the waiting carriage, and Patrick opened the doors of the brougham with a low bow and a flourish. The maids unfurled the parasols and placed them in the carriage. The footman handed first Jenny into the cool interior of the carriage and then turned to Estelle, who paused before stepping in, "How is Pepper today, Patrick?"

Patrick nodded, "Pepper is in fine fettle, Miss Estelle. Indeed, we could put her in for the Gold Cup at today's meeting. I think she could give Persimmon a run for his money."

Estelle giggled. "Thank you, Patrick, but do make sure you have a wager on Persimmon today though, Daddy says he will romp home."

"I will indeed, thank you Miss," replied Patrick gravely, privately wondering whether he would have a side wager on Valesquez as well.

With the doors firmly closed, Patrick climbed up into his seat and gently touched the pony's smooth back with a twitch of the whip, and they were off, Pepper high-trotting happily down the drive towards the open gates.

Fin was standing by the gates and lifted his cap as they passed, "Good luck to you, Pat," he called to the groom, and when he caught sight of Estelle at the carriage window, he added, "And good luck to his Lordship too."

Estelle smiled and waved. "Thank you, Fin."

Jenny, who was watching her friend closely, teased, "My, we are excited today. Now I wonder why. Could it be the thrill of the race?" Jenny cocked her head to one side, placed a finger on her chin, and appeared to think. "No," she said slowly. "I think not. I think perhaps a certain gentleman could be the cause of all this excitement."

Estelle, hiding a wide smile, shook her head at the smirking Jenny and turned to gaze out at the passing countryside.

SADIE GRIEVES-CROFT

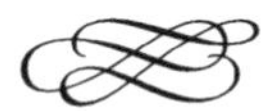

Back at Grieves Manor, the twins, Walter and William, were seated at the table in the nursery when Sadie trotted into the room followed by Florrie. Much to the relief of both nannies, the three children were still tired after a long trip home from Dawlish and had slept late into the morning, giving the ladies time to enjoy a leisurely breakfast. Now it was the children's breakfast time, and as soon as Sadie was seated, and the twins captured and strapped into their chairs, the maid served up bowls of creamy porridge.

Sadie obediently began spooning the porridge carefully into her mouth, pausing now and again to help Nanny Ryan feed the twins who were waiting, mouths open like eager young birds. Fearing that Sadie was not eating her own breakfast, Florrie offered to feed one of the twins. But Florrie's eyesight was not what it used to be, and she took the spoon from Sadie and hesitated, peering short-sightedly at the spoon hovering above Walter's open mouth. Walter was hungry and outraged and roared his disapproval when he saw William being fed before him.

"Goodness, Florrie, feed the child, he's deafening me," Nanny Ryan said with a frown.

Florrie hastily put the spoonful of porridge into his open mouth, and the howls ceased. The twins were round and vigorous, with their father's flare of red hair that was beginning to sprout up through their bald infant heads. In sharp contrast, was Sadie's delicate paleness with her head of feathery blonde hair that floated softly around her tiny face.

Nanny Ryan spread warm, buttery toast fingers with strawberry jam and divided them equally among the three children. Four-year-old Sadie slowly chewed two fingers of toast, then slipped from her chair and went over to gently wipe a blob of jam from under William's nose. William looked at her adoringly and reached out with jammy fingers to grab her hair, but Sadie laughed and moved quickly out of reach. When she was back in her chair, she said,

"Nanny, I don't think I can eat any more, thank you." The little girl's voice was soft, almost musical, and she turned her pale green eyes pleadingly toward Florrie. "May I go to the school room and read my book before our walk?"

"You haven't eaten much at all, Sadie my pet. Are you still tired?" Florrie looked concerned, and she pushed her chair back and patted her ample lap. "Come and sit up with Florrie for a cuddle." Sadie nodded shyly and trotted round obediently to where Florrie was seated.

Florrie leant forward, wrapped her arms tenderly around the tiny figure, and despite her advancing years, hoisted the little girl easily onto her lap. Nanny Ryan, who had only been with the household for just over a year, in fact only since the twins were born, looked at Sadie curiously.

"She's like a little will o' the wisp," she thought, and recalled the various stories that buzzed around below stairs about the twin's mysterious little girl cousin.

Sadie Grieves-Croft, at four years old, was a wraith-like figure, tiny-boned with white blonde flyaway hair around a small, pale face, and round green eyes framed with pale lashes. Florrie was talking softly to the child on her lap, and Sadie was smiling up into her face, "Come along then, little one, come and have a rest." Florrie put the child down gently and stood up, "I am going to pop Sadie into the school room for an hour. She is a little tired, and she wants to look through her new picture book. I'll come back for my tea, Mary."

Nanny Ryan looked at her much-older colleague. "Florrie, you look tired as well. That trip fair wore you out."

Florrie laughed, "I don't know how you cope with those little terrors; it's them two that have worn me out," but she looked fondly at the jam-covered faces of William and Walter. "Mind you, I've always had girls, but then Estelle was a real little terror in her time, a real tom boy, she was." The old lady looked down at the child waiting patiently beside her, the tiny hand lost in her large, capable one. "Come along then, Sadie, we shall get you settled down for a little while."

Walter, seeing his beloved Sadie leaving the room, howled in protest, and William's bottom lip began to quiver. Nanny Ryan stood up, "Now then, boys, let's get those faces wiped, and you can go in your play pens for a while," she said firmly, scooping up a wriggling twin under each arm. Ignoring their loud protests, she marched out to the nursery room and planted them down in the playpens.

When Florrie came back into the nursery, the breakfast things had been cleared, all was quiet from the nursery, and Nanny Ryan was seated by the open window with a fresh pot of tea. Florrie sank down gratefully into a large armchair. "I do worry about that child, she tires so quickly, although the doctor says she is well, if a little delicate."

Mary Ryan was quiet, looking out over the sunny garden, and then said hesitatingly, "You know Florrie, I have heard a bit of gossip about Sadie and how she came to be here, but I have never paid that much attention. I have been far too busy with the twins." She waited, hoping that she had not spoken out of turn. Florrie's devotion and loyalty to the family was well known, and she despised gossip, and when roused, her tongue could be razor sharp. Mary Ryan, daughter of an old friend of Florrie, had joined the household as nanny to the twins, and Florrie found that she liked and respected her younger colleague and now felt that she trusted her sufficiently to tell her about Sadie.

"Well, I daresay you heard a bit of the truth, but I wager, a lot of old gossip as well, so you may as well hear what really happened." Florrie took a deep breath and began.

"Lord Archie was an only child until he was twenty. Of course, he didn't have the title then, his father did. I had been lady's maid to his mother, Lady Grieves-Croft, for years, and they had given up all hope of having another child, so when my lady found out she was expecting another child at forty-six, it was a shock to everyone, especially young Archie, who had left Eton and joined the army."

Florrie paused and looked out over the peaceful garden. "I don't know to this day what made my lady ignore the doctor's warning not to ride, but she did. In her seventh month, her horse threw her, and although nothing was broken, she was badly bruised. The next day, she went into labour, and that is something I will never forget. My poor lady was in labour for two days and two nights. I never left her side, and she was so brave. The doctor was worried because the cord was around the baby's neck, and at one point it was feared that neither my lady nor the baby would survive, but survive they did. When the baby was born, I could see straightaway that the poor mite was not right and so could the doctor, she was so blue, and at first, they could not get her to breathe. She was such a big girl, far too big for my lady, and when the doctor finally got her breathing, she screamed and screamed. I have never heard a child scream for so long. It sent shivers down my spine."

Florrie paused again, reached into her apron pocket, took out a vast white handkerchief, and wiped her eyes. "My lady was so ill and exhausted after the birth, and after the third day, when she refused to even look at her little girl, the doctor arranged to bring in a wet nurse, and he said she must be baptized, as she was unlikely to survive. My lady would not speak about naming her, so the doctor wrapped the baby up in a shawl and went to Lord Grieves-Croft." Florrie shook her head at the memory. "But the master was so distraught, he barely looked at her and said, "Call her what you will."

The wet nurse said, "Call her Grace, because if she lives, it will be by the grace of God."

"Oh, Florrie, how sad." Mary Ryan leant forward and patted the old lady's hand. "That poor child."

The old lady nodded. "Well, Grace, as she was, was baptized here in the nursery with just the doctor and the priest, the nurse, and me. My lady refused to leave her bedroom, and Lord Grieves-Croft said he was too busy, and Master Archie said he could not get leave to come home."

"It was such a dreadful time. My poor lady got worse and worse, barely eating, just lying in her bed begging someone to stop the child screaming. By then, we had two nursemaids because the child hardly slept, and the nurses were exhausted. The doctor visited my lady and Grace every day, but one day he said to me that he needed to speak to the Master urgently. I don't know what he said, but the very next day, the Master asked me to dress my lady up warmly. When she was all wrapped up like a baby the doctor and the nurse carried her into the carriage, and the master took her to the Dawlish farmhouse by the sea. The doctor thought the sea air would help my lady to get better."

"But why didn't you go with your mistress?" Mary Ryan asked.

"I wanted to. I begged to. But it was decided that I would be needed at Grieves Manor to help with Master Archie's wedding. The doctor recommended that my lady needed a full-time nurse anyway, more care than I could give her," Florrie added sadly.

"Before they left, Lord Grieves-Croft made arrangements for Grace and her nurses to move out of the big house into Oak Lodge because Master Archie said that he did not want to bring his bride into the Manor whilst 'That child' was living there. I was glad for Grace because I liked Oak Lodge. It was a cosy little place, right on the edge of the park with its own little garden where Gracie could run around without being stared at. I think Archie knew then that his parents would never come back to live at Grieves Manor."

A loud howl came from the nursery. Mary Ryan sighed and stood up, "I'll just go and see what those two are up to now."

Florrie stood up too and rubbed her back. "I'm going to pop in and check on Sadie while you see to the boys." Sadie was fast asleep, curled up into a little ball on the day bed, with a small pink thumb lodged firmly in her mouth. Florrie drew the curtains and tucked a light blanket over the little girl and, leaving the school room door open a little, went back into the nursery. The little housemaid was tidying the room.

"Nanny Ryan has put the boys down for a little rest" she said importantly, "and she said to tell you that she won't be long."

"Thank you," said Florrie and settled back into the chair. The sun was warm on her face, and she closed her eyes. It had been a long time since she had allowed herself to think back to those dark days.

Distant howls of protest could be heard coming from the twin's bedroom, but after a while they stopped, and Nanny Ryan walked back into the nursery. "Give them five minutes, and they'll be fast asleep."

There was no reply from the figure in the chair, and she walked over to see if Florrie had dozed off. "Florrie dear, you don't have to carry on if talking about the past upsets you," she said softly.

Florrie nodded without opening her eyes. "I'm not asleep, Mary, and I'm fine. Well, now where was I? Ah yes, Oak Lodge. You know, it seemed that Grace had disappeared from our lives once she moved to Oak Lodge. She had her nurses, and the doctor went to see her regularly, and after a while, the doctor told Lord Archie that it would better if she did not have visitors, as she got very agitated at new faces."

"But why? She was just a child after all, surely she would like to see her family?" Mary Ryan was puzzled.

Florrie shook her head sadly. "The doctor said it would be better not to. In fact, I think he wanted her locked away because her rages were so terrible, but Lord Archie insisted that she was taken care of in her own home. Of course, she could not go to young Lord Archie and Miss Rose's wedding. But you know the saddest thing? My poor lady was not well enough to go to see her beloved Archie wed his lovely bride, and she had been so happy when they became engaged. Then we heard that my lady and the master would not be coming back to Grieves Manor, and soon after that, old Lord Grieves-Croft retired, and young Lord Archie left the army and took over the business."

"And did Grace get any better?"

"No, of course not." Florrie shook her head. "The doctor said she had been damaged at birth and would never get any better. Even when she was only five, reports were coming back to the family that her behaviour was getting worse. Young Lord Archie forbade anyone to go near Oak Lodge, especially Lady Rose, because by then she was expecting Master George. The lawyers set up a fund for Grace's upkeep and care, but apart from that, she was cut off from the family completely."

Florrie was thoughtful. "I saw her once you know, years later when she was almost a grown woman. Someone had left the garden gate open that led out onto the lane, and I saw a face peering through at me as I walked by. I knew it was Grace, and I was going to speak to her, but then someone pulled her back in and closed the gate, but I could hear her screaming and shouting. She had grown enormously fat, and I heard from one of the gardeners that they had to employ four nurses to take care of her. I know that young Lord Archie did his best, and although he blamed Grace for what happened to his mother, he never stopped trying to find the best nurses for her." Florrie paused. "When our little George was seven, Lady Rose gave birth to Estelle, and that baby was so perfect."

Florrie's old face creased into a smile. "That was the best time. George had a tutor, and Lady Rose asked me whether I would like to be nanny to Estelle. Of course, I said that I would. Oh my, Mary, they were such happy times, and it seemed for a while as if things were going to be all right at last, and for years it was, of course." Florrie's voice trailed into silence, and she jumped when the maid arrived with another tea trolley.

Mary Ryan stood up, "Pour us a nice cup of tea, Florrie," she said kindly, "and I'll check on the children."

The house was quiet and peaceful. Florrie could hear the gardeners mowing the lawn outside the window and the sound of low voices drifted up from the kitchen garden. She poured the tea and sat back. "It won't be so peaceful when Master George and his friends get back," she thought fondly, and allowed her mind to drift back to when George was just a small, red-headed schoolboy and Estelle was a wild-haired tomboy trying to copy everything that George and his friends did. How quickly the years had flown by, and now George was married to Lady Jenny and was a father himself, and her precious Estelle had turned from a tomboy into a beautiful young woman.

As the years passed, it seemed as if the household had forgotten about Grace, hidden away in Oak Lodge. The reports coming back from the nurses and caregivers were few and far between, but Lord Archie was assured that Grace was well-contained within the confines of Oak Lodge. But a chain of events was about to change the pattern of their lives forever, and Florrie shivered as she remembered the circumstances of Sadie's shocking entry into the world.

Lord Archie and Lady Rose were planning a stay in the apartment in Paris, when one of the long-serving nurses at Oak Lodge suddenly and without warning left, saying that she could not cope with Grace anymore. Lord Archie persuaded Lady Rose to travel to France anyway, but said that he should stay behind and find a suitable replacement. When a grave and seemingly experienced middle-aged man replied to the advertisement for a "Professional Person to assist with a Disabled Person," Lord Archibald was surprised, but agreed to see him. Dennis McCabe's references were impeccable, having been a caregiver for young adults with difficulties, and when interviewed, seemed totally unconcerned that his charge would be a grown woman. After all, he was only there to assist the nurse when her charge became violent and to walk Grace around the grounds when the nurses rested, Lord Archie reassured himself when he experienced a twinge of doubt. Much to everyone's astonishment and relief, Grace, as expected, was initially aggressive toward the newcomer, but after a few tumultuous days, slowly began to accept Mr McCabe. Although Grace's mood was still highly unpredictable, his quiet authority and soft voice appeared to have a calming effect on her.

In 1893, at the end of a hot summer, Dennis McCabe informed Lord Archie that he had received news that his elderly mother was ill, and he had to leave immediately, as she lived on the Isle of Bute, and he wasn't sure when he would be back. Florrie remembered how devastated Lord Archie had been, but, nevertheless, Lord Archie wrote him a large cheque, thanking him for everything that he had done to help with Grace, and said he hoped that he would be able to return. Then, shortly before Christmas, the doctor was summoned urgently to Oak Lodge by the nurse, fearing that Grace had appendicitis. Grace was pregnant, and in the early hours of a freezing December morning, the doctor delivered a small but healthy little girl. Grace died a few hours later from complications, but the baby girl, although tiny, was perfect.

Florrie gave a shuddering sigh recalling the moment that she was hurried over to Oak Lodge, where a shocked Lady Rose helplessly handed her a baby. Florrie, dumbfounded and bewildered, had gazed down at the helpless child in her arms and had fallen instantly in love with the elf-like infant with white, wispy hair floating around her head like dandelion fluff. For a while, despite the doctor's assurances that Sadie was perfectly healthy, the household held their breath. But soon it became clear that the calm and quiet child was indeed normal, and the first sweet smiles from her clear, sea-green eyes totally enraptured the family. Florrie, lost in her memories, was startled back to the present when Nanny Ryan came back and sat down.

"Still fast asleep, all three of them," she reported. "So, Florrie, you were saying it was all right for years and Grace stayed at Oak Lodge."

Florrie nodded. "Yes, it was, there were little upsets of course when nurses left or Grace got ill, but Lord Archie kept all that away from the house. Naturally, as the children were growing, they were curious and asked questions about the funny lady who lived in Oak Lodge. That was bound to happen, I suppose, listening to servant's gossip, but Lady Rose just said that an old aunt lived there and must be left alone, which seemed to satisfy them. When they were old enough to understand, Lady Rose explained that although Grace was their Auntie, she was very sick. I mean, George went off to Eton when he was thirteen, and even when he brought friends home in the holidays, he had no interest in a mad aunt. Estelle was the same; life was too busy for her as well." Florrie hesitated and looked across the lawns in the direction of Oak Lodge. "But then one summer, Mr McCabe came to Oak Lodge and everything changed."

Mary Ryan listened in shocked silence as Florrie related the events of the summer that Dennis McCabe came into their lives. When Florrie finished speaking, Mary Ryan leant forward and place her hands over the old lady's shaking hands.

"Oh Florrie, how awful, this poor family. So, is Mr McCabe Sadie's father then?"

Florrie shrugged and said sadly, "Lord Archie thinks so, but who knows, because it turns out that Grace escaped a fair few times and wandered around, even getting down into the village once or twice. When Grace died, and Oak Lodge was cleared out, Mrs Brent said that they found bottles and bottles of Laudanum, and when Lord Archie asked the doctor, he said he had never prescribed Laudanum for Grace. Then one of the nurses confessed that McCabe always had boxes of it delivered, and they had seen him put it in Grace's cocoa at night. But of course, the nurses never minded because it kept Grace quiet and biddable, and they could have a peaceful night's sleep."

Florrie's old eyes filled with tears at the memory. "And the worst thing is that Lord Archie and Lady Rose blamed themselves, especially Lord Archie. The family took Sadie to their hearts straightaway though, and she has been loved and cared for as if she was their own child. When Lady Rose asked me to be Sadie's nanny, I did wonder whether I was too old, but when I took that little mite into my arms, of course I said yes. Then, later, after George and Jenny married and the twins came along, my little Sadie was so excited, especially when Lady Jenny let her hold them and told her that she was the boy's big sister." Florrie's voice wobbled, and she blinked away the unshed tears.

Seeing that the old lady was visibly upset at the memory, Mary Ryan took a deep breath, stood up, and held out her hands. "Come on, Florrie, let's wake the little ones and take them down to the lake to feed the ducks before lunch. It's such a lovely day. The past is the past, nothing can change that, and anyone can see how loved Sadie is now."

HENRY AND ESTELLE

That evening, the first to arrive back from Ascot in the brougham were Lady Rose, Lord Archibald, Jenny, and Estelle. Lady Rose, looking beautiful in a misty-purple gown and a matching hat decorated with beads and feathers, was followed by Jenny, still immaculate and coolly elegant, despite the hot, dusty afternoon at Royal Ascot.

Brent, waiting in the hall, hid a smile behind his hand as Estelle, the long-abandoned hat in her hand and with her red curls dancing around her lovely face, came racing up the steps. "My goodness, Brent, that was so tremendously exciting. Persimmon won by eight lengths from Winkfield's Pride, left him standing, poor old Perry," and she burst out laughing. Waving to her amused mother, she picked up her skirt and ran up the stairs. "So hot, Mummy, I must run and change, and I want to see Sadie before she goes to sleep."

Lady Rose raised her eyebrows to Brent, who was now smiling quite openly. The superior and haughty Master Peregrine Porter was not a favourite with Brent. A giggling Jenny followed Estelle up the stairs to the nursery to check on her beloved boys. "Ma, when George comes in, please tell him that I'm in the nursery."

"And I am going into the study to count my winnings, Brent." Lord

Archie chuckled and called to John as he appeared in the hall behind Brent, "George and his rabble are on their way back, John, if you could attend to them before dinner?"

"Yes, of course, my Lord." John bowed.

Later that night at yet another riotous dinner where the guests celebrated the Prince of Wales' victory and toasted Queen Victoria with fine wines and champagne, Henry, distracted but happy, only had eyes for Estelle. After dinner, Lord Archie and Lady Rose, seeking some peace and quiet from the noisy celebration, sat together on the terrace quietly talking and listening with amusement to the loud carousing coming from the music room.

A solitary couple walked hand-in-hand in the moonlight, across the soft grass, passing in and out of the shadows of the tall trees as they strolled down toward the lake.

Further along the terrace, slouched back in a garden chair, Perry Porter slowly blew a thin stream of cigar smoke into the air and watched with a frown as the couple stopped to embrace and kiss, the man scooping up handfuls of the tumbling curls and pulling the girl toward him. Flicking the still-burning ember up into the night sky, Perry sat motionless, staring after them. It was only when the couple disappeared into the boathouse that he stood up, pushed the chair back, turned, and walked slowly back into the house.

Having partied long into the night, few of the friends were at the breakfast table on the morning of their departure back to London to begin the Jubilee celebrations. In fact, Brent, reporting back to Mrs Brent, said that at breakfast, there was just Master George and Jenny, Lord Archie and Lady Rose, Estelle, Foxy, and two more from the group.

A rather morose-looking Henry, arriving after the others were seated at the table, looked around in surprise and said, "Just we then, not even Perry this morning?"

Brent, who was serving the orange juice, paused, and without looking up, said smoothly, "Mr Porter left early this morning, sir. Patrick took him to the station. Mr Porter sent his sincere apologies but said he had to get back to London."

Henry looked astonished. "Really," he turned to Foxy. "Did Perry say anything to you, Foxy?"

Foxy, who was tucking into his breakfast with relish, shook his head. "No, old boy, not a word, old Perry's been a bit moody this trip, I have to say, perhaps because his Uncle's horse lost. I think he lost a packet."

Henry, still puzzled, shrugged. "Perry doesn't worry about things like that, Foxy, unless he lost more than he said," and shook his head when Brent offered him breakfast. "Just tea please, Brent," he said briefly.

"What time is your train today, Henry?" enquired Lord Archie, listening to the exchange with interest.

Estelle, who had been quietly talking to Jenny, stopped suddenly and looked over at Henry, who refused to catch her eye. On their walk around the lake the previous evening, they had been discussing his return to London, and Henry had been trying to persuade Estelle to ask her parent's permission to go with him to London for the Jubilee festivities. Estelle had shaken her head sadly. "Henry, I would love to, I know that I could stay in the London House, but Daddy and Mummy have arranged a huge garden party at home. Simply everyone is coming, and then there's the big party at Shaw House. It has been arranged for ages; I just can't ask to be excused. It would be most awfully rude."

Henry had been mutinous, "Please, Estelle, just ask. After all, the Devonshire fancy dress ball will be the event of the year, and you just cannot miss the parade from Buckingham Palace." But Estelle had been adamant, and Henry, not used to being thwarted, had marched off to bed, stating angrily that she obviously did not want to go with him to London.

Henry stood up, "Sir, we should be leaving. Foxy, can you make sure that the others are ready? Tell them that they are too late for breakfast."

George, who had sensed the strained atmosphere at breakfast between his sister and Henry, looked at him in surprise. "I thought you were getting the afternoon train, Henry."

"May as well make a move soon. I want to call in on Bernie before I go to London. Have another go at trying to make the old boy abandon the village for once and come to London to join in the fun."

Henry turned to his hosts and bowed. "I know I speak for my friends when I say thank you so much for making us so welcome, and we have had a wonderful stay."

Estelle kept her head bowed, and Lady Rose said graciously, if a little coldly, "George's friends have always been welcome at Grieves Manor, Henry," and she turned to her husband. "Archie, my dear, can you say goodbye to our guests please? I would like to help Jenny with our terrible twins. Are you coming with us, Estelle?" she addressed the last remark gently to Estelle, who nodded silently and left the room with her mother and Jenny.

Once out of earshot, Lady Rose put her arm around Estelle's shoulders. "Henry Maycroft always was a spoilt brat, my dear, and used to getting his own way. I suppose he wanted you to accompany him back to London and show you off at Lady Devonshire's ball?"

Estelle nodded. "He did. Oh Ma, he looks so cross, and I like him so much."

Jenny, who had remained silent, laughed gently, and taking Estelle by the shoulders, looked into the lovely eyes, filled with unshed tears.

"Yes, Henry is cross now, and I do think he is showing off, but I promise you, he will be back. Now let's go and see what mischief the boys are up to and rescue poor Sadie."

Estelle still looked anxious, "You do think he will come back, Ma?"

Lady Rose nodded her head. "Henry Maycroft will be back, my dear," she said, and taking her daughter firmly by the arm, led her up the stairs.

When Henry emerged from the dining room, his suitcases, together with the rest of the group's luggage, were arranged neatly in the hall.

"The carriage is outside, sir, and your friends are waiting." Brent checked his pocket watch, "You should be in time for the midday train."

"Thank you, Brent," said Henry, looking around for any sign of

Estelle, but it was just Lord Archie and George outside on the drive to wave them off, and, feeling rather flat, Henry boarded the carriage.

Ascot now forgotten, much of the talk on the way back to London was of the forthcoming Diamond Jubilee festivities, and as the train drew closer to Paddington, Henry, to his irritation, found his thoughts drifting back to Estelle, and he wished he had been kinder.

The next few days were a whirl of activity. Henry abandoned his plans to visit Riverside, knowing in his heart of hearts that Bernard would prefer to celebrate with the village and actively disliked travelling to London anyway. Henry had made plans to stay at Foxy's flat in Northumberland Ave to watch the Royal Parade from the balcony as it passed Trafalgar Square on its way to St Paul's.

After the thanksgiving ceremony at Windsor Castle on the 20th of June, Queen Victoria travelled back to Buckingham Palace. The grimy and sooty streets of London were hidden under waving banners and Union Jack flags festooned on every building, and the capital was a sea of patriotic red, white, and blue. Crowds of people thronged the streets, cheering and waving to their monarch, many loyal subjects happy to camp out for the night rather than miss glimpsing the Royal Parade as it wound its way from Buckingham Palace to St Paul's Cathedral. At eleven fifteen on the morning of June 22nd, a cannon in Hyde Park boomed out across London announcing the start of the parade.

Henry and Foxy, seated comfortably on the balcony above the teeming streets, touched champagne glasses, toasted the Queen, and with an open picnic basket at their feet, settled down to watch the procession.

Henry raised a sparkling glass in the air. "A moment in history, Foxy." This almost, but not quite, banished the unsettled feeling that had dogged him since he had left Grieves Manor. Henry and George had planned to meet with Peregrine at the St James club the following day, and after lunch, Peregrine was to return to the flat with them. But Henry woke feeling distinctly under the weather.

"I will convey your abject apologies to our friends, Henry," said Foxy, as he grinned, donning his top hat.

However, Foxy had returned without Peregrine, who had informed him silkily, "Sorry, old boy, I won't be staying with you and Henry after all. I decided to stay with another chum. I might see you at the Devonshire Ball."

On hearing this, Henry exploded with anger, declaring that, "Perry was bloody rude, and I haven't forgiven him for his rudeness to Lord Archie at Grieves Manor."

Foxy, listening to the outburst, raised his eyebrows and said laconically. "Perry is only sulking, Henry. Good Lord, you know how he likes to be the centre of attention, and you paid rather too much attention to the lovely Miss Grieves-Croft. Perry was most put out, but he won't miss the Devonshire party, I assure you."

Lady Devonshire's Jubilee celebration ball was to be held on July 2nd at Devonshire House in Piccadilly. Lady Devonshire was known as London's most prominent political hostess, and therefore, when the date of her costume ball was announced, no other hostesses even considered holding an event on that day. They all were, of course, hoping to be included on the elite guest list which included the crème de la crème of London society. The dress code was to be "Historical Costumes," and it was rumoured that many of the guests had spent fortunes on their costumes, keeping the wig makers, dressmakers, and theatrical costumiers busy for months. Foxy, in true character, had opted to go as a court jester, and Perry and Henry had chosen to go as cavaliers. As additional entertainment, they had planned to hold a convincing sword fight around the grounds of Devonshire House and win the hand of a fair lady. Foxy was right, Henry mused, once he had calmed down, most certainly Perry would not be left out on that day, and true to form, Peregrine strolled nonchalantly into the club a few days before the ball. Studiously ignoring Henry's glares, Peregrine suggested, almost as if nothing was amiss, "Henry, dear chap, we should collect our costumes and have a few practice fights. What do you say?" and he swished the air with an imaginary sword.

Frustrated, Henry decided to ignore Perry's odd behaviour. "If you so wish," he muttered and made up his mind to concentrate on the celebrations and not let Perry rattle him anymore.

As expected, the Devonshire costume ball was a resounding success, beginning with the celebrated photographer, Mr Lafayette, striding around in a specially-equipped marquee catching shots of the aristocrats as they paraded and posed for the camera. Foxy, a vividly decorated court jester, was hugely entertaining as usual, dancing through the guests, tweaking their hats, peering under the masks and stealing kisses from unwary ladies. Henry and Perry with their vast, black velvet hats tipped over one eye, swishing black cloaks, and white silk neck ruffs were exciting, dashing, and romantic. Perry, with a waxed, pointed beard and curled moustache closely resembled the cavalier in Franz Hal's painting.

Their well-rehearsed and cleverly executed sword fight played out in the gardens of Devonshire House, was loudly applauded, and several of the season's beautiful young debutants batted their eyelashes at the handsome pair, rushing to tie handkerchiefs to their favourite's swords. For a while, the excitement of the evening, the admiration and flattering and inviting glances from beautiful woman drove all thought of Estelle from Henry's mind. Peregrine had reverted to his charming, amusing self, whispering in Henry's ear sly acerbic comments on some of the rather portly ladies in their over tight costumes.

The evening was warm, and Henry, Foxy, and Perry were standing on the balcony enjoying a glass of wine, when below them in the darkness a young girl laughed. It was a low, throaty laugh, and Henry's heart missed a beat. For a moment, he was transported back to that last evening at Grieves Manor. He closed his eyes, Perry's voice faded into the distance, and he could see Estelle's red curls, her green eyes, and her invitingly soft mouth, and for Henry in that split second the evening died.

It was barely dawn when, after a sleepless and seemingly endless night, Henry went back to the house in Park Crescent, packed a few things, and took a cab to Victoria. He was lucky a train to Shorehill was waiting on the platform, and he arrived in the village at ten-thirty.

Bernard was in the estate office with William Hunter when he saw the determined figure of his young brother striding up over the bridge carrying a suitcase. William Hunter stopped and looked up from the accounts book as Bernard stopped in mid-sentence. "That's Master Henry, were you expecting him, sir? If you said, I could have picked him up."

"Well, yes, had I known he was coming down, I would have met him at the station." Bernard closed the books with a sigh and wondered what trouble had brought Henry down to Shorehill in the middle of the week.

William stood up. "I shall leave you to it then, Mr Bernard. I'll take the boy up to Pat O'Donnell to bag some rabbits," and nodded a greeting to Henry he left.

Bernard sat down heavily and raised his eyebrows at Henry. "Good morning, Henry. I wasn't expecting you down today. I thought you were in the thick of the Jubilee celebrations. Is something wrong? What has happened?"

"Nothing has happened, Bernard," protested Henry. "Good Lord, why do you always assume that something is amiss? Everything went very well at the Devonshire Ball, I promise."

"Then what brings you here today, Henry?"

Henry perched on the edge of Bernard's desk, looking more uncertain than Bernard could ever remember seeing him, and then listened in amazement as a somewhat subdued Henry confessed that since leaving Estelle in Berkshire, he had not really enjoyed the festivities in London as much as he hoped he would.

Bernard hid his surprise, for this was a side to his little brother that he had never seen. Henry loved a party and had never moped after a girl for more than a day. "Well, she sounds like a wonderful girl, Henry, but what are your intentions now?"

Henry shook his head. "I am not entirely sure. I just thought I should come home and have a think about it. Estelle was rather cross with me, and Perry was not on his best behaviour. In fact, I really do not know what has got into him"

Bernard frowned. "That fellow is always rather rude in my opinion. I never took to him, you know, Henry."

Henry looked taken-aback at his mild-mannered brother's terse tone. "Well, he is a trifle odd at times, I grant you. I suppose we have all got used to his manner, but he rather overstepped the mark with Lord Archie this time, I fear."

At Riverside, over dinner, Bernard listened intently with barely concealed surprise as Henry described Estelle and the few days they had enjoyed together. In fact, Henry had been talking of Estelle all afternoon. "The thing is, old man, I simply cannot get her out of my mind and that's a fact. I think I may have fallen in love with her," Henry finally admitted, swirling a large brandy around in his glass and failing to meet Bernard's eye. "I just don't know what to do now," he added miserably.

"Henry, if that is what you honestly feel, and Estelle is not another one of your little flirtations, then you must find out how she feels. But tread carefully and be sure of what you are doing." Bernard advised.

When Bernard came down to breakfast the following morning, Henry had gone. A note left on the hall table stated that he was going down to Berkshire. "Left early, made up my mind, old chap." Henry had written in haste, "I am going back to Grieves Manor, and I am going to ask Estelle to marry me. You will speak up for me with Lord Archie, I trust?"

The whirlwind romance between Henry and Estelle had taken everyone by surprise, not least of all Bernard, and now he was about to meet Henry's bride and her rather illustrious family for the first time, and he confessed to Aggie that he was feeling a little apprehensive.

But he need not have worried, for when he was ushered into the drawing room at Grieves Manor by a nervous Henry to be introduced to the Grieves-Croft family, Estelle rushed forward with a beaming smile and caught him in a bear hug.

"Estelle!" Lady Rose admonished, "Please wait to be introduced properly. My apologies Mr Maycroft, our daughter is rather too excited."

Bernard, beaming at his lovely young soon-to-be sister-in-law standing by his side, replied with barely a stutter, "Lady Grieves-

Croft, I could not have wished for a better welcome. I confess to feeling somewhat nervous about meeting Henry's new family."

Estelle squeezed his arm "I just knew you would be lovely; Henry never stops talking about his big brother."

Lord Archie walked forward to take Bernard's outstretched hand. "Welcome, Bernard. We have known Henry for many years, and we are delighted to welcome you both into our family."

Bernard took an instant liking to the Grieves-Crofts, and was introduced to George's wife, the calm and lovely Jenny. George, of course, he had known for years as Henry's friend. Brought down from the nursery, the red-headed twins, bundled up in matching pyjamas, tumbled in to bid good night to everyone, and a painfully shy, wide-eyed Sadie managed a tremulous smile when Bernard went down on one knee to solemnly wish her goodnight.

Five months later, on a clear, cold December morning, Bernard was travelling down to stay at Grieves Manor to stand by Henry as his best man when Henry and Estelle married in splendid style in the ancient Gothic Reading Minster church.

THE WEDDING

On Saturday December 18th, 1897, a bright and bitterly cold winter day, Bernard, resplendent in a long dress coat, pinstriped trousers, and a black-and-gold jacquard waistcoat, shivered under the majestic soaring arches of Reading Minster church. A strangely calm and equally elegant Henry stood beside him awaiting the arrival of his bride. In the packed pews behind them, there was an air of expectancy and excitement, as they, too, awaited the arrival of the beautiful and popular young heiress.

To Bernard, it seemed that they had been standing there for an age, when the minister standing in front of the altar nodded slightly to the organist, and suddenly the first triumphant bars from Mendelssohn's Wedding March filled the air and echoed around the church. Peregrine, silent and pale-faced and the ever-jolly Foxy, both appointed ushers, having seated the guests, took their places in the second pew behind the Grieves-Croft family. At the first strains of music from the organ, the congregation, almost as one, stood and turned their heads, straining to catch a first glimpse of the bride. All, that is, except Peregrine Porter, who kept his eyes fixed straight ahead.

Estelle, heart-touchingly beautiful in a long, white-velvet cloak and holding a tumbling bouquet of deep-red roses, stood like a snow maiden underneath the Gothic arch, the sun streaming in behind her on to the ancient flagstone aisle.

Lord Archie, stiff and proud, was tenderly holding his daughter's arm, waiting for the cue to move forward. The minister nodded his assent again, and Lord Archie turned to look at Estelle, who gave her father a beaming smile before nodding to Jenny, who was holding a shaking Sadie by the hand, and together, they stepped into the church.

A few months earlier, Estelle, casting aside Lady Rose's dressmaker's designs, had despaired of finding her perfect wedding dress. The gowns were beautiful, but too flouncy and full, or straight and dull. A young apprentice dressmaker, sewing quietly in a corner was listening as Estelle attempted to describe the wedding dress that she had in mind. She touched Estelle on the arm and shyly asked whether Estelle had seen the Paris designs by Charles Worth. A few days later, the sketches arrived, and Estelle was delighted with the elegant simplicity of the gowns. With advice from the young dressmaker, Estelle made her choice and insisted that the apprentice dressmaker supervise the making of not only her wedding gown, but Jenny and Sadie's bridesmaid's dresses also.

Estelle had chosen a breathtakingly beautiful wedding dress, a slender sheath of white silk satin with long, pointed sleeves and an embroidered lace-and-pearl bodice with rows of tiny seed pearls around the high neck.

A snow-white train of pure lace was caught up around her tiny waist, and a feather-light tulle veil fell in soft pleats over her face, held in place by a diamond-and-platinum tiara. She wore her mother's diamond-and-pearl-drop earrings. Her tiny feet were encased in silk-laced ankle boots, and as she walked, a tumble of red curls gently kissed her shoulders.

Stepping lightly behind her was Jenny, her face alight with joy, ravishing in a soft rose satin gown, with a white ermine shoulder-cape and a delicate headband of white rosebuds. Sadie, who until the last minute had declared herself too scared to walk into the church with everyone looking at her, had succumbed when her tiny white velvet dress was slipped over her shoulders, and she was wrapped in a miniature velvet cloak. Jenny carried a bouquet of pink roses, and Sadie held a posy of red and white rosebuds.

The music reached a crescendo as the entourage reached the altar, and there was a collective gasp from the congregation as Lady Rose stepped forward and gently removed Estelle's velvet cape, and the full beauty of the wedding gown was revealed. Estelle then turned to hand Jenny her bouquet. Lord Archie stood back, and Estelle, looking radiantly happy, stepped forward to stand at Henry's side. Sadie, fully recovered from her nerves, was enjoying herself immensely, and stood proudly behind Estelle, gripping her posy tightly in one hand and holding onto Jenny with the other hand.

When the service was over and the church bells were ringing out triumphantly, the happy couple stepped out into the bright sunshine to the cheers and calls of congratulations from the clapping crowd of well-wishers. A wedding carriage decorated in white and red ribbons, pulled by four white horses, whisked the bride and groom away as the guests made their way back to Grieves Manor for the lavish wedding breakfast.

The celebrations at Grieves Manor carried on well into the night, long after the newlywed couple had left on their honeymoon. Bernard, on the insistence of Lady Rose, stayed on at Grieves Manor for a few more days before journeying back to Riverside to relay the events to the household eager for news of the wedding.

Henry and Estelle's honeymoon took them first to Italy to stay in a crumbling but lovely old villa overlooking Lake Garda that was owned by a family friend of the Grieves-Croft family, and then on to Verona to visit the famous Romeo and Juliet balcony, and finally, for the last two weeks, to the Grieves-Croft Paris apartment.

HENRY AND ESTELLE MAYCROFT

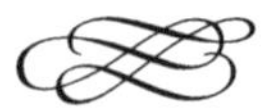

One Sunday morning, shortly after Bernard had returned to Riverside after the wedding, Betsy, the young parlour maid, knocked on the library door. She peered in nervously, "I beg your pardon, sir, but there is a gentleman outside wanting to see you." Since Bellows, the elderly butler, had died, Bernard could not see the point in employing another butler, and if Henry arrived with more than three weekend guests, Aggie could always call for help from one of her numerous relatives living in the village.

Bernard, who had been engrossed in his newspaper, looked up in surprise. "Really? Betsy, I am not expecting anyone, or at least I didn't think I was." Betsy hovered nervously. "Alright, my dear," Bernard sighed, folding his paper regretfully and placing it down on the table. "Let us see what the gentleman wants."

Lord Archie's battered old shooting brake was parked on the drive, and standing next to the car, looking around him with interest was Lord Archie's smartly dressed chauffeur. The boot of the brake was piled high with valises, trunks, and boxes of all sizes and shapes. The man touched his cap respectfully as Bernard emerged from the house. "Good Morning, Mr Maycroft."

"Ah yes, good morning..." Bernard frowned and hesitated, "Do forgive my rudeness, I seem to have forgotten your name."

The chauffeur smiled. "Manners, sir, my name is Manners. Lord Archie said to deliver Miss Estelle's," he paused and corrected himself, "I mean Mrs Maycroft's trunks to Riverside."

"Well then, yes, of course, thank you, Manners. I shall arrange to have the cases brought into the house, and I am sure that Aggie will find some refreshments for you after the long drive. Betsy will show you round to the kitchen."

Bernard turned to Betsy, who was staring at Manners. "Betsy, please show this gentleman around to the kitchen, and then go and ask Tip to send the grooms over to unload Mrs Maycroft's luggage." Betsy still stared, open mouthed. "Betsy," said Bernard kindly, "Did you hear what I said?"

Betsy started and turned scarlet. "Yes, Mr Bernard, of course," and stuttering. "Follow me please, Mr Manners," to the amused chauffeur. She fled around to the back of the house.

Riverside was sorely in need of some female influence, that was certain, and perhaps now, Bernard thought hopefully, Henry would spend more time at Riverside with his new wife instead of rushing back to London at every opportunity.

On a chill Sunday morning in late January 1898, as the congregation were spilling out of St Dominic's, the newly-wed Estelle and Henry Maycroft, returning from honeymoon, stepped off the London train and onto the still-frosty platform to be met by a beaming Bernard. Henry, looking rather pleased with himself, shook Bernard's hand vigorously, and a radiant Estelle opened her arms to hug her new brother-in-law tightly. Outside in the station yard, Pepper stood harnessed to a new, lightweight trap. Both Pepper and the smart little trap had been sent to Riverside as a surprise homecoming gift from Lord Archie to his beloved daughter.

Estelle's eyes sparkled, and she laughed in delight when she spotted her beloved little piebald. "Pepper! Oh look, Henry, it's dear little Pepper," and she rushed over to kiss the velvety nose, murmuring endearments as she stroked the little filly.

"And you must be Tip," Estelle turned to smile at the little Irishman. "Thank you for taking care of Pepper. I am so happy to see her."

"Welcome to Shorehill, Mrs Maycroft, and welcome home, Mr Henry." Tip replied gravely, giving a small nod of his head.

"Good day to you, Tip." Henry frowned when he saw Pepper. "That piebald has got a bit of a temper you know, Bernard. I'm surprised Lord Archie sent her."

Bernard shook his head, "Lord Archie said that Estelle could handle her, Henry. I must say I have driven Pepper around the village, and she seems to be a good-tempered little filly. Perhaps she will settle down in a bit. She is rather young."

"Nothing bad-tempered about the filly, Mr Henry. She is a might lively but good-tempered with it. I have stalled her next to Captain." Tip replied shortly.

Henry grunted. "Well, we shall see," and walked over to hand Estelle up onto the trap.

Tip flicked the reins lightly, turned the trap around, and they were off trotting off down Old Mill Lane toward the village. When Bernard had heard from Lady Rose that the honeymoon couple had arrived back from Paris and were heading back to Shorehill, he told an excited Aggie, who promptly told everyone in the village that Mr Henry and his bride would be arriving back from their honeymoon on the morning train.

It seemed now that the entire village had turned out to greet the young couple, and there were people lining the bridge and the narrow High Street, all waving and calling out good wishes. The children, perched on the school wall, shouted and clapped with excitement, and Estelle, in delighted astonishment, waved enthusiastically back in return.

"Thank, you, oh thank you everyone," she called. "Henry, you never told me that Shorehill was so pretty. The river is so lovely."

As Tip drove them proudly over the old bridge, she caught sight of Pat O'Donnell's giant shires dipping their great heads down in the shallows, and she jumped up with excitement. "Oh, Henry, do look at those wonderful creatures," she breathed and called out to the farmer. "Your horses are beautiful!"

Pat O'Donnell looked up, whipped his cap off, and called back with a grin, "Thank you, ma'am. Welcome to Shorehill."

Bernard, sitting opposite the excited and happy girl, chuckled to himself when he saw the pleasure on the farmer's face. Pat O'Donnell was a giant of a man, gentle but painfully shy. Bernard had a feeling that his lovely little red-headed sister-in-law would capture hearts wherever she went, and it would seem by the welcome they were receiving from the cautious villagers that they had already taken her to their hearts.

However, Henry's good humour seemed to have disappeared, and he was hunched down on the seat beside Bernard. "Estelle, please do stop bouncing around. I don't trust this pony not to tip us up."

Estelle laughed. "Rubbish Henry, Pepper would never do that, would he Tip? Don't be so grumpy, darling," and she smiled at Bernard. "Henry is a little out of temper, Bernie. We did not have a good crossing yesterday, I'm afraid."

Bernard nodded, swallowing his disappointment. "Yes, of course, I understand my dear, however, we are nearly home, and you can both rest, eh Henry?"

"Mm, yes, fine, but I just don't know why we could not have gone to London for a few days, finish off the honeymoon and all that." Henry was still frowning.

"Because, my dear husband," Estelle was amused, "I wanted to see my new home as soon as possible, and already I love Shorehill and the people are so nice. So there, cheer up do!" She leant forward and planted a little kiss on Henry's cheek.

Henry smiled grudgingly "Bloody tired, that's all. I did not get a wink of sleep all night. Damn crossing upset my stomach."

As they neared the end of the lane, the towering, wrought-iron gates to Riverside came into view, and as Pepper trotted smartly up the drive, Estelle caught her first sight of Riverside, the house by the Mill, and her new home. She stared up at the blank-eyed narrow windows and the grey flint walls of the old house, and her heart sunk a little. Everything looked so dark and damp compared to Grieves Manor, and the high oak trees surrounding the house were so dense that the clear, blue sky was barely visible.

Pushing her disappointment to one side, Estelle smiled brightly. "Henry, how sweet, do look darling," and she pointed to the staff waiting at the bottom of the steps to greet her. Estelle lifted her hand hesitantly and was heartened when the small group responded with waves and warm smiles. Henry, who seemed to have recovered his spirits, jumped down from the trap and gently handed Estelle down, kissing her hand as he did so. Bernard was relieved, he had not expected Henry to be in a bad mood, today of all days. Still holding her hand, Henry led Estelle forward and introduced her to first to Aggie. Putting an arm around the cook's plump shoulders, he gave her a squeeze and a genuinely fond smile.

"This is our precious Aggie, who cooks like a dream, and whom all my friends are in love with because she spoils them, no matter what time of the day or night they descend on Riverside."

Aggie beamed up at him, "Welcome home, Mr Henry and Mrs Maycroft," Aggie bobbed and gave Estelle a shy smile.

"Our Aggie seems to have an unending supply of relatives who help out at Riverside, and I am sure you will meet them one by one." Henry winked at the two maids who were shuffling their feet behind Aggie, almost hidden behind her enormous apron. "These are just two of Aggie's nieces, Betsy and Ruby. However, I am not sure which one is Ruby, and which one is Betsy."

Estelle was amused to see both girls rendered speechless and red-faced at Henry's teasing.

"Tip you have met, and Matthew is the gardener, and Bernard will no doubt introduce you to the estate manager, William Hunter. William is a good sort, not like his Uncle Silas, our last estate manager, miserable old bugger he was." Henry winked again at the two maids who collapsed into helpless giggles.

"Henry, language please," Bernard remonstrated, hiding a smile, and Aggie turned and glared at her nieces.

Estelle smiled prettily. "Thank you all so much for coming out to say hello and for making me welcome. Shorehill is lovely, and I know that I shall be very happy here with you all at Riverside."

Henry turned to his new wife, swept her ceremoniously up into his arms, ran lightly up the steps and across the threshold before placing her gently inside the house. "There you are, my dear. Welcome to Riverside."

If Henry and Bernard missed the look of shocked surprise on Estelle's face as she looked eagerly around the cold, smoky entrance hall, Aggie did not. Aggie, together with a team of helpers, had done her best to ensure that Riverside looked welcoming for the newly-wed's homecoming. There was a fire burning cheerfully in the old fireplace in the hall, but as the chimney had not been swept for years, a spiral of acrid smoke curled up into the darkened stairwell. The fires in the other rooms fared better, and the sweet smell of applewood logs burning in the grates filled the rest of the house. Riverside was situated so close to the river that if the fires were not lit daily, the damp seemed to permeate even the thick walls. Bernard, having lived alone for much of the time when Henry was in London, did not notice how shabby Riverside had become in the years since his parent's death. Nor did he notice the damp in the old house and the now-unloved and weed-ridden overgrown gardens. Most of Bernard's waking hours were spent either at the mill, in the estate office, or in the library with his beloved books. Aggie often dropped heavy hints about the old house needing repairs, especially the temperamental old kitchen range.

Bernard would look up from his book or newspaper, smile sweetly at her, and make vague promises. "Thank you for bringing it to my attention, Aggie, I will attend to it." But he never did, because he always forgot.

ESTELLE AND RIVERSIDE

To Henry's amazement, over the following weeks, a determined Estelle declared that she was excited at the thought of transforming Riverside, and even more surprising was that she stated that she was becoming rather fond of the old house. Bernard proved to be Estelle's willing ally, and to everyone's astonishment, he entered into the spirit of the transformation of Riverside with enthusiasm. Soon, drawings, rough sketches, and lists of ideas for the house were thrust in front of Henry.

Initially vaguely interested in the plans, Henry soon became bored when they consulted him about the various repairs and decorating suggestions. Whenever Henry found Bernard and Estelle huddled together over a new project for the garden or the house, he wandered off, sulky and dejected, but when Estelle began to make excuses and reasons not to accompany him to London, he was angry, reminding her peevishly, "Darling, we live in London, and Bernard can deal with the improvements now that you have given him the ideas. I need to get back to town and visit our customers."

"But, Henry, there is still so much to do. Bernard cannot manage without me now, and I want to finish the house and arrange the garden before summer. But darling, if you need to get back to the

London house for a while, then do go. I won't mind at all." Estelle further placated her sullen husband by promising that when the work on Riverside was finished, she would join him in London.

Henry agreed grudgingly. "After all, that was the plan, wasn't it darling? Don't you worry about leaving Bernard on his own. I rather think the old boy likes having the house to himself."

Estelle nodded, reluctant to admit to Henry that, day by day, she was becoming more attached to Riverside, especially the village, and that she had no desire whatsoever to live in London now. Consoling herself with the thought that the renovations to the house and gardens were going to take some time, she could hopefully delay moving to the London house for as long as possible, and Henry would eventually settle down at Riverside.

"The gardens used to be lovely when our parents were alive," Bernard confessed one day as he was showing Estelle the old orchard. "But Henry is always away in London, and I am always busy with the mill, and I have neglected the gardens. I do remember a rather pretty summerhouse somewhere in the orchard, and in the far meadow on the other side of the garden wall, there is an old Folly by the river."

Estelle's eyes widened. "Bernard, really? A Folly by the river? How wonderful! May I see it?"

"It's in rather a sorry state now, Estelle. No one has been there for an age, but I will tell the gardeners to begin repairing the roof of the summerhouse. It fell in ages ago. But the Folly may be beyond repair and may even be dangerous. I will have Matthew look at it."

"Thank you. I love the idea of a Folly by the river. Please don't forget to ask Matthew, will you Bernard?"

Satisfied that Tip was supervising the clearing of the grounds and garden, Estelle concentrated now on the rather dreary and broken terrace that ran along the back of the house. Watching where the sun set one golden evening, an idea began to form in her head, and she went back in the house and sketched out her idea. The next morning, she took it along to Jacob Brown, the village blacksmith.

"Are you able to make this frame-up for me, Jacob? I want to cover the old terrace and put a glass roof on it." Estelle held out her sketch and looked up at him anxiously.

The blacksmith studied the paper in her hand and shook his head. "No, Missus, no room to make it up here, but I have a friend in the foundry in Sevenoaks. I will get him to come down and take the measurements. He can make that up in the foundry."

Estelle smiled her enchanting smile. "Jacob, thank you so much. But may we go and show him my sketch now? Can you spare time to take me to Sevenoaks today?"

"It's mighty hard to refuse the young mistress. I'd like to see you try, Ernie Brown," Jacob growled at his cousin that evening in the Hop Vine. Ernie had been walking past the smithy when he had seen Jacob untie his leather apron and help Estelle gently up onto the seat of his old wagon. He had watched in astonishment as they had clattered out of the village.

"But you said you were too busy to shoe my old mare," Ernie teased. "You told me to bring her back next week, and there you were, gallivanting off to Sevenoaks at the drop of a hat."

"Well, you ain't as pretty, are you now Ernie?" Jacob grinned and downed his pint of ale.

It was a month later when the foundry lorry arrived at Riverside with a wrought-iron frame of delicate loops and swirls entwined with twisting ivy and flowers. Estelle, in the meantime, had cajoled her adoring father to import from Italy, exquisite rose-tinted Venetian glass panels to form a roof above the terrace, each glass panel etched with iridescent butterflies.

The transformation was astounding. The entire terrace was bathed in a warm, rosy glow, and the sunshine through the glass roof cast butterfly shadows flickering across the flagstones. Visitors to Riverside were entranced, and Henry, noting their admiration, proudly announced to all and sundry that it was, "A true work of art, created by my beautiful wife."

One still, frosty morning in February, after Henry had returned to London on the morning train, Estelle, finding the cold dining room empty, wandered down to the warm kitchen where Aggie was kneading a vast white mound of dough and gossiping with her sister-in-law, Bessie. Bessie Brown was housekeeper at the Vicarage and married to Aggie's brother, Ernie, the church verger. Bessie, who, as usual, had cycled through the frosty lanes to have breakfast with Aggie, was seated at the kitchen table, cradling a steaming cup of tea in her hands. Bessie looked up, a little startled to see the mistress of the house appear in the kitchen dressed only in her morning gown, and she put her cup down on the table and made to stand up. Estelle stopped her by saying. "Good Morning, Bess and Aggie. Bess, please don't get up. I'm going to join you both in a cup of tea, if I may."

Aggie smiled at her young mistress. "Mary is about to lay out in the dining room, madam. Master Bernard has had his breakfast in the library and gone off to the mill."

"Please don't bother about breakfast, Aggie. I thought I might take a walk, as it is such a beautiful morning, but I will have something to eat later." Estelle promised hastily, seeing Aggie's frown of disapproval as she poured the tea and placed it in front of her. "I hope I didn't interrupt you." Estelle sipped the hot tea, cautiously smiled, and looked at both ladies.

Aggie shook her head. "No, madam, of course you didn't interrupt. Actually, we were just talking about young Polly Dawes. Ezra, her dad, well, he worked in the mill until about a year ago until he got sick. Ezra was married to my friend, Becky, and they have just the one girl, young Polly."

Estelle, nodded, listening patiently but fighting the now-familiar feeling of nausea. She took a deep breath, put the cup down on the table, and nibbled on a corner of cold toast. When Aggie paused for breath, Bessie joined in importantly. "The Dawes, you see, they live in Meadow Cottage, madam. Well, that was until poor Ezra died of the consumption."

Aggie glared at Bessie and cleared her throat loudly. "Well, madam, as I was saying, my friend Becky is really worried that they will be turned out of Meadow Cottage now Ezra has gone."

Estelle was puzzled. "I don't understand. Why will they have to leave the cottage?"

"Ezra was foreman at the mill, you see, and the cottage goes with the job." Aggie explained.

"Oh, I see. But doesn't your friend Becky still work at the mill?" questioned Estelle.

"Oh no, madam. She's a lace maker and works in Sevenoaks with her sister. Now, young Polly might have to go into the cutting rooms at the mill, but even then, they will have to move out of Meadow Cottage."

Aggie shook her head. "It's very sad. Mr Bernard thought a lot of Ezra. Him and Cedric, they helped him a lot when the old master died so sudden."

Bessie snorted. "I told you before, Aggie, Becky won't have Polly in the cutting rooms, she promised Ezra. Polly, she's a clever one, you see, madam." Bessie went on. "Reads and writes and knows her numbers really well, and she sews so beautifully, too."

The two friends glanced at each other, Estelle waited, sensing that something else was coming. Aggie took a deep breath. "So, we were wondering, madam, whether you would consider taking Polly on as your lady's maid?" Before Estelle could reply, Aggie rushed on. "We thought, you see, that you would bring your maid with you from Berkshire, but then, that Gertie that came." Aggie shook her head. "Well, madam, she is no good is she, and you do need a personal maid, and young Polly, even though she is young, she would be a quick learner, and she is such a little lady herself." Aggie's voice trailed off.

Estelle smiled at the slightly anxious Aggie. "Ladies, I think that is an excellent idea. Perhaps I ought to see her and maybe another few girls from the village before I decide though, just to be fair. Henry has been concerned that I do not have a proper lady's maid since we arrived, so he will be pleased to know that I have listened to him for once."

"Aggie, your tea has restored me, and now I am going upstairs to dress and then have a walk around the gardens to see how the gardeners are progressing." Estelle stood up. "Please don't concern yourself about Meadow Cottage, of course I will make sure that Polly and her mother keep their home."

Aggie's face cleared. "Thank you, madam. That's very kind of you; such a relief for Becky." She looked out of the kitchen window and frowned. "But it is freezing outside. You must dress up warm and please be careful where you walk, it'll be slippery as well. Now then, where is that Gertie? She is around somewhere, I will send her up to help you dress."

"Please don't bother with Gertie, I always manage perfectly well on my own. Gertie just drops things, and that sets her crying again." Estelle winked mischievously at the cook, who sighed and shook her head in exasperation.

"Never known a body who could cry like that silly girl."

Gertie, the second housemaid at Grieves Manor, had been sent up by Lady Rose as Estelle's maid until a personal lady's maid had been found. But Gertie, who was walking out with one of Lord Archie's grooms, was heartbreakingly homesick, and her stifled sobs in the night even tried the patience of the gentle parlour maid whom she shared a room with. Estelle was finding Gertie's constant sniffing, swollen red eyes, and miserable face tiresome, and so she had already made up her mind to send the girl back to Berkshire as soon as possible.

With Aggie's additional caution, "Mind now, madam, take care," ringing in her ears, Estelle left the room smiling a little smile. Of course, she was going to take extra care, because Estelle had a secret that she had hugged to herself for over a week now. After mornings of feeling thoroughly wretched, she was becoming worried that she was really ill, until lying in the bath one day fighting a feeling of nausea, Jenny's early confinement suddenly came back to her. She remembered how Jenny complained miserably of dizziness and nausea, and spent every morning in the bathroom, listlessly refusing to take the carriage into Reading to shop.

It was then that Estelle had felt a small bubble of pure joy growing inside her. Sitting up in the bath, she excitedly began counting the weeks back in her head. They had been six weeks in Europe on their honeymoon, and of course she had not had her monthly since they had been back. Estelle smiled slowly and shook her head. "How stupid am I," she thought, and climbing out of the bath, she wrapped a towel around her and went back into her bedroom, shivering in anticipation.

She stood in front of the mirror, and dropping the towel on the floor, she looked shyly at her naked body in wonderment. There were changes, subtle changes, but changes all the same, and she wanted to shout her news from the rooftops, but Henry had to be told first, and Henry was not due home for a few days. So, hugging her precious secret to herself, Estelle told no one.

There was a short silence in the kitchen after Estelle had left. Ruby, the kitchen maid, was sniffing miserably and washing up at the sink. Aggie spoke first, "Now that is a real lady, Bess, she's going to give young Polly a chance. I knew she would. And I'll wager that she will speak to Mr Bernard about the cottage." She turned and glared at Ruby, "For goodness sake child, do stop sniffing."

Bess agreed, nodding thoughtfully. "Young Mrs Maycroft certainly is a very beautiful young lady and kind too but looking rather peaky this morning, I thought."

Aggie smiled, "Yes, and she has refused breakfast for the last few days. I might have a word later, when she comes in from her walk. It's a shame Master Henry is so busy in London."

Bessie gave a wry smile but remained silent. Bessie had her own thoughts on Henry Maycroft, and certainly did not share her sister-in-law's total devotion to him.

An hour later, Estelle, wrapped up against the cold in a thick cloak, a scarf wound tightly around her neck, a brightly coloured woolly hat pulled down low over her face, and her hands encased in thick gloves, gingerly made her way out into the frozen garden. The weak winter sun was barely visible through a milky, cold sky, and as she walked, her boots made a satisfying crunch on grass that glittered with frost.

The lily pond was covered with a thick layer of ice, and when Estelle reached over to give it an experimental prod with her gloved hand, the thick blanket of ice never moved. Petrified icicles hanging from the rockery above the pond had formed a jagged, frozen waterfall, and Estelle could not resist leaning over to snap away the nearest silvered spike. It stuck fast to her glove, the point was needle-sharp, and when she held it up to the sunlight, Estelle could see the ghostly pattern inside.

Estelle glanced around guiltily before tentatively resting the icy tip on her tongue. The icicle stuck to her tongue, and she laughed out loud, suddenly recalling when George dared Estelle to hold an icicle in her mouth for as long as possible. Nanny Florrie would scold, "Master George, there are all sorts of nasty things in that water that could poison your sister."

"Like what, Nanny?" George would ask innocently.

"Dead flies and bird droppings, my lad, that's what." Nanny's dire warnings were delivered with much finger wagging. But there was no-one to scold her now, and so she sucked as she walked, enjoying the pure, fresh feel of the icy water in her mouth.

At the far end of the garden, Matthew and another gardener were busily repairing the roof of the summerhouse. They called out a greeting as she approached, their breath vaporising in puffs in the icy air. Estelle wandered around the orchard, peering closely at the ground knowing that new life was stirring under the frozen earth. Beneath the apple trees, there was a spattering of snowdrops, the tiny white spearheads pushing up through the frost-hardened ground. Estelle looked around the misty winter garden with a sense of satisfaction. Slowly but gradually, the lovely old garden was being transformed and brought back to life. Already, Estelle could see in her mind's eye how the gardens would look in early spring. There would be purple and yellow crocus grouped around the trees, yellow daffodils in the orchard and along the riverbank, waving their trumpet heads in a gentle breeze, and winter hyacinths hidden in the fresh, green grass.

Picking her way carefully under the low branches of a giant apple tree, Estelle almost missed a little iron gate set deep in the mossy wall. The gate was fashioned in the shape of a tree with tiny birds and bugs welded onto the outstretched branches. The gate was slightly ajar, and Estelle reached out and gave it an experimental push, but the clinging ivy and the rusted hinges held fast. She tried again, and the hinges creaked in protest as the gap opened a fraction wider. Estelle frowned looking at the gap, and then, drawing a deep breath, she pushed the overhanging hawthorn branches to one side, ducked down and squeezed through the narrow gap. Smiling in satisfaction, she straightened up, brushed the leaves and twigs from her hair, and stood gazing at the scene around her.

In front of her was a meadow, the tall grasses motionless, frozen silver and petrified in the thin, cold air. To one side, she could see the river, a silky, shimmering ribbon of water flowing past the frost-hardened mossy river banks.

In a deep copse, silhouetted against a grey sky, a group of skeletal trees thrust their bare, spindly branches up into the overcast winter sky. A trio of black crows circled slowly high above the trees, and with jagged wings outstretched, they curled and dived, their harsh and haunting cries echoing around the empty sky.

Estelle looked up at the circling birds as a low winter sun suddenly split the grey sky, bathing the meadow in a misty, rosy blanket. The trees cast long shadows across the frozen grass, and she held her breath at the sheer beauty of the moment. Then, just as quickly as it had appeared, the sun vanished, swallowed up in the lowering sky, and once again the gloom of a February day descended on the meadow.

Estelle shivered, pulled her cloak tightly around her, and crunching a path through the frozen grass, she set off determined to find the hidden Folly by the river. The light was beginning to fade fast, and Estelle was on the point of turning back when, through the gloom, she glimpsed the tip of a roof behind a tangle of lilac bushes close by the riverbank, and she hesitated, "It's not too far away," she reasoned to herself. "I'll just have a quick look, and I can come back tomorrow and bring Matthew."

As she grew closer, she spotted a narrow opening in the dense lilac, and she wriggled her way through. In the centre of a circular clearing stood the ruined Folly, squat and octagonal shaped, the flint walls and narrow stained-glass windows just visible under a tangle of ivy and brambles. The thatched roof had collapsed in all but one section, leaving just a thin petticoat of straw in places. The doors had broken away from the rotted frames and lay on the steps surrounded by shards of splintered glass. Estelle picked her way cautiously up the steps, avoiding the broken glass and stepped gingerly across the threshold. It was dark inside, the air stale with the musty smell of rot and decay, and the wooden floor was littered with bunches of fallen thatch, hazel spurs, and spongy black leaves. Trembling cobwebs looped across the remains of the roofing timbers, and Estelle shuddered at the thought of the spiders grown fat on the flies and moths that had bumbled through the open doorway. The banquette seats had broken away from the walls, and the once-floral cushions were speckled white with mildew and damp.

"How sad you are, poor little Folly," whispered Estelle, remembering the look on Bernard's face when he spoke of the Folly as they sat by the fire one cold night.

"I used to play there all the time in the school holidays," he had said wistfully. "It was my own private hideaway. I fished for hours on end, ate my sandwiches by the river, and even slept in the Folly in the summer holidays."

Estelle asked eagerly, "And what about Henry? Did Henry play there as well, did you take him with you? Did he love playing in the Folly too?"

Estelle was always anxious to hear about Henry's early years, as he rarely spoke about his childhood. "Not very interesting young years, I'm afraid," Henry would reply briefly when she questioned him about his childhood at Riverside.

Bernard had shaken his head. "No, not Henry, my dear. Henry never liked being by the river very much, not even for fishing. Henry would much prefer to hunt or shoot. He used to complain that the midges feasted on him, and he said the Folly was smelly."

For some reason, Estelle had been strangely disappointed, and now she stood, looking out through the broken doors to the riverbank. Despite its sad and forlorn state, there was something about the strange little Folly that appealed to her. "It must have been so pretty once. Surely it would not take long to restore it," she mused, looking around her through narrowed eyes. But now gnawing pangs of hunger reminded her that she had lost track of time, and she should make her way back before the sun went down. Estelle touched her stomach gently and smiled to herself,

"I will ask Matthew to mend the roof and the doors, and we can make the Folly our special place, little one, somewhere to play just like Uncle Bernard did when he was small." Making her way back through the darkening afternoon, Estelle was preoccupied at the thought of the coming baby, and she was impatient now for Henry's return.

Back in the warm kitchen at Riverside, restored by a steaming bowl of Aggie's beef stew, Estelle told Aggie about finding the tree gate to the meadow and the Folly. "I found it Aggie; the Folly just as had Bernard said. I am going to ask if it can be repaired," she said breathlessly, her eyes wide with excitement.

Aggie was watching her closely. "That's all very well, madam, but you are looking a little pale. You stayed out in the cold too long and without breakfast this morning again. I was getting worried about you, fancy wandering that far on your own. That old Folly is falling to bits. It's not safe to go wandering around there." she scolded, and then added gently, "Finish your soup up. There is a nice big fire in the library. You go and get warm, and Ruby will bring some tea and a piece of my apple pie."

Estelle laughed, "All right, Aggie, don't scold. I suppose I did get a bit too cold and hungry, and it made me a bit dizzy. Nothing to worry about. I will be restored after my tea and your wonderful pie."

"Shall I get young Polly to pop along tomorrow afternoon then, maybe have a chat with her about starting as a proper lady's maid? I have asked a few of the village girls to come along to see you as well, but I think you will take to Polly. That young Gertie of yours is a good girl, but such a flibbertigibbet. Polly could be of use, especially now. Had a lot of dealings with young babies has our Polly," Aggie said pointedly.

Estelle did not reply, seemingly lost in thought.

"What do you think, madam, then, will tomorrow be convenient to see Polly and the girls?" Aggie prompted.

Estelle started. "Oh, yes, of course, Aggie, what a good idea. Silly me, I was still thinking about the Folly and what we could do to it."

"Don't know that anything can be done with that old place. Shame really, it used to be such a pretty little place. I remember the old mistress used to take her needlework down there and sit by the river."

The following day dawned foggy and damp, and waking early, Estelle lifted her head up cautiously to gaze out of the bedroom window. She was delighted to find that she felt neither dizzy nor sick, and she lay back and placed tender hands across her stomach.

"Well, little one, I think that we may see your daddy today," she whispered and shivered with excitement trying to ignore the unwelcome frisson of doubt that crept into her mind when she considered Henry's reaction to her news.

After all, they had not known each other that long before marrying, and the possibility of children had never been discussed. Pushing the lingering doubt to one side, Estelle decided against ringing for Gertie, who, without a doubt, would be more hindrance than help. She reached for her gown and gingerly swung her legs out of bed and groped around for her slippers.

It was six o'clock, and the parlour maid would be in soon to stoke up the fire, so she brushed her hair, tied her gown around her waist, and slipped out of the bedroom. She lingered on the stairs for a while wondering whether to venture into the chilly dining room, but then decided on the cosy library where she knew the fire would have been lit early. Bernard often took his breakfast and read the newspapers in the library before going off to the office. Sure enough, Bernard was stretched out in the old armchair by the fire, staring up at the ceiling, his breakfast tray on the table next to him. The *Telegraph* was open on his lap, and he seemed lost in thought.

He jumped up quickly when Estelle opened the door and peered in.

"Bernard, Good morning. I hope I haven't disturbed you?"

Giving her a warm smile, Bernard folded his paper, stood up, and ushered her into the room, seating her down gently next to the fire.

"Come, dear girl, and get warm whilst I ring for some tea, and perhaps some breakfast?" He looked closely at her shining eyes. "You're looking very pleased with yourself this morning, and you have roses in your cheeks again. I have been a little worried about you, so pale and quiet."

"Lots of tea, and yes, please, to breakfast. I am very hungry." Estelle smiled, her eyes glowing, "and I will take my breakfast in here with you if I may, Bernard." Settling herself down, she went on, "I went for a long walk yesterday and found the dear little gate into the far meadow. I remembered what you said about the Folly, and guess what? I found it. I found the Folly!"

She waited, her smile fading when Bernard frowned. "Did you indeed? I hope you did not go inside, Estelle. Matthew tells me the poor old place is rotting away, and he thinks we should pull it down before it falls down."

Estelle's eyes widened in horror. "Oh no, Bernard. Please don't let him do that, I loved it. It is so perfect, right by the river, and in fact I wanted ask you whether the Folly could be repaired."

Bernard shook his head and looked doubtful. "I would have to see what Matthew and Tip think about that. They may say that it is too far gone to repair. But let's wait and see."

"Would you please, dear Bernard, should I come with you when you ask Matthew? I shall plead for the Folly."

Bernard smiled his gentle smile. "No need, my dear. I will go and speak to Matthew before I go to the office, but please do not get your hopes up."

"I won't, I promise. Thank you, Bernard," she replied fervently. "But I will keep my fingers crossed."

But Bernard, unlike Estelle, was rather dreading Henry's return to Riverside. Estelle and her delightfully easy company and her eagerness to save the Folly had taken his mind off rather more unpleasant matters. Now, as he hurried off to find Matthew, Henry's imminent arrival reminded him of the somewhat unpleasant task ahead.

Earlier that week, Bernard had taken the London train to lunch with the company accountant, who had insisted that Bernard come up to town for a meeting. Over lunch, he had informed Bernard in no uncertain terms that Henry's consistent gambling debts and reckless spending habits were eating into the company profits, and had ended his monologue by saying, "Mr Henry is wasting his time in London. The orders have diminished, the profits are poor, and he should be looking further afield for new business." Stony-faced, the accountant had leant forward and placed a sheaf of papers in front of Bernard who read in silence the list of Henry's recent London expenses, which included an extraordinary amount of cash withdrawals.

If Bernard had hoped that Henry's marriage to Estelle would result in Henry spending more time in Shorehill and less time with the rather wild group of London friends, it was obvious now that he had been sadly mistaken. In fact, slowly leafing through the list of figures carefully compiled by the grim-faced accountant, Bernard could see Henry was spending just as much time in the theatre and at the gaming tables as ever before.

"Master Henry may have married a very wealthy young lady, Mr Maycroft. However, Maycroft Fine Paper Company cannot continue to support this level of spending," said the accountant wryly.

Brusquely, Bernard had assured the persistent accountant that he would resolve the matter without delay, and on the train back to Shorehill, he began working on a plan that would keep Henry in the Shorehill office and away from London and the gambling tables.

After a restless morning wondering whether Bernard had spoken with Matthew, Estelle was glad when it was time to interview the girls that Aggie had selected and hoped that she would like Polly. Putting all thoughts of the Folly firmly out of her mind, she settled herself at the desk in the drawing room. But two hours later, her eagerness had faded after interviewing a succession of totally unsuitable plain, dull village girls. Feeling tired and disappointed, she consoled herself with the thought that Aggie could not possibly be wrong about Polly Dawes, and Polly was last on the list of names. Estelle rang the little bell on her desk, and Polly entered the room, quietly closing the door behind her. Estelle summoned up a welcoming smile and beckoned the girl forward to sit on the chair.

Polly, having only seen the mistress of Riverside from a distance, was enraptured by the vision in front of her and hesitated for a moment before perching on the edge of the heavily embossed gold chair.

Estelle was looking particularly lovely that day. The dark, red curls bobbed around her elfin face, her green eyes, fringed with heavy dark lashes, sparkled with fun, and her welcoming smile revealed rows of perfect, white teeth. Estelle, in turn, found her spirits lifting at the sight of a tall, slim, dark-haired girl with clear, grey eyes and a ready smile.

Estelle put her pen down and studied the girl sitting in front of her, noting with pleasure the spotlessly clean clothes, the long, white hands folded neatly on her lap, and the worn but brightly polished boots. "You are Polly, aren't you?" smiled Estelle.

"Yes, madam, that's right, Polly Dawes, and I am nearly sixteen," came the quiet response. The girl reached in her pocket, pulled out a sheaf of papers, and held them out to Estelle. "I have my school reports, madam, and I am good with the needle, as my mother is a lace maker and seamstress."

Estelle leant forward and took the papers from the girl's outstretched hand, noting the quiet intelligence behind the calm grey eyes, the girl's deft, light movements, soft voice, and tranquil but confident demeanour. Estelle made an instant decision.

"I am sure that your reports are excellent, and I will read them later, but I trust my instincts, Polly, and I have a feeling that we are going to get along very well." Estelle smiled her wonderful smile, stood up, and held out her hand to Polly.

"So, Polly Dawes, welcome to Riverside. I will organise your wages with Mr Bernard, and of course, there will be the question of a uniform. We don't have a housekeeper at Riverside, but we do we have our wonderful Aggie who arranges everything. I wonder, would you pop down to the kitchen and have a word about a uniform and perhaps you could start on Monday?"

"Oh, thank you, madam. I will go down straight away, and thank you again, madam," and a beaming Polly walked gracefully to the door, gave a quick bob, and added, "I won't let you down, madam, ever. I promise."

When Polly had gone, Estelle gazed out of the window, and feeling rather pleased with herself, made a mental note to dispatch Gertie off back to Berkshire as soon as possible, which would be a relief for everyone. There was the possibility that Henry would protest her impulsive move, but Estelle was in no doubt that Polly would prove to be worthy of her trust. There was so much to tell Henry, and she felt a tingle of excitement when she thought of her husband's imminent arrival. She pushed away the tiny shadow of doubt that insisted on catching her unawares and hoped against hope that he was not bringing the wretched Peregrine Porter with him.

Amongst of all Henry's many friends, Peregrine was the one she felt at odds with. The London friends were surprised but delighted at the marriage and made every effort to befriend her. Perry, however, continued to rebuff all her overtures of friendship, and if he had to speak to her at all, he was coldly polite. Estelle knew, of course, that the hunting weekends on the Maycroft Estate were popular with Henry's shooting pals, the guests enjoying the informal atmosphere of Riverside. The Shorehill shooting seasons were eagerly awaited because William Hunter was an excellent gamekeeper, his dogs exceptionally well bred, the beaters experienced, and the grouse and red-legged partridges plentiful around the estate. This, however, was not a shooting weekend, and Estelle hoped that for once, Henry had not, at the last moment, invited a few friends to Riverside. "Just a few chums who are at a loose end, darling," he would say carelessly.

Brushing aside her disappointment, Estelle would summon Aggie. "I am so sorry, Aggie; we have a few extra guests. I wonder could you could get the maids to light the fire in the bedrooms," knowing that if it meant that Mr Henry was coming home, nothing would be too much trouble to Aggie. Now Henry was late yet again.

"Henry will be home soon, my dear," Bernard assured a somewhat dejected Estelle.

"But he said that he would be home this afternoon, Bernard," she replied sadly as the clock on the dining room wall chimed six-thirty.

"Then let us ask Aggie to serve tea and crumpets in the library, and then you will be able to see Henry as he arrives. Come along with me, I have some news that will cheer you." Bernard, quietly furious with his selfish young brother, led Estelle gently into the library. "Matthew is of the opinion that the old Folly can be repaired, but it will take a long time," he warned. "They need to thatch the roof first, and Matthew will have to fit the work in between the work on the estate."

Estelle's face lit up, and she gave a sigh of relief. "I don't mind how long it will take to restore, truly, I don't, Bernard. I have lots of ideas written down already, and I have asked Ma for the chaise longue from my bedroom. I know exactly where I am going to put it in the Folly."

But Estelle's hopes of a quiet weekend with her husband were dashed, when later that evening, after hours of anxious waiting, Peregrine's smart black landau, drawn by a pair of handsome bays, came thundering through the drive carrying a whooping threesome, Henry, Foxy, and Peregrine. Bernard was reading his newspaper, and Estelle was absorbed in listing out her plans for the Folly. At the sound of the approaching carriage, Estelle put down her sketch book, jumped up, and looked out of the window.

But the joy faded from her face. "Oh bother and bother again," she said crossly to Bernard, who had stood up at the sound of the approaching carriage. "I was hoping that just for once, Henry would be on his own," and with an angry swish of her skirts, Estelle got up and went into the hall to greet her husband and his guests.

The noisy trio burst through the door, and Henry, flinging his hat and coat onto the hall stand, strode toward Estelle and drew her into his arms. "My darling, my Estelle, I have missed you. No present, dearest, but I have a most wonderful surprise for you."

Estelle gave him a brief hug and a kiss and then pulled away from him slightly.

A beaming Foxy dumped his bags on the floor and walked toward Bernard, hand outstretched, "Thanks so much, old boy, really looking forward to this shoot, so hospitable of you as always," but his smile faded a little as the usually welcoming Bernard gave a tight smile.

"Always a pleasure to see you, Foxy," and it was, because the charming, generous, and easy-going Hon. Basil Foxborough was the perfect house guest, and of all Henry's friends, he was Bernard's favourite. Foxy grimaced and shook his head at Henry who was whispering into his wife's ear.

"Henry didn't tell you that we were coming down today, did he?"

Bernard shook his head, "No, he did not, but no matter, Foxy."

"Sorry, Bernie," Foxy was contrite, and there was an anxious look on his normally smiling face. "But Perry insisted that he wanted to visit Riverside because he has been out of town and said he missed the last shoot, and Henry said it would be fine to come this weekend."

"And it is, I assure you. Please don't concern yourself, Foxy. Aggie will cope, she always does."

Bernard looked across to Peregrine, who was leaning on his cane, head on one side silently watching Henry and Estelle with a sardonic smile on his face. Elegantly dressed as usual, tall and slim, a lock of hair as black as a raven's wing flopped across his forehead, Perry, as always, struck an imposing figure as he stood as still as a statue.

Sensing Bernard's scrutiny, he straightened up, and meeting Bernard's level gaze, he waved his cane at the newly decorated walls. In silky, drawling tones, said, "Good Lord, Henry, what's all this, what on Earth has happened to good old Riverside since I've been away? I almost didn't recognise it as the same house."

Henry looked around, laughed, and said, "Oh, I forgot you haven't been down for a while, have you Perry, went through your allowance early and you had to go pay court to that wealthy old uncle of yours! But this is nothing old chap, wait until you see the plans for the rest of the old place, and the gardens. My darling wife has transformed dear old Riverside."

Peregrine flushed at Henry's jibe about his dependence on his miserable but wealthy old relative, but making use of the fact, that he now that he had everyone's attention, he smiled slowly and pursed his lips. Through narrowed eyes, he first glanced at Estelle's unsmiling face then deliberately leant forward and pretended to examine the new wallpaper in minute detail. He sighed dramatically and stood back, tapping the wall sharply with the silver tip of his ivory cane.

"Now do tell, sweet lady, what is it meant to be? I mean, animals all over the wall, is it meant to be a jungle eh?" Perry snickered, and raising his eyebrows, he looked directly at Estelle.

"It's the new William Morris wallpaper, a woodland scene. I thought it rather pretty, and the deer in the forest remind me of Grieves Manor." Estelle's tone was cool, her face guarded, but Bernard heard the barely perceptible tremor in her voice and, sensing her vulnerability, stepped forward.

"Foxy, Perry, follow me please. I am sure that you could both do with a drink. I'll ask Aggie to prepare a cold supper in the dining room. Henry, I am sure, would like to spend some time with his wife." Bernard nodded unsmiling at Henry. "Henry, the fire in the library is lit, and I will arrange for supper to be sent in."

Estelle, normally more than a match for the supercilious Perry, had regained her composure, and she gave Bernard a smile of gratitude.

Henry looked puzzled and a little put out at his brother's unusually authoritative tone. He had been looking forward sharing to a stiff whisky with his friends after their chilly journey from London, but a look at Bernard's face prevented him from protesting, and now he was wondering what had upset the old boy. He meekly led Estelle by the hand into the library.

There was a somewhat subdued atmosphere in the drawing room after supper. Henry and Estelle had not joined them, Foxy was teaching Bernard how to play Bezique, and Perry was lounging in an armchair by the fire, his long legs stretched out in front of him. His eyes were closed, and he appeared to be fast asleep.

"Henry is better at Bezique than I," confessed Foxy, who was struggling to explain the complexities of the card game to Bernard. There came a derisive snort of laughter from the supine figure by the fire, and Perry reached out a long, pale hand and picked up the large glass of whisky from the coffee table.

"Old Henry will not be engaging in any more card games for a while, he lost a packet at White's last week."

Foxy bit his lip and looked embarrassed. "Shut up, Perry," he said sharply. "I said before, you should have stopped him After all, they were your chums he was up against, bloody professional gamblers, the lot of them." Foxy shook his head, "Sorry Bernard, I wasn't with them, not my thing really, cards, racing, and all that. I prefer to spend my time with a pretty woman."

There was a stony silence as Bernard looked from Foxy to Peregrine. Foxy, sensing that it was time to go to bed, stood up. "I am off to my bed, Bernard old chap, early shoot tomorrow. Goodnight, Perry."

Bernard, who was staring over at Perry still lounging in front of the fire, nodded. "Thank you, Foxy, and goodnight to you. The rooms are made up, and Aggie will have an early breakfast ready for you."

Perry lazily finished his whisky, placed his empty glass on the table, and stood up, yawning and stretching his arms above his head.

"Well now, it doesn't look as if we will see old Henry anymore tonight, so I may as well go up too." He hesitated and smirked. "But now, I wonder, will we recognize our rooms anymore, Bernie old boy, or will we have galloping deer all over the walls?"

Bernard pushed back his chair, walked over to face Perry, and said evenly, "Henry is married now, Perry, and this is Estelle's home. I am delighted to say she is now mistress of Riverside. Estelle has transformed this house and the gardens, and I, for one, am immensely grateful to her and also extremely proud of her. I would request that you, as a gentleman, afford her the respect she deserves as Henry's wife and mistress of Riverside."

Perry's face was set, his jaw twitched, and when he looked at Bernard, his black eyes were unreadable, but he dropped his head in a sharp nod of agreement. Foxy, who was at the door, watched the exchange then left the room silently. Bernard made as if to follow, but paused briefly and turned back to look at Perry. "Foxy was right Perry, a good friend would have stopped Henry gambling when he saw how much he was losing." Perry did not reply. He simply stared back at him, his face stony and expressionless.

When the shooting party woke the next morning, they were dismayed to see that a thick, impenetrable fog had dropped down on the valley overnight, enclosing the house and gardens in a dripping, grey blanket. The mood at the breakfast table matched the weather outside.

Foxy stared out at the dense mist pressing up against the window. "I suspect that the shoot has been cancelled today," he said glumly to the silent Peregrine, who had refused breakfast and was leaning back in his chair smoking.

Bernard poured himself another cup of tea. "Sorry, Foxy, but there is no sign of the fog lifting sometime soon. I have spoken to William Hunter, and he agreed, so we have sent the beaters home."

"Quite so," agreed Foxy. "Well then, I think I shall have some more breakfast." He looked around the table at the empty spaces, "No Henry or Estelle this morning," he enquired, glancing over at Bernard.

Before Bernard could reply, the dining room door opened, and a smiling Estelle almost bounced into the dining room, followed by Henry.

"Good morning everyone, sorry we are late down for breakfast." She apologised prettily, smiling around the table.

Henry looked out of the French doors onto the murky, dripping terrace. "Well, I guess the weekend shoot is cancelled, eh Bernie? Wretched weather, sorry chaps."

There was a murmur of agreement, and Perry spoke for the first time that morning. "We may as well go back to town after lunch then, Henry?" He ground his cigarette out in the ashtray and looked around the table, "There seems to be little point in staying on until Monday. What do you say?"

"Fine by me," said Foxy, still munching his way through his second breakfast doing his best to ignore the strained atmosphere between Perry and Bernard. Henry remained silent and concentrated on pouring himself a coffee, carefully avoiding looking across to Perry's questioning face. Estelle was humming as she took her plate to the sideboard. When she was seated at the table, she smiled across at Henry and nodded.

Henry fidgeted in his chair and cleared his throat. "Well, now I have some news. I won't be coming back to town with you chaps today or indeed for a while," and he leant across and covered Estelle's hand with his. "My darling wife has informed me that we have a rather delicate matter to attend to," and he inclined his head toward Estelle, who flushed shyly.

A long silence followed Henry's announcement. Foxy stopped eating and glanced around the table, stopping at Estelle's beaming face. "Have I got this terribly wrong, Henry dear boy, but are we talking about another young Maycroft here?" he said with laughter in his voice.

Henry nodded proudly, "We are indeed, Foxy, old chum."

Estelle held his hand tightly. "It's early days, Foxy," she said softly, "And yes, we do hope so."

Foxy jumped up and strode around the table, stopping to pump Henry's hand up and down before bending down and giving Estelle a hearty kiss. "Gosh, how bloody marvellous. I must say I am delighted, happy for you both, congratulations. I say, Perry, what about this then?"

Bernard smiled broadly and heaved a sigh of relief; his suspicions had been right. He had seen many women at the mill experiencing the same symptoms as Estelle and was hoping that he had been correct in his assumption.

"My heartiest congratulations to you both," he said, beaming at the young couple. "I am delighted for you. How very exciting."

A slow handclap came from the end of the table. "Well, well, well, bloody marvellous indeed," said Perry in his customary drawl. "Who would have thought it? Congratulations, Estelle my dear, you seem to have tamed our leader, and Henry, my congratulations to you. I guess you will be a permanent village resident now."

Perry's obvious barb seemed lost on Henry and Foxy, but not on Estelle or Bernard. Estelle gritted her teeth, determined not to let Perry spoil her moment, and said sweetly, "Perry, my dear boy, you can visit us at Riverside as often as you like. You never know, we may even ask you to be a godfather."

Bernard nodded approvingly. "Good girl," he thought but also knew that Estelle was hurt by Perry's continuing hostility toward her.

Perry smiled tightly and shuddered imperceptibly. "Dear me, I would not wish that on any infant, so no. thank you, dear Estelle," he stood up. "Foxy," he commanded. "The beautiful couple have much to do, and I think we should be on our way as soon as possible. Such a shame, it is the last bloody shoot of the season."

Shortly after breakfast, as Henry and Estelle waved the departing visitors off, and the landau disappeared into the mist, Estelle frowned and turned to Henry. "Henry, why does Peregrine dislike me so? I try so very hard, because you three have been friends for so long, but he simply does not like me."

Henry looked surprised, "Darling, don't be silly, Perry doesn't dislike you especially. He is a funny chap, I grant you, but truly, I don't think he likes many people. Don't let old Perry worry you," and he tucked her arm under his. "I have been summoned into the library to have a bit of a chin wag with big brother this afternoon, so you can take yourself off to rest."

And then, of course, came the somewhat unpleasant meeting with his brother. Bernard had not minced his words about the sorry state of Henry's finances, and Henry had guessed, quite correctly, looking at the account ledgers piled up on Bernard's desk that he had been to see the miserable little company accountant who had been hounding him in London.

Henry had listened in silence as Bernard, in a steady, reasonable tone, outlined his solution to Henry's problems and his future plans for Henry's involvement in the business. The carefully explained plans filled Henry with a growing feeling of horror when he realised how little time he would be spending in London.

"After all, Henry, if the child is a boy, there will be school fees to pay, among other things, and now that you are married, you should not be rattling around with your friends all the time. The telephone is to be installed in the office soon, and you can contact clients from here at Riverside. Oh, and I was thinking, should you not send for your valet? After all, you will need him at Riverside now, no point in keeping him in London."

Bernard had looked closely at his younger brother, trying to gauge his reaction, but seeing the dawning dismay on his brother's face, finished on a conciliatory note. "What do you think Henry? I mean, after all, you will want to spend as much time as possible with Estelle now, will you not?"

Henry quickly gathered himself together, simply nodded, and stood up to leave. Bernard took a deep breath, relieved that Henry had seemingly accepted his carefully devised plan. "Good, good Henry," Bernard said heartily. "Perhaps we can go through things in more detail tomorrow. Spend the rest of the day with your lovely wife."

Henry, with a tight smile, replied, "Of course, old man, yes tomorrow," but his heart sank further as he left the library and walked slowly into the drawing room. He poured himself a large malt whisky and slumped down into an armchair.

The fire had burned down low, and the room felt cold. He leant forward, grabbed the poker, and prodded at the logs, sparking a small flame. Whether it was the cold draught seeping under the old window frames or the prospect of living in Shorehill permanently that sent a chill through Henry, he was not sure. Either way, his spirits plummeted with the temperature.

Another bitter disappointment was, of course, the surprise holiday in Nice that he had planned for himself and Estelle. That would now have to be abandoned. That was to be the present he had promised her, but there had been no chance to tell her.

One of Foxy's far-flung, wealthy relatives had an interest in a small but luxurious hotel in Nice. Being rather fond of Foxy, he had generously offered Foxy and his chums a suite of rooms for the entire month of May at a very reasonable rate, as the hotel was being redecorated. When Foxy told his friends that the hotel was just a short walk to the casinos and the beach, there were rowdy shouts of approval.

"But you are not thinking of taking Estelle, though Henry, are you? She will be bored stiff." Perry had frowned, his elation clearly dampened at the thought.

"Of course, Estelle will come with me. She will love it, Perry. She is a great girl, always ready for some fun. Anyway, we went to the

Casino Municipal when we were in Nice, and she thoroughly enjoyed it. I thought I could take her to the flower market and the Opera also."

Flushing at Henry's sharp tone, Perry had turned without a word and left the room.

"Well then, Perry, you were right without realising it," Henry muttered to himself bitterly. "The holiday in Nice was certainly not for Estelle, now, and not for me either, so it would seem." and taking a large gulp of the whisky, he went to join his wife.

Estelle never found out what was discussed between the two brothers in the library that day, but when Henry emerged a few hours later, he was clearly in bad humour since his talk with Bernard.

"Everything is well, Estelle. We were just discussing the orders for the mill, nothing to worry about. Bernard is thinking about having a telephone installed, and then I could deal with our customers from Riverside and spend more time at home with you. You really have stirred old Bernard up, my sweet. The old boy was never one for change, and now he's talking about all sorts of things he wants to do, beginning with the telephone and renovating the old Folly of all things."

"Well, that's good, isn't it, darling? Shall we wrap up and go for a walk, perhaps look at the Folly. It might be rather fun in the fog." Estelle watched him anxiously.

Henry shook his head, "No, I am going for a canter on Captain. Tip says he could do with the exercise. Then I might have a stroll over to the estate office, that's if you do not need me for anything."

Estelle shook her head. "No, darling of course not," and looked thoughtfully at her husband's stiff and angry back as he stomped out of the room. Whatever had been said at his meeting with Bernard, Henry was clearly in a very bad mood.

The following morning. Henry woke early from a restless sleep, and even in the dim light, he could see from the dense blackness pressing against the window that the fog had not lifted, and he sighed in frustration. He could hear the muffled sound of the ever-turning waterwheel and the steady thud of boots as the first shift of mill workers made their way past the high walls and down the clinker path to the mill.

Very little had ever kept Henry awake, not even his rather pressing gambling debts, but last night, he had tossed and turned into the small hours. Lying beside a blissfully sleeping Estelle, Henry was going over in his mind the sobering events of the previous day.

The prospect of becoming a father had never entered Henry's head, and he was unsure what he felt, but he had felt a tinge of dismay when Estelle had broken the news to him. Henry was surprised and confused at how excited she was at the prospect of having a baby. "After all," he reasoned to himself, "I'm just getting used to being married, and now this, a baby of all things. It is too soon."

Henry was still miserably thinking about the lost holiday when he was startled out of his reverie by a knock on the bedroom door,

"Come in," he called out. The door was opened by a tall, slim dark-haired girl expertly balancing a laden breakfast tray. Henry sat up and gently shook his peacefully sleeping wife. "Wake up now, sleepyhead. Your breakfast awaits." he whispered in her ear.

Estelle stirred and murmured sleepily. "I am nearly awake, I promise, Henry, just a few more moments."

"Good morning, sir," said Polly quietly. "I will just put madam's breakfast down here," and she placed the tray on Estelle's bedside table.

To Polly Dawes, growing up in the small village community, Henry Maycroft was an exotic mystery. A remote, handsome figure who appeared in the village from time to time, thundering across the fields on his great black stallion. He would disappear back to London and return a few weeks later with a group of friends, and they would drink in the Hop Vine for hours. Henry would lavish drinks on all and sundry, and Becky, her mum, used to laugh, "Young Henry Maycroft, with those blue eyes of his could charm the stars and moon from the skies."

Ezra, her father, who was one of the managers at the mill, would frown and shake his head. "That's as may be, but young Maycroft is a spoilt young wastrel, and Mr Bernard is worth ten of him."

But still, the young Polly would peek adoringly out of her bedroom window, hoping to catch a glimpse of Henry as he cantered over the bridge and past Meadow Cottage. Now, here she was, face to face with the astonishingly handsome Henry Maycroft, who rubbed his hand through his tousled blonde curls and fixed her with an amused stare from a pair of piercing blue eyes.

"Good Morning, Polly. I assume that you are Polly. I have heard all about you from my wife. And Aggie, I might add. I do hope you will be happy with us. We are very nice people."

Polly, to her annoyance, felt herself blushing hotly.

"And now, Polly, when you are able to wake my dear wife from her slumber, do please tell her that I am going for a ride before I have my breakfast." Henry treated her to one of his winning smiles.

"Yes, sir, I will," Polly dropped her gaze and turned away, fussing with the tray.

Henry grinned, swung his legs out of bed, wrapped his gown around him, and strode off into his dressing room, whistling cheerfully. It always raised his spirits when a pretty girl reacted to one of his flirtatious smiles.

If Estelle was disappointed when Polly told her that Henry was out riding and not to wait breakfast for him, she hid it well. The news of the coming baby had spread through the house and village like wildfire, and Bernard had arranged for Dr Bill to visit the young couple.

"Thank you, Polly. When Dr Bill comes, I shall ask him if I can still ride out with Henry. My husband will be spending more time at home now, you see," and she blushed prettily. But when Dr Bill arrived later that day, Henry was not in the house. He had returned from his gallop and had paced around the house impatiently.

"I cannot wait around all afternoon, Estelle. I need to speak to William. We have to deal with the poachers in the woods near O'Donnell's farm."

Bill Winter examined her carefully. "Yes, you may ride a little, certainly, Estelle, but do be sensible. Rest when you feel tired, but other than that, you may lead a normal life. Now, I must go, my apologies to Henry, but I cannot wait. I have a lot of patients to see."

"Thank you so much, Doctor. Henry must have been delayed."

But nothing could diminish the surge of joy that swept over Estelle when Dr Bill had confirmed that she was indeed expecting Henry's child. She had beamed at him in sheer delight, not noticing Bill's frown of disapproval at Henry's absence.

"I will show you out, Doctor," said Polly, who had been waiting discreetly to one side of the bed.

When Polly returned, Estelle was sitting up in bed and still smiling. "Polly, I have been thinking, I would like to go home for a little while. Back to Grieves Manor so I can tell Ma and Pa in person. Oh Polly, I am so happy I could burst!"

"It is the best news, madam. I am very happy for you," Polly replied gravely. Estelle clapped her hands in excitement.

"Come, let's go to my dressing room, and we shall begin packing. You will love Grieves Manor, Polly, I just know you will," she chattered happily, taking Polly by the arm. Polly smiled. Estelle's joy was infectious. Together, they moved quickly around the dressing room, pulling out dresses and hats, skirts, and blouses. Estelle held various items aloft, pondering over each garment, putting some aside to pack and throwing others carelessly back in the closet, all the while describing Sadie and the twins and everyone at Grieves Manor to an equally excited Polly, who confessed that she had never even been on a train.

When Bernard and Henry eventually arrived back at Riverside after their meeting with William Hunter, they found an impatient Estelle taking afternoon tea in the library.

"Darling, you missed the doctor, but never mind. Dr Bill has examined me, and everything is fine." She looked at Henry and said shyly, "He thinks that the baby will come sometime in October, but he won't give an exact date until he sees me next month."

"My dear, what marvellous news. Don't you think so, Bernard?" Henry said heartily.

"I didn't know Bill was coming today, Henry. You should have been here." Bernard turned to look at his happy sister-in-law. "Wonderful news indeed. Now you must promise to take good care of yourself, my dear, and my niece or nephew."

"Oh, I will, dearest Bernard, I promise I will. But I have had the most marvellous idea, Henry," and flushed with happiness, Estelle turned to her husband. "Henry, I want to tell everyone at home about the baby as soon as possible, darling. I want to see Ma and Pa's face when we tell them. Polly and I have almost packed, and we could catch a train tomorrow."

Henry, for his part, was quietly delighted at the idea of spending some time at Grieves Manor, the sooner the better. After all, it would delay the inevitable dreary business of working in the estate office with Bernard. Also, the thought struck him that as delighted grandparents, Lord Archie and Lady Rose would, without doubt, insist on bestowing a generous allowance on their new grandchild, as they had with the twins and Sadie. "If that is what you want, my darling, then we shall make haste to Berkshire without delay." Henry reached out and took Estelle's hands in his and kissed her gently.

Estelle could scarcely contain her joy. "I told Polly that you would agree, and she will love Sadie and the twins, won't she, Henry?"

Bernard was practical. "Your family will be delighted to hear your news, I am sure, but you must let them know that you will be arriving in case they had other plans. Allow me to send Tip into Sevenoaks and send a telegram to Lady Rose to tell them that you will be arriving the day after tomorrow." He turned to Henry, whose bad mood had dissipated at the thought of a long visit to Grieves Manor. "What do you say, Henry?"

"Thank you, Bernard. You are right of course. Perhaps tomorrow would be a little too hasty," Henry agreed happily.

After Polly was told by Estelle that "of course" she was included in their travel plans, Polly couldn't wait to tell her mother. "We are travelling first class on the train, Mum. Imagine, me travelling first class. I must be the luckiest girl in the world to have Mrs Maycroft as a mistress. She is so kind. When I said that I was going to write everything in my diary so I can show you, she gave me this special notebook. Look how pretty it is." Polly held the notebook out to her mother. Becky Dawes gazed at the soft, brown leather notebook and ran a gentle finger over the line of tiny white butterflies engraved on the front cover. "Open it, Mum. See what it says," Polly urged, and Becky had opened it carefully. Inside the cover, Estelle had written, "For Polly Dawes and her notes. With love from Estelle Maycroft."

Becky turned it over and over in her hands, careful not to let her needle-hardened fingertips snag the soft leather. She smiled at her beaming daughter. "That is a lovely thought from Mrs Maycroft. You have done your Dad and me proud, my Poll," she said with tears in her eyes.

Two days later, on a dark and windy morning, Tip deposited Henry, Estelle, and Polly in the waiting room at Sevenoaks train station to await the train that would take them to Paddington and then on to Windsor. Polly, who had been awake before dawn, could not resist opening her bag to peek in and make sure that the precious notebook was tucked safely at the bottom. When they arrived at Sevenoaks, the porter had taken the cases and loaded them onto a trolley and wheeled it over to the waiting room, but Polly had clutched her bag to her tightly and refused to let it go. The porter assured them that the train was on time, but still Estelle seemed anxious and fidgeted around in the waiting room before finally standing at the open door, craning her neck to look along the line. "The train won't come any quicker by wishing, darling," Henry was sharp. "The porter said that the train is on time, so why don't you just sit down and stop fussing, and please close the door."

A bitter northeast wind had chased away the last of the lingering drifts of night fog, and the high yews around the station creaked and groaned as the icy wind shook their branches. The sky was darkening, and the first few flakes of snow swirled and danced above Estelle's head. "For heaven's sake, Estelle, come in and close the door, it's freezing," Henry repeated, shivered, and hunched further down into his great coat.

A miserable little fire smoked and stuttered in the tiny fireplace, but still the waiting room was draughty and damp. Polly stood up, "Come and sit here by the fire, madam. The train won't be long." Polly was getting used to Henry's mercurial mood changes, but she could see that they made Estelle anxious. Estelle nodded, closed the waiting room door, and perched on the edge of the bench.

Henry looked up from his paper, shook his head impatiently, and was about to speak when the long, mournful whistle in the distance signalled the train's approach, and a few minutes later, it chugged and hissed to a halt on the platform.

The porter returned and loaded their luggage onto the train, and Estelle, now relaxed that the journey had begun, settled herself contentedly next to Henry and smiled as Polly leant out of the open window to watch the other passengers boarding. Then, checking up and down the platform once more, the guard ceremoniously waved his green flag, and taking a silver whistle from his pocket, he blew hard, one shrill, piercing whistle. With a great belch of steam and a final blast, the great wheels turned on the track, and they were off, gathering speed rapidly as they left the station.

"Quickly, close the window and sit down now, Polly, otherwise you will get a face full of smuts, and that won't do at all," Estelle giggled.

Henry, also slightly mollified that they were at last on their way, grunted. "Yes, sit down do and close the window, Polly. It's damn cold."

But Polly, taut with excitement, was not at all dismayed with his grumpy manner, but she closed the window obediently, perched on the edge of her seat, and smiled, wide-eyed with nervous excitement.

When they arrived at Paddington, the snow was falling in earnest. They changed trains rapidly, Henry issuing orders to the various porters in a loud voice whilst Polly held tightly onto her mistress. The platforms were icy and wet and crowded with hurrying passengers eager to get out of the bitterly cold wind. But Estelle was strangely exhilarated, and she clung to Polly and whispered, "We are on our way Polly, and I cannot wait to see everyone's face when I tell them."

Fighting to keep her balance as they crossed to the other platform to change trains, Polly nodded grimly. "Yes, madam," she agreed. "But please, you need to hold on tightly to my arm, the ground is so slippery," and blinked as another freezing gust flung a flurry of snowflakes in their faces. It was only when they were safely settled in the comfort of their carriage and they were seated again that Polly was able to relax and look around her. Taking a deep breath in at the sheer luxury of her surroundings, she was open-mouthed when a waiter appeared in the doorway to enquire politely whether they required any drinks. Henry, his good mood now completely restored, was expansive and benign and put his arm around Estelle's shoulders, hugged her, and ordered a large whisky. As the train sped out of London and into the open country, it was clear from the snow lying across the hills and fields that out of London, it had been snowing for some time. They were hurtling headlong through the blizzard, and the blur of the passing snowflakes mesmerised Polly, who was now gazing fixedly out of the window.

Henry nudged Estelle, who had been dozing, her head on his shoulder, and nodded toward the silent girl. "Polly, are you with us?" he asked loudly and laughed at her dazed expression.

Polly started and blinked. "Yes, sir. Oh, madam, did you want something?"

Estelle shook her head at her husband and said, "No, dear Polly. Henry is teasing you, but we won't be long now, and you can meet our naughty twins and little Sadie. She is such a dear little girl." She frowned and peered out of the window. "Goodness, we are in a snowstorm! How exciting. Thank goodness Bernard suggested sending that telegram. Otherwise, we may have been stuck at the station."

When the train eventually steamed into Windsor Station, the snow was inches deep and still falling. Porters in raincoats and hats were busily sweeping the snow from the platform, whilst others held umbrellas and waited for the passengers to alight before hurrying them into the waiting room. Manners, the chauffeur, was waiting for them with one of the grooms.

"Hello, Manners," said Estelle, shaking the snow from her coat. "My goodness, what a dreadful day."

"Good Afternoon, madam," Manners touched his cap.

Henry was stamping his feet and rubbing his gloved hands

together. "Manners, can your chap organise the luggage? I want to be on our way as soon as possible and get my wife out of this weather."

"Immediately, Mr Maycroft. We have the landau just outside; the weather is too bad for the car, I'm afraid."

"No matter, thank you, Manners. Let's make a move," Henry was brusque.

The journey back to Grieves Manor was slow, the groom guiding the horse through the icy, snow-covered lanes, and Manners huddled next to him, calling the turns as he saw them. The house gates were open, and they trotted along the drive, the sound of the wheels and the horse's hooves strangely muffled in the thick snow. Solid icicles hung around the rim of the silent, frozen fountain, and thick blankets of virgin snow covered the gardens.

Brent, waiting anxiously in the hall, flung the door open as soon as the carriage appeared through the driving snow, and a beaming Mrs Brent was waiting to usher them inside the welcoming warmth. Polly was introduced to Mrs Brent, who bore her off to the servant's quarters, immediately liking the look of the calm, dignified lady's maid.

"Follow me, my dear, I shall show you to your rooms, and you can get out of those clothes."

Lady Rose, treading lightly down the stairs, opened her arms and enveloped her daughter in a tight hug. "Estelle, dearest child, you are freezing. Come into the drawing room and sit by the fire. How well you look."

At the same time, Lord Archie emerged from his study to greet his daughter and son-in-law. "My dear Estelle, how wonderful to see you both. Do come in, Henry. I am sure you could do with a stiff whisky. What awful weather to travel in."

Lady Rose kept her arm around her daughter as they walked through the hall. "Nanny says the twins and Sadie are taking a little nap. They are all exhausted as they have been playing in the snow since breakfast. Come now and sit by the fire and get warm."

"I, too, am exhausted," groaned Lord Archie. "Wait until you see the size of the snowman down by the boat house. It is no wonder that the children are tired. We have been out in the garden for hours."

"But where are George and Jenny?" enquired Estelle, looking around.

"They had to go out, darling, but they should be back for dinner," replied her mother. "Jenny's cousin has just had a baby, and they went to visit yesterday. The snow wasn't too bad then, but when it began to snow again, they sent word that they were going to stay overnight and come back later today. They are only at Sunninghill, but I expect that they did not want to travel in the snow and the dark."

"Oh, I see," replied Estelle, disappointed that she had to wait to share her news when she was bursting to tell her brother and her best friend.

Lady Rose had been a little puzzled by her daughter's unexpected visit, especially as the weather was so bad, and she had worried a little. But Estelle looked so wonderfully, glowingly happy, and was chattering happily with her father, whilst sharing tender looks with Henry. "Nothing to be concerned about then," Lady Rose thought, feeling relieved.

Mrs Brent had led a wide-eyed Polly up the beautiful staircase and laughed as Polly gazed around her in awe. "What a wonderful house, Mrs Brent, but I will never find my way around."

"Don't worry, my dear, there is always someone around to help. You are in the lady's maids' room connected to Miss Estelle's," the housekeeper replied.

When they reached the second landing, they walked halfway around the circular landing before turning under one of the soaring arches and stopping at a door at the far end of a long hall. Selecting a key from the large bunch of keys jangling around her waist, Mrs Brent slotted the key into the lock and turned the handle. "This is your room, Polly," she said, and the door opened into a warm, perfumed bedroom filled with light. It was simply furnished, a single bed with a rose-coloured silk coverlet, a pale, wooden wardrobe, and dressing table with a wash basin. A fire crackled in the fireplace, and the huge bow windows looked out over the snow-covered garden. Mrs Brent walked across the room and opened another door on the far wall. "This is the door to Miss Estelle's rooms," she said, opening the connecting door.

The enormous bedroom was full of light and beautifully furnished. The full-height, bowed windows overlooked the snow-covered gardens and the frozen lake. The heavy, red damask curtains framing the windows were held back with woven gold-tasselled ties. An exquisite little green-and-gold French writing desk sat by the windows, and on the other side of the room, a pair of French doors opened out onto a square, wrought-iron balcony overlooking the courtyard below. Thick, cream carpets covered the floors, and cobweb-fine lacy drapes looped around the fairy-tale four-poster bed. Small gold armchairs upholstered in deep, red velvet were scattered around the room, and as Polly walked across the thick carpet, she caught a faint waft of Estelle's perfume.

"Come this way, my dear," said Mrs Brent, and led Polly through another door on the far side of the room. "This is Miss Estelle's dressing room."

Polly gasped. The room was almost circular, and the crystal chandelier hanging from the centre of the ceiling was reflected over and over again in the mirrored wardrobe doors that lined the walls. Mrs Brent smiled and grasped one slim, gold door handle. The door opened smoothly.

"It's a lovely room, I know. These are the wardrobes, Polly. Clever isn't it? The doors were specially made so that Miss Estelle can check how her gowns look from the back and sides as well."

A gilded, gold-and-cream glass-topped dressing table stood in the middle of the room underneath the chandelier. Three round mirrors mounted on gold stands were arranged on the glass top, and a gold stool with a deep, red velvet seat was tucked beneath the dressing table. Polly was still standing transfixed at the sheer beauty of the light shimmering around the room.

There was a sound behind her, and two footmen moved silently past her into the room, each carrying a monogrammed valise. "Ahh good, the cases have been brought up." Mrs Brent nodded curtly to the footmen, and they disappeared as silently as they had appeared.

"Polly, if you would like to unpack for Miss Estelle, I will show you where to hang her gowns." The housekeeper swung open another wardrobe door. There were still a great many of Estelle's lovely dresses hanging on the rails, and the housekeeper slid them gently to one side. "There you are, Polly, plenty of space in here. I'll leave you to unpack. Pull the bell in your room when you are ready to come down, and I will send someone up to fetch you. Can't have you getting lost on your first visit, can we?"

"Thank you, Mrs Brent, you have been so kind." Polly smiled shyly, and hesitated. "I've never been a lady's maid before." Mrs Brent patted her arm. "You are doing very well, my dear. When you are finished with Miss Estelle's things, you will have time to unpack your own. Now, I must get on," and she bustled out into the hall.

Left alone in the beautiful rooms, Polly began happily to unpack the valises, unfolding each lovely gown before placing it on the rose-scented padded hangers and slotting them over the rail. The fine French lace lingerie and nightwear were laid neatly in tissue-lined drawers in the dressing table. When she was satisfied that everything was in place, Polly wandered over to the balcony doors and gazed across the misty, snow-covered gardens. In the distance, standing by the snow-covered lake, she spotted an enormous snowman with a black top hat on his head, a bright red cloak, and black boots at his feet. She giggled happily to herself, lost in the magic of the snowy scene in front of her. Behind her, a small mantle clock pinged the hour, and Polly started. There was no more time to linger, and she hurried through the connecting door into her room.

Her small suitcase had been placed on the silky, rose coverlet, and Polly hummed happily to herself as she unpacked. When the last of her clothes had been hung neatly in the little white wardrobe, she sat on the edge of the bed and pulled her notebook from her bag. With head bent, in careful, neat handwriting, she filled a whole page of her journal before placing it on the bedside table. Summoning up her courage, she went over and pulled on the bell cord and waited by the door. Before long, there was a sharp knock, and when Polly opened it, a cheery little maid in a blue pinafore, lacy apron, and white cap grinned up at her.

"You ready now, Miss? My name is Ethel, and Mrs Brent said you are to come along and have something to eat. Follow me if you would," and off she trotted. Polly followed behind, pausing now and again to gaze up in wonder at the soaring ornate arches. When they reached the circular landing by the central staircase, Polly stared up at the snow-covered dome high above her head. "Grieves Manor is so beautiful, isn't it, Ethel?"

"It is, Miss," the little maid said proudly and pointed up to the dome. "Just wait until the snow has melted, and then you will see something really special. It's like walking around under a rainbow sometimes."

Polly was intrigued and would have asked more, but the little maid had stopped, her hand on the banister. She turned her head, listening carefully. "There now. I think the children are waking. I must get you down to the kitchen and then come back and help Nanny to feed them. Sometimes the twins can be a bit naughty, you see," she added fondly with a smile.

Polly listened. She could hear a child's voice and then a sudden burst of laughter. "I can't wait to meet them, Ethel. I have heard all about them from Miss Estelle."

"Hmm, well, little Sadie is a dream, but those twins..." The maid shook her head, "My goodness, Nanny Ryan has her hands full with those two monkeys."

The vast basement kitchen was a hive of noisy activity, laughter, lively chatter, and delicious, mouth-watering smells. Polly was introduced to Mrs Barker, the cook, who was busily stirring a vast pot of mutton stew and watching her young assistant busily making dumplings under her watchful eye. Mrs Barker, who appeared to Polly to be quite young to be a cook in such a large house, nodded, smiled a friendly greeting through the steam, and carried on stirring. The two women, seated at the kitchen table chatting, looked up and smiled at Polly, and she could see from their uniform that they were the children's nannies, although one of them was much older.

Mrs Brent introduced them. "Polly, this is Nanny Ryan who looks after the twins, and this is Nanny Florrie, and she looks after little Sadie."

"Welcome to Grieves Manor, Polly," smiled the younger woman.

"Sorry to interrupt, Mrs Brent," said Ethel, "but I think the children are waking. I could hear the nursemaid talking to them."

Nanny Ryan sighed, stood up, and smoothed down her apron. The older woman smiled shyly at Polly. "I was Miss Estelle's nanny, you know," she said. "I hear that you are looking after my precious girl now, Polly. You make sure that Mr Henry takes good care of her as well. I remember those naughty boys, George and young Henry. Henry spent most of his school holidays here in this house, you know. Inseparable they were, those boys, always up to something. Just look at them now though, all grown and married. Master George, with his own two boys."

Nanny Florrie would have rambled on, but Nanny Ryan reminded her, "We should get back to the nursery now Flo, the twins will be screaming for their lunch. Come along, young Ethel, you can help me feed the little terrors." As the little maid scurried out after the nannies, she turned and raised her eyes to heaven.

Mrs Barker placed a steaming bowl of soup on the scrubbed-pine kitchen table. "Eat that, my dear, you must be chilled to the bone coming all that way in the snow." Taking a bread knife, she sliced into the fragrant, warm loaf sitting on the table and handed a wedge to Polly. "Fresh out of the oven this morning. Goes just right with the broth."

Polly ate her lunch hungrily, all the while enjoying the friendly chit-chat and gossip around the kitchen as the various servants came and went.

Mrs Brent reappeared and settled down next to Polly. "Only time for a quick cup of tea, Cook, please." One of the little maids trotting back and forth to the larder placed a large earthenware teapot on the table, covered it with a gaily knitted tea cosy, and following the cook's sharp instructions, hurried back with cups, saucers, milk, and sugar.

"Have you sorted out who is who now, Polly?"

"I think so, Mrs Brent. I know who the twins belong to, but who is little Sadie?"

"Sadie is a sort of cousin, dear. Her parents died, poor little thing, and so Lord Archie and Lady Rose took her in, and she is just one of the family now." Before Polly could ask any more questions, Mrs Brent stood up. "Now, if you are all finished, I'll take you up to the school room and you can meet Sadie and the twins."

In the school room at the top of the house, Walter and William Grieves-Croft, George and Jenny's rumbustious, red-headed twins were kneeling on the floor crashing toy trains together, shouting in delight, whilst Nanny Ryan sat knitting serenely by the fire. The walls of the airy and comfortably warm school room were covered with vivid childish paintings, cut-out letters of the alphabet, and times tables.

Mary Ryan looked up as Mrs Brent and Polly came in. "Twins, come and say good afternoon to Polly," she commanded, folding her knitting away into a vast bag hanging on the arm of her chair. The twin boys stood up and ran across to their nanny, burying their heads into her lap. "Come along now, boys, stop being silly." She patted their red heads and urged them forward and then beamed with pride as Walter and William, standing shyly in front of Polly, chanted together what vaguely resembled. "Lo, Polly."

Enchanted, Polly dropped on her knees and solemnly shook each chubby little hand in turn. "Good afternoon, Walter. Good afternoon, William," and then planted a kiss on each spiky head.

The twins giggled in delight and began pushing and nudging each other until Nanny Ryan intervened, promising to take the toys away unless they behaved themselves. In the corner of the room, a tiny, wide-eyed little girl was seated at a desk, staring directly at Polly. Nanny Ryan's voice was soft when she went over to the little girl. "Come to Nanny, child, come and say hello to Polly."

Sadie took Nanny's outstretched hand and walked over to where Polly was kneeling with the twins. "Good afternoon, Polly," she said, gravely holding out a tiny hand. Polly took the birdlike hand in hers and shook it very gently. "Hello, Sadie," and found herself looking into the tiny face of quite the loveliest child she had ever seen. Sadie's flyaway white hair was caught into tiny bunches on either side of her face and tied back with bright red ribbons. Her huge, emerald-green eyes underneath almost-invisible eyebrows looked back at Polly unblinking, but when Polly leant forward to kiss her pale forehead, the delicate, heart-shaped face broke into a wide smile, and her eyes sparkled with pleasure. Polly could not stop staring at her. "My goodness, Sadie, you are so pretty, just like a tiny fairy."

Sadie blushed and dropped her head, "Thank you," she whispered.

The twins, spotting that Sadie was away from her desk, held eager hands out to her. "Play, Sadie!" they demanded in unison. Polly looked anxious as they grabbed at her little hands. Nanny Ryan laughed.

"I know, Polly, you're worried that they might be too rough with her."

"Well, yes, a little." Polly admitted, "She is so very tiny."

"I know, and those two little brutes are twice her size, but watch, because however rough they are with each other, they are gentle with Sadie. They absolutely adore her, and she loves them too."

Nanny Ryan was right. Once the boys had rescued Sadie from the grownups, they sat down on the floor as close as they could get to her. Sadie spoke softly to them, and they watched quietly as she took the books with their names printed on the cover and gave them each a pencil. Then she opened the books and began to write the alphabet, coaxing them gently to repeat and write each letter after her.

Mrs Brent beckoned toward the door, "You can come back at bedtime if you would like, Polly. You could read Sadie a story. She would like that," she whispered, and Nanny Ryan nodded her agreement.

"Thank you, I will," said Polly. "I had better go and see if Miss Estelle needs me, Mrs Brent. I think I can find my way," Polly smiled.

Mrs Brent watched her go, sorely tempted to question Polly about the unexpected visit undertaken in such bad weather too, but the opportunity was lost, and she returned to the kitchen to find out whether Mr Brent knew anything more. But Brent confessed that he was as much in the dark as anyone about the new Mr and Mrs Maycroft's sudden appearance in the middle of a snowstorm.

The mystery was solved, however, when, halfway through dinner, Brent was summoned by an excited Lord Archie to "Fetch half a dozen bottles of our finest champagne, please, Brent."

When Brent returned to the kitchen, he had one of Lord Archie's large Cuban cigars in his top pocket. Tucking his thumbs inside his waistcoat and clearing his throat loudly, Brent announced with great aplomb to the puzzled staff assembled for their dinner. "Lord Archie and Lady Rose said we were to have some champagne and toast Mr and Mrs Maycroft on the news of their forthcoming baby."

Mrs Brent's face broke into a delighted smile. "There now" she said. "I thought it had to be something special to make Mr Henry bring Miss Estelle out in this weather. Did Lady Rose say when the baby is due, Mr Brent?"

"The baby is expected in early October, I believe, and Mrs Maycroft is very well indeed. As you say, she has her own personal maid at Riverside now, that nice girl, Polly. Manners is to take them all back to Shorehill when the snow clears and the roads are safer. He will collect our Gertie as she is now no longer needed at Riverside." The butler beamed, proud to be the bearer of such good news.

"Our Gertie, indeed, useless girl. I am quite ashamed of her," muttered Mrs Brent, shaking her head. "Goodness knows what Mr Bernard thought of her." But she was far too excited at the news of the coming baby to stay cross for very long.

The next few days, whilst Henry was out shooting with George and Lord Archie, Estelle spent hours being spoilt by Mrs Brent and talking babies with Lady Rose and an equally excited Jenny. Polly, with time on her hands, found herself drawn to the nursery and the enchanting and ethereal Sadie. Whilst the twins hurled themselves around in the snow, Sadie was quite content to sit by the window, quietly reading. Occasionally, a shout would make her look up, and she waved at the excited, red faces of the twins as they vainly tried to throw snowballs high enough to reach the schoolroom window. On the third morning of their visit, there were definite signs that the snow was melting, and Estelle expressed a wish to return home to Riverside. Henry, at first reluctant to return to Shorehill, perked up visibly when Lord Archie suggested that rather than take the tedious train journey home, they could travel back in his new Daimler. Manners would chauffeur them.

"Darling," Lady Rose added with a smile, "Daddy and I thought that you may like to take your little bronze with you. I am sure you can find a special place in your gardens for her."

Estelle clapped her hands in delight, "May I really, Ma. Oh thank you, but only if you are really sure, I know you both love it as much as I do."

She looked at her father's satisfied smile, "Pa, you knew I missed her, didn't you?" she said, blowing him a kiss. "You remember my bronze statue, Henry?" Henry did indeed. It was an exquisite statuette, cast in bronze, barely three feet high and much admired by all who had seen it.

Lord Archie had commissioned it for Estelle's fifth birthday, and the well-known sculptor, entranced by his lovely and well-behaved little model, had in his own words, "Created one of my best pieces of work." Pictures of the bronze, *Estelle with Butterflies*, appeared in art catalogues all over the world, and despite many requests from wealthy, disgruntled patrons, the sculptor refused to make another child bronze.

Polly, although keen to go home, knew that she would miss the children, but especially Sadie. In the hours that she had spent in the schoolroom with her, she had found herself becoming more and more attached to the little girl. When she bade the twin's goodbye, she received hearty handshakes, but Sadie wrapped her thin arms around Polly's waist and wept heart-breaking tears, her small body shaking.

Estelle, who had come to the schoolroom to say goodbye to the children, cuddled her close and promised that the next time they came, not only would they bring Polly, but a new baby cousin. Sadie blinked and nodded, the tears trembling on her lashes and falling onto her pinafore, and she gulped "Is that a real promise, Mumma?"

"That's a real and special promise Sadie." Estelle held her close and gently wiped the tears from the small face.

By the time the cases and the promised statuette had been packed carefully into the gleaming green-and-gold Daimler motor car, Sadie had recovered, having been promised a trip around the drive in the car. Snuggled in-between Estelle and Polly under several thick rugs, she squealed in delight as the car chugged around the fountain and back to the steps where the nannies were waiting. With the twins dancing around her feet, Nanny Florrie lifted the rosy-cheeked Sadie down from the Daimler and stood her safely on the ground. "Enough of that nonsense, children. Now say goodbye and let's get back inside out of the cold," she scolded, ushering her charges away.

Nanny Florrie was not in favour of the motor car and had said quite firmly to George that she did not want the children riding around in anything so dangerous. Good-natured George had indulged her, after all she was an excellent and loving nanny to young Sadie and was always on hand to help Nanny Ryan take care of his precious boys.

With Lady Rose waving them off, "Goodbye darlings, and safe journey," and Lord Archie's last-minute instructions to the chauffeur, "Drive carefully on the icy road, Manners. Take it easy, not too fast," the Daimler glided through the gates and began its long journey back to Shorehill.

It was dusk when the party finally arrived back at Riverside, and an anxious Bernard ushered them inside the warm house, but Estelle, despite Henry's grumbling, insisted on unpacking her bronze straight away. When it had been placed gently in the hall and carefully unwrapped, Bernard walked around and around the statuette, intrigued at the likeness to Estelle. Estelle looked lovingly at her beloved statuette. "I was thinking about putting her down in the Folly when it's finished. What do you think, Bernard?"

Henry looked inquiringly at Bernard, who explained, "I thought Estelle told you, Henry. Matthew has promised to repair the Folly in time for the summer."

"Yes, I had forgotten, but why? The place is a wreck, and you will get bitten to death by midges down there, darling. There is no privacy either; the village children play in the meadow on the other side of the river after school, and they make a heck of a racket. Everyone in the village uses that meadow for something or other."

Bernard raised his eyebrows and looked across to Estelle.

"I'm not worried about a few midges, darling," she said soothingly, looking at her husband's cross face. "Besides, I quite like to hear the children playing." Henry looked annoyed and opened his mouth to reply, but Bernard butted in.

"Henry, you will be pleased to know that Foxy brought the rest of your luggage down from the London house yesterday, and your manservant, Smythe, came with him. Foxy said he will lock the house up and keep an eye on it. As I said, when you do go to London, you can stay in a hotel. Much more convenient than running an entire house for overnight visits."

The wind had been taken out of Henry's sails, and he looked glum. "Well, that's that," he thought. "Stuck in Shorehill, at least until the baby is born," but aloud he replied sarcastically, "My, Bernie old chap, you have been busy." Turning to his manservant, who had been waiting patiently, he said. "Smythe, I had no idea you had been sent for, but I hope you have settled in. I wonder if you could arrange a room for Manners for the night. He's taken the car around to the stables and will be leaving early in the morning."

When Manners left for Berkshire early the next morning, taking with him a relieved Gertie, Henry's new life began with an early breakfast with Bernard, followed by a meeting in the estate office with William Hunter, whilst Estelle happily busied herself in the house and garden.

Over the following months, life took on a regular pattern. Foxy was a frequent and welcome visitor, but Peregrine Porter never visited, making a variety of excuses when Henry begged him to come down to relieve his boredom. Henry's sojourns into London were few and far between, and before long, cousin Reggie let the London house to American diplomats. "Need the income, old chum," he apologised to a silently furious Henry.

Slowly, spring emerged from the dark of winter, and the gardens at Riverside began to bloom, as did Estelle. The summerhouse had been repaired, and the garden was filled with the soothing sound of water spouting from the marble fountains and waterfalls around the grounds.

The days grew warmer, and with Polly as her constant companion, Estelle spent her days resting on the terrace, watching as the sun, though the glass roof, sent butterfly shadows dancing across the flagstones. Some mornings, Estelle and Polly wandered down to sit by the river to watch Matthew working on the Folly. Gradually, the Folly had begun to take shape, and Estelle begged Henry to come and see the transformation. "Matthew has repaired the windows and the roof now. It looks wonderful, Henry. Do come," she begged.

But Henry shrugged and replied impatiently. "No, Estelle. I'm too busy to bother with that old monstrosity. I have to plough through the estate books for that miserable little toad of an accountant." Henry was still smarting over the loss of the London house, and although Perry had offered him a room at his flat, Henry was still finding it difficult to come up with an excuse to resume his business trips to London. To make matters worse, early one morning, Smythe, who, after deciding that country life did not suit him, took Henry's new valise and caught the early morning train back to London.

One balmy May morning, when Estelle was resting on the terrace, and Polly was sitting next to her, working on a shawl for the baby, Matthew appeared from the direction of the orchard. "All finished, madam. Your Folly is ready for inspection," smiling at her shout of delight. The three, Matthew, Polly, and Estelle walked through the waving meadow grasses and wildflowers, and the newly thatched roof of the Folly came into view. In the surrounding woodland, a cerulean sea of nodding bluebells filled the air with their delicate fragrance. The river sparkled in the early summer sun, and Estelle paused and smiled at Polly. "Such an absolutely perfect day, Polly. Look at the bluebells."

Polly nodded, "I do so love the smell of bluebells. My dad used to say that if you trampled them you would disturb the fairies and make them angry." Estelle listened with delight. She loved hearing all about folklore and never tired of listening to Tip's many tales about the magical qualities of the trees and plants. The overgrown lilac and buddleia surrounding the Folly had been cut back, and the surrounding ground cleared of weeds and nettles. The web of clinging ivy had been pulled away from the flint walls, and in its place, Matthew had planted fragrant yellow honeysuckle and sweet, pink Jasmine. "Both good climbers, madam," the gardener assured her, "and the flowers will attract the butterflies." The little garden around the Folly had been planted with miniature rose bushes, purple lavender, and rosemary. Matthew had carved a bench from a fallen branch and set it beneath a willow tree on the river bank. "For when it gets too hot, madam, you and the baby can catch the breeze from the river," he said shyly, pointing it out to the delighted Estelle.

Taking a key from his pocket, Matthew proudly flung open the door to the Folly, and Estelle stepped inside. The broken banquette seats had been removed, and in one corner, Matthew had placed the little blue-and-gold chaise longue from her bedroom at Grieves Manor. Beside the chaise longue, Estelle's little bronze statuette gleamed in the sunlight. The fitted bookshelves around the Folly were filled with books from the Riverside library and Estelle's favourite books from Grieves Manor. Sweet-smelling rush matting covered the floor, the stained-glass windows skilfully repaired, and the pretty, domed roof newly thatched.

Whilst Estelle gazed happily around her, there was a shout from across the meadow, and Bernard, waving aloft his battered old Panama hat, came striding through the grass, followed by Henry, gingerly carrying bottles of champagne. A laughing Foxy, almost hidden behind a huge bouquet of flowers, was followed by Tip, laden with garden chairs. Betsy and Ruby, balancing platters of food, slowly picked their way across the meadow, scolded and guided from behind by Aggie.

Estelle turned to Polly with shining eyes. "Polly, dear Polly, did you know about this? You naughty girl. Did Henry plan this for me?" cried Estelle, giving her a swift hug.

"Actually, it was Mr Bernard's idea to surprise you," beamed Polly.

Estelle's smile faltered, and for a split second, her face clouded. "Then I must go and thank him for such a wonderful surprise."

Estelle held her arms open wide as she greeted the approaching group with a welcoming smile, and Polly felt a sudden stab of anger at Henry's indifference. When the champagne had been drunk, and the sandwiches eaten, and the others had gone back to the house to dress for dinner, Estelle reluctantly locked the Folly doors and stood for a while gazing across at the river.

Henry was right, there were clouds of midges buzzing around under the trees, but they never seemed to bother anyone. It was only Henry, who had spent most of the afternoon grumbling and angrily swatting them away with his newspaper. Her heart had sunk a little as she watched how animated Henry became after insisting that Foxy tell him about the latest London party he had attended.

"Just the usual old rubbish, Henry. Nothing exciting, I promise." Foxy had protested. Perry had made his excuses when invited to the champagne afternoon at the opening of the Folly, and Henry had sulked at being rebuffed yet again by his close friend. Much as she pushed the thought away, Estelle could feel the gap widening between them since Henry had been forced to spend most of his time in Shorehill, and in her heart of hearts, she knew that he blamed her. "But you'll make it right again, won't you my precious boy?" she whispered, laying tender hands across her unborn child because Estelle never, at any time, doubted that the child she was carrying would be a son.

Polly appeared at her side and touched her arm. "We can come back tomorrow, madam, but we should go now. Otherwise, you will be late for dinner." Obediently taking Polly's proffered arm, they walked back slowly in the gentle afternoon sun.

A hot summer followed the sweet spring of trembling catkins and white blossom, and the baby grew as the season changed. When the summer days grew too oppressive, Estelle put on her sun hat and wandered dreamily down to the Folly to sit and enjoy the cooling breeze from the river. Polly, as always, was her constant companion. When Aggie saw the couple, arm in arm, strolling through the gardens, she sent the maids down to the Folly with jugs of cold lemonade and a picnic basket of homemade cake and refreshing cucumber sandwiches.

On a particularly airless stormy afternoon, Polly was reading aloud to Estelle, who was lying along the chaise longue and drifting in and out of a light sleep. Polly looked across to her, "Perhaps we should go into the house now, madam. I can hear thunder."

Estelle yawned and swung her legs down to the floor. "Perhaps we should. I have an awful headache, Polly. I think it must be the storm," she sounded listless, her face colourless and waxy.

Polly glanced down at Estelle's feet and frowned. "Your feet and ankles are swollen again, madam. Let's get you into the house, and I will send for Dr Bill." Their progress back to the house was slow, the thunder grumbled closer, and it began to rain, heavy drops of sweet-smelling summer rain.

When they reached the house, Polly found Tip and asked him to take a note to Dr Bill. Polly hovered in the background as the doctor listened carefully to Estelle's heart. He spent a long time examining her swollen feet before taking her temperature and finally her blood pressure. "Is Henry at home, Estelle?" he asked gently.

"Mr Henry is downstairs. I will fetch him, Doctor," said Polly.

Dr Bill took the stethoscope from around his neck, folded it up, and placed it in his bag. Then he sat down at the side of the bed and took Estelle's hand gently in his. "Estelle, my dear, your blood pressure is far too high. I am ordering complete bed rest until I come back in a few days' time. After that, if I am happy that your blood pressure has settled, I will allow you to get up. But I would advise that you stay within the confines of the garden and the house until the little one arrives."

He addressed Henry, who had returned with Polly. "Henry, please be firm with your wife. It is imperative that she rests now. She has dangerously high blood pressure and must be watched carefully. Please do not wait to call me if you are concerned. I leave her in your charge."

Henry listened in silence and nodded, briefly looking a little put out at Dr Bill's tone of voice.

"I'll make sure that Miss Estelle stays in bed, Doctor." Polly's voice concealed her anger, and she avoided looking at Henry. "We will take care of her."

The enforced bed rest under Polly's watchful eye worked, and within a week Estelle was out of bed and moving around the house. But Henry, observing the gradual change in his petite Estelle, found his eyes sliding away from her rounded stomach outlined in her flimsy nightdress. One hot August morning, he walked into the bathroom and found Estelle lying in the cool water with her eyes closed. Henry stared at her heavy, blue-veined breasts and recoiled in horror. He hastily adjusted his gaze and backed out of the room. But it wasn't just the physical change in Estelle that perplexed Henry. He had fallen in love with her lively spirit, her sharp wit, and her love of adventure. After all, she had refused to go to finishing school and had opted to travel around Europe instead. But marriage and motherhood seemed to have dulled Estelle, and he found the never-ending talk about the coming baby boring and depressing.

The evening after finding Estelle in the bath, Henry casually suggested moving into his dressing room, "At least until the baby is born, darling. It's just too hot, and you must have your rest. You know that I have trouble sleeping in this heat, and I do not want to keep you awake with my fidgeting." If Estelle was hurt, she did not show it, for she was lost in wonderment at the thought of her baby growing inside her and was eagerly planning to turn her dressing room into a nursery so she could be close to the baby when it arrived.

Henry did his best to hide his disinterest, but he could not hide it from Bernard, and this, combined with Henry's increasing restlessness, worried Bernard. Recently, Henry had found more and more excuses to stay in London. When questioned about a three-day stay at Perry's, Henry had re-countered bad-temperedly, "Bernard, I deal with the customers. Telephone calls are all very well, but they do like to see a representative from the company now and again." Bernard could not argue, when, after a recent successful visit to London,

Henry had managed to secure a large contract with a prestigious London printer who supplied the stationary for some top London hotels. The quality of the Maycroft handmade paper was undeniably fine, but still, Henry had to be congratulated in securing orders from such prestigious clients.

With Perry's help, unbeknownst to Bernard, Henry had found a small ground-floor apartment in Chesterfield Street, Mayfair. The rent was very reasonable because it was in a poor state of repair.

"Anyway," Henry reasoned, when he finally told Bernard, "It is far more economical than staying in the hotels, and I don't have to keep packing away my clothes all the time." Whatever his excuses were to Estelle about his growing absences from Riverside, they were persuasive, because when Bernard expressed his disquiet, Estelle had agreed that taking the apartment in London was a good idea.

"Bernard worries too much about Henry," she confided to Polly. "I truly don't mind that he wants to stay in his own apartment rather than a hotel, and besides, it means that I don't have to entertain the loathsome Perry. I just have to be patient and wait until the baby is born, Henry won't want to stay away then," smiled Estelle, content and beautiful.

Polly agreed with her, "Of course, madam," but secretly confided to her mother, "It's not right, Mum, I do not understand why Mr Henry would not want to be with Miss Estelle at this time."

However, even Bernard had to agree that Henry was more attentive, caring, and patient with Estelle when he was at Riverside, but then, he thought wryly, Henry had achieved his goal in regaining a residence in London, and of course, Perry would ensure that he kept it.

The long, golden summer days continued into early September, and then the weather broke, and summer was swiftly forgotten as two weeks of driving rain and high winds swept across the country. By the end of the second week, Estelle became increasingly fretful and restless, resenting her confinement to the house. On a particularly wet and wild evening, Bernard was working in his study when Polly knocked on the door. "Mr Bernard, I think we should send for Dr Bill. Miss Estelle is really unwell."

Estelle was huddled in an armchair by the fire in the library. Her face was flushed and feverish, and she was shifting irritably around in the chair. "My dear, whatever is the matter?" Bernard sat down next to her and felt her forehead.

"I have the most awful headache again," Estelle confessed, tears streaming down her face.

"You have a fever. Come along now, straight up to your bedroom. Polly will send for Dr Bill, but you may just have caught a chill. Do try to rest my dear, and I will call Henry."

Estelle swallowed painfully and nodded, "Thank you, Bernard."

Henry was in London after insisting that he had an important meeting with a new client. When Bernard expressed both his disbelief and displeasure at Henry's decision to leave Estelle, Henry had laughed, "Don't be such an old hen, Bernard. I'll be back in a few days. Dr Bill said that the baby is unlikely to come before October anyway."

Dr Bill, when he arrived, examined his patient thoroughly, and by that time, Estelle was complaining of a sore throat as well as a bad headache. He ordered complete bed rest and lots of light food and fluids and said he would be back the next day as her blood pressure, once again, was rather high. Bernard was waiting in the library.

"Not too much to worry about Bernard, but as Estelle is nearly full-term, it may be an idea to send for Henry. She tells me that he is in London on business, but she is asking for him."

Bernard nodded, "I have just tried to call Henry, but rest assured I will keep trying until I reach him."

Dr Bill looked thoughtfully at Bernard, "I know that Polly rarely leaves her side, but I would advise Henry to stay close to home now. I am not very happy with Estelle's blood pressure, and I think that she also has a very nasty throat infection. I will be back in the morning, and I'll ask the midwife to call in tomorrow evening just to check up on her. I have suggested a little soup and light food until she is feeling better."

As night approached, the wind dropped, the rain began to ease, and the watery sunset held promise that the worst of the bad weather had passed. Bernard, having made three unanswered calls to the London number that Henry had given him, was becoming exasperated, but hoped, that as it was a Friday evening, Henry would be already making his way home. Bernard decided to make one last call before he went to check up on Estelle.

Perry answered the call. "Foxy, you old rogue, where are you? We are about to play another hand."

Fury flared in Bernard. "Perry," he said icily, "This is not Foxy, it is Bernard, and I need to speak with Henry urgently." Bernard could hear laughter in the background.

"Bernard, old chap," Perry replied smoothly, "Hang on, I'll get him for you. Henry," he called, "You are wanted."

There was the sound of a muffled conversation then Henry's hesitant voice. "Bernard?"

"Henry, Estelle is most unwell. It's not the baby yet, but Dr Bill thinks you should be here, at home." Bernard was terse.

"Oh. I see, well if it's not the baby," Henry paused and hesitated. "It's rather late now, Bernard, but please tell Estelle that I will leave first thing in the morning."

"As you wish." Bernard, shaking with rage, ended the call and slowly made his way upstairs. He knocked softly on Estelle's bedroom door and waited. Polly peered around the door. "She is sleeping now, Mr Bernard," she whispered. "Is Mr Henry coming, sir? She has been asking for him."

"When she wakes, tell her that Henry will be here in the morning." Bernard promised, hoping fervently that Henry fulfilled his promise and arrived early.

Henry, taking the first train from Victoria, arrived at Riverside at the same time as Dr Bill's gig turned into the drive. The sun was high in a rain-washed sky, and the air was fresh and clean with just the faintest hint of autumn in the slight breeze that rustled through the corn fields. Henry followed the doctor into the library, where Bernard was waiting. "Ah, you are here at last, Henry. Bill, Polly said that

Estelle had a very restless night, and is still complaining of a headache."

Dr Bill nodded, "I'll go straight up. Perhaps, Mr Maycroft, you could come with me?"

"Of course," replied Henry. "I came as early as I could. I had business in London." His attitude was defensive, and he avoided his brother's stern gaze.

The doctor looked between the two men and, sensing conflict, interrupted. "I suspect nothing more than a septic throat," and added, "however, this close to the birth, we must take extra care."

Estelle was still flushed and feverish, but she smiled tearfully when Henry approached and took her hand.

"Polly, now please go and get something to eat and some rest. Polly has been wonderful, Henry," she croaked, and as Polly made to protest, she added, "Henry will call if I need you."

"Of course, I will, and thank you, Polly." Henry nodded to the unsmiling Polly, who reluctantly relinquished her place at the side of her mistress's bed.

Dr Bill checked Estelle's temperature and held her wrist for some time. He looked at the bowl of water on the bedside table and noted the neatly folded flannels. "Well, your temperature has dropped, I am pleased to say. You have been applying cold flannels as I instructed, good girl, Polly."

Estelle was anxious, "Polly sat with me all night bathing my head," she said gratefully, "but is my baby all right, doctor? I have been so scared."

Henry interrupted, laughing nervously. "Of course, the baby is fine, darling. You just have a little cold."

The doctor turned away and snapped his bag shut before replying. "I am sure that the baby is well, and the midwife will be in this afternoon to examine your wife again. It may be more than just a little cold, Mr Maycroft. It is a nasty throat infection, so we have to take extra care of Estelle for the next few weeks until the baby arrives."

Over the next few days, Henry never left Estelle's bedside, fetching and carrying for her and even taking his meals with her, therefore redeeming himself in Polly's eyes, and even earning Bernard's grudging respect. By the end of the following week, Dr Bill pronounced his patient well enough to sit out on the terrace but forbade her to go any further than a short walk around the garden. The fever had weakened Estelle, and it was obvious that she had lost weight despite Aggie's determined efforts to tempt her with all sorts of delicacies. Henry went back to work in the estate office after soliciting a promise from Estelle to send for him if she needed him.

JAMES MAYCROFT

Autumn was creeping across the land, and the leaves on the trees were slowly turning russet and gold, the corn in the fields had taken on a golden hue, and the farmers had begun their harvest. At Bridge Farm, Brin O'Donnell was preparing the huts for the arrival of the hop pickers. Entire families came from London to pick the hops, and in the soft autumn evenings, their raucous laughter echoed over the fields as they enjoyed their well-earned beers by the camp fires. Estelle had always loved this golden season and was content to rest on the terrace and watch the closing of the day and the setting sun. Polly, remembering the lace-making skills taught by her mother, spent her time crafting delicate, lacy baby bonnets and tiny matinee coats. Estelle looked on, fascinated, as Polly's deft fingers moved the hook swiftly and expertly in and out of the lace.

On Sunday, October first, Estelle was woken by Polly, gently shaking her. "I have your breakfast, madam," she said softly. "It's nearly nine o'clock, and Mr Henry and Mr Bernard have gone to church."

Estelle yawned, rubbed her eyes, and winced as she moved awkwardly into a sitting position. "Thank you, dear Polly. I simply could not get to sleep last night, and my back aches so much this morning."

Polly placed the tray on the bedside table. "I'll help you with your breakfast, madam. Shall I open the windows so you can hear the church bells? It's a beautiful morning."

"Yes, please, Polly. That would be lovely," Estelle replied and groaned softly again as she tried to get comfortable.

Polly flung the windows open, and, in the distance, Estelle could hear the church bells, together with the comforting sound of the tumbling river and the hum of the ever-turning water wheel. The morning sun, slanting across the bed, was already gathering warmth as the mellow Indian summer continued after the September storms. Estelle took a deep breath and exhaled slowly, and at the sound of another muffled groan, Polly turned swiftly and was immediately at her side.

"Is it the baby, madam? Should I fetch the doctor?" Polly kept her voice calm, and Estelle grimaced.

"I think so, Polly. Perhaps we should send for the midwife as well."

It was just before ten o'clock when Edna Martin pedalled her way slowly and laboriously up the High Street and on to the humpbacked bridge. Edna paused for a while to catch her breath and loosen her heavy coat. The morning, although chilly earlier on, was becoming warmer, and she looked around her. The village was almost deserted as the church bells pealed out across the village and farms. A soft breeze rustled through the trees, and the river gurgled and chattered beneath the bridge and down toward the weir. Feeling rested and a little cooler, Edna swung her heavy frame over the bike again and made her way up and over the bridge and into Old Mill Lane. She glanced across to Poacher's Cottage, where her friend Dottie Hunter lived and thought she might stop and ask for a cooling glass of water. But the windows were closed and the curtains drawn, so, sighing regretfully, she carried on. The dense bushes by the side of the lane were laden with ripe blackberries, and as she pedalled slowly past, the brambles snagged Edna's thick wool stockings, and she tutted crossly.

Edna had been enjoying a nice, soft-boiled egg from one of her hens when young Betsy from Riverside had come banging on her door to say that little Mrs Maycroft had started her labour, and "Polly said she must come straight away."

Edna sighed as she regretfully swallowed the last of her toast. "Take my bag, girl, and run on ahead."

Edna had delivered enough babies to know that she would not be needed for a while yet, but the lovely, young Mrs Maycroft was one of her favourites, and so she did not hesitate. By the time she had reached the gates of Riverside, the sun was well and truly up, and as she puffed red-faced up the drive, she could see Aggie waiting anxiously by the side of the house.

"Dr Bill should be on his way, Edna, we sent for him a while back," she said as the breathless midwife propped her bike up against the wall and wiped her brow.

"Take my coat, Aggie. I am fair sweating, and for goodness, sake stop your fussing. If Mrs Maycroft has just started, we have a long way to go yet, and you should know that. Now, please fetch me a glass of water; I'm as dry as a bone. I was going to stop at Dottie's, but no one was around."

Aggie ushered the large midwife into the kitchen, and Edna plonked down heavily into a chair and fanned herself with a giant white handkerchief.

"Hurry up with that water, girl," Aggie ordered, as a wide-eyed Ruby scurried across the kitchen and thrust a glass of water in her hand. Aggie was fussing. She didn't want Edna, unconcerned, sitting in the kitchen sipping her water; Aggie wanted her upstairs with Estelle.

"Well, they would all still be at church wouldn't they, Edna?" she snapped. "Mr Henry and Mr Bernard are at church as well, but we have sent Tip to fetch them. Polly is upstairs with Mrs Maycroft."

"That's all right. Young Polly is a sensible soul, and I don't think Mr Henry is needed at the moment. We have a fair time to go yet." The midwife smiled calmly at Aggie. "Let's have a nice pot of tea sent up for Mrs Maycroft whilst we wait for the doctor. Has young Betsy taken my bag up?"

Aggie nodded. "Good," Edna said as she drained her glass and heaved herself to her feet. "Shall we see what's happening upstairs?" The midwife moved ponderously out of the kitchen door as Aggie tutted with irritation.

Edna was right, and the household held their breath throughout the long day and evening. James Henry Maycroft was born on October 1st, 1898, waiting until almost the stroke of midnight to put in an appearance. Polly, flying up and down the stairs at intervals, reported to Aggie that all was well. Dr Bill, taking a rest and a quick lunch and then dinner with Henry and Bernard was smilingly reassuring.

When Polly escorted a nervous Henry into the bedroom, Estelle was sitting up in bed with her arms wrapped around a tiny bundle. Dr Bill, with his sleeves rolled up, was washing his hands in a bowl, and the midwife was waiting with a towel.

"Henry," Estelle looked ecstatic. "We have our son."

The bedroom window was open, and although there was a breeze moving the drapes, Henry detected the strong odour of carbolic, and another smell which he could not identify, and he gave a faint shudder. He approached the bed, and Estelle turned a beaming, if pale, face up to him, and he took a deep breath and bent to kiss her damp forehead.

"Well done, darling. Let's have a look at him." Henry's tone was jovial, and the midwife beamed her approval.

"Just one quick look, sir, then we have to get Mother ready for feeding."

Estelle gently unfolded the shawl from around the baby, and Henry looked down into the misty, grey, new-born eyes. A tiny pink fist seemed to be clutching the edge of shawl, and the baby's head was covered in fine, fuzzy, carrot-coloured curls. Estelle waited, her smile fading a little as Henry continued to stare at the baby, not saying a word.

"Henry?"

At the sound of her voice, Henry recovered his composure. "He's very small, but beautiful, darling."

Dr Bill walked across to the bed and looked thoughtfully at the baby. "He is a little underweight, which is why we want to get Mother feeding as soon as possible. Your wife has had a long and difficult labour, which she handled with great courage, Henry."

The midwife bustled over. "Now, Mr Maycroft, if you would like to wait outside whilst we make Mother comfortable, we will call you when she is ready."

"Yes. Yes, of course," and turning to Estelle, Henry touched her hand briefly. "I'll be back soon, darling." Bernard was waiting at the bottom of the stairs. "Well," he said. "Is everything all right Henry?"

"Splendid," said Henry with false jollity. "I have a son, and you have a nephew, Bernard!" Bernard relaxed and slapped him heartily on the back.

"Then we should drink a toast to your wonderful wife and son."

Polly, who had been in the kitchen with Aggie, appeared in the hall and said softly, "We have laid out some tea and sandwiches in the drawing room, Mr Henry."

"Thank you, Polly, but no tea, something stronger is called for. And if you are going up to my wife, please tell her that I will be up directly, just celebrating with my brother."

Polly nodded happily and ran lightly back up the stairs.

Bernard watched her go and said, "That girl, as young as she is, has been a tower of strength. Come along, Henry, it's all over, and Estelle is fine, and you have a son and heir, something to celebrate."

An hour later, Dr Bill put his head into the drawing room to say that Henry could go up to see Estelle, and that he was leaving, but the midwife would stay until the morning.

"Tell Estelle that I will come and see her and the baby tomorrow, Henry. I am off to my bed now." Bernard thanked the doctor before walking with him to the front door.

When Henry crept into the darkened bedroom, the midwife who had been sitting in the chair next to the bed jumped up. "Ahh, good. Just in time,sir. Baby is feeding nicely, and when he is finished, I shall take him so Mother can get some rest."

Estelle looked up. "Thank you so much, Edna. I think he's nearly finished, greedy little boy. Henry darling, come and see. He is so sweet and good." Henry forced a smile. The baby, with his eyes closed tightly, was snuggled up against Estelle's exposed breast and snuffling softly as he sucked. Estelle, spellbound, looked lovingly at the tiny face.

Neither the midwife nor Estelle saw the look of distaste that flitted across Henry's face as he watched his wife breastfeeding his tiny son, but Polly, emerging from Estelle's dressing room where she had been preparing a bed for the midwife, saw and was shocked.

Henry cleared his throat. "Darling, I won't disturb him whilst you are feeding, shall I come back later?"

Estelle looked up, and although she looked tired and pale, her face was glowing with joy. Henry glimpsed for the first time in months the beautiful girl he had fallen in love with. "No, Henry, please don't go. I have been waiting for you. Sit here with me, please," and she patted the side of the bed and looked down at the sleeping baby. "Edna," she said proudly, "I think he's finished. He's fallen asleep."

Henry sat down on the edge of the bed but positioned himself so that he could not see Estelle tenderly remove the baby from her breast and hand him gently to the waiting midwife.

"Well done, Mrs Maycroft. That seems to have settled the little chap," and to Henry she said, "Would Father like a cuddle before I put Master Maycroft to bed?"

The midwife's tone was playful, and Henry felt all eyes on him. "Yes, of course, let me have the little fellow," and he held his arms out.

Edna placed the small bundle into his open arms, and he took a deep breath, holding his son almost at arm's length. The baby stirred and made a faint mewling sound. "Hold him closer, Father. Baby is missing his mother already," urged the midwife.

Henry nodded and pulled the baby closer to him and looked down once again into the unseeing, unfocused, milky eyes. But there was a smell drifting up from the tightly wrapped baby and Henry nearly gagged. "Good God," he said. "What is that awful smell?"

The midwife smiled indulgently. "Master Maycroft," she scolded. "What manners! We need a nappy change, I think."

Behind him, Henry heard Estelle giggle as he hastily handed his son to Polly, who stepped forward to take him. "I'll change him, nurse, if that's all right. I know where everything is," Polly said, and the look she gave Henry from her cool, grey eyes was unfathomable.

Back in his dressing room after spending an hour with Estelle, Henry sat smoking by the open window. Whilst the baby had slept, he was able to hold Estelle gently in his arms until she fell into an exhausted sleep. But he was unable to sleep, because his mind was in a complete turmoil. Everything had happened so fast, and in one short year, he had married and had a baby, and the longing for the freedom of the life he had led before was now even stronger. He loved Estelle, he reasoned, of course he did, but the life he had imagined was a life together in London, not entrenched in a village that he had never liked even as a child. He was trapped, he realised with a sinking heart, because he knew that despite Estelle's reassurances, she would never move to London now. And now a child, a new life, another human being that he was responsible for.

As he stared into the early morning sky, already streaked with the orange light of dawn, Henry wondered what he should have felt when he had looked into his son's eyes, because he had felt nothing. He was living in a house that he had never felt at home in, married to a lovely girl that he now realised he hardly knew, and he had a son that he had never wanted. Henry threw the remains of the cigarette out of the window, and as a rush of bleak despair enveloped him, he dropped his head into his hands.

He must have dozed off, because when he was awaked by the parlour maid coming in to make up the fire, the morning sun was streaming in through the bedroom window. Henry waved the parlour maid away, locked the door, undressed slowly, washed, and climbed into bed, overcome with a suffocating weariness. After all, he thought as he pulled the covers over his head to shut out the morning light, it was too early to disturb Estelle, and the midwife was sure to be fussing around. There was Polly, the maid, as well, and he frowned when he remembered the barely concealed look of dislike in her clear, unwavering stare when she had taken the baby from him.

In one way, Henry was right, because for the next few weeks, the entire household revolved around his infant son and Estelle. The tiny boy was so small and slow to gain weight, and the midwife expressed her concern to Dr Bill.

Dr Bill took Henry to one side. "Perhaps you should consider having the little chap baptized, Henry?"

Henry looked alarmed. "What should I say to Estelle? I don't want to upset her any more. She weeps all the time now anyway."

"Don't concern yourself with that, Henry. Your wife is exhausted, and all new mothers tend to be emotional. I am going to check on Mother and baby now, and I will talk it over with Estelle." Bill Winter responded with barely concealed exasperation.

Estelle watched anxiously as he examined the baby, then he came and sat on the side of the bed.

"Now then, my dear, the baby has a slight cold, nothing to worry about, and you are still a little unwell from the throat infection, and you have had an arduous labour. That is why you are feeling a little teary and tired, you were very brave. Now, have you and Henry thought about a name for your son?"

Estelle brightened, "Yes, and we both rather like James Henry."

The doctor looked at her thoughtfully. "You know, Estelle, I am all in favour of early baptism. It is going to be a while before you feel strong again, and I wondered whether you would consider holding the christening at Riverside."

Estelle nodded, and looked across to Polly. "Do you know, I think that is a wonderful idea. How lovely to have the christening at Riverside. If the vicar agrees, I would like that." The elderly local vicar agreed, and on a sweetly warm late October afternoon, and with most of the village invited, he performed the christening ceremony at Riverside.

Jenny and George were delighted to be elected godparents, but the twins and Sadie, recovering from measles, were advised to stay home with the nannies. Foxy and Perry sent apologies and presents and a message to say that they were taking another short break in Foxy's uncle's hotel in Nice. Even a large cheque from the besotted Grieves-

Croft grandparents could do nothing to lift Henry's bad mood when he heard that once again the friends had gone on holiday without him.

James Henry Maycroft was baptised in the white satin christening robe that had been passed down through generations of Grieves-Croft babies and had been worn by Estelle at her own christening. After the christening, Henry was standing on the terrace, gloomily sipping champagne. Estelle was walking around the garden with Lady Rose, who was proudly holding her grandson, whilst his father-in-law chatted to Bernard about the mill. Even George had deserted him and was engrossed in a conversation with Doctor Bill about the twin's measles.

Since the baby's birth, Henry was more than ever convinced that he had to find a solution that would release him from the constraints that family life had inflicted on him. He would suggest to Estelle that it was time now to employ a full-time nanny. After all, George and Jenny had employed a nanny almost as soon as the twins had been born, and Jenny declared that she could not manage the twins without her.

Lady Rose had offered to pay the nanny's salary. "It will allow you some freedom, my dear. Please think about it," Lady Rose had urged her reluctant daughter.

Henry sighed heavily but forced a smile when he saw Estelle heading towards him, and he put his champagne glass down on the nearest table.

"James is getting restless, darling. Would you take him into the nursery? Polly will put him down for his nap." After Henry had thankfully handed his son to a silent Polly, he proceeded to down as many glasses of champagne as he could in an effort to dispel his misery.

As the golden October days shortened and winter beckoned, Polly became concerned about her mistress, and although Estelle assured her that she was perfectly well, Polly could see how thin she had become since the birth. James was a difficult baby, fretful and restless, but Estelle had endless patience, and although she fed him when he demanded, James never settled for more than an hour or two at a time. On some days, when his ceaseless crying brought his exhausted mother to tears, Polly gently removed James, and singing softly to the restless baby, she paced around the terrace until he finally slept. One night, when James had been particularly fretful and his crying had woken Henry for the third time, Henry lost patience.

"Estelle, you have been feeding that child on and off all night. What on Earth is wrong with him? It cannot be right, this endless crying. James needs a nanny, and you look dreadful. I think you should speak to the doctor and then employ a nanny for James."

Estelle looked at him levelly, and her voice was low and controlled.

"Please do not raise your voice, Henry, you are upsetting James. Go and sleep in your dressing room. I can rest later; James will settle soon. We do not need a nanny. Polly and I can manage perfectly well. Dr Bill is coming in the morning as usual to check on James, and I will see what he says."

There were signs of the old Estelle in her steely tone, and Henry gave a reluctant smile. "As you wish, darling, but I am worried about you. I will move into my room for a while, but only if you promise to speak with Bill Winter."

Estelle gazed at her handsome husband and felt a sudden rush of love for him. "I will. I promise, Henry. Sleep in your room, darling. We will be fine. I know that this is a difficult time for you, adjusting to working with Bernard, and when James is a little older, you can spend more time in London with your customers."

Henry visibly relaxed and gathered Estelle into his arms. He dropped a kiss on his son's downy head. "I am so sorry, my dearest, I am being very selfish. I will do whatever makes you happy, and if you are sure that you and Polly can manage, then we will not speak about a nanny just yet."

A repentant Henry was hard to resist, and Estelle smiled tearfully when Henry stroked his son's tiny face. "Now then, James Henry Maycroft, it's about time you began behaving yourself, young man, you are wearing your poor mother out."

But the following morning, when Dr Bill came to see James and weigh him, he frowned and looked thoughtfully at Estelle's anxious face.

"How often are you feeding, him my dear," he asked gently and looked across at Polly who was hovering close by.

"All the time, and it seems that I never stop feeding him." Estelle replied tremulously. "Why, is something wrong?"

Doctor Bill sat down next to her and took her trembling hand in his. "James is not gaining weight, Estelle, and he is hungry, which is why he cries all the time. I'm afraid that you do not have sufficient milk for him." He held his hand up, as Estelle made to protest, "Please, listen, my dear, we need to consider finding a local wet nurse, or we could try him on a bottle. It's for his own good and yours. You are not getting enough rest; you are too thin, and you will make yourself ill." His tone was firm enough to brook no further argument from Estelle, and her eyes filled with tears.

Polly rushed over and put her arms around her shaking mistress. "I wanted to feed him myself. I should be able to. I am his mother, and I have failed him." Estelle wailed.

Dr Bill laughed. "That is pure nonsense, Estelle. Many of my new mothers employ a wet nurse. If James is nourished and well fed during the day, there is nothing to stop you feeding him at night, my dear. I have just the lady in mind."

"Lizzy Dacres was just saying the other day that she was thinking of weaning her little boy even though she still had plenty of milk. She would be glad of the money, as this last baby made number six." Looking at Estelle's anxious face, he added, "Lizzy is a kind and gentle soul. I would not entrust young James to anyone. You know that, Estelle."

Within a week, Estelle had to admit that James was a different baby, quiet and contented, sleeping peacefully in his pram on the terrace. Estelle enjoyed giving James his nightly feeding, although Henry secretly hoped that Estelle would abandon feeding altogether, as it was something he still could not bring himself to watch. However, he was delighted to see Estelle returning to her lively, beautiful, and loving self, even though James was always by her side, in her arms, or sleeping in a cradle close by. One evening, when he went upstairs to say goodnight to James, he said casually,

"Darling, I was thinking of spending a day or two in London now that the baby has settled down. Visit a few customers and try and get some new orders. What do you think before I have a chin wag with Bernard?"

Estelle hid a smile as she tucked the blanket around a sleeping James before placing him gently in his cradle. "Of course, Henry. James and I will be perfectly fine at Riverside. When were you thinking of leaving?"

"Oh, fairly soon, actually, darling, but of course, I will come home every weekend," he added hastily. "Now, if you are sure, darling, I'll go down and have a word with Bernard and sort it out."

It proved to be a difficult conversation with Bernard, but Henry remained calm and reasonable, fortified by Estelle's assurances, and eventually, Bernard reluctantly agreed. Henry would spend Monday to Thursday in London, visiting existing customers and making new contacts, and long weekends at home in Riverside. There was an unspoken agreement that Henry had a restricted budget to be used for entertaining clients, and as Henry would not be in London at the weekend, Bernard had to be content with that.

One Sunday evening after dinner, when Henry had left for London, Estelle asked Polly to settle James and went to find Bernard, who was sitting on the terrace enjoying his evening pipe. It was a mild evening for early November, and the sky was clear, with just a few lacy clouds drifting across a full moon. Somewhere in the trees, a fox barked, and in the stillness of the night, they could hear the hum of the waterwheel and the slap of the paddles in the river. Estelle sat down in the rocking chair next to Bernard, "Henry has just left, Bernard. He said to say goodbye."

Bernard took the pipe from his mouth and sighed. "Yes, well, my dear, Henry always leaves as soon as we have finished dinner, does he not?" Estelle was not taken in by his quiet tone. "Bernard, I know that you are not happy with this arrangement, but it does suit us both, you know, and I hope not having Henry in the office has not caused too much of a problem, although he says not."

Bernard laughed, "No, my dear, I do not miss Henry in the office.

However, I confess that I do not understand why he would want to stay from you and that delightful child."

"Henry and I do love each other, but since James was born, I have realised that we never had time to really get to know each other. James came so quickly after we were married. It is partly my fault, Bernard. I knew how much Henry loved living in London, and I was excited at the thought of it as well. Whenever Henry took me to London, we had such good times, but when we came to Shorehill, I found all sorts of excuses not to leave, and I did not have the courage to confess to Henry that I no longer wished to live in London." She smiled sadly. "The thing is, Bernard, when I found out that I was expecting a baby I was sure that Henry would settle down, and again, I was wrong, because, if anything, it has made him more restless."

Bernard went to say something, but she stopped him gently. "We have spoken about the situation, Bernard. The solution for the time being seems to be Henry has his time in London and then comes home to us. However, and we have agreed on this as well, he will not let the dreaded Perry influence him as he did before. I like and trust Foxy, but not Perry. Perry resents me and James." she added simply.

"I hear and accept what you say, my dear, and heavens only knows what your family thinks of this arrangement, but I have to say that I am still very disappointed in Henry. I too, must accept some blame, because I allowed Henry such a free reign after our parents died, and I fear he has become extremely selfish. However, I will do my best to ensure that he does not drift back into his old ways. Henry must wake up to the fact that he has family responsibilities now."

"And that, my darling Bernard, is precisely what has frightened Henry away: those very responsibilities. We shall have to give him time to learn to accept the fact that he is a father now."

Bernard, who knew this to be the truth, nodded, and they sat together without speaking. Bernard glanced at the calm, beautiful face of his sister-in-law and wondered whether Henry would come to his senses before it was too late.

It was surprising how quickly life at Riverside settled into a routine. Henry kept to the timetable, religiously visiting the Maycroft clients, and under the accountant's watchful eye, he even kept his spending within the monthly budget. Foxy and other friends still visited Riverside for the shooting and fishing. Peregrine, however, always had an excuse not to visit, and Estelle breathed a sigh of relief every time Henry appeared minus Perry. However, when Estelle and James went to Grieves Manor to visit Lady Rose and Lord Archie, Perry always seemed to find time to come to Riverside for the weekend, blatantly ignoring Bernard's cool and somewhat offhand welcome.

James thrived, a peaceful and happy baby and when a brand-new bassinet arrived as a gift from James's generous and doting grandparents in Berkshire, both Estelle and Polly delighted in wheeling the baby around the village to be fussed over and admired. When the weather was good, they would take it in turns to carry James through the garden across the meadow to picnic in the Folly and paddle in the shallows of the river. Estelle delighted in their days together, teaching James the names of the birds flitting across the river. When the sun shone, they collected wildflowers and chased butterflies through the meadow before returning tired, happy, and browned by the sun. The school children playing on the opposite riverbank would wave and shout to James, and to the small boy's delight, they sometimes joined him and Estelle to paddle and splash in the river.

At four years old, James was a shy but happy child, and Henry began to raise the question of his education. Estelle, with a sinking heart, brushed the matter aside, promising that she was already looking into James's schooling.

"But he doesn't speak much, does he? It is clear that James needs to mix with other boys." Henry frowned as he looked across to where James was happily building blocks with Polly. He lowered his voice. "Apart from that, he seems to have a bit of a stammer. You must have noticed it, Estelle?" Henry's tone was slightly hectoring. "You do know, Estelle, that Bernard also stammered as a child, and he inherited that from my father. I worry that James has inherited it as well, and I think he needs to, well, learn to rough-and-tumble a bit."

Estelle was defensive, "It's not a stammer, Henry, it's simply that he gets a little shy when there are a lot of people in the house, that is all, and you do tend to talk loudly to him. Perhaps when you are at home, you could spend a little more time with him. He is a very bright little boy."

But Henry had already made up his mind to pursue the question of James's schooling after speaking with George and Jenny.

George and Jenny's riotous red-headed, seven-year-old twins had been enrolled as boarders at Barrow Hill, the feeder school in Berkshire which prepared boys for Eton College. Henry was quietly determined that when the time came, James would join his cousins but decided not to mention this to Estelle for the time being.

But Henry had worried her, and Estelle voiced her concerns to Bernard. He was reassuring.

"I have been thinking about young James's schooling also. Henry mentioned to me a while ago that he thought James was a little slow and would benefit from boarding school later on." He laughed at Estelle's indignant face, "Don't worry my dear, I assured him that young James is very bright, but Henry doesn't always see the best of him. I have been making enquiries around the village, and as it happens, there is an excellent lady, a widow, who has just moved into Nut Cottage with her daughter."

"Mrs Blanche Dove used to teach French and drawing at the Catherine Lodge School in London until it closed a few years ago. I had a word with her after the service at church last Sunday, and she said she would be delighted to come to Riverside and tutor James at home."

When Blanche Dove presented herself to Estelle in the drawing room at Riverside, Estelle looked at the trim and gentle-faced schoolteacher and visibly relaxed. "Mrs Dove, I am so pleased to meet you. Please sit down, and I will ask Polly to fetch James."

Blanche Dove smiled, and her blue eyes twinkled. "I am looking forward to meeting James, Mrs Maycroft. We haven't lived in the village very long, but when I walk through the meadow, I sometimes see you playing with James on the other side of the river. In fact, you often both wave to me. I was delighted when Mr Bernard suggested that I call on you."

Blanche handed Estelle a three-page letter, a reference from Mrs Field, who had been a principal at the Catherine Lodge School. Estelle studied it in silence. When she had finished reading, she handed the letter back to Blanche, who had been waiting, composed and confident. "What a wonderful testimonial, Mrs Dove. I think we would be very fortunate should you agree to tutor James. I am sure we will all get on famously."

So, Blanche Dove came to tutor James every weekday between ten and three and watching the shy little boy blossom under Mrs Dove's tender guidance filled Estelle with joy. Estelle could hardly wait for Henry to return home, when after a month, Mrs Dove declared that, "James is a naturally bright child, who enjoys his letters and his numbers, and is showing an aptitude for the French language."

Henry, hearing this, was reserved in his praise and stated privately to Bernard, "Well, at least the boy will be prepared for Barrow Hill when the time comes." Bernard, knowing how Estelle felt about the subject of James boarding away from home, was silent on the subject.

RIVERSIDE 1908

Late one humid afternoon in August, in the year of James's tenth birthday, Henry arrived back at Riverside with his shooting friends for the annual grouse shoot. Some of the shooting party would be staying at Riverside, and others were booked in at the Hop Vine. The Glorious Twelfth was the one Shorehill shoot that Peregrine Porter would not miss, and Estelle was dismayed to find that he would be a guest at Riverside, and not, as she had hoped, booked in at the Hop Vine. James, having completed his lessons and not keen to be around his father's overpowering friends when they arrived, had asked whether he could play down by the Folly with Billy Hunter and his friends. Estelle readily agreed, for although Billy was adventurous and noisy, he and James had built up a solid friendship, and through him, James had been accepted by the village boys.

Whilst the group of friends argued loudly amongst themselves for the best bedroom, Peregrine, who knew that Henry would have allocated him his usual bedroom at the front of the house, was idly relaxing on the terrace with a large whiskey. In the distance, he could hear the sound of boys shouting and hooting with laughter. He was intrigued, and lighting a cigarette, he debated lazily whether to leave his comfortable chair and find the source of the merriment. The boys were not in the garden, and curiosity overcame him, so picking up his glass, he wandered across the lawn and through the apple orchard. Pushing open the little gate in the garden wall, Perry ducked under the overhanging hawthorn branches and found himself standing in a meadow of high grasses, a shimmering sea of gold in the late afternoon sun.

Above the rush of the river, he could hear the boys' shouts of laughter louder now and in the distance, could see a thatched roof, the lower half of a building hidden behind a neat circle of lilac bushes.

"Well, I never," Perry said to himself. "I guess that must be the infamous Folly." The afternoon sun was hot on his bare head, and he debated whether to go back for his hat, but instead, he set off across the meadow, following a path where the grass had been trodden flat. The Folly was further away than he anticipated, and when he finally reached the shade of the bushes, he was sweating and uncomfortable. He took his jacket off, wiped his forehead with his handkerchief, and looked over the hedge at the oddly-shaped Folly. Honeybees buzzed lazily in and out of the sweet-smelling jasmine and vibrant honeysuckle that clung to the walls and windows.

A small, white fence surrounded a garden full of shrubs and flowers of every colour and description. Smooth, round stepping-stones led across the grass through an open gate and disappeared down to the riverbank.

The doors to the Folly were wide open, and Perry walked softly up the steps and peered inside the cool interior. Sunlight streamed through the stained-glass windows onto the wooden floor. On the far wall was a pretty brocade chaise longue and next to it a bronze statuette of a child that looked oddly familiar. To his right was a small bookcase crammed with books of every shape and size, and in the centre of the room, stood a round table and four cane chairs. The Folly was sweet with the scent of the crimson roses that filled a tall glass vase, and a few velvety petals had fallen on the deck of playing cards scattered on the table. Perry gazed around with interest, and although there was no one around, everywhere in the Folly there were signs of frequent visitors. His curiosity was aroused even further, and he went back outside, blinking in the sudden glare of the sun. Heading in the direction of the voices, he followed the steppingstones down toward the riverbank.

The sound of the river grew louder, and when he reached the steep bank, he could see below him the crystal-clear water flowing rapidly over the pebbled riverbed. A weeping willow tree sat at the edge of the river, its curtain of drooping branches swaying in the rush of the river. Under the tree, a roughly carved wooden bench was piled high with shirts, socks, and shoes.

Perry hesitated then side-stepped slowly down the slope until he was standing on the soft, mossy riverbank. He could see them then, a small group of boys attempting to build a dam by dragging fallen branches into the river and filling the gaps with mud and stones. They were the very essence of carefree youth as they jostled each other, shouting and bent double with laughter at each unsuccessful attempt. They did not see Perry lounging against the tree, hidden in the shadow of the whispering willow tree. Perry spotted James immediately, his likeness to Henry was breathtakingly unmistakable, as he threw back his head in laughter. His strawberry curls glistened with droplets of water; his slim body swift and golden brown as he dived around in the river collecting pebbles.

Perry watched silently until he finished his cigarette, then, tossing the stub to one side, he stepped out of the shadows and called out the boy's name. "James," and again edging closer to the boys, he called louder, "James." This time, the boys heard him, and as one, they turned to look up at him, shielding their eyes against the glare of the hot sun. Perry saw in an instant, the flash of dislike flit across James's face as he recognized him.

James turned to the group and muttered something in a low voice before wading to the water's edge. Ignoring Perry's proffered hand, he clambered nimbly up the bank. "Hello, Uncle Perry. Is Father here already?" he asked, politely avoiding Perry and walking over to the bench.

"Yes, indeed, young James. He is, and no doubt he is wondering where you are."

Perry masked his annoyance at the boy's direct snub. James dried himself roughly with his shirt before pulling it over his head.

"Mother knows where to find me, sir." James's reply was cool and offhand. "I expect she is waiting for me in the Folly," and he ran sure-footed up the riverbank deliberately keeping ahead of Perry, who stumbled after him.

Estelle was waiting at the Folly, standing in the open doors and shielding her eyes with her hat, she saw James running toward her. She waved, smiling broadly, but then her smile faded when she saw the familiar, dark-haired man striding along behind him.

"Oh no," she said under her breath, then as the man came closer. "Perry! What on Earth are you doing out here?" she said crossly, and turning to her son, "James, darling, I was just coming to fetch you. Daddy is back, so run home and change for dinner. Polly is waiting in your room with some dry clothes." James needed no second bidding and sped off, disappearing into the long grass toward the house.

"Well, dear lady, I was enjoying a quiet drink on the terrace, and I could hear all this noise, and I was curious, so I came to investigate." Perry said smoothly, his dark eyes fixed on her unsmiling face. "And lo and behold, I came across young James, frolicking half-dressed in the river with a bunch of village boys, or of course, they could have been gypsies."

"Don't be so ridiculous, Perry. I knew he was with Billy Hunter and his friends from the village." Estelle could barely contain her anger but watching a faint smirk of satisfaction cross Perry's face, she felt a sinking feeling that the odious man would find a way of using this against her and James.

After a pleasant dinner, during which, to Estelle's puzzled surprise, Perry did his utmost to charm, even going as far as to tease James, which brought a reluctant smile to the boy's face. Henry declared his intent to stroll down to the Hop Vine and meet with William Hunter and the beaters.

"Arrangements for tomorrow's shoot, darling," he explained as he put his arm around Estelle and dropped a kiss on her head. Estelle exhaled in relief. Perhaps she had done Perry an injustice, as Henry appeared to be in high good humour.

But her relief was short-lived, when the shooting party returned late afternoon the following day, it was only Henry who was grim-faced. The rest of the party were noisily celebrating the fact that after a successful day shooting, all the guns had achieved their bag limit.

"Perry," said Henry curtly, not meeting Estelle's eyes as she moved among the guests. "Give me a hand sorting out the beaters and the birds, will you? William has them over at the Lodge."

They were gone for several hours, and it was obvious when they returned for a late supper, that Henry was extremely drunk, and Perry was sober. Bernard had no heart for shooting, and whilst he insured that the guests were well taken care of, he tended to spend his time in the library or in the estate office until they had departed. It was in the library that Estelle found Bernard, long after Henry had stumbled up to bed.

Bernard listened without comment as Estelle tremulously explained how Perry had come across James playing in the river. "I know Perry has made up some story about James 'frolicking' with gypsy boys, but he was with young Billy, the blacksmith's twins, and a few others. Blanche said that he had finished lessons, so I said he could play with his friends, but Henry is so angry, Bernard, he went up to bed without saying a word to me. What shall I do if he wants to send James to Barrow Hill? The problem is that Walter and William have been boarding there for over a year, and George told Henry that they love it. Even Jenny said in front of Henry that perhaps James was a little too sheltered."

Bernard looked with compassion at Estelle. "I will talk with Henry. Tell me, is Henry aware of how well James is progressing with Blanche Dove?"

"Yes, of course he does, I tell him all the time, and I show him James's books and the lovely report that that Blanche wrote about James."

"I will do my best, dear girl, I promise, but Henry listens to Perry above all else. I fear that Perry thinks that Henry will spend less time at Riverside and more time in London if James is away at school."

Estelle thanked him tearfully, knowing in her heart of hearts that Henry had already made his mind up, and it was only her determined efforts that had kept James with her for so long. Very early the next morning, the shooting party returned to London without Henry, and Estelle's heart sank when, after last guest had departed, Henry strode into the drawing room where she was seated at her desk. She stared up at him defiantly. "Well, Henry?"

Unable to meet her direct gaze, he thrust his hands into his trouser pockets and walked around the room before turning back to her. "First of all, Estelle, I want you to know that my decision has nothing to do with how Peregrine came upon James with a bunch of young ruffians, whom I understand were trespassing on our land."

Estelle, trembling with anger, gritted her teeth but said nothing.

"You see, I had already made up my mind, darling. It is time for James to join his cousins at Barrow Hill, and when George and Jenny enrolled William and Walter a few years ago, I also enrolled James."

Estelle gasped, and Henry, still avoiding her eyes, carried on. "Everything is in place for James to start Barrow Hill in September, so you should inform Mrs Dove that her services will no longer be required."

"And you have done all this behind my back, you, George, and Jenny plotting, and I suppose my parents. Everyone appears to know my own son better than me. When exactly did you intend to discuss this with me, Henry?" Estelle's voice was shaking with fury.

Henry blustered. "George and Jenny were under the impression that we had already discussed it, so do not blame them. I delayed telling you because I knew you would make things difficult. This is the best thing for James, and he has to be prepared for Eton." He hesitated and cleared his throat. "Estelle, I explained to James last night that he would be joining his cousins at Barrow for the autumn term. I was waiting until we were alone this morning to tell you."

Estelle looked aghast, "You were drunk when you told our son that he was going away to school in a few weeks, and I wasn't there to explain anything to him. He is a small boy, Henry; he will be confused and frightened." She stood up shakily and confronted her husband. "I will never, ever forgive you for this, Henry Maycroft," she said icily as she left the room.

When Estelle knocked gently on James's bedroom door, there was no reply, and she knocked again. "James, it's Mummy, darling. May I come in?"

The door opened, "Sorry, Mummy, I was waving to the men."

James's bedroom was at the very top of the house overlooking the clinker path to the Mill and the tumbling river. When he was tiny, Polly used to hold him up to the window to wave to the mill workers as they went past the house. They still looked up and called out a cheery greeting if they saw him leaning out of the window.

"James," said Estelle softly, kneeling and putting her arms around him. "Daddy has just told me that you both had a little talk last night about going to school."

James pulled away and walked back toward the window. "Yes, we did, and school sounds awfully good fun, Mummy," but his voice was tremulous, and Estelle felt the tears gathering in her eyes. She brushed them away and joined him at the open window, and together they leant out and looked down on the river. The morning sun was warm on their arms, and the air was filled with bird song and, in the background against the rush of the river, the hum of the engine that turned the vast water wheel.

"James, I want you to know that you can always come home if you are unhappy, and you do not have to fully board. You can spend the weekends at Grieves Manor, and I will come and join you there." Estelle put her arms around the boy's shuddering shoulders.

"Thank you, Mummy, but Daddy said that the twins stay at school at weekends. Daddy says that it will be more fun staying in school with the full boarders."

Estelle took her son's face in her hands and bit her lip when she saw the panic in his eyes and the tears now streaming unchecked down his white face. "James, I promise that you can come home to Grieves Manor every weekend, and I will be there."

James gulped and nodded silently. "Promise, Mummy," he whispered.

"I promise James, and sometimes I will bring Polly."

James took a deep breath. "Daddy said we have to go to a shop in Victoria tomorrow, so I can be measured for my uniform. Will you come?" Estelle forced a laugh. "My darling boy, we will spend every day together until you go to Barrow, I promise. Now let's go down and find Uncle Bernard and tell him the exciting news."

That night after James had gone up to bed, Estelle, who had deliberately missed dinner on the pretext of having a headache, went in search of Henry. She found him sitting in the drawing room by the open window.

He stood up as she entered the room and looked at her warily, a cigar in one hand and a large whisky in the other. "Sit down Henry," Estelle said coldly. "This will not take long, and please do not interrupt me. When I have finished speaking, I am going for a walk in the garden and when I return, I expect you to have removed yourself from our bedroom." She paused and took a deep breath. "As from tomorrow, James will have no further lessons or tuition from Mrs Dove. I intend to spend every possible minute with my son until he leaves. I will oversee all the preparations for his move to Barrow. James and I will spend the weekend with my parents before term begins. Every weekend whilst he is at Barrow, I will spend at Grieves Manor, and if he does not want to board at the weekend, then he can come and spend the weekend with me. Just because William and Walter choose to board seven days a week does not mean that James must, and I will not allow you or anyone else to coerce him into staying if he does not want to. James will always have the choice to come to Grieves Manor for the weekend."

Without waiting for a reply, Estelle turned sharply on her heel and left the room. The evening was warm and still, and Bernard, sitting in the shadows on the terrace, was enjoying a late-night brandy. He started, when behind him the dining room doors were flung open and Estelle, white faced, stormed onto the terrace.

Bernard jumped to his feet. "Estelle, what on Earth is wrong? Is it James?"

"No, Bernard, please don't concern yourself," her voice trembled. "I am going for a walk around the gardens. I shall not be long," and before he could stop her, Estelle had picked up her skirts and fled down the steps and into the soft twilight.

Bernard stared in consternation at her disappearing figure, uncertain what to do next. He had kept well away from Henry, aware of the turmoil his brother's decision to dispatch James off to Barrow Hill had caused within the household, but now he decided to find out what had caused Estelle's obvious distress. Bernard found Henry in the drawing room still seated by the window.

"What is going on Henry? I have just seen Estelle, and she seemed most upset."

"What is going on indeed, my dear brother? My wife has thrown me out of our bedroom." Henry's tone was bitter. "I am doing the best for James, and this is the thanks that I get. The boy must go to school, and why on Earth Estelle cannot see that is beyond me. The boy will be ten years old in October. I simply do not understand what all of this fuss is about."

Bernard looked at his younger brother's furious face and decided that it would be pointless to reason with him now, so he shook his head and went in search of Estelle. He found her sipping tea in the kitchen with Aggie and Polly. She gave him a trembling smile. "The deed is done, Bernard, and we have to accept it, but Henry will not get all of his own way in this, believe me."

Bernard shook his head sadly, "I am so very sorry my dear." Unable to sleep that night, he tossed and turned, wondering whether time would heal the rift between Henry and Estelle and prayed that James would settle at Barrow Hill like his cousins.

Over the next few days, Henry, unsure how to deal with Estelle's obvious hostility, found he was also faced with Bernard's unspoken disapproval, and a silently mutinous Polly who avoided him whenever she could. He weathered this for a week before deciding that he may as well go back to his flat in London and wait for the storm to pass.

After all, it was obvious that he was not to be invited to accompany Estelle and James on their shopping jaunts, and it was extremely difficult to work with Bernard in the office, so he announced his intention to return to London over dinner one night.

"Calling on clients, Henry?" Bernard enquired, without looking up from his meal.

Henry flushed darkly. "Yes, of course. Why else would I be going? Estelle, perhaps we could all meet for lunch when you bring James up for his uniform?"

"If we find time, Henry, I will let you know," Estelle replied coolly, and that was the end of the conversation.

Henry left early the next morning before breakfast. When Foxy, Perry, and a few friends strolled into St James's Club at Sunday lunch time, they were startled to see a morose Henry slouched in a chair nursing a large whisky. Perry raised his eyebrows.

"Long way to come for Sunday lunch, Henry, as excellent as the roast beef here is, but as I recall, it does not compare with your Aggie's Yorkshire puddings."

"Yes, very amusing as usual, Perry," Henry snarled and sat up, his unread newspaper falling to the floor.

"Just my little joke old boy, another one for you before lunch?" smirked Perry as he caught the waiter's eye. "Another large one for my friend here."

Foxy sat down next to Henry. "Is everything alright at Riverside, Henry?"

An aggrieved Henry told him about his decision to send James to Barrow Hill. "Honestly, Foxy, had I committed murder, I could not have been treated any worse. I am simply insisting on the best education for the boy. George's boys fare very well at Barrow, and so will James."

Foxy was thoughtful, "William and Walter have each other, Henry, and anyway, James is not like his cousins, you know. He's a quiet lad; he prefers his books to sports."

"Exactly," said Henry triumphantly. "James needs to toughen up and learn to play a decent game of cricket like a gentleman instead of mucking about fishing and climbing trees with the village boys. Barrow Hill will do that for him. Get him ready for Eton. James spends too much time with Estelle and Polly, and Bernard is far too soft with him."

Foxy frowned and looked across to Perry, who was watching them through narrowed eyes whilst swirling a large brandy around in his glass. Foxy looked back at Henry. "Henry, this rush to send James to school, it has not got anything to do with our friend has it, because I sense Peregrine's fine hand in all this? Much as I love the dear chap, he does like to call all the shots, and he likes his friends to be around when he needs them."

"Good God. Not at all, Foxy," blustered Henry. "My decision totally. It had to come sooner or later, and Estelle will come around once the boy settles down."

But Foxy detected an uncertain look flit across Henry's handsome face, because no one knew better than Henry that underneath Estelle's beautiful face and sweet nature was a lady with a will of iron when it came to protecting her son. Several hours later, following an excellent roast dinner and a few bottles of Claret, Henry was feeling rosily optimistic about the future. By early evening, he had accepted Perry's casual invitation to, "Drop round to my gaff for a couple of games of poker," and promptly lost a rather large sum of money.

"Well, it serves old Bernard right." Henry was defensive and petulant when questioned by Foxy about just how much money he had gambled. "Bernard should have backed me up, instead of siding with Estelle."

For James and Estelle, the next few weeks passed in a blur of trips to London for uniform fittings, the purchase of cricket whites, stiff collars, top hats, and riding boots. The trips were tempered with visits to museums and art galleries ending in afternoon teas in the Savoy.

When the shopping was completed and with no timetable to keep to, James and Estelle spent the shortening summer days in the Folly, or down by the river where Bernard would often join them for tea.

On the soft, misty September mornings that were left to them, Estelle and James would rise early, harness Pepper into the pony trap, and trot smartly through the peaceful, narrow lanes. Together, they watched as the rising sun dissolved the drifting mist that clung to the fields and hovered over the river. As they approached the village, they could smell the sweet, wood smoke curling lazily up from the chimneys into the awakening sky.

Often, Blanche Dove, on hearing Pepper's hooves clattering on the bridge, opened her door to call them in for breakfast. Fresh eggs, warm from her hens, were poached and placed on homemade bread, the rich orange yolks trickling over the melting creamy butter.

All too soon, they had run out of time, and James, stiff and pale, his strawberry curls cut and tamed, green eyes brimming with tears, stood in the hall by his smart new trunk, labelled and strapped, "JAMES HENRY MAYCROFT. BARROW HILL." Estelle shivered when she read the label. Aggie and Polly stood close together. Aggie was wringing her hands, and Polly stood, openly weeping.

Henry held out his hand, and James leant forward to shake it. "Good luck, James. Be a good scholar. I hope to visit once you have settled in," but his tone, attempting to be jovial, was too loud.

"I will, sir, and thank you," James shook his father's hand briefly then turned away and held out a trembling hand to Bernard.

"Goodbye, Uncle Bernard. I will miss you so."

Bernard, ignoring the outstretched hand, scooped his nephew up in a bear hug and held him tight. "I will miss you too, my boy, and I will write and tell you all the news, and I promise to visit soon."

Estelle stood stiff and proud as Tip and a groom came to collect the trunks. "Polly, my dear, would you like to come to the station with us to see James off?" Her voice was coolly composed.

Polly shook her head wordlessly, rushed forward, and going down on her knees, she cradled James close, the child she had watched being born and loved with all her heart as he had grown into this lovely, sweet boy. "My James," she whispered. "Your Polly will always be here for you. Come back to us soon."

James clung to her and gulped, "I will Polly. I promise. I have left Bear on my bed, Father said not to take him. Can you take care of him for me, please? He will be lonely without me." James's precious Bear was a grumpy-faced, much loved teddy bear, and had spent most of his short life tucked underneath James's arm. Bear, the friend who had comforted him through measles, tummy aches, and scared away the under-bed monsters. Precious Bear, the little teddy bear that his Mummy had tucked next to him in his cradle a few days after he was born and whispered, "James, meet Bear," was to be left behind.

Polly gave him one almighty hug and said fiercely, "James, I will look after Bear. I promise he will never be lonely, and he will be here when you come home."

Henry watched stony-faced, as with a final goodbye, Estelle and James climbed up into the trap. Tip touched Pepper's rump with the whip, and they were off to the station and Grieves Manor. Bernard stared after them until the trap disappeared into Old Mill Lane and turned to look at Henry. "I hope for your sake, Henry, that you have sent James away for the right reason, and I hope he is happy at Barrow Hill, because otherwise, Estelle will never forgive you."

Henry was defiant. "Oh, for goodness sake, Bernard, the boy is only going away to school, and I wasn't even allowed to go and send him off. I offered, you know, Bernard, pleaded to be allowed to travel with them and spend a weekend with James at Grieves Manor. I wanted to take him on his first day, but it seems that I am surplus to requirements."

Bernard looked his brother's handsome face, sulky and resentful, and he turned and walked away without saying a word.

The day after James took his place at Barrow Hill, Estelle returned to Riverside, and unannounced, she arrived at Shorehill Station on the early train. "Good Morning, madam," Percy touched his cap and looked around uncertainly. "Are you being met, Mrs Maycroft?"

"No, Percy. I'll send for my bags later. It's a lovely morning, so I shall walk home," and she smiled briefly at the astonished station master and hurried through the station and into the lane.

It was an exceptionally lovely day, soft and mild, a few turning leaves drifted down around her, and through the trees, she could see ears of ripe corn trembling in the breeze, and beyond, the sheep-cropped green and gentle hills.

It was still too early for the children to start school, and she was glad. Estelle could not bear the thought of hearing their shouts of carefree laughter or their young voices as they made their way to the tiny schoolroom. Inside her chest was a frozen lump, a hard knot of tears that would not flow. She had tried so hard not to cry over the last few weeks, but now she found she needed the release of tears. She reached the bridge, leant on the warm parapet, and stood staring down into the glistening water, watching the duckweed and the yellow king cups move gently to the rhythm of the river. Overcome with despair and sadness, she dropped her head down onto her hands, her body wracked with dry sobs.

Blanche Dove, standing outside Nut Cottage, saw the slender woman leaning on the bridge distraught with grief. "Oh, my dear, stay there, Estelle, I'm coming," she called out and hurried up onto the bridge. When she reached Estelle, she took her shawl off, and wrapping it around Estelle's shuddering shoulders, she guided her back across the bridge and into Nut Cottage.

"Come along my dear, you are shivering. Let me make you a hot drink. Sit here by the stove."

"Blanche, what am I to do? He never cried, you know, James, when I left him. I said goodbye and kissed him, but he just walked away. Does he blame me as well, Blanche? Do you think my darling boy blames me as well? I just cannot bear it if he does."

Blanche held her close, trying to still the racking sobs that engulfed the thin frame. Fighting back her own tears, she said firmly, "You are going to have some tea, and you are going to stop crying because James does not blame you, Estelle, and never will. No more tears now, my dear. Come and talk to me whilst I make our tea."

Estelle, her sobs slowly quieting, wiped her eyes and wandered into the kitchen. Blanche smiled. "That's better. Now tell me, is James a full boarder at the school?"

"No, but he may as well be," Estelle sniffed miserably. "He can come home on Saturday afternoon, but he must be back on Sunday night in time for supper and evening prayer. The headmaster said that some boys don't bother going home if they live a long way away. I have arranged to stay with Ma and Pa at Grieves Manor every weekend, and James can come there."

Blanche set the teapot down on the kitchen table, poured out two cups of tea, and sat down opposite Estelle. "Well then," she said comfortably, "That's not so bad, is it? It will be the holidays before long, and then you can both come back to Riverside. Will Mr Henry be staying at Grieves Manor at the weekend as well?"

Estelle was staring out of the window as the first trickle of children began to make their way across the bridge to school. It was a while before she replied. "No, Blanche, my husband has business in London. He is too busy to visit every weekend. James does understand that, but I have promised James that Polly will visit. I am sure that James will not miss Henry in the least."

She leant forward and picked her teacup up, her face expressionless and her jaw tight as she sat straight-backed in the chair. Beneath the tumble of red curls, the tears were drying in salty streaks on her pale face, and her lips were set in a straight line.

"Estelle, you know how very fond I am of James and of you too, and I am here if ever you need someone to talk to. But it will get easier, my dear, and before you know it, he will be home for Christmas and talking about all the new friends he has made."

Leaving Nut Cottage, Estelle returned to find Riverside completely deserted apart from Aggie, who was dozing in a chair in the garden, her knitting needles abandoned on her lap, and Betsy, who was busily adding the final touches to a large apple pie. After James and Estelle had left, Henry had wandered aimlessly around the house for a few hours and had then caught the train back to London, much to Bernard's relief. Polly, too upset to stay at Riverside without James, had asked Bernard for the day off to visit her aunt and mother in Sevenoaks. "I will be back this evening, Mr Bernard," she had promised.

Betsy looked up, flustered, when she saw Estelle standing in the doorway. "Oh, madam, we were not expecting you." She put the pie down and wiped floury hands on her apron. "I'll wake cook directly. Mr Bernard is out, so is Mr Henry, and our Polly is off visiting her

Ma. Now, madam, can I get you something?" Betsy asked, looking anxiously at her mistress's pale face.

Estelle smiled. "Don't bother to wake Aggie. I've just had tea with Blanche Dove, so I really don't need anything. But I walked from the station, and I wonder if you could send Tip up for my bags?"

Betsy hesitated. "I hope you don't mind me asking, madam, but is Master James alright?"

"Master James is absolutely fine, Betsy, I promise." Estelle assured her gently. "Oh, and Betsy, if Mr Bernard comes in, I shall be in my room."

It had upset Bernard far more that he imagined it would to see his young nephew miserably leaving for boarding school, and Estelle's deep distress was painful to watch.

After Henry had stomped off back to London, Bernard went first to the estate office and later to the Hop Vine. He was not inclined to return to Riverside, and it was late when he finally returned to the house. Riverside was quiet, far too quiet. The kitchen table had been cleared, and there was a solitary cold ham supper on the table. Aggie had left a note to say that she was taking supper with Bessie and Ernie, and of Estelle, there was no sign. Ignoring the food, Bernard, with a gnawing niggle of worry, searched through the empty rooms. Perhaps Estelle had returned and was resting in her bedroom. But there was no sign of her in the empty, silent house.

It was growing dusk when he went outside to see if she was sitting on the terrace. Tiny bats were swooping soundlessly through the trees, the moon was bright, and the sky clear, but the terrace was empty, and instinctively Bernard headed for the Folly. She was curled up on her little chaise longue, sleeping peacefully with Bear held tightly in her arms. Bernard stood for a while looking down at her. "Poor, dear child," he whispered then turned and went back to the house. He returned, carrying several blankets, a picnic basket, and a bottle of wine and two glasses.

Estelle blinked sleepily when he woke her then smiled at the small feast laid out on the table. "Bernard, I am sorry. I just needed to be out of the house for a while, but I was so tired, and it was so cosy in here. I just fell asleep."

"Never mind that, my dear. I understand you must be exhausted, but you should eat a little, I doubt that you have eaten much today." Bernard's voice was gruff with emotion. "And then you can tell me all about James. That is, if you are ready."

"Bernard, of course. I want to tell you about James and the plans we have made."

"Good. Eat first, then we can talk."

They ate together in silence, and when Bernard poured the wine, he ventured to ask, "So tell me, my dear, did our boy go off all right, and what are these plans?"

"Yes, he did, and Bernard you would have been so proud of him. I am ashamed to say he was far more composed than I, but he looked so awfully small and lost somehow. A few of the other new boys were crying, but James was so grown-up, and I was just so proud of him." Her voice wobbled, and she laid her head on Bernard's shoulder.

"James is a strong boy, Estelle," said Bernard, tucking the blanket around her. "Just remember, very soon you will have two entire days to spend together."

Estelle snuggled closer to Bernard, "I know, and I have made up my mind despite what Henry says. James will not board at the weekend. I plan to go back to Grieves Manor every Friday, and James can stay with us for the weekend. I have promised James, and I will not let him down."

"Then we shall drink to your plan, my dear, and you must be as strong as James, for Henry will oppose you on this as well, but I will always support you."

Catching the last bus from Sevenoaks, Polly called into Poacher's Cottage on her way back to Riverside. Becky Dawes had made her friend, Dorothy, some lace gloves for her birthday, and Polly promised her mother that she would deliver them. It was close to midnight when Polly arrived back at Riverside, and she stared curiously at the untouched supper on the kitchen table before making herself a cup of hot milk and taking it out into the kitchen garden. She was standing in the shadows, lost in thought and enjoying the mild night, when she saw them, Estelle and Bernard walking, hand-in-hand slowly across the moonlit garden. A harvest moon, perfectly round, hung in a midnight sky, and Polly could see clearly that Bernard was carrying a picnic hamper, and Estelle, with a garland of daisies around her head, was holding Bear by one paw, swinging him gently back and forth. As they approached the house, Estelle turned a smiling face up to Bernard, and he bent to whisper in her ear. Polly moved further back into the shadows and slipped silently back through the kitchen door. She placed her empty cup carefully in the kitchen sink and made her way slowly to her bedroom.

The next morning, when Polly brought Estelle her breakfast tray, she found her sitting by the open bedroom window gazing out over the misty garden. Polly set the tray down on the table, "Good morning, madam. I am so sorry that I wasn't here when you came home yesterday. Mr Bernard gave me leave to visit my mother." Estelle turned and smiled shakily. Polly could see the fresh tears glistening on her cheeks.

"That's all right, Polly. I hope you had a nice day with your mother. James wanted me to tell you that he was very grown-up and not to worry about him, and he will see you soon. I was going to stay at Grieves Manor, but my parents thought I should come home and let him settle into Barrow and perhaps visit in a couple of weeks."

"Please don't cry, madam. You will make me cry as well," Polly said shakily. "I am sure the time will pass very quickly, and Barrow Hill is not far from Grieves Manor is it?"

Estelle stood up and put her arm around Polly's shoulders. "I know how upset you were to see James leave Riverside, Polly. I know how much you love him. I have promised James that when I visit, you shall come too."

Polly nodded, brushing away her tears, then laughed and pointed to the chair where Estelle had been sitting. "Oh, do look, madam. There's poor Bear, and what on Earth is that on his head?" James's beloved Bear was squashed in a corner, a wilting daisy chain drooping down over one black button eye.

Estelle leant forward, picked the small bear up and gently removed the daisy chain. "Darling Bernard found me asleep in the Folly last night and brought me food and blankets. I was so tired and upset Polly, I just couldn't settle in the house. Do you remember how James loved sleeping in the Folly"?

"I do, and once when we picked daisies in the dark, James called them star daisies."

"I told Bernard about our star daisies, and the dear man made a crown of daisies for me. He cares so much for James, and I know he thinks that James is far too young to be sent away from home."

Polly knew that Estelle's unspoken reproach was intended for Henry and said nothing.

The weekend of James's birthday approached, and the family gathered together in the gardens of Grieves Manor to celebrate. Walter and William were a little sulky and would have preferred to spend the weekend at school with their friends as they found they had little in common with their quiet cousin. They complained to both parents that James's shyness was both tiresome and embarrassing. The daredevil twins, red-headed and roundly robust like George, were madly keen on sports, both played rugby for the school, and both represented Barrow Hill in the under-fifteen cricket team. James, in stark contrast, was tall for his age, slender and thoughtful, and generally scorned for being "bookish."

The twin's strengths were out in the field, and whilst James enjoyed cricket, he loathed riding, rugby, and football, and thus, to Henry his son was a mystery. When he complained about this to Estelle, she told him coldly of James's preference for books and study groups, and Henry decided it was time to have a private talk with his son. Taking James to one side, he patted him on the back. "Now, James, how are you finding Barrow Hill. Not so bad is it?"

But James was reticent and guarded with his replies which frustrated Henry. "School is fine, Father. Thank you for asking."

"There you are. You see, I knew you would enjoy it once you started. Why not bring some chums home to Riverside at Christmas?" Henry was hearty and loud. "What about the Junior Rugby team,

James? George said the boys were both selected in their first term. You have to join in, you know." Henry frowned at James, who nodded stiffly but remained silent.

Estelle was standing close by and overheard Henry's hectoring tone. "James do come and speak with Sadie. She has a present for you. Polly has something for you too."

Henry sighed in angry frustration. "Off you go then, boy, your Mother is calling you."

In reality, James found Barrow Hill almost unbearable, and when his pillow was wet with stifled tears of loneliness and the long lonely night stretched ahead of him, it was the thought of coming back to Grieves Manor at the weekend that gave him the courage to deal with the bullies and the taunts. Driving a miserable James back to school after the weekend, Manners confided to Brent, "I feel sorry for that little blighter, you know, always being compared to those twins. He's a different kettle of fish, that one, cosseted by his Mother and bullied by his father. Something wrong at Riverside, if you ask me."

Whilst Brent protested loyally, "Mr Henry is not a bully, he just wants what's best for the boy," later, however, talking things over with Mrs Brent, they agreed that things were not right between young James's parents.

Sadly also, it was painfully obvious to the family that there was also a clear rift between Jenny and Estelle since James had joined Barrow Hill. Estelle was deeply hurt at what she perceived to be Jenny and George's betrayal in supporting Henry against her. Jenny had attempted on many occasions to explain to Estelle that both her and George had understood from Henry, that James's entry into Barrow was with Estelle's blessing. But the intimacy between the two old friends had gone, and Jenny was heartbroken. Estelle, too, was upset, and felt that her only true friends, apart from her parents, were Bernard and Polly, and she found peace and comfort in the company of her gentle brother-in-law.

As 1908 drew to a close and Christmas approached once again, it was decided that the Grieves-Croft family would come to Riverside for the holidays. In truth, Bernard, if not Henry, thoroughly enjoyed the traditional village celebrations. Henry, for his part, finding the village celebrations somewhat tedious, enjoyed the Boxing Day Hunt, where he was able to show his prowess in the saddle.

The rift between Estelle and Henry had healed only marginally, but Henry nursed a secret hope that he could persuade Estelle and James to, at least, celebrate the New Year in London. Peregrine Porter would be out of town for the holiday period and would not able to attend Foxy's lavish New Year party that was to be held in a Knightsbridge Hotel. But Henry's hopes were short lived, as after a very successful Christmas Day, followed by the Boxing Day Hunt, with Henry as Hunt Master, flamboyant and dashing as always, basking in the admiration and attention, Estelle went down with a sudden bout of sickness which confined her to bed.

As New Year's Eve drew closer, it became apparent that Estelle, although out of bed, was still too unwell to travel to London, and Henry's mood spiralled downward. Traditionally, Bernard would attend the New Year's party in the village hall, and Bernard, giving the morose Henry a hearty slap on the back, assured him that the food was always excellent, and Mick Carey, landlord of the Hop Vine, had promised to provide some decent barrels of ale. "I promise you will enjoy it, Henry, and apart from that, James was looking forward to spending some time with his village friends again."

Polly, however, was concerned about Estelle, who was still pale and listless and refusing to see Dr Bill. "It's nothing Polly, something I ate at Christmas, I expect" but Polly remained unconvinced.

1909

New Year's Eve was a gloomy day with drizzling rain and a biting cold north wind. James, Bernard, and Aggie had left the house soon after breakfast to help to prepare the village hall for the New Year celebrations. Estelle was half asleep and curled up in Bernard's armchair by the fire in the library, when James popped his head around the door, "I am going with Aggie and Uncle Bernard to help put the buntings up in the hall, Ma."

Estelle looked up and smiled at her son's excited face. "James Maycroft, I think that you are secretly rather happy that we are not going to Foxy's party," she said teasingly.

James flushed. "I am really sorry that you are ill, and I would like to see Foxy, but…" his voice trailed off, and he looked guilty.

Estelle put her fingers to her lips and whispered, "I don't like being ill, darling, but I am very glad that we are not going to London. I much prefer to be here with Bernard and Polly for the New Year. But I am going to send Daddy to London because Foxy will be very upset if none of us are able attend his party. So, darling can you go and find Daddy for me and ask him to come to come to the library?"

Henry put up a token resistance to his wife's cool suggestion that he should go to London, but he could barely contain his excitement.

"Darling, that is so very sweet of you, and of course I do not want to disappoint Foxy. I shall just go and pack a few things." When he returned, Henry managed to look contrite. "Now, are you sure you don't mind, dearest? I must say you do look awfully pale," and he frowned, looking closely at his wife. However, before she could reply, he had taken his watch from his waistcoat pocket. "If I hurry, I can catch the midday train to Victoria."

"Henry, yes, please do go now. The others will be ages getting the hall ready, and I can have a rest whilst everyone is out." She was firm and raised her face for his hasty kiss, and then he was gone, calling as he went, "Wish everyone a Happy New Year for me, darling, and I shall be home tomorrow, and we can celebrate bringing in 1909 altogether."

It was no surprise to either Bernard or Estelle that Henry did not return the following day, but, much to James's secret delight, only returned a few days later.

"Sorry, darling, sorry Bernard, old boy. I must have caught Estelle's cold. I have been laid up and far too unwell to travel. I hope that your New Year went well."

"Well, I have to say Henry, you seem to have made a remarkable recovery, and it would have been courteous to have kept Estelle informed. We were expecting your return on New Year's Day." Bernard, after looking up briefly at Henry, returned to his paper. Henry flushed and began to bluster an apology, but Estelle was disinterested, remote, and cold. She was still feeling unwell, sickly, and dizzy. Just a week later, Estelle, accompanied by Polly, returned a reluctant and silent James to Grieves Manor ready for the spring term at Barrow.

Following the mid-April Easter break, Estelle surprised Bernard and announced that she was going to stay with her parents at Grieves Manor throughout the coming summer.

"But I thought James had settled in school now. He seemed fine at Easter, and his letters are cheery." Bernard was puzzled and disappointed.

"Yes, he has, and being able to come home at the weekend has helped enormously," Estelle's tone was bright. "But I'm not going just for James, Bernard. The parents are off to Europe again, and they have asked whether I could stay with Sadie. I'll take Polly with me, of course. George and Jenny are taking the boys to Italy for the holidays, and it means that Nanny Ryan can have some company."

Estelle beamed at Bernard, and he thought, not for the first time lately, how very well she was looking. She had even put on a little weight.

"What does Henry say?" He was curious.

"Oh, Henry understands, and of course he will come and stay at Grieves Manor sometimes. Anyway, I know that Henry has planned a little trip to Nice, and I am quite happy for him to go," she added wryly.

"Perhaps I arrange to visit Grieves Manor sometime in the summer and spend a few days with you? It's going to be rather lonely at Riverside without both you and Polly."

Estelle was strangely evasive. "That would be lovely, Bernard dear. Yes, do come and see us. You will be most welcome, but you must let me know when you plan to visit. I may take James to Dawlish if the weather is good, and I don't want you to have a wasted journey."

Bernard nodded slowly, "Of course, my dear, of course," he agreed, a little puzzled at the sudden decision to visit Dawlish, but he relaxed when Estelle gave him an impulsive hug. "You must come, of course James would love to see you."

Riverside was strangely empty in the weeks that followed, and even the lovely gardens that Estelle had created drooped and wilted without her tender care. When, after a particularly lonely Sunday lunch in early May, Bernard was wandering aimlessly through the garden, he found himself in front of the gate into the meadow. Glossy green ivy had entwined tough stems through the hinges, and Bernard pushed hard until the gate sprung open. Once on the other side, he could just see the roof of the Folly in the shimmering afternoon sun. The grasses had grown over the once well-trodden path, and he made his way slowly through the ears of ripening corn enjoying the spring sunshine.

The little fence around the folly had been broken down, probably by a fox or badger, Bernard thought as he reached for the key above the door. Inside the Folly, it was hot and airless, prisms of light danced on the dusty floor, a vase of long-dead flowers drooped sadly on the table, and the books and bookshelves were covered in dust. He sat down on the chaise longue and looked sadly at the little bronze statuette standing on the table next to him. *Estelle with Butterflies*, he murmured as he reached out and placed a gentle finger on the ring of bronze daisies set on the tight curls. Outside, the bees hummed busily through the dense honeysuckle, and he could hear the rush of the river close by. He remembered the last time he had been in the Folly, the night when he had brought blankets and food to comfort a distraught Estelle, the night when at last, he had held her in his arms.

The heat inside the Folly was soporific, and Bernard was lost in thought when he heard a boy's voice raised in laughter followed by the sound of splashing. Taking a deep breath and shaking his head to clear the bittersweet memories, he stood up, took the dead flowers from the vase, and threw them outside. Then he locked the door and made his way down to the river.

Young Billy Hunter and his friends had rigged a rope onto an overhanging branch and were taking turns swinging from one side of the riverbank to the other. Billy, whose turn it was, stood holding the rope on the opposite bank and was about to swing, egged on by the shouts of his friends, when he looked up and saw Bernard watching him. He hesitated, but when Bernard gave him a nod of encouragement, he gave a triumphant whoop, and accompanied by cat calls from his friends, Billy jumped high in the air and hovered precariously above the water before dropping like a stone into the river below.

Years later, on a grim winter's day in 1917, when the world was caught in the bloody turmoil of an horrific war, and Bernard was anxiously scanning the casualty lists, he would recall that golden summer afternoon, the careless laughter of the fearless young boys, and remember the names and faces of those boys hovering on the brink of manhood and prayed fervently that he did not see a name he knew on that grim list.

When Bernard wrote to Estelle to say that he could spare a few weeks away from the mill and suggested he visit sometime in June, he received a hastily written response from Polly to say Estelle had gone to stay with a pregnant cousin for a week or so.

Bernard was not too surprised at this, as the Grieves-Crofts, unlike his own family, seemed to have an endless stream of cousins, aunts, and uncles all over the country. But he was disappointed, and when Henry came to Riverside accompanied by Foxy to discuss the August shoot with the game keeper, he mentioned it to him.

Henry had been disinterested. "There is always some cousin or other producing offspring in that family. My esteemed father-in-law has a large family, so I have no idea which cousin Estelle is visiting. Why don't you come down with me? James will be home from Barrow in a fortnight."

Two weeks later, Henry duly arrived at Riverside, and together they caught the train to Paddington and then on to Windsor. Manners collected them from the station in the Daimler, and it was late afternoon when they rolled through the open gates of Grieves Manor.

As they drove through the immaculate lawns and past the trickling fountain, the afternoon sun glinted on the elegant arched windows, and Bernard was once again struck by the peaceful beauty of the lovely house. Mrs Brent had laid afternoon tea out in the gardens, and while Henry strolled around the grounds chatting amiably to James, Bernard sat with Estelle in the shade of the apple trees.

"Henry always appears to be on his best behaviour in your parents' house," Bernard chuckled as they watched James and Henry disappear in the direction of the boat house. Estelle was unusually quiet and appeared distracted. When she did not reply, Bernard turned to look at her. "Are you alright, my dear?"

Estelle jumped and gave him a quick smile. "Sorry, Bernard. I was daydreaming. Why yes, of course, I am well. Why do you ask?" Her voice was light, but her eyes were anxious darting past Bernard in the direction of the house.

"Because you seem pre-occupied, and you are a little pale. Have you been doing too much, taking care of your cousin all these weeks? Did she have her baby?"

"My cousin, Delfie? Oh yes. Well, actually, we have the baby staying with us for a while. Her husband is in the Household Cavalry and is rarely home. Delfie is taking a little time to recover from the birth. Of course, we have the nannies to take care of him, and young Sadie, of course, is already besotted with him. Did I say, it's a dear little boy called Rupert."

Just at that moment, before Bernard could respond, a tall, thin girl came running from the side of the house, her blonde pigtails flying behind her as she charged up to where Bernard and Estelle were sitting.

Polly followed sedately behind. "So sorry, Mumma," said the girl breathlessly. "I was helping Nanny Ryan bathe Rupert, because he was sick all down his new clothes."

Estelle touched the girl's arm gently, "Thank you, Sadie. Please say good afternoon to Uncle Bernard."

Sadie smiled shyly and held out her hand, "Hello, Uncle Bernard."

Bernard shook the delicate hand gravely. "It's very good to see you again, Sadie. You have grown very tall, how old are you now?"

Sadie giggled, her clear, green eyes filled with merriment. "Mrs Brent said that I am growing like a weed, and I will be sixteen in December." She searched the garden, "Where has James gone? He promised me a game of tennis."

"James has gone down to the boathouse with his father, Sadie. I expect Henry wants to hear all about his schoolwork." Estelle replied, raising her eyebrows at Bernard.

"Come along then, Sadie, let's go and find them. Nanny will take care of Rupert." said Polly.

As Sadie scooted off in the direction of the lake, Estelle shook her head, "No wonder she is so thin. That child simply cannot stand still."

"What's wrong with the baby, Estelle? Nothing serious, I hope?"

"Nothing now, but he was born far too early and was rather poorly for a while. It was a difficult birth." Estelle smiled her lovely smile,

"Sadie has been rather lonely since the twins went to Barrow and having the baby has been such a lovely distraction for her."

"Nanny Ryan is thoroughly enjoying having a baby in the house again, and of course, we have our darling Polly. Old Florrie has retired now and lives in Oak Lodge, but she loves to wander over and sit with the baby, so we have plenty of help here."

Bernard was watching her closely. There was still an air of fragility about Estelle, and she seemed on edge. "I see. Well, don't do too much, my dear. As you say, there is plenty of help, and you look as though someone should be taking care of you. Are you sure that you are alright?" His tone was tender, and Estelle flushed.

"Perfectly well, Bernard, I promise. Oh look, here comes Henry, and it looks as though James and Sadie have abandoned him," she sounded relieved.

Henry came striding across the lawn and threw himself down on the grass in the shade of the trees. Wiping his face with his handkerchief, he grinned up at them. "Whew, it's hot. You two look wonderfully cool. My son has deserted me to play tennis with Sadie and Polly." He yawned, stretched his arms above his head, and closed his eyes. "Darling, I wonder, could you find Brent and see if he can provide something a little stronger than tea?"

Estelle laughed and pushed him with her foot, "Go find him yourself, Henry, you lazy thing," she said playfully.

Henry opened one eye, squinting against the bright sun streaming through the branches of the old apple tree. This sounded like the old Estelle, he thought, her sharp tone and coldness toward him seemed to have melted away since she had been staying at Grieves Manor. He groaned and got to his feet. "Well then, I will, my darling. What would you like me to fetch you?" he gave an exaggerated bow.

Estelle turned to Bernard. "What would you like to drink, Bernard?"

"Some more cold lemonade for me, please, Henry, nothing stronger."

"Lemonade, and some for the children when they come back." Estelle agreed.

Henry strolled toward the house, hesitated, turned, and called out, "Talking of children, what's this James tells me about that baby still living in the house?"

"Rupert." Estelle called after him. "Little Rupert is staying with us for a while. Cousin Delfie's little one. I brought him back with me. Delfie is a little unwell."

"Oh, I see," and Henry, already disinterested, went to find Mrs Brent.

Bernard was unusually quiet and thoughtful during the short visit, claiming to be just enjoying the rest. Sadie was happy to have James at home whilst Henry, delighted that Estelle seemed to have forgiven him at last, was good humoured and relaxed with James. Henry only once enquired about the whereabouts of Rupert, and Estelle reported that he had a slight cold, and Nanny Ryan was keeping him in the nursery.

The lazy, warm, summer days slipped by, and before long, it was time for James to go back to school. Henry, now clearly restless, was keen to return to Shorehill in time for the August shoot, and Bernard reminded them that sadly, he, too, needed to return to Riverside and the mill. As the party departed for the station, Estelle waved them off, promising to return to Riverside as soon as the baby was settled.

"Well, when is the mother going to collect him Estelle? Soon, I hope." Henry enquired a little crossly.

"In a week or so, darling," Estelle replied vaguely and gave Henry a warm hug, which he returned, dropping a kiss on top of her red curls.

"I miss you," he said simply.

Overhearing, Bernard interrupted, "We miss you too, dear Estelle, the garden and the Folly are looking very sad and forlorn."

Estelle laughed a little awkwardly. "I will be coming home in week or so, I promise," and she kept to her word.

It was a changed Estelle who returned to Riverside after her long summer break. She seemed happier and relaxed, even welcoming a wary Peregrine to Riverside on one occasion. Estelle, accompanied by Polly, still went to spend almost every weekend with James at Grieves Manor.

"Do you have to go so often?" Henry asked petulantly on one occasion when he arrived at Riverside one Saturday with some friends.

"Darling, we were not expecting you this weekend. Anyway, it's not for long, Henry. When James goes to Eton, he will board all the time, so I am just making the most of the time we have. I know you understand." Estelle pouted prettily at him.

Henry gave a reluctant laugh. "You and Polly spoil the boy, but of course, I do understand," and the matter was closed.

Lord Archie and Lady Rose, secure in the knowledge that Sadie and Rupert were well looked after by both nannies, spent more time in Paris, whilst Estelle and Jenny spent valuable healing time together. Gradually, the rift between the sisters-in-law began to close, and they once again enjoyed that special closeness that had been lost. But Bernard remained perplexed that Estelle and Henry still seemed content to spend long periods apart. Strolling together across to the Folly one frosty afternoon in late November, he once again asked if Estelle was happy.

Estelle confessed, "Henry and I could not endure to spend all of our time together. I do love Henry, Bernard, and I think he loves me, but he must have his freedom." She grasped Bernard's arm. "You are my dearest friend, and I know that you understand when I tell you that Henry was not ready to be a father, and I don't think he ever will be a good father to James. Also, there is the matter of the children. I love Rupert with all my heart and dear Sadie as well, and Henry will never understand that. So, you see, what we have is a different kind of marriage."

It was a while before Bernard replied gruffly, "My dear, I cannot imagine Riverside without you and James, so I will be content with any arrangement that keeps you both here for at least some of the time. Rupert and Sadie will always be welcome at Riverside, Estelle. They are part of our family."

Estelle's arm, tucked under his, appeared to tremble, and he turned to her in concern. Her head was bent, and a few curls escaped from under her hood as she reached inside her cloak for a handkerchief. Bernard watched in alarm as she dabbed her eyes with the handkerchief. "Estelle, are you crying? Whatever is the matter? What have I said?

"No, no. I'm not crying, I promise. The wind is a little sharp, don't you think?" and she raised her head and gave him one of her brilliant smiles. "My dearest Bernard, whatever would we do without out you?"

"I will always be here for you, Estelle," he replied simply. "But now, you are cold, my dear. I can feel you shivering. We shall go back to the house and have some hot chocolate. My brother is an odd salt, and that's a fact."

1911

In the September of 1911, James joined his twin cousins at Eton. He was now nearly as tall as his Uncle Bernard but fell short of his father. He was a mixture of both parents. He had Henry's height and Estelle's wild curls, although his were a soft, strawberry blond, and he had inherited her startling green eyes and her slender frame. He loved reading, music, and painting, but loathed most sports, and Estelle secretly worried how he would deal with this at Eton. However, although sports and school societies characterized Eton the strongest, in James's first season, he had proved to be an extremely adept cricketer, his long legs serving him well. He joined the debating societies. He was a spirited talker and found to his amazement that he enjoyed Eton far more than Barrow Hill, despite the stricter regime.

Estelle was a little disappointed that James's visits home during term time were few and far between, as he was quite happily settled as a full boarder at Eton. Christmas came around, and this year the celebrations were to be held at Grieves Manor. Henry was happy with this but insisted that the party return to Riverside in time for the Boxing Day Hunt. Bernard, however, was staying at Riverside for

Christmas, and when James heard this, he approached Henry and asked tentatively whether he could stay with his uncle.

Henry laughed. "Absolutely not, James. You will be at Grieves Manor with your family. Your uncle Bernard is invited to spend Christmas with us, of course he is, but he has decided that it is his duty to be in Shorehill. Apart from which, George says that your grandfather has something important to tell us. Anyway, I thought you would want to see William and Walter at Christmas."

James snorted, "I see them all the time at school, Father, I do not need to see them in the holidays as well."

Henry patted him on the back, "Well, sometimes we all have to do things we don't want; it keeps the family happy. I must say, James, Eton has served you well. It's given you some confidence," he added admiringly.

Urged on by James, Estelle made one more plea to Bernard to accompany them. "Please, Bernard, Christmas will not be the same without you."

"No," he replied firmly. "I need to be here for the children's Christmas Eve concert. Miss Dove has worked so hard, and I like to hand out the children's presents. I know that William Hunter will stand in for me, but I like to be here in the village at Christmas. It's only for a day, after all. You will be back for Boxing Day."

At the last minute, much to James and Estelle's dismay, Polly, after some soul-searching, made up her mind to stay behind with Bernard.

"My mother wants to come and visit with Dorothy Hunter, and I am quite happy to stay at Riverside." Polly could not be persuaded, and for that, Bernard was secretly grateful. Riverside without James, Estelle, and Polly at Christmas would be rather too quiet, even for him.

Lavishly decorated as usual, Grieves Manor was a blaze of lights when James, Henry, and Estelle arrived on a gloomy and damp Christmas Eve. Manners had driven the Daimler to Shorehill to collect them, and as they tumbled out, loaded with their festive parcels, an excited Sadie was waiting impatiently on the steps.

Nanny Ryan scolded, "Come inside and put a coat on Miss, if you please."

"I'm not a baby, Nanny," Sadie was indignant. "Please hurry, James, I have been waiting for simply ages. Come and see the Christmas tree, it's huge this year," and she grabbed him by the hand and dragged him up the steps.

The tree was huge indeed, beautifully decorated with paper and glass ornaments, flowing garlands, white, waxy candles, red ribbons, and pink-and-white sugar mice. It reached high up into the stairwell. Statuesque urns, filled with crimson-berried holly and trailing ivy, decorated the entrance hall, and the drawing room was filled with the scent from the exotic, white stargazer lilies that overflowed from every vase in the room. Fires burned bright in every room, and the Christmas stockings had been hung from the fireplace in the dining room.

It was a noisy but happy and excited family that sat down to the traditional Grieves-Croft Christmas Eve cold supper. The elegantly-dressed dining table was laden with platters of cold roast beef, succulent slices of moist pink ham, a golden-crusted game pie, and the centre piece, a whole Scottish poached salmon on a silver platter dressed in fresh lemon and dill with tiny triangles of brown bread. Bowls of fresh fruit had been placed around the table, black, shiny grapes, golden pineapples, tangy oranges, and sweet figs shimmered in the candlelight.

At one end of the table, Sadie was talking happily with James, and on the other side of the table, William and Walter argued noisily. Lord Archie sat at the head of the table, flanked by Lady Rose and George. Henry sat next to George, and Jenny and Estelle sat opposite their husbands. Rupert, in his highchair, was tucked in next to Estelle.

When at last, the last remnants of the jellies and ice puddings had been cleared away, and Brent had laid out cheese and bread on the sideboard, together with the port and claret, the servants retired.

"Sadie, come, we should settle Rupert in the nursery, and then you may come down into the drawing room for a short while with the ladies." Estelle pushed back her chair. Jenny rose from her chair and looked enquiringly at Lady Rose, who had remained seated. Normally, Lady Rose would suggest that the ladies retire to the drawing room and leave the men to their port and cigars, but Estelle and Jenny were waved back by Lady Rose.

"Sit down, my dears. Rupert is perfectly happy for the moment," she instructed in her low musical tones. "Archie and I have a surprise for you all," and she turned, smiling to her husband.

Lord Archie stood up and cleared his throat. Henry looked at George, who gave him a wink, which said he knew something about this announcement that his father was preparing to make.

Lord Archie took his time, lighting a fat cigar before he began speaking. "As you know, it has been a very exciting year in shipbuilding, and in May, George and I were privileged to attend the celebration dinner in the Grand Hotel in Belfast following the launch of the Titanic." He paused and looked at the expectant and puzzled faces around table.

"In view of the special relationship between our company and the White Star Line, we were given the opportunity to secure first-class cabins on the Titanic's maiden voyage to New York. We sail on 10th April from Cherbourg."

The stunned silence that greeted Lord Archie's speech was followed by a collective gasp and then whoops of joy from the twins. Henry, barely able to contain his excitement, turned to look at George, who laughed.

"George, you traitor. You have known about this all this time and did not tell me."

"Henry, George did not tell his own wife, so I am as surprised as you, I promise," said Jenny ruefully, shaking her head at her delighted husband as he reached across the table to grasp her hands.

"Sorry, my Jenny Wren, but Father and I were both sworn to secrecy until the sailing date was announced, and then Father thought it would be a great idea to announce it at Christmas. Mother knew, of course, but she could not say anything, could you Ma?" George appealed to his laughing mother.

Jenny interrupted, "George, Oh I don't care, really I don't. It's just so exciting. First Class to New York," she said breathlessly. "Just think about it, Estelle, we can go shopping in New York."

"But why are we travelling from Cherbourg, sir?" Henry addressed his triumphant father-in-law. "I thought Titanic was sailing from Southampton."

Lord Archie nodded. "She is Henry, but I thought if we spent Easter with my cousin Clarence, in Le Touquet, we could board Titanic at Cherbourg."

The twins, who by now had left their seats and had rushed over to where their grandfather was standing, were firing questions at him without waiting for replies. Lady Rose held her hand up to still the chatter of excited voices. "Boys, go and sit down please. There are several matters we all need to discuss." Their grandmother's voice was low but carried authority.

George stood up and sternly pointed his sons in the direction of their recently abandoned chairs. "Sit," he ordered sternly. "Do not leave the table without asking."

Estelle, who had remained oddly silent throughout, now burst out, "Pa, Ma, I can't possibly go. What about Rupert and Sadie?"

Henry looked first shocked and then angry. "What are you talking about Estelle? The boy is going back with his family, surely?"

"Yes, of course he is, Henry, but not for a while." Estelle retorted; her face now flushed with anger. "And if you had listened to anything I said to you, you would know that Rupert will be staying at Grieves Manor. Nigel has taken his commission and has been posted to India. Delfie is going with him, and Rupert is far too young to go. Nanny Ryan will be taking care of Rupert. It has been arranged for months."

Henry looked sulky. "Well, perhaps I do recall something about that," he muttered. "Surely, Sadie will be coming with us anyway, and as you say, Nanny Ryan can care for the child."

Estelle looked enquiringly at both parents. "Is Sadie to come with us then, Pa?"

Lord Archie raised his eyebrows and nodded to his wife. "Over to you, my dear," he said, reaching across the table for the whisky decanter.

"Sadie is not able to accompany us on the voyage." Lady Rose explained. "The doctor does not think it is a good idea, as she is still prone to chest infections. Sadie has already expressed a desire to stay at home and help Nanny with young Rupert."

Sadie, who was sitting quietly next to James, smiled serenely and nodded. "I really do not want to go. I promise, and anyway, I can't wait to help Nanny with Rupert. It will such fun, and after all, you won't be gone forever, will you?"

Lady Rose looked enquiringly at her daughter. "So you see my dear, you really are fussing over nothing, and your father was so looking forward to giving everyone the good news," her voice held a note of mild rebuke.

Estelle flushed and forced a laugh, "Sorry, Ma. I'm being silly, and of course I am excited, Pa. We shall shop in New York, Jenny, just as you say."

Jenny nodded. "We shall indeed shop" and laughed as George pretended to groan.

The moment had passed. Henry recovered his good humour, and was soon caught up once again in the excitement. Sadie squeezed James's hand and whispered. "Are you excited too, James? Just look at the twins. Please don't worry about me, I love helping Nanny with Rupert, and you can tell me all about it when you come home."

James swallowed the lump of panic in his chest and fought to keep his voice calm. "Of course, Sadie. It is very exciting news, but I still wish you were coming with us."

In the New Year, James and the twins went back to Eton, and Estelle, although reluctant to leave Sadie and Rupert, returned to Riverside. As the weeks went on and the plans for the voyage on the Titanic unfolded, it was decided that as each party had their own "on board" stewards, only Lady Rose and Jenny would take their maids, and Polly would accompany Estelle. The Easter holiday approached, and James, who, had been given leave to finish the term a week early, arrived back at Riverside to find the house in turmoil. His mother was flying around the house, her bed littered with hats and dresses, and she and Polly were in a frenzy of deciding what was to go in the large steamer trunks that had been purchased for the momentous voyage.

"Dearest James, go and have a look in your bedroom. Your case is packed. I am really busy, and I think Daddy and Uncle Bernard are going over some final bits and pieces in the office, so why don't you pop over and surprise them, darling?"

"I really wanted to talk to you first, Mumma," James was strangely subdued, and Polly looked at him quickly.

"Alright dear, but Polly and I will just finish this, and then we can have a chat in the library. Will that be alright, James?" Estelle appealed, giving him a swift kiss.

"Yes, of course, Mumma," James agreed and wandered downstairs.

Outside, the gardens were a riot of daffodils, and the flower beds were dotted with winter hyacinths and early primroses, but the air was thin and cold, and James shivered as he trudged the familiar path down to the river and the Folly.

The village school had not yet broken up, and the meadow on the opposite side of the river was empty and quiet with no sign of his friends. He wandered over to the Folly, took the key from the ledge above the door, and let himself in. It was warm inside even though the sun was weak. The red biscuit tin was still on the table, and he took the lid off and peered hopefully inside. There were a few crumbly shortbreads at the bottom of the tin, and he took them eagerly and sat down on the chaise longue. A fitful spring sun broke through the clouds, and watery beams flickered through the stained-glass windows. James, chewing slowly, sighed, and idly traced a faint butterfly shadow with his toe, watching it slowly fade as the sun was lost behind the clouds. James wondered again how to tell his father that not only he did he not want to go with the family to France, he also had no desire to accompany them on Titanic's maiden voyage.

He was cold and hungry and was steeling himself up to go back to the house and find Henry when Bernard opened the door. James jumped, but when he saw it was his uncle, he heaved a sigh of relief. "Golly, you made me jump. I thought it was Father."

"There you are, old chap," Bernard came inside and stood in front of him. "Everyone is asking where you are, especially your father. Is anything wrong? Polly wondered whether you felt unwell, but if there is trouble at school, you can tell me if you don't want to bother your parents."

"No, sir, no trouble at school, I promise, and I'm not ill, although I jolly well wish I were." His tone was gloomy, and he ran his hands through his hair.

"Then why are you avoiding Henry, and why on Earth do you wish you were ill?" Bernard was mystified.

"Because I do not want to go to France, and I really do not want to go on the Titanic." James burst out. "There now, I've said it, and I know it's dreadfully ungrateful, and the masters and other fellows are awfully jealous and think that we are so lucky to be going on the Titanic. But before you ask why I don't want to go, I don't really have a good reason. I would have to share a cabin with the twins, and although we get on alright at school, they do think that I am a bit wet. I don't see them that often, and it would be awfully awkward. Apart from that, Father would be there all the time. "Do this James. Do that. Stop reading. Put the book down. Join in with the games. Sit up. Eat up." James sighed. "I would rather stay with you and Sadie and Rupert."

Bernard sat down next to his nephew. "Well now, I doubt that Henry will understand, James. I am sure you know that he will be very angry."

"Well, I don't want to go, and I won't, and Father cannot make me!" the words came out in an angry rush.

"Hold on, hold on," Bernard said calmly. "Nobody is going to make you do things you really don't want to do James, but please speak to your mother first and explain how you feel. It's no good pretending that your father will not be furious, but knowing your grandfather, I think he will respect your feelings. I understand, and if you want to stay at Grieves Manor until the family returns, I am sure Nanny Ryan and the staff will be pleased to look after you until you go back to Eton. Or of course, you could stay here at Riverside. Now let's go and face the music."

Bernard was right of course, Henry was in turn, incredulous, angry, perplexed, and then furious when a white-faced James refused to budge. Bernard stood steadfast by his nephew's side until it looked as though Henry, completely frustrated, would strike the boy, and then he led James firmly away. Estelle, disbelieving at first, then tearful, was consoled by Polly, who reminded her that it was not for long, and James would be happy with Sadie and Rupert. To James's eternal gratitude, Estelle agreed to reason with Henry and urge him to respect James's decision. She would explain the situation to the rest of the family when they arrived at Riverside the next day for the farewell dinner.

Lord Archie, summoned to the library by Bernard just before dinner, listened quietly, and without comment as his nervous but steadfast grandson asked to be excused from the voyage. James gave no reason, simply because he did not have a valid reason, but then neither did his grandfather ask for one. Instead, Lord Archie placed his hand on the boy's shoulder, "James, I am disappointed, but not in you, just disappointed that you won't be joining us. Do not concern yourself further. Your Mother and I will explain to the family. Leave your Father to me."

Throughout the dinner that followed, James sat close by Estelle and Bernard whilst Henry glowered at him from the far end of the table. Lady Rose was gentle with him, George and Jenny quietly accepting, and the twins were secretly relieved that James would not be sharing their cabin, as they found their young cousin puzzling.

It was an awkward meal, and when Henry ordered the champagne to be brought out, James, who had barely eaten any of the delicious dinner, asked to be excused and left the room, closely followed by Estelle. Gradually, however, the thrill of the coming voyage dispelled the tension at the table, and as the champagne flowed, the guests relaxed, and soon the room was filled with laughter and excited chatter.

After a while, Estelle returned with James who, avoiding Henry's glare, sat down next to his mother and uncle. When Henry suggested a toast of thanks to Lord Archie and Lady Rose, Estelle stood by his side and raised her glass with the rest of the dinner guests, all the while watching her silent son.

TITANIC 1912

Early on Tuesday morning, April 2nd, 1912, the same day that the mighty Titanic left Belfast for Southampton, the voyagers left Riverside and Shorehill and travelled to Dover to catch the cross-channel ferry to Calais. James and Bernard had waved them off bravely, with Estelle calling one last desperate message, "See you in a few weeks, James darling. I will write every day."

Bernard was a little guilty at the sense of relief he felt as the party disappeared. Henry had been odious to James, and this had clearly upset Estelle. However, James had stayed resolute against Henry's fury and remained silent as Henry continued to demand an explanation for his refusal to embark on the Titanic voyage.

Despite Polly's fears, the channel crossing was calm, and the family finally arrived in Calais, where they were met by Clarence Grieves-Croft, accompanied by an elderly chauffeur driving a stately Rolls-Royce.

"My goodness, Archie, I have been looking forward to this visit," said Clarence as he greeted his cousin fondly. "Rose, my dear, you are as beautiful as ever." Clarence Grieves-Croft, white haired, tall, and elegant, kissed each lady's hand in turn with great aplomb. This promptly reduced Jenny's lady's maid, Belle, to nervous giggles.

Clarence turned to Archie. "Etienne is following up in the shooting brake to transport the other ladies and the luggage to the Villa. We shall go now, and Etienne will catch up."

As the Rolls-Royce purred through the blossoming countryside, Estelle breathed in and smiled at her father. "Daddy, I can smell the seaside." Lord Archie replied gravely, "I am sure you can, my dear."

Lady Rose and George burst out laughing. Henry frowned and looked from one to the other. "Sorry, Henry," George laughed. "When Estelle was little and we had just boarded the train for our Dawlish summer holiday, before we had even left the station, she used to lean out of the window and say that she could smell the sea. Pa always said the same thing, although we were miles away."

"Oh, I see," replied Henry, and although he considered the ensuing conversation rather trite, he was pleased to see Estelle relaxed and smiling. Obviously still angry with him for not making his peace with James before they left, Estelle had said very little to him on the crossing, seeming to prefer the company of her maid and her sister-in-law.

As they turned from the town onto a narrow, sandy track, Clarence tapped the chauffeur on the shoulder, and the car stopped. Clarence stepped out and walked to the front of the car. He pointed up through the trees, and with a dramatic wave of his arm, announced triumphantly, "Voir la famille, la Villa Champagne!"

La Villa Champagne was perched high on a hill, just visible through the towering pine trees and bathed in early spring sunshine. Even from far below, the Villa looked large, with many turrets and encircled by a balcony covered in tumbling purple bougainvillea. The chauffeur opened the car doors, and one-by-one, the family clambered out, the twins first, anxious to be free of the confines of the car. They all stared up to where Clarence was pointing.

There was a moment of silence, broken by Henry. "Is it pink, Clarence? Because it looks bloody pink from here," he spluttered, and the elderly chauffeur gave a snort of laughter.

"Indeed, it is Henry, sparkling pink, just like my best champagne," replied Clarence with amusement.

Estelle burst out laughing, "Uncle Clarence, your Villa is utterly magical."

Clarence gave a small bow. "Why, thank you, my dear, I think so too. Now, shall we move on as my cook has prepared the most wonderful lunch for us all, and she does get rather cross when I am late."

Lord Archie looked at his cousin in amusement. "I agree. Your Villa looks wonderful, Clarence, and, no doubt, we shall enjoy sampling pink champagne from your excellent wine cellar."

"It will be my pleasure, Archie," replied Clarence with a broad smile.

For the next few days, Clarence took great delight in showing his family the delights of Le Touquet Paris-Plage. Since its incorporation as a town, Le Touquet Paris-Plage was fast becoming the most fashionable resort for chic Parisiennes. However, Lady Rose declared herself content to spend most afternoons relaxing on the balcony with her playing cards.

When invited to join the others she replied, "No, thank you, my dears, I find the views quite intoxicating, and I shall enjoy myself just as much sitting here with Clarence." Dottie, her faithful maid, shook her head sternly and said, "No, thank you. I will not leave my Lady in a foreign country." Belle, Jenny's maid, cried in her bedroom because she was "too scared of them foreigners" to go out.

So, it was left to Estelle, Polly, and Jenny to explore the hidden delights in the steep, cobbled streets that led down into the town. They discovered elegant, bow-fronted dress shops and tiny jewellery shops tucked away deep in the winding lanes and were even more delighted when they chanced on a busy street market selling fragrant pastries and candied sweets.

Most afternoons after lunch, Henry, George, and Lord Archie went to play golf, leaving Clarence happily gossiping with Lady Rose. William and Walter begged to be allowed to take Clarence's silver Saluki hounds down to the sand dunes. Clarence consented, but on the condition that the hounds were groomed thoroughly when they came back to the villa.

"Boys, not one grain of sand must be left in their coats. They have very sensitive skin. They have their own brushes and combs with their initials on the back. The taller one here is Cain, and his brother is Abel." Clarence laughed as he gently patted each aristocratic head in turn. "But they will answer to either name when called. Salukis, I am afraid, are known for their beauty and not their brains, but they are gentle creatures, so treat them well."

Every evening, the family came together to enjoy a leisurely, candle-lit dinner, and whilst the soft spring days held a growing warmth, there was a chill in the evening air, and so they ate in the elegant dining room with the balcony doors open to enjoy the scented night air. After dinner, Henry departed to try his luck at the Casino, and the rest of the family were content to luxuriate in the lovely drawing room, drink champagne, and share the day's experiences with each other. As promised, on Easter Sunday, Clarence took them to celebrate Mass in a tiny medieval church tucked away in the narrow back streets of Le Touquet. The little church was packed with gaily-dressed families, and after the service, they followed the singing procession through the streets to the cafes and restaurants that had been laid out especially for the celebration meals.

Estelle, watching the families rejoicing together, felt something akin to panic when she remembered that soon she would be moving further away from home and James. "Stop being silly," she chided herself and hooked her arm through Jenny's trying to stem the panic.

Jenny, feeling the tight grip, turned to look at Estelle pale face. "What's wrong, Estelle? Are you ill, my dear?"

"No, I am not ill, Jenny, but suddenly I feel most awfully home-sick." She forced a laugh. "It is watching all of the families, so happy to be altogether. I feel so far away from home and James. I know that Rupert and Sadie are safe with Nanny Ryan, and of course, Bernard is devoted to James, so I know that I am just being silly."

Jenny could see that Estelle was close to tears. "Have you said anything to Henry?"

Estelle shook her head, and her tone was determined. "Gracious me, no Jenny, and you must not say anything either, or to Ma and Pa.

It's very selfish of me, and I do not want to spoil it for anyone. Don't worry, it was just a silly feeling, and I feel better now."

Estelle knew instinctively that her telephone calls both to Riverside and Grieves Manor irritated Henry, and even more so when she explained that she just wanted to know that the children were well and not missing them too much.

"Good God, Estelle," Henry had replied testily. "Of course the children are all right. We have barely begun our journey, and already you are fussing. Your parents have gone to a great deal of expense and trouble to arrange this trip to New York. You are just being overprotective."

All too soon for Estelle, their time in Le Touquet was over, and it was time to leave La Villa Champagne and begin the next step of their journey and make their way to Cherbourg and Titanic.

On the afternoon of April 10th, 1912, the Grieves-Croft party arrived at the bustling port of Cherbourg. There was a brisk wind blowing through the crowded harbour, and the sea was choppy. Lord Archie and Lady Rose bade a fond farewell to Clarence Grieves-Croft and thanked him profusely for his hospitality. The excited twins jostled their way through the harbour to see if they could spot Titanic arriving, but their grandfather laughed and explained that Cherbourg did not have the docking facilities for a ship the size of the Titanic, so the passengers would have to go out on a tender and board Titanic using a gangplank.

Although due to dock in Cherbourg at five p.m., Titanic had been delayed leaving Southampton, and so she finally arrived at six-thirty, dropping anchor in the Roads, just off the Cap de la Hogue. The excited passengers and their luggage, together with bags of mail, were loaded onto the two White Star tenders. The Grieves-Croft party were on the Nomadic, and as she pulled out of the harbour, a sudden squall swept in from the open sea. The crew had difficulty holding onto the connecting gangway as it bucked and twisted in the wind, and some of the older passengers held back and gasped in fright.

Eventually, encouraged and helped by the amused crew, one by one, the passengers began to carefully negotiate the swaying gangway.

First, George and Henry escorted Jenny and Estelle, who clung to each other, giggling nervously. They were followed by Lady Rose, as elegant and composed as usual, holding on tightly to her hat with one hand whilst clasping onto Lord Archie's arm with the other. The twins, now beside themselves with excitement, were about to make a dash along the gangway when George called them sharply to them. "Boys! Remember your manners and help Polly and Belle."

The boys turned back sheepishly, and Walter gallantly crooked his arms around a determined Polly and a shaking, weeping Belle. William managed to hold onto Dottie, who much to the twin's intense delight, had closed her eyes tightly whilst whispering a prayer and was about to step onto the walkway just as William grabbed her arm.

When Polly, with trembling legs, felt herself stepping onto the solid deck of the great ship, she eventually felt safe enough to release her iron grip on Walter and look around her.

The Titanic officers, immaculate in double-breasted blue coats with White Star gilt buttons, proudly saluted the passengers as they boarded, and the stewards, in snow-white jackets and black bow ties, welcomed the arriving passengers into the lavishly furnished Reception Room. Lord Archie and Lady Rose, who had already registered the Grieves-Croft party, had been given the deck plans, and the stewards dedicated to Grieves-Croft were arranging for the luggage to be taken down to the first-class cabins. As Estelle's personal maid, Polly had stayed in some of the finest stately homes in the county, but nothing could have prepared her for the opulence of the Titanic. Polly and Belle, like many others, gazed around, rendered speechless, and even the seasoned trans-Atlantic passengers seemed awestruck at the sheer grandeur of the great ship. Walter and William, eagerly studying the deck plans, were excitedly pointing out to their grandfather the location of the squash courts, the indoor swimming pool, the gym, and the elevators. Lord Archie held up a calming hand.

"Now, boys, you will have plenty of time to explore later, but for now, the stewards are waiting to show us to our cabins, and we all need to get our bearings," their grandfather reminded them benignly. The Grieves-Croft party had reserved four first-class cabins on B deck, and Polly was delighted to find that she had a single cabin close to Henry and Estelle. Dottie and the still-shaking Belle were shown to their double cabin, and the twins, wide eyed, who had expected to share with James, could not believe their luck when they found they too had a first-class cabin to themselves.

When a smiling steward opened the door to Polly's cabin, she stood transfixed, lost for words. The walls were painted duck-egg blue, and a sumptuous cream carpet covered the floor. The single bed was covered in a pretty, lacy bedspread, and one end was piled high with soft pillows. At the side of the bed was a small cupboard with drawers, and on the top sat a bedside lamp with a blue shade and a pocket-sized Bible. There was a marble-topped wash basin with gold taps and a round mirror fixed on the wall above the basin. Opposite the bed was a single wardrobe, a dressing table with a mirror, and a stool with a blue-and-cream padded seat.

Polly took a deep breath and turned to the waiting steward, "Are you sure that this is my cabin, just for me, on my own?"

The steward looked down at the list in his hand. "Miss Polly Dawes, lady's maid to Mrs Estelle Maycroft?"

Polly nodded wordlessly,

"Then, miss, you are in the right cabin, and Mr and Mrs Maycroft are four cabins along. Your trunk is on its way, and the stewardess will be along to unpack for you, and here is your cabin key."

Before Polly could protest, the steward gave her a saucy wink, handed her the key, and disappeared down the corridor.

Without waiting for the stewardess or her trunk, Polly, eager to tell Estelle about her cabin, closed the door, walked along the thickly carpeted hall, then counted each door before nervously on the fourth door along from her cabin.

She tapped lightly on the door. "Madam? It's me, Polly."

"Polly, come in," Estelle called out. "Tell me now, what do you think of the famous Titanic?"

But Polly gasped at the sheer luxury of Estelle's cabin. The walls were panelled in rich, red walnut, the thick carpet was pale gold, and the richly upholstered chaise longue was piled high with sumptuous silk cushions. Against one wall was an ornate curved-leg writing desk, and in the centre of the cabin, stood a polished dining table and four gold-backed chairs. The faux marble fireplace was fitted with an electric fire, and heavily beaded chandeliers hung on all the walls.

"How wonderful," breathed Polly, but where is your bed, madam?"

"There are two bedrooms and a bathroom through that door, and look at this, Polly." Estelle flung back the heavy damask curtains to reveal double doors which opened onto a private deck. "See, we even have our own promenade. Now tell me, do you like your cabin, Polly?"

"It's the loveliest room, madam. It is so pretty, and I have it all to myself. Has your luggage arrived? I thought I would come and unpack for you."

"Henry says we have a steward who will do that, but I'm glad you are here. Henry, George, and Pa have gone to find the Lounge, and Ma wants to rest in her cabin. Jenny has been dragged off by the twins to explore. I said I would join Henry in the Lounge in a little while, but first I want to find the purser's office. If I write to the children now, the letters can be posted when we get to Queenstown."

Arranged neatly on the desk was a stack of post cards with Titanic's great black hull surging through the ocean leaving waves of creamy foam in its wake, the black-topped funnels belching tunnels of steam, white against the fiery setting sun. The stationery, the post cards, the writing paper, and even the fountain pen carried the White Star Logo, a fluttering triangular red flag with a white star in the centre.

"I am still writing in my notebook every day," Polly said proudly. "I have kept the newspaper cuttings with pictures, my ticket for the ferry, my boarding pass, and I'm going to keep anything else, just to show Master James."

"How good you are, Polly. I am missing the children so much." Estelle brushed away sudden tears. "Now, I am just being silly, and Henry will be so cross if he sees me crying again. My first letter to James is just to let him know that we are safely on board and tell him what it is like to be on Titanic."

Estelle sat down at the desk, took a sheet of the thick creamy writing paper, and began writing rapidly, every now and then stopping to tap the pen against her teeth. Her brow furrowed in thought. She finished the letter with a line of large kisses, folded it, and placed it an envelope. "All done. Ring for the steward, Polly, and he can show us to the purser's office."

Within minutes, there was a sharp rap on the cabin door. Polly opened it and found herself looking down on a diminutive steward in pristine white jacket and navy trousers with a knife-edge pleat. The man gave a small bow. "Good evening. My name is Gerry McBride, and I am your steward for the voyage. How can I help you today?" he said in a gentle southern Irish accent.

Polly explained that they wanted to be taken to the purser's office. Gerry, who had been with the White Star Line for many years, smiled a greeting at Estelle who appeared behind Polly.

"Are you our steward?" Estelle asked. "How lovely. I am anxious to send this letter, and I understand that the post will be collected when we dock at Queenstown?"

"That is so, and you've plenty of time, madam. If we sail on schedule this evening, we should dock in Queenstown tomorrow around midday. Now ladies, if you come along with me, the purser's office is on C deck, and we can take the elevator to save time."

Polly guessed at once that Gerry had picked up the veiled anxiety in Estelle's voice.

There were a great number of other passengers milling around in the sumptuous reception area, fur-coated ladies and gentlemen in top hats, all openly admiring the Grand Staircase that swept all the way down to the lower decks. Gerry acknowledged each group respectfully as he skilfully guided Estelle and Polly through the crowd, but Estelle hurried past with barely a nod. She did not want to be delayed in conversation.

Three uniformed lift attendants stood smartly to attention by the First-Class lifts. The grills were closed, but the doors were open, ready for passengers and inside each elevator there was an upholstered couch. Gerry waved them inside the nearest lift and waited until he was sure they were comfortably seated before nodding to the waiting attendant, who had his finger poised over the button. But then he paused as a woman's voice called out urgently, "Wait, please, wait for us."

Estelle leant forward and recognised the slim figure of her sister-in-law rushing towards the lift, followed by the tow-headed twins.

"Gosh, Estelle, I have been looking everywhere for you," said Jenny breathlessly, and she grinned. "Well, then, what do you think about all this," and she gestured toward the Grand Staircase. She peered inside the elevator. "And, oh my word, seats in an elevator," she added, raising her eyebrows.

"Jenny, behave," replied Estelle, smiling at her irrepressible sister-in-law. "I've been in our cabin writing a letter home to the children, and now Gerry, our lovely steward here, is taking us to the purser's office."

Estelle fondly ruffled the twin's spiky hair, who, for once were not talking ten to the dozen.

At fifteen, Walter and William were startlingly like their father; red headed, stocky, and full of never-ending energy. "Jenny, what on Earth have you done to my nephews? They are far too quiet, and moreover, they are standing still."

Jenny looked sternly at her twin sons. "I said that if they wanted tickets for the swimming pool and squash court, they had to be quiet and stay with me until I found the purser's office. I am useless at reading the deck plan, and we got lost," she said, airily waving the deck plan around. "But, no matter, because now we are saved. Gerry can escort us to the purser," and she sent the patiently-waiting Gerry a beaming smile.

The purser's offices were on the starboard side of the ship, and as the elevator doors opened, they could see that the area around the purser's desk was already filling up with passengers eager to obtain tickets or send mail. Most were waiting patiently in orderly queues between the gilt partitions, but the queues were growing rapidly, and Estelle clutched at Polly's arm. "Oh, my goodness, Polly, so many people. How long is this going to take?" Her voice was high, and her face once again had an anxious frown. Polly looked at Jenny to see if she had noticed the panicked tone in Estelle voice, but Jenny was busy watching where her boys were going.

The twins had quickly joined the end of one queue, determined to get tickets to the swimming pool, and Jenny heaved a sigh of relief. "Right boys, you have your deck plan, so when you have your tickets, I want you to go straight back to your cabins and dress for dinner, no wandering around the ship. If you are late for dinner, Grandpa will be very cross. Estelle, my dear, do give your letter to the boys, and they will give it to the purser, then we can wake Ma and join the men for lovely cocktails before dinner."

But Estelle tensed and shook her head and clutched her letter tighter. "You go on Jenny, and I will join you later."

Jenny looked surprised, and Polly quickly intervened. "Let me have the letter, madam. I will make sure it goes in the post." Estelle still looked uncertain, and Gerry, who was watching quietly, placed a gentle hand on her arm.

"My nephew is on the desk, madam, and I will take Polly around to the side, so we won't have to queue."

Estelle visibly relaxed and beamed at him. "Thank you so much, Gerry."

Gerry flushed. "You are welcome, madam, and if you let me know when you want to send another letter, I will attend to it myself."

Jenny nudged her. "Another conquest, I think, you naughty lady. Now do buck up, my dear, relax and enjoy yourself, because I most certainly intend to enjoy every second. I know that you miss James, and he was a silly boy to miss all this, but he has Bernard and Sadie and Rupert, and anyway he will be back at school in a few days."

"Your mistress seems a little anxious. I hope you don't mind me saying," remarked Gerry thoughtfully as he watched Jenny and Estelle make their way back to the elevators.

Polly bit her lip and nodded. "I think she is just worried about leaving the children behind. I am sure she will be alright in a day or so."

The four officers behind the desk were busily dealing with the queue of passengers, but Gerry called over to a young officer with the longest black handlebar moustache that Polly had ever seen. "Joe," he called out, and the young man looked up. "Can you take this letter for the Queenstown post? It's very important to Polly's mistress."

The young officer looked around him quickly, took the letter, and put it in the mail bag at his side, flashing a smile at his uncle as he did so. "Course I will, and if you have any more, miss, just bring them straight to me. Always look on the notice board for any information. Once we have left Queenstown, your mistress can send a radio telegram home. We have the Marconi system on board," he added proudly.

Gerry looked at his watch. "We must get back now, miss. It's almost time for the dress call before dinner, and you can assure your mistress that her letter has been posted."

Since their arrival on the Titanic, Estelle had become even more uneasy and nervous, but amidst the general excitement, none of the family had noticed, not even Jenny. Polly had, and so when she went back to the cabin to find that Estelle had recovered her spirits and was happily discussing with Henry what dress to choose for their first family dinner aboard the Titanic, she relaxed.

"The letter has gone, madam, and the purser assures me that the post will go ashore at Queenstown. Shall I help you dress for dinner now?"

"Thank you, dear Polly," Estelle lowered her voice and pointed to the bathroom. "It would seem a stewardess has been sent along as my dresser, so don't worry tonight. I am sure that you need to go and get dressed for dinner. Can you go along and see how poor Belle and Dotty are coping with life aboard? Perhaps when you have eaten, you can come and find us. Have you found your dining salon yet, Polly?"

"Yes, madam, the maid's and valet's dining salons are on C deck by the staircase. I just hope that we can persuade Belle to come to dinner with us."

Belle, Jenny's maid, had recovered sufficiently to dress her mistress for dinner and was fluttering around deciding whether she had anything suitable to wear. Stout Scottish Dottie had no such qualms and had donned her usual sensible skirt and blouse and reported that Lady Rose was resting and would take her meal in her cabin.

"Well, can we go to dinner now that you are back at last Polly?" Dottie was hungry, tired, and testy. "How do we know what time to go, and where to go?"

Belle once again was on the verge of tears. "I want to go home. I feel sick," she whispered.

"Belle, you are a silly goose. Do stop crying," laughed Polly. "Gerry, the steward, told me that we should listen for the bugler to play *The Roast Beef of Old England*, and that lets us know when to go to dinner."

"Good Lord," said Dottie. "How extraordinary! How often does that happen?"

"Half hour before luncheon, and the same at dinner time. I know where our dining room is, I found it on the deck plan," Polly informed them with some importance and added, "Gerry says that we will be leaving France and on our way to Queenstown whilst dinner is being served, now isn't that exciting?"

"How extraordinary," Dottie said again, shaking her grey curls.

At nine p.m., Titanic departed Cherbourg for the next step of her journey, the overnight sailing to Queenstown. The more experienced passengers lingered over the sumptuous first night dinner served in the luxurious dining room, whilst some of the older passengers decided to retire as soon as they had finished their meal. The new travellers wandered the ship, spellbound at the sheer beauty of their surroundings.

Walter and William, anxious to be part of the explorers, hurried through their dinner, and George had cause to reprimand them several times. Lord Archie intervened. "Let them be, George. They just want to explore. They do not want to be sitting here with us."

George nodded. "Well, boys, your grandfather has given you permission to leave the table. Do not get lost, and do not be a nuisance to anyone." He looked at his watch. "We are going to the lounge on A deck after dinner, and remember, our cabins are on "B" deck, so meet us in the lounge no later than half-past eleven."

Gabbling their assurances and thanking their grandfather, Walter and William sped off before their father could change his mind. "I cannot keep up with those two, never still for a second," George shook his head.

Henry, who had been enjoying some banter with the twins during dinner, looked at their departing figures and said somewhat bitterly, "Well, at least they are here with their family and enjoying the experience of a lifetime." There was an awkward silence, and Estelle dropped her head and fiddled with her napkin whilst Henry glowered.

Jenny placed a sympathetic hand on Estelle's arm. "Come, Estelle, let's leave these men to their port and cigars and see how Lady Rose is faring."

Estelle looked at Jenny gratefully. "Yes, lets. Ma might welcome some company now after her nap. You don't mind if we leave you, Pa?"

Estelle looked across to her father, and he smiled at her gently. "A good idea, Estelle, and see if your mother feels well enough to join us in the lounge later?"

Lord Archie stood up and gestured to the hovering stewards who sprung forward attentively. "The ladies are leaving us."

Henry and George stood up, and Henry, studiously avoiding his wife's furious glare, bowed slightly as she swept past him.

"Pay Henry no mind, my dear," said Jenny, and she linked arms with Estelle, who was controlling angry tears. "I think we are all a little tired. It has been such a long, exciting day. Now, let's see if we can find our way back to your Ma without getting lost."

They found their way with ease, but when they entered quietly, Lady Rose remained unwilling to leave her cabin, declaring herself to be perfectly comfortable, just a little tired.

"Pa would like you to join us for drinks later," Estelle said hopefully.

"I don't think so, my dears," Lady Rose shook her head. "I shall look forward to hearing all about the adventures tomorrow when I am well rested," and so saying, she settled herself more comfortably in her chair and smiled at them. "Tell your father that I had a perfectly wonderful dinner." Lady Rose held up her face for a kiss. "Off you go, my girls, and enjoy yourselves."

They would have lingered, but Dottie fixed them with a look. "Lady Rose needs to rest now," and she ushered them to the door, closing it firmly behind them.

"Golly," said Jenny, giggling. "That is Dottie at her most fearsome. I think I'll let her loose on the twins if they misbehave."

Estelle laughed; it was hard to stay low in spirits when her vivacious little sister-in-law was around. "She absolutely adores Ma, but I am sure that she scares Pa, although he would never admit it. Are you going back to your cabin now, Jen?"

"Certainly not," replied Jenny firmly. "I want to make sure that the boys do as they have been told and meet George in the lounge. I don't want them wandering all over the ship at night. What about you?"

"Well, I don't think I could sleep yet," Estelle looked undecided.

"Then come with me and we could sample some of those delicious-looking cocktails on the bar menu."

Estelle shook her head. "No, I don't want anything else to drink. I think I will pop along to Polly. Can you tell Henry that I may join him later, but not to wait for me?"

Jenny looked doubtful, not wanting to leave her alone. "Well, if you're sure, but you do need a good rest, Estelle. I know how much you are missing James."

Estelle nodded, and at the mention of her son's name, she felt the hot tears threaten once again, and she shook her head and gulped, furious that she could not control the tears. "I think you are right, Jenny. I am just tired. Wish everyone goodnight from me, please."

Jenny still lingered, but Estelle, with a determined smile, strode purposefully toward her cabin.

Tucked away in her cabin, Polly was absorbed writing in her notebook when Estelle knocked on the door, but she flung the door open and proudly invited her inside.

"What do you think; isn't it wonderful, madam? I have to pinch myself to make sure that this is all really happening to me. Oh, and look here, I am writing everything down for James and Sadie too, so that she can explain where we are to Rupert. There is so much to remember, isn't there? The lovely food, how nice everybody is, all about Gerry and Joe; I can't write fast enough," she laughed.

"I am sure that James and Sadie will love reading all about our travels. I hope I didn't disturb you Polly, but the family are having some late night drinks, and I was feeling rather restless."

Polly looked at her mistress keenly as she fidgeted around the cabin. "I have an idea, madam. Why don't you help me with my journal, and if you see something that James would like to know about or something that would make him laugh, just write it down. It will be really special if we both wrote about something that happened to us every day."

Estelle stopped pacing around the cabin, and her eyes lit up. "Polly, what a good idea. Yes, yes, let's do that. James will love it. We shall call it Polly's Diary on the Ship of Dreams, with contributions from Estelle Maycroft. Thank you, Polly."

Estelle hurried along the corridor toward her cabin, her mind full of the funny little sketches and stories she could send to the children. Strains of a catchy song floated across the dark water, and Estelle paused and smiled. The orchestra had assembled on A deck for an impromptu concert and were enthusiastically playing the popular *Alexander's Ragtime Band* to a delighted and appreciative audience who were enjoying coffee and sipping after-dinner cocktails.

For a brief moment, Estelle deliberated whether to join the family, but she was still too cross with Henry, and so she went back to her cabin. When a slightly inebriated Henry slipped into the cabin in the early hours of the morning, Estelle was in a deep, untroubled sleep, her first in many days. Titanic departed, leaving Cherbourg behind her, and began the next leg of her journey, the overnight sailing to Queenstown, Southern Ireland.

THURSDAY 11TH OF APRIL 1912

At around mid-morning on Thursday the 11th of April 1912, the Southern Ireland coastline came into view, and Titanic slipped into Queenstown harbour to pick up the remaining passengers on the last stop of its voyage across the Atlantic Ocean.

Like Cherbourg, the harbour could not cater for large vessels, and so again the White Star tenders transported the disembarking passengers and the mail bags to shore and ferried the boarding passengers to the great ship.

It was a pleasantly warm, if cloudy, morning with a brisk wind, and the Grieves-Croft family, after an early breakfast, had once again parted company to explore the great liner.

The twins, who had discovered the less formal Café Parisian, went to meet their newfound friends. Cafe Parisian, which typically resembled a Parisian Café, had windows that could be rolled down if the weather permitted. It was furnished with wicker tables and chairs and walls of trellis work with ivy and exotic plants in large pots. It opened at eight o'clock in the morning and did not close until eleven o'clock at night, and it was proving to be a popular meeting place for the younger passengers, especially as it was on the same level as the Poop deck where the deck games were played.

Lord Archie, Henry, and George were sent off to the barber's shop with strict orders from Estelle to purchase some of the White Star souvenir trinkets to take home for the children, a hat for Rupert, a doll for Sadie, and a penknife for James.

Jenny, Estelle, and Lady Rose went in search of the reading and writing room.

"It's away up on A Deck. It is a lovely, quiet room for the ladies to relax and write their letters home. The gentlemen tend to prefer the smoking room and the bar, of course," Gerry had confided to Estelle.

"Well, what a perfectly delightful room. It reminds me a little of home," said Lady Rose, her face breaking into a contented smile as she stood looking around at the softly painted, panelled walls. Fluted columns decorated with delicate plasterwork divided parts of the room into little private alcoves. Each alcove was furnished with beautiful silk-covered armchairs, little sofas, writing desks, and crystal wall chandeliers.

"Clever, Gerry," Lady Rose turned to Estelle. "This is ideal, my dears," and picking the alcove closest to the magnificent sweeping bay window overlooking the promenade, she settled herself on a yellow-and-blue silk-upholstered chaise longue. Resting her feet on a foot stool, she looked up at them. "I can read my book and watch the world go by as well," she said contentedly.

"You do look nicely comfortable, Ma. Will you be all right if Jenny and I go and explore a bit more"?

"Of course, I will, Estelle. To be truthful, I am feeling a little under the weather this morning. I did not sleep very well because of this wretched cough." Lady Rose confessed, "But please do not tell your father," she ordered as an afterthought. "I am sure it's just a little chill. Dottie has gone to find the doctor for some aspirin."

Just as she said that, Dottie bustled into the room with Polly following behind. "I've some aspirin and a tincture for that cough, madam." Nodding to Jenny and Estelle, she said quite sharply in her broad Glaswegian accent, "The mistress needs a little rest now, if you please. I will take care of her, and she's not in need of a lot of chatter."

"It seems that we are not needed yet again, Ma," said Estelle wryly, who was used to the good-hearted but abrupt Dottie.

Lady Rose smiled a little wearily. "Thank you, Dottie. Now off you go, girls, and do enjoy yourselves."

When they turned to wave, Dottie was tucking a soft cashmere shawl gently around her mistress's shoulders.

"Let's go out on deck and see what's happening. Come with us Polly, we can watch the new passengers boarding." Jenny suggested.

"It's breezy today, madam," said Polly. "I am going to fetch a coat for Miss Estelle. Shall I ask Belle to fetch a coat from your cabin?"

In truth, there was not a great deal for Polly or the other lady's maids to do on board. The stewardesses and dressers who had been allocated to Estelle and Jenny's cabins were swift and skilled in dealing with their first-class ladies and always politely refused all offers of assistance. But Lady Rose's dresser had been summarily dismissed by Dottie, outraged that anyone other than Dottie herself should assume to dress her mistress. But Belle, Jenny's maid, gratefully relinquished her duties as she had been unable to control her terror at being at sea, and apart from dashing to Jenny's cabin, she rarely ventured from her cabin.

On the deck, there were plenty of curious onlookers pointing and peering over the rails, and Jenny, Polly, and Estelle found a space and joined them.

The two tenders, having dropped off the mail sacks and the disembarking passengers from Titanic, were already speeding back with the last of the passengers to join the ship. At one-thirty, there was a long blast from Titanic's whistles, and a great cheer went up from the excited passengers crowded on the deck as the great liner weighed anchor and began the westward journey across the Atlantic. As the grey Shehy mountains gradually slid out of view, another great cheer went up from the flag-waving crowd on the quayside. After one more stop to drop off the pilot who had guided the ship in and out of the harbour, Titanic headed out into the Atlantic, following the breathtakingly lovely Irish coastline. Many of the Irish migrants had crowded silently on the Poop deck for one last glimpse of their homeland, and amid the excitement there was also tears and sadness.

When Henry, George, and Lord Archie met for pre-luncheon drinks, the girls were still on the deck, and it was only Lady Rose and the twins waiting for them in the Verandah Café. Lord Archie frowned at the small amount of food on his wife's plate. "Rose, you should eat something more than that, my dear, you are very pale."

"Well, perhaps just a little more consommé, and perhaps some cheese, darling. I did eat rather well at breakfast." Lady Rose smiled at her anxious husband.

"It really was the most delicious breakfast," George agreed. "I am surprised to find that I am hungry again. It must be the sea air."

"We are starving," declared William, looking hungrily at the buffet table piled high with smoked sardines, platters of roast beef, buttery potatoes, sausages, and great slabs of veal and ham pie.

Henry sipped his whiskey, "I agree. It must be the sea air. Lunch looks very tempting," he said appreciatively."

"We should wait for the ladies," Lord Archie said sternly to the twins, who began to protest, just as Jenny, Estelle, and Polly joined them, wind-blown and breathless.

"George," Jenny lifted her face for her husband's kiss. "You should have been up on deck. Everyone was waving and cheering from the quayside, so exciting, can you believe it, we are really on our way now."

"How lovely, girls, I would like to have seen that," Lady Rose said wistfully. "Perhaps we can have a walk after luncheon, if I can escape from Dottie, that is."

Later that afternoon, except for the twins, who had begged to be excused from tea, the family met together in the reception room.

"You look better, my dear. You have roses in your cheeks. The fresh air has done you good," Lord Archie beamed at his wife.

"We had a very pleasant stroll and met some interesting people, didn't we girls? Perhaps you three gentlemen should have followed our example," teased Lady Rose. "Where have you been since luncheon? In the smoking room, no doubt."

Lord Archie admitted to falling asleep reading his paper by the fire, and Henry and George confessed to playing a long and innocent game of cards. "No betting, Ma, honestly."

William and Walter appeared briefly to enquire whether they could go down on G Deck to play squash with their friends. They were given strict instructions by George not to miss the bugle call to dress for dinner, which was booked for seven-thirty. It was not only Lady Rose who appeared to have benefitted from the sea air. Estelle appeared relaxed and cheerful and did not once mention James during tea but sat with her mother enjoying the orchestra.

Lady Rose felt well enough to join the family for dinner that night in the magnificent dining salon and shook her head in disbelief at the lavish, ten-course menu. The mood was relaxed and leisurely as, apart from the twins, the family all agreed that an early night was called for, and even Henry said that he was too tired for the after-dinner drinks. George sent the twins to bed, firmly insisting that they needed to rest and catch up on sleep as there had been too many late nights. Furious protest followed. "It's only ten o'clock. We are going to look complete fools being sent to bed like children." They pleaded to a laughing Jenny, but she agreed whole-heartedly with her husband.

Lady Rose stood up and put her arms around their shoulders. "Come along, my sweet boys, help me to my cabin." William and Walter, who adored their grandmother, instantly linked arms with her and escorted her from the room, protests forgotten.

By nightfall, Ireland was behind them, and leaving behind the mild, dry weather, for a sharp northwest wind, bringing with it a bitterly cold front that was lurking in the West.

FRIDAY 12TH OF APRIL 1912

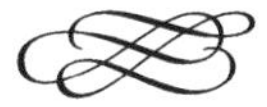

Titanic was now well out into the Atlantic Ocean, and had covered 386 miles since leaving Ireland, and although it was noticeably colder, the sky was clear and the sea was calm. Messages of congratulations and good luck wishes poured in from other vessels to the Marconi wireless operators on the Titanic, and these were conveyed to Captain Smith. Each message also contained warnings and advice about sightings of icebergs.

At breakfast that morning, the family gathered to discuss plans for the day ahead. Lady Rose was again troubled by an irritating cough and had little appetite. After a light breakfast, she retired to the peace and quiet of the reading and writing room, accompanied as always by the ever-faithful Dottie.

The twins, as usual, disappeared after breakfast, explaining that there was to be a quoits competition on the Poop Deck, and with permission, they would like to be excused luncheon. Jenny and Estelle, having ensured that Lady Rose was settled with the ever-watchful Dottie watching over their beloved Ma, strolled along the companionway and around the Promenade Deck enjoying the sea air and the views of the sea from the stern. Polly excused herself from the walk and settled in a deck chair, with a steamer rug wrapped around her against the breeze. Only the top of her head was visible as she sheltered against the wind, lost in thought as she scribbled busily in her journal.

"There's Polly," Estelle exclaimed spotting her at the end of the deck. Jenny giggled, "Shh. Let's see what she is doing." They tiptoed up behind her. Jenny bent down and whispered in Polly's ear.

"Don't forget to tell James about your Joe, now, will you, Polly?"

Polly, absorbed in her writing, jumped. "Ohh, madam, you scared me."

"Well, did you write about Joe in your little book?" Jenny laughed at Polly's red face.

"I may have mentioned him once or twice, madam," Polly replied shyly.

In fact, every time the young purser was off duty, he managed to sneak away from his friends to spend time with Polly. This had not gone unnoticed by the twins, who teased Polly at every opportunity. "Is Joe your beau, Polly?" They would call out until a grinning George scolded them, but then could not resist a little teasing of his own.

Polly took this all in good part, but her pretty, glowing little face bore testimony that she was indeed taken with the young officer. Joe, for his part, came in for jibes and jokes from his shipmates and strongly defended himself and admitted that he was very taken with Polly, and she was indeed a "Grand girl."

Henry and George had amused themselves first in the gymnasium and then the squash courts before joining the family for luncheon, although Lady Rose excused herself and settled for a snack in her cabin. Lord Archie joined his wife and ordered the faithful Dottie off for a break. Dottie reluctantly folded up her knitting and placed it in her work bag. "I shall be back in two hours, my lady," she said firmly and nodded to Lord Archie briefly as she left.

Later, when Jenny and Estelle arrived, brandishing the latest novel by Lady Rose's favourite author, they found Lord Archie reading his newspaper, and a rather wan-looking Lady Rose dozing with an open book on her lap.

Lord Archie looked up and held his finger to his lips. "She has just dozed off, my dears. That wretched cough is troubling her again," he whispered. "Leave the book. She will like that. I will stay with her until Dottie dismisses me."

Dinner that night was a quiet affair for the Grieves-Crofts, as Lady Rose had developed a temperature and was confined to her cabin. After dinner, Jenny insisted that the twins spent some time with her and Estelle, and so the four of them settled in the Verandah Cafe for an evening of chess. George and Henry retired to the smoking room for their habitual game of cards.

Keen-eyed Gerry was on duty and saw that Henry was eagerly watching card games being played at other tables. Spotting a few familiar faces, Gerry drew Lord Archie into the purser's office. "Keep an eye out for those fellas, Lord Archie. I have just spotted a few regulars at the tables," and Gerry pointed to a caution notice on the wall warning about the "Boat Players," professional gamblers who preyed on wealthy passengers.

Lord Archie was grateful for Gerry's vigilance, but when told of the notice and warned about being drawn into gambling with them, Henry was outraged. "Great Heavens," he snorted derisively. "How old do they think we are? A caution indeed."

Lord Archie exchanged glances with George and said mildly, "You would do well to heed that warning, Henry. We would not want to upset the ladies by gambling and losing, now would we? A small, friendly gamble is acceptable, but these men are professionals."

Henry, silently fuming at the rebuke, strode away shaking his head. Lord Archie made a mental note, if George went to bed after the friendly game, he would not leave Henry at the tables on his own.

SATURDAY 13TH OF APRIL 1912

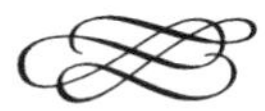

Another clear but chilly day dawned, and Lord Archie sent a message via Dottie to say that he and Lady Rose would take breakfast in their cabin as Lady Rose had suffered a sleepless night and was now resting.

Estelle and Jenny had decided the evening before to skip breakfast and have an early morning swim in the heated, saltwater pool. There was a female-only session held from nine o'clock, and after that they were eager to try the Turkish baths before meeting for luncheon. Feeling that they both needed some form of exercise following the amount of food and drink they had consumed over the last few days, George and Henry challenged the twins to a squash match. The delighted twins sped off to tell their friends, and when George and Henry arrived at the squash courts, George for one, was dismayed to find a collection of the twins' newfound friends had arrived cheer Walter and William on.

When Polly arrived at Estelle's cabin, she was surprised to find that Henry had gone and Estelle was still in her dressing gown.

"Jenny and I are going for a swim and then to the Turkish baths. Come with us, why don't you, Polly?" Estelle urged, winding her unruly curls up on top of her head and securing them with a net.

"I don't swim, madam, but I would love to see the Turkish baths," Polly was intrigued.

"That's settled then, have your breakfast and then meet us in the swimming baths. Do you think Belle may like to come and see the baths? Is she any better, poor little thing?"

Polly giggled, "No, madam. I don't think that she has even seen the water. Dottie scolds her, but that just makes her cry, and Miss Jenny says to just leave the poor thing alone."

The heated saltwater swimming pool was at least thirty feet long and seven feet deep. There was a line of changing rooms, several showers, and a raised wooden walkway with marble and teak steps leading down into the water. Estelle was speechless with delight, but Jenny looked around nervously. "Goodness. It's like a giant tank," she said, looking up at the iron girders above her.

"Come on Jenny," urged Estelle. "Don't forget, we only have until twelve o'clock to use the Turkish bath as well, and I want a massage. Go on and get changed."

Jenny nodded, "Alright, but if it's cold, I'm not getting in," she warned.

When Polly opened the heavy door to the pool and peered in, Jenny and Estelle were swimming idly up and down, chatting.

"It's half-past ten, madam," Polly called out, her voice echoing eerily around the cavernous pool.

"Thank you, Polly, we are coming out now." Estelle waved, and they swam to the side of the pool and climbed up the steps and ran into their changing rooms.

"What about your hair, madam? Where can I do your hair? Polly said as Jenny and Estelle emerged from the changing rooms with towels wrapped around their wet hair.

"Don't worry about my hair, Polly. We can shampoo our hair in the Turkish bath," Estelle assured her.

The Turkish baths were situated close by the pool, and two smiling attendants were waiting to greet them. Both were clad in loose-fitting peach tunics with white gloves, and both were wearing white plimsolls. "Are all three ladies experiencing our Turkish baths today? May I have your tickets, please," one of the attendants asked politely.

Somewhat nervously, Jenny handed her two tickets. The attendant smiled and slipped them into her tunic pocket and turned to Polly, who was hovering in the background. "Madam, will you be having a steam and massage too?"

Polly hesitated "I'm not really sure," and looked at Estelle, who urged.

"Come on Polly, hand over your ticket."

"Perhaps madam would like to look inside first?" the attendant enquired with a superior smile, and with practiced ease, swung open the ornate gilt-and-cream panelled door.

Nothing could have prepared them for the Arabic interior of the extraordinary room. Polly gasped open-mouthed. Jenny was silent, but Estelle clapped her hands in sheer delight at the sight of the exotic room facing them. The walls were panelled in blue and green, the ceiling cornice and beams were gilded, and the ceiling was painted crimson. The floor was a rainbow of multi-coloured mosaic, and dangling from the ceiling beams, large bronze lanterns glittered and swayed, casting flickering shapes across the floor and walls.

Around the vast room, towering teak pillars, intricately carved with tiny birds and insects, reached up to the ceiling, whilst drinking fountains set in arched recesses bubbled gently in the background. Around the room, long, low buttoned couches were piled high with gaily coloured cushions. On the far side of the room, a group of ladies, seated in teak-and-canvas folding chairs and wrapped from head to foot in white robes, were idly smoking and chatting.

Polly took a deep breath and shook her head firmly. She thrust her ticket back into her pocket and turned anguished eyes to Estelle.

"No, no, thank you, I'm sorry, but I have changed my mind. I am so sorry, madam."

Jenny leant across and patted her arm. "Don't fret Polly, It's perfectly all right. We understand, in fact," and she raised her eyebrows at Estelle. "I'm not sure that I am comfortable with all this myself."

Estelle laughed. "Off you go, Polly, then. We shall tell you all about it, and you can write it up in your journal," and with one more apologetic smile, Polly backed out of the door.

The attendant raised her eyebrows and closed the door behind her. "It doesn't suit everyone, of course," she said coolly, clearly put out. It was obvious that she was very proud of her domain, and Estelle looked at Jenny and stifled a giggle. The attendant opened a tall cupboard and produced fluffy towelling robes and identical white, open-backed slippers and handed them to Jenny and Estelle.

"If you would, please do remove your shoes and put the slippers on, and I will take you to the changing rooms, and you can change into your robes. Now ladies, our suite comprises a steam room, a hot room, a warm room, and a shampoo room. First, we carry out a full body wash and massage, and then we like you to rest for a while in the cooling room." She took a deep breath and paused. "We do, of course, offer our ladies a chance to try the electric bath."

Jenny looked alarmed, but Estelle was bubbling with enthusiasm.

"How very exciting," she exclaimed, and the attendant looked suitably satisfied at her response.

"Well," she explained importantly, "The electric bath is just like a comfortable bed but with an overhead cover and electric lamps on a timer. The heat from the special lamps relaxes the muscles and gives the body a lovely glow."

Jenny looked even more nervous. "May I ask, have you, yourself, tried the electric bed?"

The girl shifted uncomfortably. "No, madam," and hurried on, "But I have seen lots of ladies use it, and they were very happy."

The attendant waited expectantly, her head on one side. Estelle turned to Jenny, her eyes twinkling with mischief,

"Come on, Jenny Wren, shall we try everything?"

"Certainly not," said Jenny firmly, and addressing the attendant said, "Thank you, but we will just have the body wash, shampoo, and massage please." Before Estelle could protest, Jenny led her firmly by the arm toward the changing rooms. Estelle turned to the disappointed-looking attendant,

"I may come back tomorrow morning to try the electric bed, and without my dubious friend."

When Jenny and Estelle arrived for luncheon, Henry and George were relaxing with cocktails.

"We were well and truly thrashed by your wretched boys," admitted Henry to Jenny, and they sat down at the table, "Now they have been carried off by their chums to celebrate their victory in the Café Parisian."

"I hope you did not gamble with the boys, George," Jenny said severely.

"We just had a little bet, my dear," admitted George. "Henry convinced me that we could beat them, anyway," he said, hastily changing the subject. "Do tell us about the Turkish baths. Henry and I thought we would try them after lunch."

"Actually, it was very relaxing and enjoyable," admitted Jenny.

Estelle interrupted. "But if you do go you must try the electric bath, Henry, and let me know what it is like. Jenny would not let me try it."

"I may, darling, I may. It sounds like quite an experience." Henry smiled amiably.

Estelle looked around. "Are the parents joining us?"

George shook his head. "No. Pa sent Dottie up to say that their morning walk had tired Ma out, and they would lunch in the cabin."

Estelle frowned. "I should go and see how she is feeling. I am beginning to worry about her. Her cough is dreadful."

George shook his head, "No, Estelle. Pa is with her, and he will send Dottie to find us if we are needed."

That morning, after breakfasting in their cabin, Lord Archie had persuaded his wife to take a gentle stroll along to the Café Parisian. "I think it will do you good to get out of the cabin for a while, Rose, and the boys tell me that there are outstanding views across the ocean from the Café Parisian." Although he hid it well, Lord Archie was alarmed that even the leisurely stroll appeared to exhaust his normally vivacious wife, and she was clearly out of breath when he settled her gently into a comfortable wicker chair in front of the picture windows.

However, after several cups of coffee and some delicious French pastries, she seemed to recover her spirits, and her cheeks had regained some colour. "What a pretty room," she said, taking in the delicate vine-covered fretwork around the walls. "And the sea looks so still you would hardly believe we are moving, Archie."

"Well, we are, Rose, and a trifle too fast for my liking. The temperature has been dropping for the last two days, and I suspect we could encounter some ice."

"You worry far too much, Archie my dear," she replied and put her cup and saucer down on the table quickly as another bout of coughing overtook her.

Lord Archie frowned and handed her a handkerchief from his top pocket. "I think we should pay another visit to the doctor. Your cough is no better, Rose."

Lady Rose shook her head and regained her breath. "I think it's a little better than last night, and my headache has gone. Please don't fuss, dear. I don't want to spoil things for the children."

When, later that afternoon, Estelle and Jenny knocked gently on the cabin door, Dottie answered the door, "My lady is resting now, and Lord Archie has gone up to the smoking room with his newspaper."

"Perhaps Ma will feel better now. Let's hope she can join us for dinner," said Estelle.

But that evening, when they met for drinks in the reception room, Dottie was waiting for them. "Lord Archie says please begin dinner and do not wait for him and Lady Rose. They may take dinner in the cabin later as Lady Rose does not feel like eating yet."

Estelle's heart sank. "Oh Dottie, is Ma unwell again? Should we come back to the cabin with you?"

"Certainly not, madam. I am sure Lord Archie will join you later."

But Lord Archie did not join them. He sent a steward to tell the family that "All was well, and he and Lady Rose would join them for breakfast, and to please remember the church service will be in the dining salon at ten-thirty."

SUNDAY 14TH OF APRIL, 1912

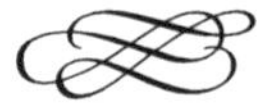

Sunday morning dawned fine and clear, with an early morning sun glittering across the surface of the ocean accompanied by a brisk and invigorating breeze. George, Jenny, and the less-than-enthusiastic twins had risen early to enjoy a sunny stroll along the promenade and boat deck before joining the others for breakfast. Lady Rose had woken with a bad headache and was having breakfast in her cabin.

"I am worried about your mother," Lord Archie confided to Estelle, as arm-in-arm, they made their way to the dining salon for the church service. "She cannot seem to shake this chill, and nothing the doctor prescribes seems to help, and that wretched cough is keeping her awake at night. I am going to ask the doctor to come and have another look at her. It's so unlike her; she does not want to leave the cabin."

Estelle, although concerned herself, sought to reassure him. "I am sure it is just a cold, Pa. After the service, Jenny and I will go and sit with her for a while. You should go for a walk or ask George or Henry for a game of chess."

Lord Archie hugged her gratefully, "Do you know, my dear, I think I shall."

Having finally rounded up their reluctant sons, Jenny and a hot and cross-looking George were already seated in the crowded dining salon.

Henry was waiting outside leaning against the door, and he flicked his cigarette away as Estelle and Lord Archie approached. "Estelle, there you are. I was just coming to find you. George and I had to go and find the twins who went missing as soon as they heard about the service."

"I thought George was looking a bit harassed," Lord Archie chuckled.

George, catching his father's eye, raised his eyebrows and shook his head.

"I'm not surprised he's angry," replied Henry, lowering his voice. "Little blighters were down in steerage mucking about and playing with some rough Irish types."

Estelle hid a smile and avoided looking at her father, whom, she suspected, had known exactly where his grandsons had spent much of their time aboard, and he did not object to them having a little fun.

The short service finished with some rousing hymns, the twins singing loud and lustily out of tune, but this did not redeem them in their parents' eyes. George and Jenny had guessed what they were up to, and as the congregation began to disperse, George grasped each twin firmly by the arm. "Oh no, you don't, my lads," he said. "We are off to the gymnasium, but if you behave yourselves, I will set you free after luncheon. Are you coming, Henry?"

"No, thank you, George. I was thinking of taking a turn around the deck."

Lord Archie, who had a strong suspicion that Henry had planned to indulge in a little gambling, clapped him on the shoulder. "Henry, have your walk and then perhaps join me in the library later. We could have a cup of coffee and a game of chess. The girls are going to spend some time with Rose after Estelle has sent her usual telegram home."

Henry, thwarted, was grouchy. "Another telegram," he complained.

"Estelle is either writing letters or sending telegrams to James. The boy should have come with us."

"Well, James chose not to, and if it makes Estelle happy to write to the boy, then I see no harm in that." Lord Archie's tone was mild with an edge of steel, and Henry, who knew better than to argue with his father-in-law, remained silent and sulkily prepared to spend the morning playing chess when in fact, he was hoping for a little serious poker in the smoking room.

Polly was waiting in Estelle's cabin when she hurried through the door. "There you are, Polly. Can you take this telegram to the purser and get tickets for deck chairs and blankets please? If it is not too cold, Jenny and I thought that we may sit out in the sun. We must, of course, see Lady Rose first, so please bring our tickets to the reading and writing room. You are welcome to join us on deck if you wish."

Polly smiled and took the telegram, "Thank you, madam. I'll take it straightaway."

"Oh, and Polly, I just wanted to say if Joe is on duty, I am sure that you won't have to queue for long." Estelle giggled, and Polly blushed.

Gerry had let slip to Estelle that his nephew had said how "Remarkably pretty" Joe thought Polly was, and Estelle had teased her unmercifully ever since.

The purser's office was busier than usual, and there were long queues of passengers hiring cars ready for when they docked in New York. Some passengers were booking onward train tickets, whilst others were waiting to purchase activity passes, but the longest queue was the postal desk to send telegrams and letters ashore. Polly slipped around the side of the queue where Joe, unmistakable with his black moustache, was standing, patiently putting passenger's telegrams in the canister before placing them in the tube that would transport them to the Marconi radio room. He looked bored and was yawning when he spotted Polly, and his face lit up immediately. "Another telegram! Polly, your mistress sends more telegrams and letters than anyone else on Titanic. Are you sure you don't ask her to send more letters as an excuse just to see me?" he teased.

"Don't you be so sure of yourself, Joe," retorted Polly but could not hide a shy smile. The telegram was duly dispatched, and Polly returned to the reading and writing room where Jenny and Estelle were waiting for their deck chair tickets.

"Here are the tickets, madam. It is cold outside, and Joe says that it is going to get colder, so if you are going out on deck, you should wrap up very warm." Polly said solemnly.

"Then we shall follow your Joe's excellent advice, Polly," Estelle teased. "Come Jenny, let's see how Ma is feeling before we fetch our coats."

"Lord Archie is very worried about Lady Rose, isn't he, Estelle?" Jenny mused as they strolled along the deck toward their cabins.

Jenny loved her parents-in-law deeply and was concerned to see her normally calm and composed father in law so visibly worried about his lovely wife.

"It is so unlike Ma to be ill. I expect that is why he is fussing," Estelle replied. They had reached her parents' cabin, and Estelle knocked softly on the door. It was opened almost immediately by an anxious-looking Dottie.

"Oh madam, I am so pleased to see you. I was just about to come and find Lord Archie," she said glancing back over her shoulder. "My lady is not at all well, and I am worried that she is getting worse, and she refuses to let me to call the doctor. I've been trying to get her to drink something, but it just sets her off coughing again."

Estelle put her arm around the distressed maid and said firmly, "All right, Dottie dear. I will send for the doctor, and you go with Jenny and find Lord Archie. I will stay with Lady Rose and wait for the doctor. Hurry now."

Lady Rose's voice called weakly from the direction of the bedroom. "Estelle, is that you, my dear? Please do come in. Dottie is fussing so," then her voice was cut short by a racking cough, and Estelle hurried into the bedroom.

Her mother was sitting propped up on a mound of pillows, her still-brilliant Titian curls spread across her shoulders, and she was holding a lavender-scented handkerchief to her mouth. Her normally sparkling eyes were heavy, and her cheeks a dull red in an ashen face.

Estelle took one look at her mother, and her heart sank. She reached over and rang for the steward. "Sorry Ma, but you do need to see the doctor. Dottie was right. Jenny has gone to fetch Pa. You should have allowed Dottie to call the doctor earlier," she scolded, taking care not to show her mother just how worried she was as she straightened the ruffled sheets.

Lady Rose shook her head weakly. "Such a fuss. It is just a chill; no need to bother anyone," she croaked and leant back wearily, closing her eyes, her hands moving feverishly over the covers.

Estelle grasped her mother's beautiful hands gently in her own. They were hot and dry, and Estelle fought back a threatening sense of panic. It frightened her to see her strong, calm mother looking so helplessly weak, and when the steward arrived, she urged him to hurry and find the doctor. When Jenny came back with a grim-faced Lord Archie, the doctor was waiting for him.

Having made a thorough examination of his patient, he addressed Lord Archie. "I'm afraid that her ladyship may have a chest infection," he said, slowly removing his stethoscope and folding it up into his bag. "Lady Rose is very poorly, and I would like to move her to the infirmary where she can have complete rest and I can keep a closer eye on her." He stood up and looked directly at Lord Archie. "With your permission, my lord, I would like to move her to the infirmary straightaway."

"Of course, Doctor, whatever you think is best." Lord Archie turned to his wife, who, having heard the word infirmary, was struggling to sit up. "No, my dear Rose, lay back, because, for once, you are going to do as you are told. Follow the doctor's orders, and then you will feel better when we get to New York." Lord Archie was gentle but firm.

Estelle nodded. "Just rest, Ma. Jenny and I will get your things together."

"Excuse me, Miss Estelle, I will be doing that, there is no need for you to bother yourself. I will get my lady ready." Dottie's broad accent became even more indecipherable when she was annoyed, and now she stared at the group, daring anyone to challenge her.

A soft chuckle came from the direction of the bed, and Lady Rose, who had accepted defeat, winked at her husband. Lord Archie looked ruefully at the doctor. “I am afraid, Doctor, that you will have to make up a bed next to my wife, because if you don’t, Dottie here,” and he waved his hand toward the glowering little maid, who had stationed herself close to her mistress, “Dottie here will sleep on your hospital floor.”

Dottie nodded grimly, still staring at the doctor who looked mildly alarmed. “So, I will,” she assured him.

Once Lady Rose was settled in a cool quiet corner of the infirmary with two smiling nurses in attendance, Estelle and Jenny were asked politely to leave and allow the patient to rest. The doctor administered a small dose of Laudanum.

“Laudanum will ensure Lady Rose gets some sleep, and it will help to subdue the urge to cough,” the doctor reassured Lord Archie and Dottie who was watching closely.

“Then I will stay until my wife falls asleep.” Lord Archie said firmly.

The doctor agreed reluctantly. “If you wish, sir, but then you must leave. Lady Rose needs as much rest as possible if she is to recover.”

“Archie, do go my dear.” Lady Rose turned her head to look at him. “Tell the family that I am fine, they will be so worried,” but already her voice was fading, and within half an hour she was sleeping deeply and peacefully.

When Lord Archie was sure that his beloved wife was settled, he whispered to the hovering Dottie. “I will be back soon, Dottie. Please watch her carefully.” Dottie nodded grimly.

Once outside the infirmary, he lingered for a while, completely forgetting that he had arranged to meet Henry in the library. He considered going up on the boat deck for some fresh air, but instead he made his way up to the smoking room. He was not in the mood for company, and the smoking room was not normally busy during the day, although it was a popular venue for gambling gentlemen most evenings.

The smoking room, which resembled a gentlemen’s club, was

saved from being austere by an array of elaborate stained-glass windows and panels. Elegant mahogany and red, plush velvet settees were grouped invitingly around a crackling log fire and dimly-lit, beaded chandeliers glittered from the ceiling, creating a mood of calm and quiet.

When Lord Archie arrived, the room was almost empty. In one of the dim alcoves, a group of diehard card players were bent over the green baize card table engrossed in their game, and a couple of bored-looking stewards were leaning idly up against the bar.

The comfortable-looking armchairs by the fire beckoned, and Lord Archie, suddenly weary and cold, sank thankfully into the one closest to the fire. One of the stewards appeared beside him, "May I fetch a pot of coffee for you, sir, or perhaps something stronger?"

"Thank you, but just coffee, please."

Fortified by several cups of the pleasantly strong brew and feeling more relaxed, Lord Archie closed his eyes and allowed his head to fall back. In the background, he could hear the low voices of the card players and the comforting crackle of the burning logs. Gradually, his tense body relaxed, and his mind drifted back easily over the years, and to the time that he had met Rosie Tremaine.

Archibald Grieves-Croft was a nineteen-year-old Captain in the 1st The Royal Dragoons when he met and fell in love with eighteen-year-old Rose Esther Tremaine. Despite being heir to the Grieves-Croft fortunes, when he left Eton, he immediately took a commission in the army.

Rose Esther Tremaine was the only child of General Lancelot Tremaine of the 1st Royal Dragoons and Captain Archibald Grieves-Croft's commanding officer. Rose's mother had died in childbirth, and the army was the only life that Rose had ever known, although her father ensured that she enjoyed as normal a life as possible in the care of carefully vetted nannies, before going to a suitable boarding school. In the winter of 1862, as Christmas and Rose Tremaine's eighteenth birthday approached, the General considered taking his daughter to the Regiment's Annual Christmas Ball and searched around for a suitable escort for her. The serious young Captain Archibald Grieves-

Croft came to mind, and he summoned the surprised young captain to his office, informing him brusquely that he had been chosen to escort his daughter Rose to the Regimental Christmas Ball.

Then as an afterthought, he asked sharply, "Are you otherwise spoken for, Grieves-Croft? Are you? If so, speak up, man."

The bemused young officer replied, "No, sir."

"Good." The General appeared satisfied. "Thank you, you may go now, Captain."

Archibald's fellow officers had teased him unmercifully when they heard. "No one has ever really seen the young Rose Tremaine. You know, Grieves-Croft, she could be a plain Jane."

But to their dismay, Rose Tremaine was far from plain. In fact, she was quite beautiful, tall and slim with an abundance of red curls, dancing green eyes, and a quiet demeanour that hid a glorious sense of fun.

Archibald Grieves-Croft was as tall, with thick, black hair and dark brown eyes and carried with him an air of calm and quiet confidence that belied his young years. For the following couple of years, they spent as much time together as possible, and within three years of meeting, and with the General's blessing, they were married.

When old Lord Grieves-Croft announced his intention to retire from the company, Archibald resigned his commission, took a degree in Naval Architecture, and joined the family firm to replace his father. Lord Archie sighed and opened his eyes briefly, pushing away the unwelcome thought that maybe his lovely wife was ill, although this was something he simply could not contemplate.

Whilst Lord Archie dozed by the fire, a disgruntled Henry was pacing around the library waiting for his father-in-law to join him. "Perhaps," Henry thought, hopefully, "something has happened to change his mind."

Estelle and Jenny were with Lady Rose, George was with the twins in the gymnasium, and knowing that he would not be missed until after luncheon, Henry decided to wait no longer and headed off in the direction of the smoking room. Henry was disappointed to see that the room was empty apart from a group of four who were so engrossed in their card game that they never raised their eyes from the table. An air of tension hung around them, and Henry recognised one of the players as a professional gambler and his pulse quickened.

With any luck, there may be a chance of a game after all, he thought, but then with a shock, he spotted the unmistakable figure of his silver-haired father-in-law, who appeared to be fast asleep in a chair by the fire, his long legs stretched out in front of him.

Henry swore silently under his breath and turned to the watching steward, "How long has Lord Archibald been in here?" he hissed. "He was supposed to meet me in the library at least half an hour ago."

The steward looked across to the supine figure stretched out in front of the fire. "Only a short while, sir. His Lordship appears to be sleeping. Would you like me to wake him for you?"

"No, no, don't bother," Henry snarled, turned on his heel, and walked away.

A smouldering log rolled onto the hearth, and the steward hurried forward to grab the tongs. But the tongs had been placed too near the fire and he dropped them with a clatter, cursing under his breath.

Lord Archie woke with a start and looked around him. "Good God, man, what was that?"

"So sorry, sir, the tongs were hot." The steward, red-faced was nursing his burnt hand under his arm.

Lord Archie shook his head, irritated with himself for being so jumpy. "Are you alright, old chap? Apologies for shouting; you startled me. I must have dozed off." He yawned and stood up. "I should get that hand looked at by the doctor."

"Thank you, sir, I will. There was a gentleman looking for you just a moment ago. He said he thought he was meeting you in the library?"

"Damn, I'd forgotten all about Henry. That was my son-in-law, thank you," and he made mental note to apologise to Henry.

On the way back to the infirmary, he was feeling slightly apprehensive, but when he passed the doctor attending to a child with a cut hand, the doctor looked up and gave him an encouraging smile. The screens were still drawn around his wife's bed, and Lady Rose was still sleeping, serene beneath crisp, white sheets. Dottie was knitting quietly in a chair next to the bed. She looked up when she saw him.

"My lady seems much better, sir. The doctor says her fever has gone, and she has not coughed for a while."

Lord Archie put his hands together in semblance of thanks and touched Dottie gently on the shoulder. "Then, Dottie, I insist that you go and have a rest and something to eat. I will sit with your mistress for a while, and I promise I won't disturb her."

Dottie hesitated, but then nodded, folded her knitting away into a capacious tapestry bag, and stood up. "Very well, Sir. I will just pop out for a cup of tea," and went promising to return within the hour.

Lord Archie settled into the chair and rested his eyes on his wife's beloved face. The bright spots of fever had gone, and her skin had lost its deathly pallor, and he sent another silent prayer of thanks to Heaven, because truthfully, he had no idea how he could go on without her by his side. She had been so young, yet so mature when, united together, they endured those dreadful days with Grace, but she was unendingly kind and patient with his demented sister, far more than he was able to be.

Then came the shocking birth of little Sadie, and all through this, Rose had stood steadfast and calm by his side, promising always to take care of the infant girl. Together, they had shared the joy of the birth of their grandchildren, William, Walter, and James, and had seen joy from tragedy as little Sophie grew to be a beautiful young woman. When Henry Maycroft had approached him and requested his permission to court their beloved Estelle, Lord Archie, for one, had been a little dismayed.

Whilst the family had welcomed Henry into their home as George's friend from Eton, they agreed that Henry lacked a certain steadiness and work commitment, albeit that he had inherited with his older brother a successful, if small, paper mill in a lovely Kent village.

But George had loyally backed Henry's cause, and their precious Estelle was very obviously deeply in love with the handsome and charming Henry. Lord Archie had consulted George about finding a job for Henry in the family business, but George had confirmed his own reservations stating that, "Old Henry is a law unto himself, Pa, but I do know that brother Bernard has Henry firmly under control now. Henry does love Estelle, Pa, and she loves him."

When Lady Rose and Lord Archie were introduced to Bernard before the wedding, they had relaxed and come to the same conclusion as George, that the quiet and steady Bernard could control his charismatic and flamboyant younger brother.

But then James was born, and it seemed that Henry drifted back to his old ways once more, and even more puzzling was the fact that Estelle did not seem to be concerned about her husband's frequent absences but found fulfilment in her beloved son.

As James had grown into a quiet, polite, but rather remote child, Lady Rose had voiced her concerns about Henry's unsettled relationship with James. On his wife's insistence, Lord Archie had brought the subject up with George at a company dinner just before the Titanic voyage. George had admitted that Henry was spending too much time in London with the old set. "Foxy and the others are decent fellows, Pa, but Perry," and he shook his head. "Perry gambles and drinks too much, and Henry gets drawn into Perry's set."

"Thank you for your honesty, George. Your mother and I have had our concerns for some time, because Estelle spends far too much time at Grieves Manor, and of course we don't mind that, but I confess we do worry about their marriage. Thank heavens that James seems to have settled in quite well at Eton. I know he was unhappy at Barrow Hill, but he has Estelle's strength and determination, and he stuck it out."

Of Rupert Grieves-Croft's sudden appearance at Grieves Manor, the family spoke little, other than to present to the outside world that, due to family circumstances, the child would remain living at Grieves Manor as a much-loved cousin to James and the twins.

He was still musing over Henry's antipathy toward James, when Lady Rose's soft and much-loved familiar voice jolted him out of his reverie. "Hello, my darling. I have been watching you for a while. Why are you frowning? What are you thinking about?" she teased.

He sat bolt upright in the chair, reached across for her hand, and pressed it to his lips. "Rose, my dearest Rose, what a fright you gave us. How do you feel, darling? Should I fetch the doctor?"

"You can fetch me something to eat, Archie. I am very hungry and thirsty," she smiled and freed her hand to stroke his head. "I am so sorry I worried everyone. How silly, but I promise that that I am better now." .

Lord Archie laughed out of sheer relief. "Doctor first though, dear-est, then food."

The doctor nodded in satisfaction, "I see that sleep has restored you, my lady. But complete rest and very little excitement is on the menu for the remainder of the voyage, and before you ask, you may not get up for dinner this evening. After dinner, you may have visitors for a short while, but not too many." He nodded to Lord Archie and looked at Dottie. "And I am sure that I can trust this good lady here to ensure that you all follow my orders."

Dottie nodded vigorously. "I will make sure they do indeed, Doctor."

He left his wife comfortably chatting with the doctor and hurried to find his family, chiding himself for feeling so close to tears. He found them gathered quietly together in the reading and writing room. Surprisingly, even the mercurial twins were engrossed in a game of chess. Jenny and Estelle were reading and discussing the merits of some fashion magazines, and George was dozing, an open book on his lap.

Henry was nowhere to be seen. "I wager that he has slipped off to find a game of poker," he thought wryly, but he was feeling far too happy to make a fuss. Lord Archie approached his family, arms outstretched and with such a wide smile on his face that all the eager and anxious questions hovering on their lips were answered, and the worry disappeared from their eyes as he related the doctor's assur-ance that their beloved matriarch was on the road to recovery.

"I think we should celebrate your mother's recovery with cham-pagne, and tonight, as it is our last night at sea, I have booked dinner at the A La Carte restaurant. Pre-dinner drinks will be in the foyer on

B Deck." Lord Archie beamed around the group. "Now, I see that we are missing Henry. George, if you would be so good as to find him, we shall take our champagne in the lounge."

Chattering happily together, the family headed off, and Lord Archie took his son to one side. "George, I rather think that you will find Henry in the smoking room."

George sighed and nodded. "That was to be my first port of call, sir," he said resignedly.

When Henry reappeared with George, he appeared in high good spirits, and for the next hour they celebrated Lady Rose's imminent return to the family group. Jenny and Estelle then went to see if the doctor would allow a short visit with Lady Rose. George, Henry, and the twins, after some deliberations, decided to try the Turkish baths.

Lord Archie left the girls to enjoy some time alone with their mother and went up to the Promenade Deck. The air was crisp and cold with little or no wind. It was a lovely late afternoon, and the sea was calm without a cloud in the sky. There were a number of other first-class passengers strolling around, enjoying the sea air.

"What a wonderful voyage this has been," remarked a fur-clad lady standing next to him, admiring the view.

Her companion, huddling down into his greatcoat, added, "Jolly cold though. I heard the purser say that the Captain had received some warnings of icebergs from other ships in our area."

Lord Archie raised his eyebrows, "Really?"

The man nodded. "But he assured us that it was nothing to be concerned about. It was only to be expected in the Atlantic in April."

"I'm sure," Lord Archie agreed thoughtfully as he looked out across the glassy sea. "Well, I bid you good evening; I really must take myself off and dress for dinner. Have a good evening."

When the polite goodbyes had been exchanged, Lord Archie made his way through the vestibule to the Grand Staircase and found himself pondering over the man's seemingly innocent remark about the possibility of encountering icebergs. But, he reasoned, as the temperature had dropped so rapidly since lunchtime, it certainly seemed to be a possibility that there would be icebergs in the area.

Lord Archie, as a much-respected naval architect, had been privy to inspect and comment on the early designs and sketches of the Titanic, and now, as he stood at the head of the Grand Staircase, he had to marvel at the fine craftsmanship of the sweeping sixty-foot-high staircase. Constructed of polished oak, with finely-gilded balustrades and beautiful, wrought-iron railings, it truly was magnificent. Each newel post was intricately carved, and atop each one was a fine, pineapple-shaped filial. At the base of the staircase, on the central newel post, a bronze cherub sculpture held aloft an illuminated torch, and he touched it gently as he passed.

It reminded him of the precious bronze of the child Estelle, and it also brought to mind James, his absent grandson. Fingers of weak sunlight filtered through the immense wrought-iron and glass dome above the staircase and glanced off the magnificent crystal-and-gilt chandelier that hung from the centre. "The Ship of Dreams indeed," he murmured to himself and made his way back to his cabin.

Perfectly attired in an immaculate dinner jacket, he hummed as he brushed back his unruly thatch of silver hair. With his head on one side, he viewed his reflection, nodded as if in approval, and adjusted his cuffs as the steward ran the clothes brush once more across his shoulder.

"Very smart you look, sir, if I may say so," and his steward stood back and admired the tall, distinguished figure.

Lord Archie acknowledged the compliment with a slight smile, "Thank you," and as was his usual practice, he gave the steward a tip. He took his watch from inside his waistcoat. "If I hurry," he thought, "I can spend a little time with Rose before dinner."

Striding through the infirmary, he heard a familiar throaty giggle coming from the end of the ward. A young nurse was sitting in Dottie's place by his wife's bedside, and judging by the mingled laughter, it was obvious that they were sharing a joke.

"I would know that laugh anywhere," he teased as he approached the bed and bent to kiss his wife's cool forehead. "My dear, you look radiant," and she did. The wonderful red curls were brushed and shining, the green eyes were clear and sparkling, and she was smiling her heartbreakingly lovely smile.

"Archie, dearest, you look very handsome, quite the dandy. Are you off to charm the ladies? Marie," and she turned to the wide-eyed nurse, "Marie, this is my husband, Lord Archie."

Marie blinked, stood up, and bobbed a small curtsey, her small face flushed. "Good evening, my lord," and stared at the tall, handsome man who was smiling down at her.

"Good evening to you, Marie, and please do sit down. It is lovely to hear my wife laugh and, I think that has something to do with you. You are taking very good care of her I can see, and you have even managed to unseat our Dottie."

The little nurse, visibly relaxed by his easy manner and gentle voice, at once became efficient. "I'll just check your temperature and pulse, madam, and then you should rest before the doctor comes back."

After straightening the bed covers and plumping up the pillows, she gave Lord Archie a shy smile and bustled off down the ward.

"Oh, my darling," Lady Rose laughed, "Another smitten female."

"Now, enough of that, Rose. What has the doctor said?" and he sat in the chair by the bed.

"My orders are that I am to stay resting for today, and if I have a good night's sleep, and I am not coughing, I can get up for breakfast tomorrow." Before he could reply, she carried on. "I shall dine very well here tonight. Dottie is determined to stay with me, and little Marie is on duty all night, so you see I shall be perfectly all right."

Despite her husband pleading to be allowed to stay and have dinner with her, she firmly refused. "It is a very special night, my darling, and you must dine with the family. Then you may come back and tell me all about it, only of course if the doctor allows," she teased.

Lord Archie looked crestfallen. "I will do as you say, I promise, and I will come back after dinner to say good night, whether the doctor allows or not." and he kissed her tenderly once more.

There was an air of barely concealed excitement among the first-class passengers gathered in the B Deck foyer. The air was filled with laughter and wafting cigar smoke mingled with expensive perfume. He stood for a while, surveying the almost-perfect scene, beautiful women dressed in satin and silk with mink stoles carelessly flung across creamy shoulders. Under the many-faceted crystal chandeliers, priceless diamond rings, bangles, and necklaces glittered from elegant necks and slender arms. Their escorts, attentive, immaculate, and debonair completed the scene whilst in the background the string quartet played a selection from *The Mikado*.

Even among the glamour and the glitz of other guests, Lord Archie spotted his family at once and was filled with pride.

There was George, jolly and laughing loudly at something Henry, his tall and incredibly-handsome brother-in-law, was whispering in his ear.

Jenny, dear Jenny Wren, smooth and elegant in a tight-fitting emerald green silk gown, her cap of shining hair unadorned, apart from a diamond-studded band circling her forehead and looking far too young to be the mother of the strapping twin boys standing by her side. Walter and William, the irrepressible twins, looking so grown up as they listened patiently to what Jenny was saying to them.

Then there was Estelle, his precious daughter, the living image of her lovely mother, ethereal and sylph-like in a cloud of cream lace, her famous red curls loose and tumbling around her bare shoulders.

Almost as if sensing his presence, she turned and smiled her special smile. At the sight of her pale face, something caught at his heart. She was too thin, too fragile. Why hadn't he noticed before? He hurried across the room to her. The concern must have shown on his face because her smile faded, and she reached out and caught both his hands in hers.

"What's wrong? Is it Mama? Is she worse?" At the sound of her anxious tone, Jenny stopped teasing the twins, and Henry stopped whispering to George.

"No, Rose is absolutely fine and still well on the road to recovery I am told." Lord Archie's tone was hearty and reassuring, and the group relaxed as one. He turned to his grandsons. "Walter and William, I would not have recognised you, you both look very handsome." The twins, for once, were standing still, and they self-consciously both reached up to smooth down their rebellious tufty red hair.

"Now," said Lord Archie, "Let us go and sample which is reputed to be the finest of French Haute Cuisine."

Many heads turned to watch as Lord Archibald Grieves-Croft, proud and dignified, led his family through the crowded room. They watched, because even amongst the rich and famous first-class passengers, there was a close unity, an air of cool elegance, confidence, and glamour surrounding the Grieves-Croft family that drew lingering glances from the other passengers.

The "A La Carte" restaurant on the Titanic was the very last word in luxury, and whilst Lord Archie and George had seen the plans and sketches for this exclusive dining area at the Harland and Wolfe offices, nothing could have prepared them for the sheer beauty and elegance of the room.

George gave a low whistle and ran his hands appreciatively over the exquisitely carved French walnut panelling. Stylish oval mirrors had been placed within the panels imitating windows, and the seating bays were separated by tall, fluted columns. Rose du Barry Axminster carpeting covered the floor, and the walnut chairs were upholstered in rose-patterned Aubusson Tapestry.

As the family entered the restaurant, a waiter stepped forward and introduced himself as their waiter for the evening, and then guided them toward a reserved bay halfway along the softly-lit room. The dove-grey table was decorated with crystal vases of dusky pink roses and white daisies. The seating places were beautifully laid out with heavy solid silver cutlery and gilt-and-cobalt-blue Spode place settings.

Once everyone was seated in their luxuriously upholstered chairs, the waiter, with great aplomb and a flourish, handed each one a menu, beautifully handwritten in copperplate.

Lord Archie, happier now than he had been for several days, ordered his favourite wine, Heidsieck and Co Monopole champagne. The family studied the menu and discussed it in detail. The choice was exotic and included clear, green turtle soup, Russian caviar, whole pink lobsters served with Béchamel sauce, a lime sorbet to freshen the mouth, followed by spiced quail from Egypt. The desserts were simple, tender, blush peaches, sweet hot-house grapes, and to finish, a selection of the finest cheeses served with an aged port and sweet liquors for the ladies.

Time and time again, the pure-cut glass champagne flutes were filled with the bubbling golden wine and raised to toast each other, the Ship of Dreams, and to the absent Lady Rose. The mood around the table was relaxed, and the general air of informality, combined with gentle music from the trio of violinists seemed to ease away the tension that had hovered over them for the last few days.

Lord Archie looked around him with a dart of sorrow that his beautiful wife was not sitting by him, and he made a silent vow, that when they reached New York, he would take Rose to De Beers and buy her a diamond ring to celebrate their anniversary.

Henry was sweet and attentive to Estelle, who blossomed under his attention; the twins were quiet and well behaved, but secretly sharing a pact to slip away as soon as possible after dinner. Their new Irish friends in steerage were planning a riotous last night party and had invited the twins to join them. Walter and William had no intention of missing it, as there was always the chance of enjoying an illicit beer or two.

George and Jenny exchanged knowing looks, having discussed and guessed the reason for the twin's unusually suppressed demeanour.

At nine-thirty, George and Jenny excused themselves, saying that they were going for a stroll on the deck, and after much pleading, William and Walter were given permission to say goodbye to their Irish friends on the condition that they would be back in their cabin by eleven-thirty.

Estelle agreed with Jenny and George that she, too, would like some fresh air, but when invited to join them, Henry shuddered. "Far too cold for me out there, darling. With your permission, my sweet, I think I will pop along for one more game of cards."

Lord Archie raised his eyebrows. "Henry, watch out for the boat men, remember what Gerry said. They are seasoned gamblers, and this is their last night to make money by fair means or foul."

Henry's good humour seemed to dissipate in the face of his father-in-law's rebuke, and he scowled as he strode away.

Lord Archie put his arm around his daughter's thin shoulders and gave her a warm hug, and Estelle looked up at her father in resignation. "You will never change Henry, Pa," and smiled to reassure him, but her glow had disappeared. Before her father could reply, Polly appeared suddenly by their side, flushed and a little out of breath.

"Polly, how pretty you look. Have you had a nice evening with your Joe?"

Estelle teased her gently and Polly blushed, "Not a whole evening, madam, just the last hour, because Joe has to go back on duty now, and he was telling me how fast we are going and all about the icebergs we might see."

"What's all this about icebergs, Polly?" Lord Archie tried to moderate his voice, but he felt a flash of alarm.

"Did I tell you that our Polly has an admirer, Pa? Gerry's nephew Joe is a junior officer in the purser's office, and he has taken a liking to Polly. Why do you ask about the icebergs?"

"Nothing, Estelle, really, but another passenger on deck mentioned icebergs that is all. But, if you are going for a stroll on deck you should wrap up, it is freezing outside."

"Polly, would you fetch my grey fur from the cabin?"

Of course, madam," Polly looked at Jenny. "Should I fetch a wrap for you too, madam?"

Jenny nodded "If you would, dear Polly, we will wait here for you."

Lord Archie frowned. "Where is your maid, Jenny, Belle wasn't it? I cannot recall seeing her at all since we left Ireland."

George, who was standing with his arm around his wife, raised his eyes to heaven. "Nor has anyone else, Pa. It turns out that the girl is petrified of the water, and whilst she helps Jenny in the cabin, she won't go anywhere where she can see the sea."

Lord Archie snorted, "Then why on earth did you bring the silly creature?

Jenny smiled her sweet smile and tucked her arm through his. "Because, darling Pa, her brother works on the docks in New York, and she hasn't seen him for five years, and it's the only family she has. I knew she was nervous, but the poor thing is beside herself with fear."

"Then I suggest that she stays in New York with her brother and does not undertake the return trip." Lord Archie sounded exasperated. "Ridiculous child. Wait until I tell Rose."

"Oh, Ma knows about Belle. She thinks it is awfully funny," replied Jenny serenely and smothered a giggle.

Lord Archie shook his head and walked away, calling out as he went. "I'm going to sit with your mother for a while. Pop along and see her before you go to bed, and don't stay too long outside."

On his walk back to the infirmary, the question of the icebergs was still going around in his head, and remembering where Polly had gained her information, he decided to make a detour to the pursers office on C Deck. Despite the relatively late hour, the Grand Staircase was still milling with passengers on their way to their cabins, or simply enjoying the last night on board. The reception area in the pursers office, for once, was most nearly empty, just a few passengers sending last minute messages. Lord Archie spotted Gerry, their steward, sitting at one of the writing desks talking quietly with a young officer with an enormous handlebar moustache and another passenger.

Gerry sprung to his feet as soon as he saw Lord Archie approaching. "Good evening, my Lord. May I help you? I am off duty, but is there is anything I can assist with?"

"Thank you, Gerry; I was going to have a word with the purser."

The young officer stood up, "I am on duty here, sir. May I help you?"

Lord Archie guessed at once that this was Polly's Joe, and Gerry's nephew, and he waved them to sit down again.

The third man at the table spoke. "Good evening, Lord Grieves-Croft, my name is Price, and I am employed with Harland and Wolff as an engineer. Of course, you may not remember me, but I was at several of the launch meetings, and I do remember seeing you there."

Lord Archie recalled that some of the Harland and Wolff engineers were to be assigned to the Titanic's maiden voyage to assess the performance of the ship, keep a log, and report back on their return to the Belfast Office.

He leant forward and held out his hand. "Good evening, Price. It is good to meet you." The three men looked at him expectedly.

"A question, if I may. I have heard several titbits of information about icebergs in the vicinity, and that we expect to arrive in New York ahead of time. I have almost my entire family on board with me, and honestly, I am a little concerned."

Price cleared his throat and said with a degree of pride, "Well, sir, we may well arrive ahead of time, travelling at nearly 23 knots, and Titanic is performing superbly. Since noon yesterday, we have covered five hundred and forty-six miles, and I have heard many passengers comment on how smoothly Titanic travels."

"So, you are not concerned about icebergs?" Lord Archie pressed him.

"Not a bit, sir," the man responded promptly, but Lord Archie thought he saw a flicker of concern pass between Gerry and Joe.

"We were just talking about the very same thing," Gerry confessed.

Price spoke up again. "I assure you, as I have just assured these gentlemen, Lord Grieves-Croft, there is nothing to concern yourself with."

There was an awkward silence.

"Thank you, Price. Please do not get up, gentlemen," Lord Archie walked slowly away and could tell that Price had him marked as an interfering old fusspot.

By ten-thirty, Jenny, George, and Estelle had abandoned their walk, leaving a few hardy souls on deck enjoying the exceptionally lovely night. There was no wind, the sea was flat calm, and the stars shone brightly from a clear night sky, but the temperature had dropped below freezing, and Jenny complained that it was too cold. They had arranged to meet Henry in the lounge for coffee and brandy, but when they arrived, they found only Lord Archie waiting for them nursing a large whisky.

"Golly, it's freezing out there. That whisky looks good. What are you doing here, Pa? I thought you were sitting with Ma," said Estelle sitting down and snuggling up to him.

Her father put his arm around her. "So, I was darling, but when I got to the infirmary, the nurse said she had been asleep for a few hours, and I could hear Dottie snoring in the next bed. The nurse said that we can collect your mother after breakfast tomorrow, and it wasn't worth disturbing her tonight, so here I am. Where are twins and Henry? I thought Henry was meeting us here?"

"The boys will be still with their chums, and Henry is in the smoking room. I looked in after our walk, and he promises that he will be joining us soon," Estelle's tone was defensive.

"Then I am sure he will my dear, but if you will excuse me now, I am off to my bed." Giving her a warm hug, Lord Archie bade everyone goodnight and left. But he was restless and unable to sleep and was tossing and turning fully-clothed on his bed when he felt a long judder that seemed to reverberate throughout the ship. A few moments later, the engines stopped, and after four days of hearing the steady thrum of the engines, it was eerily quiet, and he felt a chill run down his spine.

There was a creak as one of the wardrobe doors swung open. He started, then sat up and found himself staring at three lifejackets stacked neatly in a pile at the bottom of the wardrobe. He waited. There was nothing; no sound, just the ticking of the clock on the bedside table, but he was uneasy, and swinging his legs off the bed, he padded shoeless across the floor and opened the cabin door. He walked out and looked up and down the corridor, but it was deserted, no sign of activity or of anything amiss. He hesitated in the doorway, uncertain what to do, and then he saw the familiar figure of Gerry and the young purser hurrying down the corridor toward him.

"Ah, I was hoping to find you in here, Lord Archie. May I ask the whereabouts of the rest of the family? Are they in their cabins?" Gerry's voice was level, but Lord Archie sensed that the steward was exercising every ounce of control to keep calm, and he knew with awful certainty that something was seriously wrong.

"Tell me. What exactly has happened? Why have the engines stopped?" he commanded.

The young purser spoke. "It appears that we have hit an iceberg, Lord Archibald, and some of the compartments have been breached. Price said that the carpenter has been sent to do the soundings."

"Hell and Damnation," the curse was uttered under his breath, but Gerry heard it and repeated his question.

"Please, Lord Archibald. Where are the rest of the family, sir? We are not sure what the damage is but, Joe here thinks you should all go up to the Boat Deck with your lifejackets just as a precaution."

"Wait for me," Lord Archie strode back into the cabin, put his shoes on, and reached inside the wardrobe for the three lifejackets. "Gerry, take these for me, please," and as an afterthought, pulled two fur coats from their hangers. As he did so, he caught the evocative woody aroma of his wife's favourite perfume, and his stomach twisted in fear.

"Take a warm coat for yourself, sir," Gerry urged and reached inside the wardrobe for Lord Archie's Norfolk. "Now we need to collect the family together."

"I am not certain where the rest of the family are, but my wife and her maid are in the infirmary. I suspect that Henry is still in the smoking room; my daughter Estelle should be in her cabin, and so should George and Jenny. The twins were instructed to be in their cabins by now, and Polly, my daughter's maid, is in her cabin, and Belle, Jenny's maid is in her cabin."

Joe nodded, and his voice was firm and calm. "Sir, if you collect your wife and her maid from the infirmary, I will check the cabins, and Gerry will go up and collect Mr Henry. There will be spare life jackets in the smoking room. Wait on the starboard side of the Boat Deck for me."

Jenny, having sent George to locate William and Walter, was reading and dozing in the armchair when she felt the shudder. She sat bolt upright and put the book down on the table, sensing immediately that something was wrong. She was halfway across the cabin when Joe knocked on the cabin door. He was standing outside with an alarmed-looking Polly, who was wearing her lifejacket over her dressing gown but had managed to push her feet into her shoes.

George was on his way down several flights of stairs to F Deck, the third-class dining salon where the twins had said the party was to be held, and the sudden jarring stopped him and several other passengers in their tracks. When he reached C Deck, a junior officer was standing at the bottom of the stairs encouraging the passengers to return to their cabins and collect their life jackets.

"There is absolutely nothing to worry about, ladies and gentlemen," he assured them. "But please collect your life jackets and muster on the Boat Deck."

George confronted the man blocking his path. "What is happening? My sons are in the dining room on F deck, officer, and I am going to collect them."

The officer hesitated. "As I said, sir, I am sure there is nothing to concern yourself with, but collect your sons and ensure that all of you have your life jackets and make your way to the Boat Deck as quickly as you can." The man, despite his assurances, was clearly nervous.

"Did we hit something? Are we in any danger?"

But the young officer avoided meeting George's eye. George pushed past him impatiently and hurried on down the stairs, his heart pounding and his mouth dry with fear.

Lady Rose and Dottie, fast asleep in the infirmary, did not feel the impact but were woken gently by the doctor.

"Please ladies, we must go up on deck. Nurse will assist you."

"Why, what has happened?"

Lady Rose was instantly awake and sat up to see her husband striding along the ward with two fur coats over one arm and carrying three lifejackets in the other hand. The doctor greeted him warmly.

"Thank goodness you are here, Lord Archie. We have been instructed to go up to the Boat Deck. I have no idea what has happened."

"We have hit an iceberg," Lord Archie replied grimly.

Dottie was already helping Lady Rose to get dressed, whilst the nurse hurried along to wake the only other patient, a child from steerage with a hacking cough.

"Please remember, Lady Rose, take things very slowly. You may still be weak from the fever," the doctor instructed.

Lord Archie nodded. "Take care of the child, Doctor. I will take good care of my wife, never fear, and thank you. Now sit down, my dear, and I will slip the lifejacket over your head."

"Is this really necessary, Archie? Are you sure that you are not fussing too much? You know you do sometimes."

"I hope that I am wrong this time, my dear, I really do," and his voice was grim.

Dottie, already attired in her lifejacket, took her mistress's arm gently. "Come along, my lady, I have my lifejacket on and very comfortable it is too. Now, if you would just lean on me, madam, we can go up on deck and see what all this fuss is about."

Lord Archie shot a grateful look to the sturdy, calm maid. The doctor held the sick child in his arms, and the nurse followed behind with their lifejackets and several blankets, and together, the five made their way slowly up to the Boat Deck.

Estelle, tired and irritated, was on her way to the smoking room on A Deck to locate Henry, who had very clearly lost track of time. Two stewards were lounging by the smoking room, idly chatting, and they hastily straightened up as Estelle approached. Estelle stood in the doorway and gazed around the room. She spotted Henry in an alcove close to the fireplace.

"May I help you, madam?" One of the stewards asked politely, but before she could reply, a sudden jarring seemed to shake the ship, and she put a hand out to steady herself.

The steward who had spoken to her turned to his companion in alarm. "What the hell was that?" The older man frowned. "No idea. Go and find out," he ordered and then to Estelle, "Are you looking for someone, madam?"

"I seem to have found him," replied Estelle shortly and pointed to the table in the alcove.

Henry and two other men were seated around a table with green baize top and brass slide rails. The first, a large, bald man, was gripping his cards tightly in one hand whilst in the other, he was wiping his forehead with a large handkerchief. He was sweating profusely, but his eyes never left the splayed cards in his hand. Henry was no less relaxed; he was hunched over the table, his card-hand held tightly against his chest. The third man, in complete contrast, was completely relaxed, leaning back in his chair, his bowler hat tipped jauntily over one eye. Smoke from the thin, black cheroot he held loosely between his lips drifted up into the air, and he was smiling as he watched his companions through narrowed eyes.

"Ah, Mr Henry," said the steward. "Yes, I see, madam. If you would like to follow me to the Verandah area, I will let your husband know that you are here," and he led her through a revolving door and seated her in a comfortable chair overlooking the Promenade Deck. "May I fetch you a drink?" he enquired.

Estelle shook her head. "No, thank you. Could you please just let my husband know that I am here?" and then she hesitated and listened. "Why have the engines stopped?" she asked curiously.

"I am sure it is nothing to worry about, something routine, I expect. I will go and inform your husband that you are waiting," and he hurried away.

When the steward failed to return after five minutes, Estelle, cold and exasperated, ventured back through the door and spotted not only the steward who had spoken to her, but Gerry speaking earnestly to the three men. Angry now, she strode across to the table.

"What is going on? Did the steward not tell you that I have been waiting for you, Henry?"

Henry was flushed and clearly furious. He ignored Estelle and addressed Gerry through gritted teeth. "How dare you interrupt my game with some cock-and-bull story about an iceberg? I suppose my wife or her father put you up to this."

Gerry remained calm as Estelle looked at her husband in astonishment. "Gentlemen, this is not a practice. We have hit an iceberg, and the orders are to collect your life jackets and assemble on the Boat Deck."

Then he stared hard at the lounging man who was openly grinning. "Murphy," he said. "I didn't know you were on board, you managed to avoid me, I see. Mr Henry, please leave this game. Mr Murphy here is a boatman, a professional gambler who will allow you to win until the last night of the voyage and then he takes it all back and much more."

There was an inward gasp of breath from the fat man who stood up, puce-faced. He flung his cards on the table, snatched his jacket from the back of the chair and, stormed out.

"Ah now, Gerry, at least give Henry here a chance to win his money back." Murphy's voice had a musical Southern-Ireland-lilt, and he spoke without removing the cheroot from his lips.

Gerry shook his head. "Be sensible man, did you not hear me? We have hit an iceberg, and it's serious. We must get down to the Boat Deck right now."

Henry, his anger fading, turned aside and took Estelle's arm. "Estelle, please, darling, I need to finish this game," he pleaded with a desperate look in his eyes.

"No, Henry, please, come with me," she begged with tears in her eyes.

Henry shook his head miserably. "I can't," he replied simply.

"Right," said Gerry, taking Estelle by the elbow. "Madam, I am going to take you down to Lord Archie, then I am going to fetch some life jackets and come back for these gentlemen."

There was no arguing with the little steward. She was held in an iron grip as he propelled her out of the room, and she flung a last desperate glance back at Henry, whose head had already turned back to the cards he was clutching in his hand.

When Joe, Jenny, and Polly arrived on the Boat deck, there were already large groups of people gathering. Some were fully clothed in heavy coats and furs, and others, who were in their night clothes, were clearly irritated.

There were mutterings of "waste of time, totally unnecessary."

Some watched in amusement as the crew began uncovering the lifeboats, arranging the oars, and coiling the ropes. Others, seeing nothing visibly amiss, and despite the urgings of the crew to stay on the deck, went back to the warmth of their cabins.

"Stay here. Stay close together," ordered Joe to Polly and Jenny, and positioned them next to a lifeboat. "Keep together by this lifeboat, and I will know where to find you. I am going to look for Lord Archie."

Polly looked around. "Where is Belle? I thought she was behind us." Polly had managed to persuade a near-hysterical Belle to don a warm coat and a life jacket.

"She must have run back to the cabin." Jenny said with exasperation and put her arm around Polly who was shivering. "Cuddle close to me; we can keep each other warm. Joe or Gerry will go back for Belle, but we must stay here until Joe comes back," and all the time she was scanning the crowd, anxiously looking for any signs of a familiar red-head. Ten minutes passed before they saw Joe shouldering his way through the drifting crowds, closely followed by Lord Archie and Lady Rose with Dottie close behind.

"If you stay here with the ladies, I am going to see what I can find out, sir," said a grim-faced Joe.

Lady Rose was clearly out of breath and, distressed, leant against her husband. "Archie, where are the rest? Where are Henry, Estelle, George and the twins, and where is little Belle?"

Lord Archie held her close, "Now then, don't fret my dear. Gerry has gone for Estelle and Henry, and George is fetching the twins. Joe will find Belle, I am sure."

They waited in tense silence as gradually the Boat Deck began to fill up, and then, thankfully, Gerry appeared followed by Estelle.

"Here we are, Sir Archie. Mr Henry is following on."

Estelle was white-faced but controlled. "Pa, thank goodness you are here." Estelle put her arm around her mother. "Dearest Ma, don't worry, the others will be here soon," and whispered to her father, "Is it true Pa? I just heard a crewman say that we are sinking. We cannot be sinking?" and there was desperation in her voice.

"Rubbish," said Lord Archie roundly. "but, you should put your lifejackets on anyway, my dear, and it will save carrying them around."

The lifejackets, cork panels covered in white canvas and tied with ribbons at the side, were light, but cumbersome, and Estelle, Jenny, and Polly all stood nervously as Gerry helped to settle the lifejackets over their heads and tie the ribbons.

"Gerry, please go and hurry Henry up, will you?" Estelle was anguished.

"No, Estelle. Henry will be along very soon, I am sure." said her father firmly. "We should all stay here until Joe comes back to tell us what is happening. Look, here he is now."

Joe came hurrying towards them and took both men to one side. "Six compartments gone, the soundings are back, and Orlop is flooded," he said in a low voice. "They have sent out a CQD to all vessels. We need to get the ladies into a lifeboat immediately."

Lord Archie looked out at the cold, black sea and then up at the brilliantly beautiful starlit night and felt a moment of sheer terror. "Worse than I thought then, gentlemen," he said steadily.

"If that's the case, then I estimate that we have two hours at the most."

Jenny, standing close by, overheard, gasped, and grabbed Lord Archie's arm. "I am sorry, Pa, but I can't wait any longer, I must find George and the boys, and Belle has run back to her cabin."

"I will go with you, madam," Gerry said instantly and added, "Joe, stay with the family until I come back." Then he was gone, pushing his way through the crowds as Jenny dodged people as she went racing ahead of him.

Estelle pulled Polly to one side. "Polly, I have to find Henry. I should have made him come with me. He does not have a lifejacket, and Gerry said he would go back with one, and now he has gone with Jenny. Should anything happen to me, you must take care of my boys and Sadie. You must do anything to save yourself and get back to them. Promise me that, Polly, and always remember our secret. Have you your notebook with my messages to James?"

Polly nodded, her teeth chattering with cold. "I have the notebook here, madam, tucked inside my lifejacket. I will take care of the children, I swear, but please don't go, madam, just wait here for Mr Henry."

Estelle shook her head, and her voice was desperate. "I must go back for him, Polly. He will be waiting. Now, take this and do exactly as Joe tells you." She shrugged the soft grey fur coat from her shoulders and wrapped it around Polly, who was shivering violently. Polly grabbed at the fur as it almost slid down on to the deck. "Madam, please don't go. You must stay with us," she pleaded frantically, turning to Joe, who was shifting from foot to foot, anxiously scanning the crowded deck. "Joe, please go and find Mr Henry. Please stop her," she begged.

But in that split-second, Estelle was gone, weaving her way through the clamour of the rapidly-filling Boat Deck and ignoring Joe and Lord Archie's frantic cries for her to come back.

"Miss Estelle has gone to find Mr Henry, sir, I begged her not to," Polly sobbed, clutching tightly onto the fur coat.

"Damn and blast that man," Lord Archie swore vehemently, lifting his eyes to heaven. "But we must stay together, Polly, otherwise, the others will not be able to find us, and we will all be lost."

By twelve twenty-five, there was still no sign of Henry, Estelle, George, Jenny, the twins or Belle, and Lady Rose was weeping silently against her husband's chest.

"Don't worry, my dear," Lord Archibald fought to keep his voice steady. "Just you see, they will be here soon, I promise."

Joe could wait no longer, and he touched Lord Archie's arm. "I must go and see what is happening, sir. Please stay here, and I beg of you, do not move."

Lord Archie nodded. "Of course, but be quick, man."

Less than a minute later, Joe appeared, pushing the crowds to one side and calling "Lord Archie, we are ordered to get the women and children on the lifeboats straight away."

Then suddenly, the cry went up, and the ships officers were striding up and down the decks shouting, "Women and children first, please! Woman and children by the lifeboats please. Quick as you can now, please, the crew are there to help you."

There was a clamour of voices, confusion mingled with fright and nervous laughter. Then above the noise and chaos, came a deafening boom and a shrieking hiss of steam escaping through the tall funnels, and all the while the orchestra, positioned together on the deck, determinedly played a medley of cheerful ragtime tunes.

Lord Archie stiffened as he sensed a slight list to portside, and he adjusted his feet and held tightly onto to his trembling wife. With a jerk of his head, he motioned to Joe. "We are going down, Joe. Quickly give me a hand to get the ladies into the lifeboats."

Suddenly, there was a loud whoosh, and a rocket shot upwards into the clear, starry, night sky. Watched by a sea of upturned faces, the rocket shot higher and higher until it exploded into a brilliant white arc sending showers of sparks into black sea. There was a collective gasp from the passengers and cheers from the children but there could be little doubt now that this was a clear distress signal and a desperate call for help. The grim reality that Titanic was indeed sinking suddenly dawned on the confused passengers milling around the deck. There were sudden frantic and panicked calls for missing friends and relatives and a rush to don carelessly held lifejackets. Men began urging their wives forward, thrusting children and babies in their arms, pressing and begging them to get into the lifeboats. Some passengers, still in night clothes went racing back to their cabins for their money and jewellery pushing aside stewards pleading with them to stay on the Boat Deck

Teams of crewmen were frantically turning the cranks, and the lifeboats swung out, hanging clear above the icy, dark water far below. Slowly and disbelievingly, groups of woman and children began to gather together by the ship's rails, urged on by the pleading ships officers, and their menfolk.

Lady Rose, clinging to her husband, watched in terrified silence as the men pushed and carried their protesting wives and sobbing children into the lifeboats, tucking them in tenderly with blankets and coats, and promising, "We will follow on. We promise we will be in the next boat, you will see." And to the children, "Be brave, be strong soldiers, help Mummy. Daddy needs to stay and help, and then we will follow you."

Here and there came a plaintive plea from a desperate woman. "I want to stay with you. Don't make me leave you, dearest, please."

But when Lady Rose spoke to her husband, her voice was strong. "Before you ask, my darling Archie, I am sorry, but I am not leaving without you or the children. But please, Dottie and Polly must go now," and she remained resolute and upright against Lord Archie's desperate pleadings. He begged her. "Rosie, dearest, please, I implore you, you are still unwell, it will be better if you go now. I can search for them easier on my own. Joe will help me. I will make sure the children are safe, and we will be on the next boat, my darling, I promise."

"No, Archie, I will not go. The children will be here soon, Gerry will find them. We just have to wait for them, and then we can all go together." Her voice, although desperate, was firm.

Joe reappeared at Polly's side. "Right my Lord, the ladies can board now if they would like to follow me."

Lord Archie shook his head with resignation. "Lady Rose will stay with me until the others get back, Joe, but we think Polly and Dottie should go with you now."

Dottie stepped closer to her master and mistress and shook her head firmly. "I won't go without Lady Rose, so it's no good asking," and she clung on tightly to Lady Rose.

Polly closed her eyes, and Estelle's pleading face swam in front of her eyes, and she turned to Lord Archie and Lady Rose.

"I have to go. I made a promise to my mistress, and I won't break it. I have to get home, you see, for the children, James and Sadie and Rupert. I promised, you see," she repeated.

Lord Archie was too distracted to listen clearly to what Polly was saying, but Lady Rose reached out and pulled Polly into her arms.

"I know you do, Polly, and nobody could have been a better friend to Estelle, watch over our boys and Sadie as best you can." she whispered, the tears once again rolling down her stricken face. "This is such a burden for you to carry alone, my dear. I am so very sorry."

Polly hugged her close. "I will take care of the children, Lady Rose."

Pulling away, she wrapped Estelle's fur coat around her tightly. "I'm ready, Joe," she said simply, and not trusting himself to say a word, Joe handed Polly tenderly over to the waiting crewmen.

Looking straight ahead, Polly took her place in the lifeboat, never turning her head as, little by little, the lifeboats, like tiny toys against the great hull of the giant ship, were lowered down into the icy-black water of the Atlantic far below. Not once did Polly dare look back at the stricken Ship of Dreams, but resolutely closed her eyes and ears to the screams and sobs of the people floundering and drowning in the icy water, remembering only her promise to her beloved mistress.

Inch by inch, the lifeboat pulled away from the floundering ship, and Polly became aware of another sound close by, the sound of a child sobbing and a mother's low, consoling voice. Seated next to her, a young woman wrapped in a thin blanket was cuddling a flaxen-haired girl of about six years old. The child was in her nightclothes, and her tiny feet were blue with cold. The mother was pulling the blanket tighter around the little girl whilst trying to tuck her feet inside.

"Here, please take this coat," Polly urged, slipping the soft fur across the mother's shoulders. "I don't need it, and it will keep your little girl warm."

The woman did not argue but turned desperate, tear-filled eyes to Polly, "Thank you. Thank you. We only had time to grab a blanket; my husband just wanted us to get away quickly."

Polly pulled the fur coat closer round the distraught mother, and after a while, both child and mother slept, huddled close together, exhausted whilst the sailors rowed desperately through the cruel black sea.

APRIL 1912 RIVERSIDE

Long after the carriages bearing the Titanic voyagers had disappeared through the gates of Riverside, James Maycroft stood staring bleakly out of his bedroom window. It was a dreary morning, cool and showery, and he wished with all his heart that it was time to return to Eton, but the summer term did not start again until mid-April. In between, there was Easter without Estelle and Polly. He hoped that when he went back to college, he would not feel the unbearable emptiness that he was feeling now. Being back at college would make the time pass quickly until they returned.

Unlike Barrow Hill, where there were eight boys to a dormitory, at Eton, James had his own room with a folding bed, a tiny fireplace, a bathtub, and desk. The fellows in his House, The Trimbralls, were a lively bunch. Each House had their own debating society, cricket and football teams, and House Fours on the river. The food was decent, and a fellow was left to do as he wished in his free time without being ragged for cramming or joining a debating team. There was a knock on his bedroom door.

"James," said Bernard. "May I come in?"

"Of course, Uncle."

Bernard walked across to the window and placed his hand on

James's shoulder. "James, you know if you change your mind about going with the family, you can meet up with them at Cherbourg. I am sure Henry has kept your ticket."

James shook his head slowly. "No thanks, Uncle. I haven't changed my mind about the voyage, but it will be rather lonely here without Mother and Polly."

Bernard tactfully ignored the fact that James had not mentioned Henry. "Come downstairs with me, James. There is something I want to discuss with you. You ate hardly anything at breakfast, and Aggie will not stop fussing at me. There's a decent fire in the library, and we can eat in there."

James smiled reluctantly, "At least I still have Aggie to nag me until Polly and Ma come home."

A pot of tea and a plate of fresh toast with game pate were waiting for them in the library, and once James had been cajoled into eating, Bernard set out his plan.

"Now, let me see," said Bernard, consulting the notes that Estelle had prepared for him. "Term begins on 15th, but you have to be back in your House by Friday 12th? Anyway, that's what your mother has written down here."

James nodded, mystified. "Yes. That's right, back at House before lock up."

"It is Easter weekend next week, and I don't suppose it will be much fun here at Riverside. So. I thought, if you like, we could go down and spend the time with young Sadie and Rupert. They will be feeling a little lonely as well I expect. I could send a note to the Brents to prepare for us?" Bernard waited expectedly.

"You know, Uncle, I think that's a splendid idea." James said slowly. "I mean, we could pack my trunk ready for Eton and take it with us, and I can go straight from Grieves Manor. Yes, a perfectly splendid idea. If you're sure you can spare the time, I mean."

"Of course, I can spare the time. I would like to see Sadie and Rupert again. Cedric and William can take care of things here, and I always enjoy a trip to Berkshire."

Without further delay, Bernard dispatched Tip to the village post office to ask Grace Peabody to send a telegram telling Brent to expect them and confirmed the train time. Mrs Brent responded very quickly, stating that everyone was looking forward to the visit, especially Sadie, and that everything would be ready for Bernard and James arrival.

The weather was still unsettled and a little drizzly when they arrived, but that did nothing to dampen the rapturous welcome that awaited them on their arrival. Sadie and Rupert were waiting for then in front of the house, Sadie holding tightly onto Rupert's hand as he bounced up and down waving frantically as the car approached.

Rupert adored James, and whilst he loved Sadie, she was not very good at football. Neither could she find very good hiding places, and James always found the most amazing places to hide in. Rupert was nervous of his other cousins, the loud, red-headed twins. They were seldom home, but when they were home, they largely ignored him or teased him until he cried and Sadie came to rescue him.

The spring nights were still chilly, but the early April days were glorious and sunny, and the next day after breakfast, the threesome headed off down to the lake, taking lunch in a picnic basket.

Bernard settled himself contentedly on the covered veranda at the back of the house, perfectly happy with his paper and his pipe.

From the veranda, he could hear their happy voices and shouts of laughter. Now and again, he glimpsed Estelle's old swing flying high in the branches of the giant oak by the lake. After lunch, Mary Ryan joined Bernard on the veranda. She took her knitting out of her bag and sat down with a sigh.

"A little peace and quiet, Bernard," she said. "It is so good to have James home again for a while. What a treat to have you all here for Easter. Sadie has been very quiet since the family left; it is so lovely to hear her laughing. She adores Rupert, of course, and she is very good with him, but she misses the twins so much."

Bernard was curious, "What about Rupert's parents, Mary? Are they still in India? He is such a lovely little chap and so like James in many ways. His parents have missed so much of his young life. How old is he now"?

"Master Rupert will be four this summer, and the family have a big party planned for him. We are keeping it a secret because Miss Estelle has promised to bring him something special back from New York." She looked up from her knitting and stared out across the immaculate lawns, a frown on her face. "Do you know, Bernard, I have never seen his parents. The year that Rupert was born, Miss Estelle and Polly stayed with them all summer. Then, when the baby was born, Miss Estelle brought him straight back to Grieves Manor saying that her cousin was too delicate to look after a baby. I do wonder sometimes if they will ever come back for him. I worry, because it will break Sadie's heart if they take Rupert away."

"And Sadie," prompted Bernard. "She is quite the young lady now. What does she do when she is not helping with Rupert?"

"She is a real pet, that one," said Mary fondly, her round face creased in smiles. "Sadie helps around the house and does a few afternoons in the village nursery reading with the little children. But of course, she is quite delicate, so we must watch out that she does not tire herself too much."

"And what of you, Mary? How did you come to the family?"

"Oh, I looked after my mother after my father died. They had me rather late in life, you see. Nanny Florrie was my mother's friend, and when my mother died, Nanny Florrie found me a post at Grieves Manor with her."

"Young Mrs Grieves-Croft had just had the twins, and they were looking for a nanny, and here I am even though the twins are almost grown. But now, of course, we have Master Rupert, and I am very happy to stay with the family."

"The family are very lucky to have you, Mary."

Mary Ryan blushed. "How about you, Bernard? You have never married?"

"No." Bernard shook his head. "I never had the time to find a wife. Running the mill and the estate takes all of my time, although of course I would have liked to marry, but I am a little too set in my ways now."

They sat together in companionable silence, and soon the afternoon sun and the steady click of Mary's knitting needles sent Bernard into a light doze, still pondering on the mystery surrounding Rupert's absent parents. When Mary looked at him, he was fast asleep, gently snoring.

At breakfast on Easter Saturday, Sadie laid out their plans for the day. "After breakfast, we should go through the woods and pick some pretty flowers to weave through the Easter baskets before we put the eggs in."

James looked a little put out and chewed his toast thoughtfully. He pulled a face at Bernard who was hiding a smile.

"Sadie, actually that's a bit sissy for me, collecting wildflowers. I'll do something else."

Rupert looked up quickly. "And me, Sadie, same as James. I want to go with James," he said, frowning.

James grinned at the rebellious, small face next to him. "It's not sissy for you, Rupert. You should go with Sadie, and it will be fun to pick the flowers."

Rupert dropped his head, and Sadie could tell from the trembling of his bottom lip that Rupert was about to go into a full-blown rebellion.

"I have an idea, Rupert." she said quickly. "You come with me this morning and collect the flowers, and James can go and collect the eggs for painting. Then this afternoon, after Cook has boiled the eggs, we can paint pretty patterns on them and put them in our baskets."

Rupert thought about this for a while, and his sunny nature prevailed. He gave Sadie a tearful smile. "And James will help me to paint the eggs?"

"That's exactly right, Rupert, so we three have a very important job," said James approvingly, and Rupert's face broke into a wide smile

The storm had been averted, and after breakfast, Rupert trotted off quite happily with his basket in one hand and holding Sadie's hand with the other. After tea, when the dyed and painted eggs had been placed carefully in the flower baskets, Manners drove them to the village school, where the parents and teachers were waiting to hide them, ready for the children to find the next day. It was a happy and excited small boy who went to bed very late that night, not even staying awake for one of Sadie's stories.

But when, on the Thursday evening before James's departure, Rupert spotted James's school trunk standing packed and ready in the hall, his face crumbled, and he knew that James was leaving. He refused his tea and clung to Sadie, and not even his beloved Nanny Ryan could comfort him.

James went up to the nursery to say goodbye, and he stood outside listening to the little boy's heart-wrenching sobs. He opened the nursery door and peered in. Rupert was curled in a tight ball on his bed, and Sadie was stroking his rigid little back. Nanny Ryan was standing by the bed with Rupert's pyjamas in her hand.

James walked across to the bed and sat down. "Rupert, what's all this fuss about? Be a good boy and put your pyjamas on for Nanny," he said gently.

Rupert raised a scarlet, tear-soaked face, shook his head, and hiccupped. "I don't want you to go back to school, James, and I want my mumma."

James had long ago accepted that Rupert thought that Estelle was his mummy too, and it bothered him not at all. He loved the little boy and moved closer and drew him into his arms.

"I need you to do something very special and grown-up for me, Rupert," he said as he held the hot, shaking little body close. "While I am away at school, I need you to take great care of Bear until I come home. Can you do that for me?" From behind his back, James produced the scruffy little teddy bear with his crooked eye, James's precious Bear, and Rupert nodded, hardly daring to breathe.

"You see, Bear is rather old, and he needs lots of cuddles, especially at night."

"Like me, James? Is Bear just like me? I like cuddles too," Rupert was breathless with wonder.

"Bear is just like you, Rupert, and if you get scared in the night, Bear can blow bad dreams right out of the window, and if ever you are sick, he sits with you until you feel better."

Rupert sat up and sniffed loudly and held out his arms. "Hello,

Bear, I'm Rupert," he said tenderly. "I am going to take care of you until James comes home."

"That's better, Rupert. Now put your pyjamas on for Nanny. Sadie knows a super story about a teddy bear, and don't forget, I will be back at half-term, but until then Sadie will help you to write and tell me all about your adventures with Bear. When Mumma comes home, she will be so proud of you and how grown-up you have been."

The following morning, whilst Sadie and Rupert were in the school room at the top of the house, Bernard tried to persuade James to let Manners drive him back to Eton, but James refused.

"No thank you, Uncle. I have already arranged to meet some chums in South Ascot at midday. It's only about an hour on the train to Windsor and Eton Riverside, and then it's just a walk across the bridge. Our trunks will get sent on. But if Manners could drop me off at South Ascot, that would be useful. Come along with us if you wish?"

"Thank you, James, but I think that I will stay and enjoy the remainder of my stay at Grieves Manor, and then I shall make my way back to Shorehill on Monday."

Rupert was subdued for most of the following day, and Sadie did her best to amuse him, but he was fretful and fussy with his food. Mary Ryan laughed when Bernard expressed his concern about leaving. "Don't you worry about Rupert, Bernard. He played up the last time Master James went back to school; he'll get over it. The family will be back soon. You just enjoy the weekend."

"Thank you, Mary. You know, I didn't realise that the child was so attached to James."

Mary Ryan nodded, briskly folding towels and putting them in the linen cupboard. "They both adore James. Sadie writes to him every week and sends him little sketches of the family, and the dear boy always writes back with a special little note for Rupert."

As she was talking, Bernard began to see a side to his nephew that James never revealed when he was at Riverside. When Henry was at Riverside, James was contained, polite, and quiet in the house, and spent much of his holiday out on the river and in the fields with the boys in the village.

Bernard had no doubt in his mind that when Henry stayed at Riverside during James's holiday breaks, it was not a pleasurable time for James. Now, he had seen how happy James was with Rupert and Sadie, and he did not blame his nephew for preferring to spend his holidays at Grieves Manor.

Mary Ryan could not deny that Henry Maycroft was a handsome man, but she was not fooled by his outward charm. Neither Sadie nor Rupert were happy in Henry's company, and James was a different boy to the one she knew when his father was around. Mary found herself drawn to Henry's dignified and kindly older brother whom she had guessed to be in his early fifties, and it was obvious that James adored his uncle. When Bernard had arrived at Grieves Manor with James, he looked pale and strained, and it was clear to see that the family friction about James's refusal to take the Titanic voyage had taken its toll on Bernard.

Now, after just over a week, Bernard had colour in his face from his time in the garden, and it seemed to Mary that he was far more relaxed and cheerful. "Stay another day or so, Bernard. Surely that old mill can run without you for a while?"

Bernard shook his head and said ruefully. "I wish I could stay, Mary, but duty calls, and I should get back to Shorehill. But you must visit us some time with Rupert and Sadie. Shorehill by the river is rather lovely."

Manners drove Bernard to Windsor Station, arriving rather late due to a stubborn flock of sheep dithering around in the middle of the lane. The train was already on the platform when Bernard arrived, and there was no time to purchase his newspaper. He had barely settled in his seat when, with a great belch of steam, the train heaved out of the station. The first-class carriage was empty apart from a couple of men in suits and bowler hats. One man nodded a greeting and the other was totally engrossed in his newspaper, rustling it now and again with a muttered comment. A steward, balancing a tray of drinks, appeared, and the man with the newspaper flung it down on the seat with an irritable frown.

"Nothing much in there then today, old chap," enquired his companion mildly, taking a proffered drink.

"Asquith and his third Irish Home Rule bill, bloody suffragettes causing trouble again, and strikes and unrest. I ask you, what is this country coming to?" the other man replied crossly.

His companion raised his eyebrows at Bernard, "Nothing pleases my friend today, not even the weather."

Bernard smiled politely and closed his eyes until the train arrived at Paddington, where he thankfully changed for Shorehill. Percy Potts, station master and porter, tipped his hat and hurried forward as Bernard alighted from the train. "Ah, there you are, Mr Bernard."

"Good afternoon, Percy, did you want to speak to me?"

Percy nodded importantly. "Not me, Mr Bernard, but Dr Bill does, and he is in the waiting room, been here for nearly an hour."

Just then, Bill Winter emerged from the waiting room and took Bernard to one side. "Bernard, I wasn't sure what train you would be travelling on, and so I waited. I called Grieves Manor and the house-keeper told me you were on your way home."

"Why, what's the matter, Bill? Nobody ill, I hope."

The doctor shook his head. "Not as far as I know, but Aggie sent Tip up to the surgery because she wasn't sure what to do. There have been a number of telephone calls for you from a chap who said he is a friend of yours from the Board of Trade and needed to speak to you urgently."

Bernard frowned, and then his face cleared. "That could be Davis. I sometimes meet up with him when I go to London, although why on Earth he would want to speak to me urgently, I don't know. Anyway, thanks, Bill. Can I hitch a lift with you? I was going to walk, but perhaps I ought to find out what it is that is so urgent."

As they approached Riverside, Bernard could see Aggie was hovering by the open door, "Good to have you back, Mr Bernard, you are looking very well."

"Thank you, Aggie. Now, what did Davis want?"

"He just said to call him back as soon as you get home. Three times since lunchtime he has called, Mr Bernard. I said I thought you would be back today."

Bernard, still not unduly alarmed, thanked her. "I am sure it is nothing of concern, Aggie. I must have missed a business meeting, that's all. I will call him back now."

~

Arriving back at Eton with a few other House boys, James enjoyed the relaxed holiday atmosphere in the college that still prevailed before term officially had begun. Now it was the fifteenth of April, the first day of the summer term, and the day began in the usual fashion with coffee or cocoa, buns or biscuits, followed by Early School. Returning to the House for breakfast, James was accosted by one of the prefects.

"Titanic due to arrive in New York today, Maycroft? Can't understand you missing a trip like that. Your cousins went, didn't they, the Grieves-Croft twins?"

"Yes, they did," James replied shortly.

It was after lockup when James was eating tea in his room, when his House Master appeared in the doorway. "Maycroft, there is a call for you in my office. Your uncle would like a word."

The House Master had a short conversation with Bernard before calling James to the telephone, and now waited at his desk until the call finished. A white-faced James silently handed him back the telephone. The master placed his hand on James's shoulder.

"Sit down, Maycroft. It is not necessarily bad news. Your uncle said that the latest information that he received today was from a friend in the Marine Department. The reports are that the Titanic had collided with an iceberg with no loss of life. Try not to worry. Your uncle has promised to ring if there is any more news."

But when Davis from Marine Department called an anxiously waiting Bernard the next morning, he confessed that the information he was receiving from the White Star offices was both confusing and conflicting. "There are reports that Titanic is being towed to Halifax, and another report says that she is sunk, but all passengers are safe."

"What do you suggest I do, Davis? My brother, his wife, and her family are all on board." Bernard's voice was sharp with anxiety.

There was a short silence. "If I were you, Maycroft, I would go to the White Star offices in London tomorrow, and if I hear anything further, I will ring you tonight."

Bernard made a decision. "Davis, I am going to give you the number at Grieves Manor, please call me on that number. I am going to collect my nephew from Eton and bring him home until we know what exactly has happened."

After calling the Headmaster at Eton College to inform him that under the circumstances it would be better if James came home, Bernard called Grieves Manor and arranged for Manners to pick him up from Riverside and take him straight to Eton College to collect James. In the next hour, Bernard held a meeting in the Estate office with Cedric, manager of the Mill, and William Hunter, the estate manager, briefly explaining the situation.

"Tis in the paper this morning that Titanic hit an iceberg, but everyone is safe, and no lives lost," Cedric reported dourly.

It was nearly midnight, when Bernard and James arrived back at Grieves Manor to the anxiously waiting staff. Nanny Ryan took one look at James, and brooking no argument from the exhausted boy, she took him off to his bedroom and asked for a supper tray to be sent up immediately.

Bernard thanked Manners profusely for his help throughout the day, and after gratefully accepting Mrs Brent's offer of supper asked, "Brent, has there been a call for me from a Mr Davis?"

"No, sir," Brent shook his head. "Is there any news of the family, Mr Bernard?"

"Nothing yet, I am afraid. James and I will be leaving early tomorrow to catch the London train. Davis works in the Marine Department at the Board of Trade, and he advised that we should go directly to the White Star Offices in London for information. Brent, how much does young Sadie know?"

"Sadie knows that the Titanic hit an iceberg, but that's all, sir." Brent's face was expressionless, but Bernard had heard the tremor in his voice.

"Brent, I can trust you to ensure that whatever the news, it is kept it from the children until James and I return."

"You can trust all of the staff, sir," Brent promised.

The call from Mr Davis came at approximately 1:30 a.m. on the morning of the 17th of April. The call was short and, Brent, hovering in the doorway, watched as Bernard said simply, "I see. Thank you, Davis." He placed the receiver back on the cradle, dropped his head into his hands and slumped forward.

Without a word, Brent came into the room, picked up the whisky decanter, poured two large glasses, and placed one in front of Bernard. Then he drew up a chair, sat next to Bernard, and placed a comforting arm across his shaking shoulders.

"Don't worry about anything at the house, sir. Me and Mrs Brent will take care of everything. Just look after Master James. Mr Maycroft, I think we should wake Master James now."

When the six-thirty train arrived in Charing Cross, James and Bernard walked silently through the crowded station and out into the spring sunshine to join the growing crowd outside Oceanic House, the London office of the White Star Line.

The flags on the buildings around Trafalgar Square, Pall Mall, and Cockspur Street were all flying at half-mast, and there was a deathly hush as the nervous crowd waited for the White Star office doors to open. At seven o'clock precisely, an official from the company opened the doors and said quietly with a look of unutterable sadness on his face, "Ladies and gentlemen, please come in."

There was a clamour of voices, and the sound of muffled sobbing as the crowd surged forward into the White Star Booking Office. Some were desperately calling out the names of their relatives, other were waving pieces of paper in the air. The officer held up his hand, and there was a sudden silence.

"Ladies and gentlemen, please. The clerks are here to help you." He waved to a semi-circular desk where a line of solemn-faced clerks stood with passenger lists lined up on the desk in front of them. The very same clerks who had previously sold tickets for Titanic's maiden voyage now had the task of listing who, out of the passengers and crew, had survived and who was missing, presumed dead.

"As more information comes through, we will post the lists of the survivors onto the bulletin boards. The offices will stay open all night, and I pray for you all. God help you." The head clerk could no longer contain his distress, and he wept openly as his colleagues rushed to his assistance.

After a gruelling twenty-four hours in London, a disbelieving and grief-stricken Bernard, accompanied by a stony-faced James, began the heart-breaking journey back to Berkshire. Of the entire Grieves-Croft party who had boarded the Titanic at Cherbourg, Polly Dawes was the only name that appeared on the list of survivors. Junior Purser Joe McBride also survived, despite suffering a severe head injury. His uncle, Gerry McBride, did not survive. With an over-whelming sense of unreality and after a nightmarish journey, Bernard and James arrived back at Grieves Manor.

James went immediately to his bedroom and spent all the following day in Estelle's bedroom eating very little and saying almost nothing, just asking to be left alone. A heavy pall of grief hung over the lovely house that was once so full of life and love. Grieves Manor was now quiet, sombre, and echoing empty.

Bernard's concern was for his shocked and silent nephew, whilst Nanny Ryan was taking care of a distraught Nanny Florrie and a disbelieving, broken-hearted Sadie who was refusing to eat or leave her bedroom.

James eventually came downstairs. He found Bernard in the library talking to Brent. "Have you heard anything about Polly, Uncle?"

"Not yet, James. Davis says that there is to be an enquiry, and after that, Polly can return home."

"Then I would like to go back to school if you have no objection, Uncle. Can you please keep me informed about Polly?" James asked politely.

"I will, my boy, as soon as I know when she will be coming home. I will call the school. My dearest boy, I wish with all my heart that I could make this easier to bear. I pray that it is all a mistake, and we shall hear that they are all safe and sound."

James looked with compassion at Bernard, who seemed to have aged ten years within the space of a day. His uncle's face was drawn and grey, and his eyes were red from weeping. James looked down and slowly shook his head.

"I don't want to think about what happened to them, and I cannot speak of it, Uncle. I just need to go back to school. Please understand."

Bernard nodded sadly. "I do, James. I do, but I have a favour to ask of you. Before you leave, would you please speak to Sadie? Mary says that she will not come out of her room."

James dropped his head forward onto his hands. "I cannot, Uncle," he whispered brokenly. "Truly, I cannot. I don't know what to say to her."

Bernard did nothing to dissuade James from leaving. Everything and everybody in the house held heart-breaking reminders of the lost family, whereas at Eton, James could resume his school life, detached from the tragedy and the all-enveloping air of grief and sorrow that filled every corner of Grieves Manor. Rupert, of course, was far too young to understand, but he knew something had gone awfully wrong in his small world. His Nanny Ryan kept crying, and Sadie, his Sadie, had locked herself in her room, and Rupert was scared. He picked at his food and cried for his Mumma and Polly.

James went back to school, and eventually, Nanny Ryan told Sadie that Rupert was fretting and refusing to eat, which scared Sadie. Encouraged by Mary Ryan and the staff at Grieves Manor, day by day, she appeared to grow stronger.

Afterwards, Bernard knew that he could not have dealt with the horror of the days that followed without the support from everyone at Grieves Manor. From the lowliest stable boy to the Brents, the entire staff rallied around, and when Bernard made plans to return to Shorehill and Riverside, Brent assured him that they would take care of everything until Clarence Grieves-Croft arrived from France.

On April the 18th at nine-thirty, on a chill, damp evening in New York, after three days of rough seas, fog and thunderstorms, the Carpathia, carrying some of the Titanic survivors, docked at Pier 34. The US senate had passed a resolution to hold an enquiry to investigate the sinking of the Titanic. The hearings began on the 19th of April, 1912 at the Waldorf-Astoria Hotel. Polly Dawes, first-class passenger and the only known survivor of the Grieves-Croft family, refused to make a statement, claiming not to remember anything about the night, apart from the extreme cold.

Davis made one more call to Bernard. "Your Miss Dawes will be on the Adriatic, leaving New York on May 2nd and arriving back into Liverpool sometime on May 11th. If you are meeting her, then please go to the Princess Landing Stage. I can tell you no more than that, Maycroft, because there is to be a Board of Trade enquiry."

"Of course. Thank you, Davis, and thank you again for all your help."

Bernard, desperately heartbroken, grimly kept to his work routine running the mill. His workforce were loyal to a man, and with the assistance of Cedric, his elderly but fiercely-loyal manager, the mill carried on running smoothly.

Bernard had little doubt that William Hunter, with the assistance of his game keepers, was perfectly capable of running the estate office and dealing with the farms. The company accountant, on hearing of the tragedy, packed his office up for an indefinite period and arrived in Shorehill to assist William Hunter with the monthly collection of the rents and took over the time-consuming paperwork which Bernard would normally have dealt with.

It was Dr Bill Winter who travelled to Liverpool to collect Polly. "Bernard, I have an aunt and uncle who live close by the docks. I can stay with them overnight, and if the Adriatic docks late, we can travel back the next day. Stay home and be ready to welcome her."

It was a largely silent group of Titanic survivors that arrived home to a crowd of jubilant friends and relatives waiting eagerly to greet them.

Polly Dawes, pale, thin, and hollow-eyed, was one of a small group of passengers escorted gently through the throng by a ship's nurse.

Bill Winter hurried over to the group and introduced himself after giving Polly a gentle hug. "Miss Dawes is still recovering from the effects of exposure and has been rather poorly, but she insisted on travelling." The nurse was fiercely protective, and it was only when she was assured that Polly was in good hands, did she relinquish her charge with weary gratitude.

On a glorious, mellow May afternoon, Polly Dawes arrived back at Riverside, clad in borrowed clothes donated by kindly New Yorkers. The mountain of luggage that had accompanied the Grieves-Croft family on their ill-fated voyage was now at the bottom of the sea. One thing that had survived was Polly's journal and her envelope of keepsakes which she had tucked deep inside her lifejacket and protected with a ferocity that had astounded her rescuers when they attempted to remove her freezing-wet clothes.

Polly slept for almost a full week, waking only to eat the nourishing food carefully prepared by an ever-attentive Aggie. When she was strong enough to come downstairs, she sat with her mother Becky or Bernard on the terrace, saying little except to continually ask about James, Rupert, and Sadie. When Bernard had satisfied her that they were safe and well, she wept tears of relief.

After her return, Polly stayed close to Riverside for weeks, venturing out to the village on rare occasions. She recovered gradually, but steadfastly refused to speak about any part of the voyage, shaking her head silently even if gently questioned by Aggie or her mother.

Bernard, who could only begin to imagine the horrifying scenes of death and despair that Polly had witnessed, watched over and guarded the traumatised girl, who had been so devoted to his beloved Estelle. He forbade anyone to speak of Titanic, warning that to question or to sympathise would bring the horror of what she had witnessed back to haunt her.

However, Bernard did not have to explain this to James, as it was obvious from the stilted and brief calls that James made to Riverside that he, like Polly, had no desire to hear any details of the loss of his family. "I try not to think about what happened to Titanic. I have said the same to the pastor at Eton and my house master. Polly understands," he explained simply.

The weeks passed, and Bernard, despite the hollow feeling of deep sorrow that dogged his waking hours and the ghosts that haunted his nights, fought to contain his grief and focus on the mill and the estate.

When Bernard found himself unable to go into the rooms at the top of the house previously occupied by Henry and Estelle, he decided that the rooms should be closed.

The curtains were pulled closed across the windows to block out the sunlight, and the furniture was covered in dust sheets. The house staff had been reduced to just Aggie, several maids, and an assortment of Aggie's numerous nieces who could be called on when needed.

Dottie Hunter collected the weekly laundry, returning it crisp and clean and perfectly ironed. Outside, Irish Tip took charge of the stables with the help of a few boys from the village, and Matthew took care of the gardens.

Except for Captain, Henry's great black stallion, and Pepper, Estelle's smart little piebald, the remaining horses stabled at Riverside were sold to a friend of the Grieves-Croft with liveries in Berkshire.

Henry, a skilled and fearless rider, had been a familiar figure racing around the countryside, but now it was Tip, Henry's devoted groom, who rode Captain sedately across the fields and through the village. Shorehill villagers smiled sadly to see the tiny little Irishman astride the great horse, remembering the dashing and romantic figure of the handsome, fair-headed Henry in his flamboyant red riding jacket.

Polly found solace and comfort in her journal and her precious keepsakes. The Folly became her hideaway, and it was here that she opened her eagerly-awaited letters from James.

Bernard watched from the terrace as the slight figure, locked in silent grief, slipped away in the direction of the Folly. He called Tip to one side, "Tip, please make sure that Matthew looks after Estelle's

Folly. Keep it watertight, clean it regularly, and take care of her little garden. Ensure that the Folly is locked every night."

"I will, sir. I will keep it just how Miss Estelle liked it," Tip promised.

The first time that Polly returned to the Folly and breathed in the familiar woody smell, it felt for a moment that nothing had changed. She walked over to the little bronze statuette and touched it tenderly with trembling fingers, and overcome with grief, she sank down onto Estelle's chaise longue and sobbed as if her heart would break.

A glancing shaft of sunlight through the window cast prisms of colour dancing across the floor, and she cried afresh at a piercing memory of Estelle and little James, chasing the "baby rainbows" around the room. When exhausted from crying, and with no more tears left, she reached in her pocket for her precious notebook and ran tender fingers over the soft brown leather and then counted the tiny white butterflies engraved on the front cover. She opened it and whispered the precious words that Estelle had written. "For Polly Dawes and her notes. With love from Estelle Maycroft."

The journal was full of notes written in excitement and anticipation, some written hastily, precious little stories and amusing little sketches of some of the passengers that had captured Estelle's imagination. Every adventure and funny story they had planned to show to James on their return, the messages and jokes that Estelle had written for James. Polly could not bring herself to read the last entries, the last special day when Jenny and Estelle had found her writing and teased her about Joe. Estelle had taken the notebook and done one of her lightning sketches which had reduced all three to helpless giggles. Polly could not show her notebook to James now. It would break his heart all over again, and she put it resolutely back into her pocket.

When she closed her eyes, she could see again the desperate look in Estelle's lovely eyes as she whipped the fur coat from her own shoulders and wrapped it around Polly. She could smell again Estelle's favourite French perfume and hear her lovely, low, husky voice just as if she was standing next to her. "Dearest Polly, if anything happens to me, you must take care of my boys and Sadie. Keep my secret. Promise me that, Polly."

They did not come every night, the nightmares. Sometimes two entire nights would pass before they came back, the screams and the desperate cries for help, the black, unforgiving, icy water and the splash of the oars, but the promise that Polly had made to Estelle in the last minutes before Joe handed her into the lifeboat was with her day and night.

When Dr Bill deemed Polly fit to travel, she began to plan her first visit back to Grieves Manor, and she approached Bernard.

"Dr Bill says I am well enough to travel, so with your permission, I would like to spend some time with Sadie and Rupert." Her voice faltered. "I made a promise to Miss Estelle, you see."

Bernard agreed readily, "Polly, dear Polly, you do not have to explain anything to me, and if your visits help you or the children, then of course you must go." He hesitated. "There is just one other thing that has been concerning me, my dear. Mary Ryan told me about Rupert's parents. I just wondered what will happen to the dear child now, and Sadie of course."

"Rupert's future was all taken care of a while ago. Miss Estelle arranged it all," Polly replied quickly. "Rupert's legal guardians were Lord Archie and Lady Rose, but he is happy at Grieves Manor and believes that Sadie and James are his brother and sister. I am sure Mr Clarence will know what to do about Rupert and Sadie. Sadie wrote and told me that James has entrusted his beloved Bear to Rupert," and she gave Bernard a searching look. "You do remember Bear, don't you, Mr Bernard?"

"I do indeed," smiled Bernard, but he was still distracted and worried about Rupert, and finally decided that he should consult a solicitor. After all, Clarence Grieves-Croft was a bachelor and had resided in France for many years. Bernard was in uncharted waters, but he was certain of one thing. Rupert needed a guardian, at least until his parents returned. "But I will let things settle down first. Too much to think about now, and the child is happy," he thought.

1912 – AFTER TITANIC

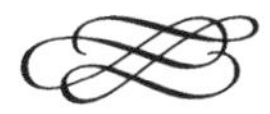

Without anyone realising it, a routine was gradually established. Clarence Grieves-Croft kindly insisted that Manners drive up and collect Polly every other weekend and bring her back to Riverside at the end of the visit. Sadie refused to leave Grieves Manor, but on one occasion, Polly brought Rupert back to Riverside.

"Just for a short visit," Polly had explained. "I promised to show him where James's other bedroom was in Riverside, and where Bear used to live."

But the visit was almost spoiled when Rupert, on a walk with Polly, lost his beloved tin soldier, a French Legionnaire horseman that Bernard had given him to play with. But Bernard had retraced their steps and discovered the little soldier tucked in a crevice in the church wall.

Early in July, on a dismally damp Sunday evening, Bernard, seated alone at the long dining table, was half-heartedly picking at his dinner. He disliked the cold emptiness of the dining room and avoided it as often as he could, preferring to take his breakfast and lunch in the library, but for a reason he was unsure of, Bernard carried on the tradition of eating the evening meal in the dining room.

Gazing down at the lamb chops and gravy slowly congealing on his plate, he gave up all semblance of eating, pushed his plate away, and reached for his wine glass.

Leaning back in his chair, Bernard turned to gaze through the rain-streaked French doors to the terrace. A wind had picked up, and the rain hammered down on the glass roof above the terrace. The rose bushes at the bottom of the steps danced together wildly, bending this way and that at the whim of the summer storm.

Bernard took another sip of wine. It was smooth and rich and as it hit his empty stomach. His head began to swim, and he felt himself relaxing back into his chair. He closed his eyes, and instantly, the memories swam into his head, vivid and clear. This time, however, he did not push them away as he had resolutely done whenever they threatened to intrude in an unguarded moment. They were here, in this room, just as they had been on that last night a few short months ago.

The family and friends were seated around a laden table, raising their champagne glasses high, the travellers and the well-wishers, touching glasses. "Bon voyage. To Titanic!" was the cry, over and over again.

There was Henry, a golden god, his face glowing with wine and excitement, reaching out to pull Estelle to her feet, "Darling, raise a glass to our wonderful benefactors, Lord Archie and Lady Rose," and Estelle, reaching out her hand to her silent son, still seated beside her.

Had he imagined it, that shadow of fear, almost panic, flit across her lovely face as she grasped James's clenched hand tightly. Feeling Bernard's eyes on her, she had beamed her wonderful smile across the table at him and joined her husband in the toast.

The guests clapped and cheered loudly, a chorus of voices joining in with the congratulations. Estelle had sat down then, bending low over James, and Bernard could hear again her soft voice, cajoling James. "Please eat a little, my darling boy."

Had he heard a stifled sob in her voice? He was certainly seated close enough to hear. Had shock dulled his memory of that last night, or was it in his imagination?

A staccato of hailstones rapped sharply against the French doors, and Bernard woke with a jump. The memories of that night melted away as quickly as they had appeared. He pulled himself upright and, with shaking hands, placed his wine glass down on the table and reached inside his jacket pocket, feeling for the familiar shape of his pipe and the soft pouch of tobacco. Filling the round, smooth bowl with his special brand, he lit the pipe and drew in deeply. The aroma of the fragrant leaf soothed his racing heart, and he was thankful to find that his hands were no longer shaking.

Tentatively, he allowed his thoughts to go back to that final day and the morning of their departure. As they had gathered in the hall, ready to leave, Bernard had shaken Henry's hand and quietly asked him to try and understand and respect James's decision.

How tightly Estelle had held onto her beloved James, her eyes shimmering with tears as she begged Bernard to write often and take care of James. How furious Bernard had been with Henry when, at the last minute, he turned to his son, and just giving James a brief handshake had said curtly, "Behave yourself for your Uncle." Bernard had held James tightly across his shaking shoulders as the boy waved a last goodbye to his parents before turning away abruptly and racing up the stairs to his room.

Another rush of grief threatened to overwhelm Bernard, and he stared, unseeing, into the rain-drenched gardens and clenched his teeth around the stem of the pipe, fighting to control the hot tears filling his eyes. The dining room door suddenly opened.

"Sir, Aggie was just wondering whether you would like some apple pie." Polly paused in the doorway, quickly taking in the uneaten meal on the table and the half-empty bottle of red wine. She walked across the room and laid a gentle hand on the grieving man. Bernard looked up, and she saw the tears glistening in his eyes. "Sorry Poll," he smiled weakly, reaching up to pat her hand. "Just memories. It's this room, you see, full of ghosts."

"Yes, I do see," she nodded slowly, allowing her gaze to fall on the empty chairs.

Bernard stood up, pushed his chair back, took the pipe from his mouth, and slowly tapped the still-glowing embers into an ashtray. "I know Agnes is not going to be very happy with me, but I'm just not that hungry tonight, Polly," he said ruefully. "It's this awful weather, not like summer at all."

"Why don't you come and eat with us in the kitchen?" suggested Polly a little shyly. "It might be better than sitting here on your own surrounded by, well..." she stopped.

"Ghosts for dinner companions?" he finished the sentence for her, smiling wryly. "My dearest girl, I accept the invitation wholeheartedly, and I would love to join you for dinner and every night if I may. It will be a relief not to sit at this table again."

"Good, that's settled then. Aggie can warm this up with a little gravy," and placing the dinner plate on a tray, Polly reached for the bottle of wine.

"Leave the wine here, Polly, I think one of Aggie's strong cups of tea will warm me up." and they made their way out of the chilly dining room across the hall toward the warm kitchen.

Aggie, surprised at first at to see the master seated at the kitchen table every night, was however, relieved to see him finishing his meals for the first time in months. Even Tip, who felt that everyone should keep to their place in life, soon became used to Bernard's easy, genial presence. For Bernard, the gripping sense of loneliness and loss diminished a little in their comfortable company, and James wrote to say that he thought it a most sensible arrangement.

But something else was troubling Bernard. James and Bernard had attended the memorial service for the entire Grieves-Croft family in Reading Cathedral, but there had not been a memorial service for Henry and Estelle in Shorehill.

When the elderly vicar of St. Dominic's died suddenly, a suggestion was made that the vicar of St. Swithin's in Sevenoaks should conduct the services at St Dominic's until a replacement vicar was found.

The Rev. Baxter of St Swithin's was a hollow-cheeked wraith-thin man in his middle sixties who bitterly resented being dispatched twice a month to take the services at St Dominic's. When he swooped down into the village on his ancient bike, with his black cloak flying behind him, and often late for the scheduled service, the children whispered. "The witch hunter is in the village."

Bernard and Ernie rallied as many reluctant parishioners as possible to attend the services, but even the church organist refused to play after the Rev. Baxter accused him of playing poorly. The services were dismal, long, and rambling, delivered in a deadly monotone, and the Rev. Baxter narrowed his cold eyes if any child coughed or wriggled restlessly. When he raised his eyes up and quoted from the scriptures his voice grew louder, and his wispy goatee beard quivered on the end of his chin as he pounded the pulpit with a bony fist, promising hell and damnation to all sinners.

St Dominic's was the very heart of the village, and generations of Maycrofts and village families had been christened, married, and honoured in death under its ancient soaring beams. The weathered old door was seldom closed, and the scent of fresh flowers welcomed those who wanted just to sit or kneel in private prayer, and so to wander through the churchyard and see the door firmly closed caused Bernard great sadness. But Bernard and James had agreed vehemently that a memorial service for Henry and Estelle could not be held anywhere but the village church, and so they would wait until their own vicar had been appointed.

Ernie Brown had approached him again and asked tentatively, "Mr Bernard, is there any news from the bishops? It is just that we would like to pay our respects, and I have cleared a lovely spot under the cherry tree."

"Thank you, Ernie. I will approach the bishops again. I am sure that Shorehill will have our vicar very soon."

In early August, a letter arrived to say that, at last, a suitable candidate had been found to take up the post as Vicar of Shorehill.

The Rev. Andrew Wellbeloved and his wife, Annie, would be arriving in Shorehill at the beginning of September, and the bishop had written to Bernard to request if the vicarage could be made ready for the new arrivals. Little did Bernard know that Andrew and Annie Wellbeloved's arrival in Shorehill would bring new life to the village and cement friendships that would last for a generation.

Thus, it was in the summer of 1912, whilst the community was still coming to terms with the tragedy that had devastated not only the Maycrofts, but the whole village, a new vicar and his wife were destined to arrive in Shorehill.

When Bernard pinned a triumphant notice inside the church lynch gate, and Grace Peabody pinned a large notice in the window of the post office, announcing the appointment of a new vicar at St. Dominic's, a frisson of excitement swept through the village. It was a packed village hall that greeted Bernard at the Parish Council meeting, and there was an enthusiastic round of applause when he announced that the new arrivals were Andrew and Annie Wellbeloved and that they would be arriving in Shorehill on the midday train on the 4th of September.

Once the welcome news had spread through the village, there was no shortage of volunteers to make ready St Dominic's and the vicarage for the new arrivals. Various work parties were organized by Bessie Brown and dispatched to St. Dominic's to clean the brass candlesticks, dust the pews, polish the pulpit, lay out the embroidered knee pads and fill the church again with fresh flowers. Bessie, Aggie, and Polly descended on the forlorn old vicarage, which had been empty since the old Vicar had died.

"Poor old chap only lived in two rooms," sniffed Bessie. "The other rooms were closed up, so there will be a lot of work to do."

The doors and windows were flung open, the vast linen cupboard was emptied, the boiler lit, and soon the washing line was filled with billowing white sheets, pillowcases, table cloths, and towels. Rugs were taken out into the garden and severely beaten until the last vestige of dust had disappeared. Ethel, one of Aggie's numerous nieces, kneeling on her hands and knees, waxed and buffed the beautiful old wood floors vigorously until Bessie declared them to be "passable." Ernie mowed the grass, weeded the paths, and cleaned the windows.

Finally, on the day before the Wellbeloved's arrival, Aggie stood back, plump hands on ample hips, and nodded with satisfaction to the linen cupboard stacked high with fresh sweet-smelling linen. "There now, Bess, a good job done," she announced proudly.

Bessie, who had been black-leading the vast old kitchen range since early morning, nodded grudgingly, looked at her own blackened hands, and grumbled, "Some people always manage to pick the easy jobs."

Polly, who was standing on a chair wiping down the top shelves of the dresser, listening to Bessie and Aggie gently quarrelling, gave a small giggle. Despite the fierce rivalry between the sisters-in-law, everyone knew that they were the best of friends. At the sound of Polly's small snort of laughter, Aggie gave Bessie a nudge and said severely, "Are you laughing at us, our Poll? Mind you, I'm not complaining; it's always good to hear you laugh."

There was a short silence. Polly stopped dusting and looked down at the upturned faces of her two dear friends, roundly comfortable Aggie, and narrow, waspish but kind-hearted Bessie.

"Well, you two would make anyone smile, trying to outdo each other as always," she teased as she climbed down from the chair. Handing the duster to Aggie, Polly untied her apron, folded it neatly, and laid it on the kitchen table.

"If everything is finished here, then ladies, I'm going back to Riverside." She stopped at the door. "Mr Bernard is having dinner with Dr Bill tonight, isn't he, Aggie?"

"Yes, to make arrangements to collect the new vicar from the station tomorrow, that's what he said," Aggie agreed. "So, we'll just have a cold supper later."

Bessie straightened all the chairs briskly and gave the old farmhouse table one more wipe, then turned to her friend, who was gazing out of the kitchen window watching Polly walk down the path. "Penny for them, Aggie."

Aggie sighed and turned away from the window, "I'm still worried about Polly, Bess. She says she's alright, but she is still so quiet, far away, and lost in thought. She goes off to Berkshire every other weekend, although I must say she always seems a bit brighter when she comes back."

Bessie looked puzzled. "Why does she do that, then, go down to Berkshire? I thought all the family had been lost on Titanic?" She paused awkwardly.

Aggie nodded. "Most of the family died, but there is Sadie, Miss Estelle's young cousin. she's a bit delicate, and that is why she didn't go with them, and another cousin, a small boy, I think. Polly said that she made a promise to Miss Estelle that she would always look after them, but that's all she will say. You know what Bess? I can scarce believe that Mr Henry has gone forever, and Miss Estelle, I can still see her laughing with old Tip in the garden. She used to tease him until he could not help but laugh."

"I thank God every day that he spared our Polly, although she is a changed girl. Heartbroken she is, she was that close to the mistress. I would say they were more like friends." Her voice wobbled, and she turned away, wiping her eyes with her apron.

"Come on Aggie, don't upset yourself. Nothing can change the past. It's happened, and life goes on. Polly just needs to get away from Riverside for a while and all the memories, that's all." Bessie replied, briskly pinning a large black hat firmly on her head.

"Come on, I think we are done here now. I'll lock up, and we can have a stroll along the river to the pub for a glass of stout. I think we deserve it. I'll wager that's where we'll find our Ernie."

After one last look around the spotless kitchen, she nodded in satisfaction, and, taking Aggie firmly by the arm, closed the vicarage door and stepped out into the garden. It was hot in the late afternoon sun, and Bessie paused to look around the garden. "Hmm, not bad, I suppose," she allowed, looking with approval at the trimly cut grass and a path swept clear of fallen blossoms.

"Not bad? Ernie's worked really hard here, Bessie," Agnes scolded. "It looks a real treat now compared to what it was like when the old vicar was here. I reckon our Ernie deserves that pint."

Bessie pursed her lips, careful not to give her husband too much credit. "I suppose," she said grudgingly. "Aggie, what you said about young Polly. You know, you can't expect her to be the same after everything that she's been through. Poor child must have been so scared, in a boat in the middle of the night, not knowing where everyone else was. It was only a couple of months ago, after all, so I expect she is still in shock."

"I know that Bess, honestly I do. I keep telling myself that, but there's something else troubling her. I can tell, and so can Master Bernard. We've both tried, but she won't talk to anyone about it, not even to her mum. Becky thinks it something to do with the young cousins at Grieves Manor."

The two friends had paused on the brow of the bridge, grateful for the slight breeze that whispered through the willow trees, stirring the branches.

"Are you sure you not imagining it, Aggie? I mean, perhaps it really is only just a matter of time until the memory fades a bit, and there must be other family who can take care of the children." Bessie sounded exasperated. She was hot and tired and in need of a cold drink.

Aggie shook her head; her round face was pink with exertion, and a curl had escaped from under her hat and clung damply to her forehead.

"I don't know about that, Bessie. I just worry over Polly. She goes off on her own a lot, you know, wandering by the river, or just sitting in that Folly. Mr Bernard says leave her be, she is still recovering. I think he's hoping that she will be able to talk to the new vicar, someone not connected with what went on, if you see what I mean,"

"Maybe she will, Aggie, or maybe she won't, and again, maybe it's just too awful to remember. Oh Lordy, Aggie, look, Blanche Dove has spotted us."

"Aggie, Bessie," a soft voice called out to them, and they turned to see Blanche Dove standing outside Nut Cottage waving. Her face, under an enormous straw hat, was wreathed in smiles. "Ladies, I have made some fresh lemonade, and there is warm shortbread just out of the oven. Please do come over and rest awhile."

Soft-hearted Aggie smiled. "Of course we will, Blanche, how kind," and she nudged Bessie, who grumbled. "What did you say that for, Aggie? I was looking forward to a glass of stout with Ernie in the pub."

"Well, you'll have to wait and have your glass of stout later." Aggie scolded her cross little sister-in-law, guiding her firmly back over the bridge and down to Nut Cottage, where a beaming Blanche beckoned them to sit on the bench in front of the cottage. The overhanging thatch provided welcome shade from the hot sun, and Aggie plumped herself down with a sigh.

"Thank you, Blanche. Phew, it's nice to get out of the heat," she said, looking down ruefully at her swollen ankles wedged inside her old black shoes.

Bessie perched down next to her and unpinned her hat. "We can't stay long, Blanche," she said, placing her hat on the seat.

"Of course, dear. I know you've been busy at the vicarage." Blanche gestured inside the cottage.

"Bessie, perhaps you could bring a table out for the lemonade," and she bustled back into the cool, dim interior of the cottage. Bessie followed her and emerged holding a small table.

She placed it down next to Aggie and whispered, "You know that she will try and keep us chatting here until Grace arrives home, don't you?"

"Well, I think Blanche sometimes gets lonely, and anyway, you know that I can't resist Blanche's shortbread," Agnes said peacefully.

An hour later, slightly mollified by a few glasses of iced lemonade and several slices of warm, crumbly shortbread, Bessie sat back with a contented sigh. "Well, Blanche, not long now and we shall be welcoming our new vicar at long last."

Blanche clasped two small white hands together, "It is rather exciting, isn't it? Grace and I are both so pleased, and of course, poor, dear Mr Bernard has been trying for so long to get a new vicar for the village, so it must be a relief for him as well. And how is our dear Polly?" Blanche chattered on. "I saw her the other day as she was going into Meadow Cottage. Quite early in the morning, it was, and she had a sweet little boy with her. Of course, she often pops in, just to keep an eye on the cottage. Would you like another piece, dear?" and Blanche held the plate out to Bessie.

Aggie gave a gentle snore and Bessie, a glass of lemonade poised in her hand, looked across sharply at the bright-eyed little lady nodding at her.

"No more for me, thank you, Blanche, but I will take a bit back for Ernie. He does love your shortbread. Now, I wonder who the child was with Polly. It couldn't have been James, as he's a young man now and at Eton."

"Gracious me, I know that Bessie, I used to tutor the boy at Riverside. I do recall that there was mention of a small boy who lived at Grieves Manor with the family." Blanche smiled gently and gazed into the distance.

"Yes, Polly mentioned another cousin, but what would he be doing here at Riverside, I wonder. Bit of a mystery about the parents, I understand."

Blanche shook her head. "Perhaps I was mistaken then, or perhaps it was a village boy."

Both ladies were silent for a while, and inside the cottage, a clock chimed five o'clock at the same time as Aggie, mouth slightly open, gave another snuffling snore. Bessie put her glass on the table and gave her friend a gentle shake.

"Wake up Aggie, its five o'clock already." She brushed the crumbs from her skirt and stood up. "That was delicious, Blanche, but we must get on. I promised my Ernie kippers for his tea, and Aggie needs to get back to Riverside. Polly will wonder where she has got to."

She gave Aggie another shake. Aggie woke with a start, yawned, and struggled to her feet. "Oh my, I dozed off. It is so nice and cool here under the thatch. Blanche, my dear thank you so much. It was just what we needed. It was hot work up at the vicarage, and your lemonade was just perfect."

Blanche beamed and nodded. "Please do come again. I do so love having company. Oh now, ladies look," she stood up and pointed up to the bridge. "Here comes my Grace. She's been collecting the children's welcome letters to the new vicar. Wait here a second, Bessie, I'll just wrap Ernie's shortbread," and she scurried back indoors.

Grace Dove, spotting the two ladies outside the cottage, gave a cheery wave. As the little schoolteacher trotted towards them, Bessie elbowed Aggie and said under her breath, "Please don't start chatting again, Aggie. I really do need to get on."

Blanche came out of the cottage with Ernie's shortbread, neatly wrapped in a square of greaseproof paper. "There you are, Bess, two pieces for Ernie."

"Ladies, have you been keeping Mother company? How very kind of you both," Grace said brightly. "Won't you stay for another cup of tea?"

"No, thank you Grace, time to make a move." Aggie said quickly. "Goodbye, and thank you again, Blanche," and they hurried off, closing the gate behind them.

Grace gave her mother a kiss on the cheek. "I'll make some fresh tea, Mother, and then I'll walk up and put the children's letters in the vicarage. How nice of the ladies to visit you."

"Yes indeed, very nice," murmured Blanche, taking off her hat and patting a few stray strands of hair back into her neat silver chignon. The late afternoon sunlight danced on the gently flowing river, and the bees hummed drowsily in and out of the lavender bushes. Blanche watched the backs of her two visitors as they disappeared over the hump of the bridge, quick, impatient Bessie next to the large, rolling frame of the gentle Aggie.

Had Bessie turned around then, she would have seen the familiar, dreamy-faced old lady, a wry smile on the little nut-brown face, and two sharp little eyes dancing with amusement. It sometimes suited Blanche Dove to play the forgetful, vague old lady with her head in the clouds, but Blanche was far from that; her mind was still as sharp as a tack, her eyes seeing more than most from her vantage point in Nut Cottage.

But she was cross with herself now for mentioning Polly and the boy. It was just a moment's lapse in concentration. Bessie Brown was a good woman, sharp, but kind-hearted, but like a lot of people in the small village, Bessie was forever curious about the goings on at Riverside, and especially so since the Titanic disaster.

Aggie, on the other hand, even though she had been in service at Riverside for many years, never gossiped about the family and loyally refused to answer any questions, and so Bessie had long ago given up asking. Blanche hoped that Bessie was putting the question of Polly and the unknown child down to imagination or confusion in Blanche's mind.

Blanche chuckled to herself, remembering how cross Bessie had been when she turned up at the children's Christmas Party with her tray of chocolate nests and yellow iced chicks perched in the centre.

Bessie's eyes had widened with irritation. "Blanche," she spluttered. "What on Earth?" but Polly had swooped down and claimed them with forced enthusiasm.

"Blanche, how clever! The children will love them, something different," but then catching Blanche's slight twitching of her mouth, had realised quite quickly that Blanche had not mistaken Christmas for Easter, but rather had decided to do things a little differently.

And of course, this was why, when Miss Dove announced that her mother, Blanche, would be taking story time on Friday afternoons, the school children whooped with delight.

Blanche Dove allowed her imagination to take over when it came to devising stories to keep a large group of five to ten-year-old children amused. Her captivated audience were transported from the school room to faraway lands, remote islands, magic woods, castles, fair ladies, and brave knights. They listened transfixed with wide eyes and open mouths as dragons were slain, fair damsels rescued by handsome princes, and pirates vanquished.

Many of Blanche's adventure stories were played out in the old barn in Lower Meadow, and she smiled with contentment when she heard her children whooping around the meadow, sailing the seven seas and fighting pirates in the hay loft. But now, Blanche could not help wondering again about the child and cast her mind back to the day she had seen the little boy with Polly.

It was a Sunday afternoon toward the end of May, and Blanche was on her way to the churchyard, curious to see how the memorial to Henry and Estelle was progressing. It was a day of fitful sunshine and racing clouds, chased by a stiff breeze and chilly for late May. The tall elms creaked in the wind, and Blanche shivered and pulled her cardigan around her tightly.

Beneath a lovely, flowering cherry tree, a partially completed little wrought-iron enclosure marked the memorial site. A beautifully-chiselled marble plinth stood in the centre of the enclosure in readiness for the memorial statue, and Blanche felt the sting of tears at the back of her eyes.

Those bright young people, so full of life, their parents, and the twins not yet into manhood, almost the entire family had simply gone, disappeared forever, lost in the freezing waters of the North Atlantic. She thought of Bernard Maycroft, grief-stricken but striving so hard to stay strong, James Maycroft, silent and stony-faced, her one-time pupil, now an Eton boarder, and sweet Polly, now so remote and lost without her beloved mistress.

Blanche was so lost in thought that she had not noticed the gusty wind and the blossoms drifting down from the trembling branches above. She shivered. The lowering clouds were heavy with rain, and whispering a last prayer, she turned to go, then hesitated. Somewhere, not too far off, a young child was laughing, a high, joyous laugh. Blanche moved to the edge of the trees, and the child laughed again. She saw them then, close to a low wall at the far end of the churchyard.

Polly was lifting a small boy onto the wall. His curly head was thrown back in laughter as he wobbled on the top stones. Polly was laughing too, her hair blowing about her face, looking up at him, holding one of his hands tightly. At that moment, the sun broke briefly through the clouds, and Blanche glimpsed the boy clearly. Polly seemed to be urging him to let go of something that he was clutching tightly in one hand. The boy shook his head, still laughing, and Polly reached up, took the toy from his small fist and, tucked it into his trouser pocket.

Then in one swift movement, she grabbed him under his arms and lifted him high in the air as the boy screamed in delight.

As she did so, something dropped from his pocket and into the grass below. Blanche moved closer until she was clear of the trees.

The small boy was giggling and squealing with excitement, his chubby legs paddling the air wildly. In a swinging arc, Polly deposited him firmly on the other side of the wall where he collapsed on the grass, convulsing with laughter. Polly scooped him up and set him tenderly on his feet, and together they turned back in the direction of Riverside.

Blanche stared after the retreating figures, Polly with her long stride and bouncing brown hair, and the small boy dancing through the tall grass ahead of her. There was something about the child, his wild curls, the lift of his chin, and his slight frame that reminded her of someone, and she hurried over to where the boy had been standing on the wall.

A toy soldier lay in the long grass, and Blanche bent to pick it up, turning it thoughtfully over in her hands. It was a beautifully painted lead soldier. A French Legionnaire wearing a jaunty red hat with a tassel, and his breeches were tucked into long, black riding boots. A yellow kerchief was tied around his neck, and his jacket was a brilliant blue. It was obvious that he was a horseman, and although she searched carefully through the grass, there was no sign of his horse.

Blanche deliberated for a while whether should she go after them, but something stopped her, and deciding against it, she placed the toy soldier carefully between two stones on the top of the wall. Blanche was certain that Polly would come back to look for the little soldier and was equally certain that Polly had not wanted to be seen that day, and so she had pushed the incident to the back of her mind.

Blanche was still chiding herself for mentioning the child in front of Bessie, when Grace tapped her lightly on the shoulder. "You were day-dreaming again, Mother," Grace scolded gently. "You were miles away. What were you thinking of?"

"Oh, nothing really," replied Blanche lightly. "If tea is ready, I'll come in now. Off you go, up to the vicarage with those letters."

September fifth dawned clear and bright with just the slightest hint of an early autumn mist drifting up from the river. Aggie and Polly had left early to put the finishing touches to the vicarage, leaving Bernard to breakfast alone. It was rare for Bernard to take a day off from the mill these days, but today was special, a day he was looking forward to.

He finished his breakfast and made his way across to the stable yard where Tip was grooming Pepper. "Steady now, little lady, got to make you look smart for the new vicar."

"Good morning, Tip. What a lovely day." Tip looked up, brush in hand, and touched his cap respectfully. Pepper skittered around impatiently on the cobbled yard.

"Nearly finished, sir. Just one last brush, and I'll harness her. Pepper can't wait to be off, can you?" and he stroked the white blaze on the pony's forehead affectionately. "Should only be about half an hour now. The train due in about midday, you said?"

Bernard smiled and patted the pony's smooth, warm back. "That's fine, Tip. Don't rush. I'm going to walk up to the vicarage to see if the ladies need anything."

Tip nodded. "Oh, and I made sure that Captain had a good gallop this morning as well."

"Yes, I saw you bringing him back. Thank you, Tip."

Bernard settled a battered old Panama on his head and strolled down the drive toward the gates. Tip looked after him thoughtfully, and giving one long last brush to the pony's gleaming coat, said with some satisfaction, "There now, Pepper, Mr Bernard looks happy. This is going to be a good day for our master, I think."

The air was still and hot, with just the hint of a breeze blowing up the river, barely stirring the trailing willows. Behind him, Bernard could hear the reassuring, steady hum of the engine turning the great wheel, the sound of a working day at the busy mill. The heat from the sun penetrated the worn old hat, and he stopped under the trees to loosen his tie and wipe his handkerchief across his forehead.

In the distance, he could see the bell tower of St Dominic's and, beyond, the tall, red chimneys of the vicarage. A couple of whiskered

Ancients were resting on a bench by the riverbank, and the thin smoke from their pipes curled in the air as they watched two small boys paddling and splashing in the pebbly shallows under the bridge. They nodded a greeting, and Bernard lifted his hat in response.

The solid old front door of the vicarage was slightly ajar, and he pushed it open and made his way into the cool, wood-panelled hallway. Muted voices were coming from the direction of the kitchen, and there was a sudden burst of laughter. An enticing aroma of fresh-baked bread floated into the hall, and he breathed in appreciatively. The kitchen door was open, and he stood in the doorway unseen for a while.

Bessie, hot faced, was bent over the kitchen range, gingerly taking a batch of freshly baked bread from the oven.

Aggie and Polly were arranging cups and saucers on the kitchen table. Grace Peabody, the postmistress, was standing by the sink, humming and swaying her well-padded hips, as she filled a large vase with water. A bunch of deep-red roses sat on the draining board.

Bessie, who was now balancing the hot tray of bread in both hands, turned around and slid the tray onto the worktop close by the sink. She wiped a floury hand across her forehead and frowned at Grace.

"Don't you be splashing any water onto my bread, Grace Peabody," she snapped at the postmistress.

"Of course not, Bessie," Grace hesitated. "I'm nowhere near your bread, though, but I'll put the vase on the table. See?" She put the vase on the kitchen table.

"And I hope you're not thinking of leaving them flowers in my kitchen either," snapped Bessie.

Grace shook her head uncertainly, "No, Bessie. I'm going to put the roses on the hall table," and she looked for reassurance at Aggie and Polly, who had kept a discreet silence.

"That's the perfect place for your lovely roses, Grace," Aggie soothingly reassured the flustered postmistress, at the same time shooting her sister-in-law a reproachful look.

Bessie tossed her head defiantly and muttered under her breath, "I bet we have blooming black flies all over the kitchen now from those roses."

Polly, trying hard not to smile, looked up and saw Bernard watching with an amused grin, and he raised his eyebrows when he caught her eye.

Since Grace Peabody had joined the village bell-ringers, Ernie Brown had been fulsome in his praise of her determined commitment. Bessie, far too short to be a bell ringer, had become increasingly irritated. Ernie, always ready to score a point against his sharp-tongued little wife, spotted an opportunity to tease her. Much to the amusement of the regulars in the Hop Vine, Ernie announced loudly, and on more than one occasion, "That Grace Peabody certainly knows how to ring a bell."

But few knew that poor Grace Peabody's heart belonged to another, and it had been lost the moment she had arrived as the new postmistress and her namesake; trim and pretty little Grace Dove had trotted into the Post Office for some boiled sweets for Blanche.

Both Aggie and Polly strongly suspected that Ernie knew where Grace Peabody's devotions lay, but had decided not to tell Bessie, all the while immensely enjoying the attention.

Now, Bernard smiled gently at the nervous postmistress and stood aside as she bustled past him with the vase of roses.

"Miss Peabody, your roses are beautiful, and all of you ladies have done a sterling job. The vicarage looks wonderful. Thank you very much."

There was a murmur of approval, Grace blushed, and even Bessie managed a grim smile.

Outside the vicarage, the pony traps were waiting. Tip was chatting to Bill Winter, and Star, the doctor's little pony, stood quietly next to Pepper. Pepper, however, was tossing her head, impatient to be off, and Tip reined her in smartly.

"Steady, Pepper," he commanded crossly as Bernard climbed up onto the seat next to him.

Bernard lifted his hat in a greeting to Bill Winter. "New vicar and his wife are catching the village at its best, I think, Bernard," said the doctor cheerfully.

"We're off then, trot on," said Tip with a slight twitch of the reigns. Pepper trotted along smartly followed by the more sedate Star.

Bernard, watching Pepper high-stepping proudly up the lane, remembered how cross Henry had been when Estelle insisted on bringing the little horse up from Berkshire. "That pony has a wild streak. Leave her with your parents, and I will buy you another," he had demanded, but Estelle had laughed, stroking Pepper's soft nose. "I know she's lively, and that's why I like her. Anyway, she was a present from Daddy, and I feel safe with her." But Henry had never warmed to the little horse, and Pepper, sensing his dislike, had tossed her head and snickered nervously when Henry approached her stall. Tip, surprisingly, had disagreed with Henry and said firmly to Henry that he admired the little pony's spirit and courage, and so Pepper had stayed.

Shaded by the high trees, Old Mill Lane was cool and peaceful. the only sound to disturb the still air was the steady clip-clop of the ponies' hooves and the lazy hum of bees hovering in and out of the wild honeysuckle tangled through the hedgerows. Bernard looked through the trees to the golden cornfields at the foot of the downs. Far off in the distance, he could see a solitary tractor, the driver leaning up against the massive wheels, eating his lunch. A small flock of corn buntings hovered in the blue sky above, and Bernard wondered what the London couple would make of this tiny pocket of rural England and his beloved village.

He thought then of the temporary vicar who had so disappointed him and everyone in the village, and he prayed fervently that the new vicar was a different kettle of fish to the whey-faced Rev. Baxter.

He was jolted out of his musing when Tip announced, "Here we are then," and made a sharp right turn up the station approach, followed by Bill Winter and Star.

As they trotted to a stop by the station, Percy Potts, station master and porter, unkindly nicknamed "Potty Potts" by the local children, was standing importantly in the entrance, checking his pocket watch.

Looking very hot in his heavy uniform, Percy nodded solemnly. "Good day, gentlemen. The train from London is a little delayed. Nothing to worry about, just about fifteen minutes late. Would you like to wait in the waiting room?"

Tip looked across at him. "Looking very smart, Percy, if you don't mind my saying so, but you do know it's not the king arriving today, don't you?" Tip sniggered as he climbed down from the trap. "Give me the reins, Dr Bill. I'll take the horses over for a drink and wait in the shade under the trees." Then he leant forward and whispered, "Get Mr Bernard to tell you the story of old Percy and his rifle," and, still grinning, Tip led the horses over to the horse trough and tethered them firmly before reaching in his pocket for his pipe.

"Good day to you, Percy," Bernard said, and then looked closely at the uncomfortably perspiring little man. "My goodness, you do look very smart. But if you are too warm, I am sure that the Rev. Wellbeloved would not be offended if you took your jacket off in this weather."

Percy was scandalized. "But then I would be in my shirt sleeves, Mr Maycroft, and that would not do at all, thank you. Now if you would like to follow me," and straight-backed with indignation, he marched through the station and onto the platform, Bernard and Dr Bill following obediently behind.

The little station was immaculately tidy as usual, not one piece of scrap paper dared to litter the platform. The brass lamps, swinging gently outside the waiting room, gleamed blindingly in the midday sun. Old Mrs Potts had filled the flower tubs outside the waiting room with red hot geraniums, trailing ivy, and golden marigolds. The green and red benches had been freshly painted, and the waiting room windows gleamed. Percy and his beloved station stood ready to welcome the new vicar and his wife. In the station house, old Mrs Potts had positioned herself in a chair by the window, waiting and watching behind the snowy-white nets for a first glimpse of the newcomers.

"Good old Percy takes his job very seriously," Bernard whispered, as they made their way onto the platform. "I stand duly chastised."

Dr Bill laughed. "Bernard, while we're waiting, Tip said something about Percy and a rifle."

Bernard sighed. "I swear Bill, Tip is the worst gossip in Shorehill, however, it is an amusing story, so I will tell you."

Percy Potts lived in the tiny station house with his elderly mother, and it seemed that Percy was never off duty. In between the trains arriving and departing, Percy swept the platforms with vigour, polished the brass station lamps, and cleaned the waiting room. When the trains steamed into the station, Percy was always there on the platform standing to attention with his trolley ready to collect the passenger's luggage.

This was Percy's world, and when following a visit from a rather self-important official from the London, Brighton, and South Coast Railway resulted in a letter commending, "Mr Percival Potts" on the well-run station, Percy was beside himself with pride. After agonizing for several days on exactly where to display the letter, Percy had decided to glue it inside the waiting room on the window. That way, he hoped passengers would see it as they passed.

Old Mrs Potts worried that not enough people would see it and shyly asked Grace Peabody if she would place a notice in the post office window informing the village of the commendation, and, of course, kindly Grace Peabody did exactly that.

Next to the immaculate little station house was a small, walled orchard where Percy and his mother grew the sweetest and finest Cox's Orange Pippins. The delicious fruit won first prize every year at the Harvest Festival Competition. As autumn approached, the apples ripened high in the trees, tantalizingly just out of reach. Lured by the thought of the mouth-watering fruit, the village boys, giggling nervously, crept up the lane, staying close to the wall. When the lookout gave the signal, the boys would nimbly scale the orchard wall by climbing on each other's shoulders.

Every year, old Mrs Potts, sitting in her rocking chair by her back door, broom at the ready, would peer through the twilight for the young marauders. Wobbling on top of the wall and hastily grabbing the apples from the closest tree, the boys dropped the stolen apples into the bag held open by the eager boys below. Mrs Potts, surprisingly agile for her age, would haul herself out of the rocking chair and sneak through the trees hoping to catch a few unwary ankles with her broom. It was an annual game that Mrs Potts quite enjoyed. After all, scrumping was a time-honoured tradition in the orchards around the village.

But Percy did not see it like that at all, and his spotless reputation and high standing with the LB and S Railway was nearly marred forever by an unfortunate incident. Percy was a veteran of the Boer War, and when he returned to England, he managed to smuggle home the broken barrel of a Lee-Enfield rifle in his kitbag as a souvenir. One warm autumn evening, returning to the station house to make himself a sandwich, he found Mrs Potts fast asleep in her rocking chair by the garden door. Moving around the kitchen quietly, so he didn't wake her, he was buttering his bread when, through the open door, he heard the unmistakable sound of muffled giggling. Percy put the knife down on the bread board and crept out into the garden. Standing on the garden wall, silhouetted against the evening sky, two shadowy figures were busily helping themselves to the apples on the high branches.

Percy was outraged and sneaked softly into his shed. "It's them twins. I'll give them the fright of their lives," he muttered under his breath, looking around for a stick. His eyes alighted on the broken rifle propped up by the door. He picked it up and marched purposefully out of the shed toward the wall. "Hands up!" Percy shouted, and the startled boys found themselves looking down the barrel of a Lee-Enfield.

The boys froze for a split second. "Quick jump," Jacky Dales cried, and together they slid down the wall, scraping the skin from their knees as they did so.

"Old Potty Potts has got a gun," Toby Brown said to his startled twin, Theo, who was holding the bag of apples on the other side of the wall.

All three fled down the lane, giggling and pushing each other, all the while looking behind them to make sure Percy wasn't following.

But Percy, grinning with satisfaction, had gone back indoors, reassured his confused mother, finished making his sandwich, and went back on duty to the station without giving the matter another thought.

"Wasn't a real gun, just a bit of one," puffed Jacky, as the three drew close to their cottages.

The other two boys, Toby and Theo Brown, twin sons of Jacob Brown, the blacksmith, nudged each other. "Course, we knew that," scoffed Toby. "But it might be fun if we pretended that we thought it was real. You know, tell our dads that we were scared."

Jacky hesitated. His dad had forbidden him to steal Percy's apples, but it was always fun being with the twins, so he had gone along.

Theo looked down at the bag of apples at their feet. "And we didn't even get that many, anyway," he grumbled.

"Look, you two have them; I don't want any. Honestly, I promised my dad I wouldn't," said Jacky. He was already late for tea, which was going to land him in trouble anyway.

"Right," said Toby. "But put a few in your pocket, and your dad won't find them," and he leant forward and stuffed two large apples in Jacky's coat pockets.

Jacob Brown, the blacksmith, stood at the door of his cottage, a frown on his face, his muscled arms folded across his chest, and looked up and down the road for the twins, who, once again, were late for tea. Jacob's wife, never having fully recovered after giving birth to the two hearty boys, took to her bed and died before their first birthday. With the help of his good-hearted neighbours, Willy and Gladys Dales, Jacob raised the boys on his own as best he could whilst still running the smithy. Boisterous and mischievous, a few in the village, victims of some of the twin's pranks, grumbled that they should be called the terror twins.

After a few minutes, when there was still no sign of the boys, Jacob went back indoors and was preparing to put his boots back on to go and find them, when the cottage door burst open and the boys rushed in, both talking at once.

The table was laid for tea, a plate piled high with sliced ham, a bowl of boiled potatoes, and a fresh loaf sat on the bread board next to the butter dish. At the head of the table, waiting silently, stood their grim-faced father.

Jacob pointed to the clock on the mantelpiece, and the boys fell silent. "Tea is at half-past six, and it is now past seven o'clock. Where have you been?"

Looking at the bag of apples at Toby's feet he said, " Are they from Pott's orchard?"

Toby was silent.

"Well, I'm waiting?" Jacob insisted.

"It was only a few apples, Dad, honestly." Toby pleaded, then seizing the opportunity carried on, "But guess what? Potty Potts suddenly came chasing out, pointing a rifle, and said he was going to kill us."

Jacob stared at Toby in disbelief then turned to look at Theo, who was standing miserably next to his twin.

"Well, Theo?" he said quietly.

Theo flushed and dropped his head, "No, he didn't Pa. Anyway, it was half of a rifle, and Potty just said 'hands up'."

There was an audible gasp from Toby. "Traitor," he muttered.

Jacob shook his head and said sternly, " Quiet Toby. I expect you took young Jacky with you, did you?"

Both boys nodded, and then, Jacob, much to the twin's dismay, began clearing the table, spooning the potatoes back into a pot on the stove, wrapping the ham, and putting it back in the larder, and placing the bread into the bread bin.

"Well then," said their father. "I don't suppose you are hungry now; you must be full of Percy's apples. So off you go, both of you, wash and straight to bed, and I am going to have a word with Willy and see what Jacky has to say about this before I go and see Percy."

There was something in Jacob's tone that silenced the twins, even Toby, always ready with a cheeky reply. He sat down, removed his boots, placed them next to Theo's, and in silence, they walked past their father to the washhouse. Jacob waited until he was sure that the boys were in bed and then called up the stairs, "I am going next door to see Willy. Go to sleep. I will have a lot of jobs for you both to do after school tomorrow."

Upstairs in the bedroom, Toby glared across at the hunched figure of his twin on the other bed. "What did you say that for?" he said accusingly.

"Shut up, Toby. Dad would find out that you were lying anyway. It's your fault we got no tea, and I'm starving." Theo sounded furious.

It was not often that the twins argued, and Theo rarely challenged his twin, but Theo sounded so cross that Toby wisely let the matter drop.

Listening at the bottom of the stairs, Jacob grinned to himself. Old Percy meant no harm, he was sure, but he did need to sort it out before the story got out of hand.

Willy was leaning up against his front door, smoking his pipe. "Been waiting for you, Jacob," he nodded, and calling over his shoulder, "Going for pint with Jacob now, Gladys," and without waiting for a reply, pulled the door closed.

"Jack told us what happened with Percy. What did your boys say?" Jacob relayed the conversation to Willy, who let out a shout of laughter, "He's a quick one, that Toby, but my boy said the same as Theo, it was just a bit of an old rifle, and when they scarpered, he heard old Potts laughing to himself."

"That's all very well, Willy," said Jacob gloomily. "But that boy of mine, Toby, is a bit too wild for his own good, and if Charlie Briggs gets wind of this, he will be in trouble again."

Charlie Briggs, the local constable, was stationed in Sevenoaks but came down to the village on his bike every Tuesday evening to deal with any non-urgent breaches of the law. Anybody in the village who wanted to report a crime or minor misdemeanour could find him at Lovett's tea rooms, notebook open on the table, pencil at the ready. The Lovett sisters would flutter around, piling the constable's plate with fresh cakes and making endless pots of tea, all the while hoping to pick up some gossip. Charlie Briggs would sit for an hour or so before making his ponderous way back to the station. In fact, there was rarely anything to report, the villagers finding that it was quicker to pay a visit to the police station in Sevenoaks rather than wait for "old Charlie" to write everything down in his notebook.

One scorching hot afternoon, on one of his regular weekly visits to Shorehill, Charlie Briggs, the overweight and pompous constable, was pedalling slowly and laboriously across the bridge. His helmet was balanced precariously on his faded, thinning hair, and the sweat trickled down his scarlet face. The ancient bicycle creaked under his weight, and he puffed loudly as his short, stubby legs pushed down hard on the pedals. Just as he reached the brow of the bridge, he was distracted by a scrabbling sound to his left, and he turned his head in time to see a boy's grinning face pop up over the parapet.

"Boo!" the boy shouted.

Startled, the constable jumped, and clinging to the handlebars, he fought desperately to control the bicycle and wobbled on for a few more feet before falling heavily on his ample rear. The helmet slid slowly down over his face, and with two fat legs waving in the air, Constable Briggs rolled around on the bridge before heaving himself to his feet.

Blanche Dove, hearing the commotion, looked up from her knitting to see Toby and Theo Brown and little Jacky Dales hiding in the shallows under the bridge, helpless with silent laughter, fists stuffed into their mouths.

Then she looked up to see the furious and red-faced Charlie Briggs leaning over the bridge, shaking his fist in the air, shouting, "I know you're down there. I saw you. I know who you are!" He looked down at Blanche. "Madam, did you see those boys? Can you see them now? Where did they go?"

Blanche shaded her eyes and squinted up at the constable, and smiling vaguely, she shook her head.

"Who are you looking for, Constable," she called out, and from of the corner of her eye, she saw the three boys, holding their shoes high above their heads, creeping out from under the bridge and scrambling up the opposite bank.

"Bloody fool woman," Charlie muttered, and knowing full well that the boys had made their escape, limped back to collect his bicycle and his helmet.

Nothing ever came of the incident, because Charlie, although he was certain in his mind that it was the blacksmith's twins, had no proof, and strangely enough, no witnesses. Instead, he had a strong word with Jacob, who in turn rebuked the twins, who claimed it was just a bit of fun.

Blanche Dove, who had seen exactly who was responsible, was barely able to control her amusement but decided anyway to have a quiet word with Jacob. Blanche was rather fond of the motherless twins and could see that their scrapes were harmless. They were high-spirited and daring but extremely likable, which was fortunate for them. Since that day, Jacob knew that Charlie Briggs had his eye on the boys, so when Willy said, "My missus wants to call Charlie Briggs in, she thinks old Percy shouldn't get away with threatening the boys," Jacob's heart sank.

That would be playing straight into the constable's hands.

By now, they had reached the Hop Vine, and Jacob ducked under the low-beamed entrance and into the smoky interior. The old pub was full, and Willy, following, stopped to nod and call out to some acquaintances, but Jacob, lost in thought, moved up to the bar.

Mick Carey, the relatively new pub landlord, was at the end of the bar talking quietly to his wife Sylvia. The Carey's had moved to the Hop Vine over two years ago from Ireland but were still thought of in the village as newcomers. Michael Carey was a soft-spoken Irishman, and when questioned by curious villagers about his past, divulged only that they came from Kilmore Quay, a tiny fishing village in County Wexford. His father had been a fisherman, and Mick had run the local bar with his uncle. When their only daughter, Moira, came to train to be a nurse in England, they had decided to follow her and set up home to be close to her, and he confided to Bernard in his quiet manner, "There is big trouble brewing in Ireland, Mr Bernard. I wanted my family out of it."

Sylvia looked up and smiled as they entered the pub and said something to her husband, who turned around, raised his hand, and walked toward them. Wiping down the already-immaculate bar, Mick smiled. "Evening Jacob, Willy. What can I get you two gentlemen?"

"Two pints of your best ale, Mick, please." Jacob leant against the bar and Willy settled himself on a stool next to him.

"Willy, I think we should have a word with Percy before your Gladys gets the constable involved. After all, we don't want to get Percy in trouble. It was the boys' fault, pinching apples again."

Mick set two foaming pints of ale in front of them, and Willy took a large gulp, wiping the foam from his straggly moustache before replying. "Have a word with her when we get back then, Jacob. She might listen to you. But she worries about your two as much as our Jack," he said doubtfully.

"I know that," the big blacksmith rubbed an enormous hand across his forehead and sighed, "The boys can be a bit of a handful, but they mean no harm."

Mick, who was listening thoughtfully as he polished the glasses, "I was going to have a word with you about the boys, Jacob."

Jacob straightened up and frowned. "Now what," he thought, but before he could say anything, Mick carried on, "I could do with a couple of strong lads at the weekend, working in the cellar, stacking the barrels, and helping with the drays. Keep them out of trouble, what do you think? Have they been in a bit of bother again, then?"

Jacob explained about Percy Potts, and Mick grinned and pulled himself a pint.

"No need for the law. You know what Charlie Briggs is like, makes something out of nothing. Bernard Maycroft is a magistrate, isn't he? And a good man, I hear. Why not have a word with him?"

Moving off to serve another customer, Mick called out, "And I'll expect your boys bright and early on Saturday morning, Jacob?"

Jacob nodded, "Thanks Mick. They will be in the yard at eight sharp."

Gladys agreed not to speak to the constable but thought that it was a good idea for Mr Maycroft to have a quiet word with Percy Potts and added grimly, "And I will deal with the boys, tormenting that poor man."

Bernard Maycroft was working in the library going through the accounts, when Polly tapped on the door and said that Jacob Brown would like to see him. "Of course, Polly, do please show him in." Bernard put his pen down, closed the book, and stood up to greet the burly blacksmith. "Jacob, what can I do for you?"

"Thank you for seeing me, Mr Bernard. I just wondered if you can help." Jacob explained the situation about the boys and Percy Potts.

"If you could have a word with Percy, Mr Maycroft, I wouldn't like the old boy to get into trouble with the railway, and if we tell Constable Briggs, he will have to file a report. I am dealing with the boys, and I have warned them that if they say Percy threatened them with a gun, even though it was just an old part of a gun, poor old Percy could get into trouble and could lose his home. My boys can be a bit wild, Mr Maycroft, but I know they wouldn't want to get anyone into trouble, and Mick Carey is giving them some work. I will make sure they stay out of trouble."

It was a long speech for the quiet man, and Jacob took a huge breath in and waited anxiously, twisting his cap between his hands, but he need not have worried.

Bernard smiled. "I understand completely, Jacob. I am sure Mr Potts meant no harm, but we don't want that kind of thing getting back to the railway, and I know that I can trust your boys not to mention the incident to anyone. On this occasion, I don't think there is any need to trouble the constable. I will deal with it, and don't worry too much about your boys."

Polly showed the grateful blacksmith out, and Bernard, watching him go, smiled to himself.

The incident with young Toby Brown and Constable Briggs on the bridge had caused a great deal of hilarity in the village. The constable was regarded as somewhat lazy, and the sight of the overweight figure on his backside in the middle of the bridge was a talking point in the Hop Vine for many evenings after.

The next morning, Bernard, good as his word, took a stroll up to the station. Percy was sitting in the waiting room reading his newspaper but jumped up when he saw Bernard. After exchanging a few pleasantries, Bernard went on to gently explain the reason for his visit. Percy, who had put the whole incident out of his mind, was visibly shaken, but grateful that Constable Briggs had not been involved. He promised to lock the rifle barrel away. Bernard patted him on the shoulder and suggested that perhaps Mrs Potts could put some windfalls into a bag and leave them by the orchard wall, adding that the Potts apples were famous for their fine quality and passers-by would appreciate them.

At this, Percy perked up, and later told his mother proudly about Mr Maycroft's suggestion. Mrs Potts agreed a little reluctantly, as she rather enjoyed the sport of catching the boys out, but at least Percy's reputation with the railway had been saved.

When Bernard had finished telling the tale of Percy Potts, the twins, and the rifle, Dr Bill threw back his head and roared with laughter.

"Wait till I tell the wife. They are a handful though, those twins of Jacobs. I had the devil's own job making them stay indoors when they got the measles. I've seen them working with the barrels in the back yard of the pub. Mick Carey seems to keep them in check, and of course, Sylvia keeps a motherly eye on them."

Their conversation was interrupted by the long, piercing shriek of the train whistle as it rounded the track and chugged into the station, billowing great clouds of steam that enveloped the two men on the platform.

Percy hurried forward importantly with a luggage trolley. "Stand back, if you would, gentlemen," he ordered as the great wheels ground slowly to a halt. The carriage doors were flung open, and a few figures emerged through the steam: local people who waved a greeting to Bernard and Dr Bill. Bernard spotted a tall, fair-haired man, who, having jumped lightly onto the platform, turned and held his hand out to a slim woman in a simple grey dress and wearing a pretty veiled hat. They stood for a while, smiling at each other, the man's hand under his wife's elbow.

Bernard stepped forward and raised his hand in a greeting. The man waved back with a cheerful smile, said something to his wife, and arm-in-arm, they came towards Bernard and Dr Bill. "Mr Maycroft. I am so pleased to meet you," Andrew held out his hand. "How very good of you both to meet us. May I present my wife, Annie, and of course, I am Andrew Wellbeloved."

Bernard shook his hand, "It is a great pleasure to meet you at last, Andrew. I am Bernard, by the way, not Mr Maycroft, and this is Dr Bill Winter."

Andrew leant forward to shake Dr Bill's hand. "Delighted to meet you, a real welcoming committee."

Bernard turned to Annie Wellbeloved and held out his hand. "Annie, I am delighted to welcome you both to Shorehill."

Bernard's first impression had been of a rather ordinary face under the frivolous little hat, but then Annie Wellbeloved gave him a wide grin, and her entire face was transformed. "I am so very happy to be here, Bernard." Her voice was light and quick with a hint of hidden laughter, and she reached up, removed her hat, and shook her head lightly.

"Gentlemen, I do hope you don't mind, but it's far too hot for a hat today. I gather from Andrew that you have had to put up with old Hellfire-and-Brimstone-Baxter for a while. How awful for you."

There was a moment of silence as she looked at them with amusement, her head tipped to one side. Dr Bill burst out laughing, and Bernard, despite struggling to contain himself, could not help joining in. Anne looked at them in satisfaction and gazed around her.

"What an absolutely heavenly place, Bernard. I love Shorehill already."

"Wait until you have seen the rest of the village and the river," Bernard replied with pride.

Andrew, in the meantime, had walked over to where Percy was busily unloading the luggage from the train and onto the trolley.

"Good afternoon. I hope they are not too heavy," and he held out his hand. "I'm Andrew Wellbeloved."

Percy wiped his hand down his trousers and shook the outstretched hand. "Good afternoon, Vicar. Welcome to Shorehill. I am Percy, Percy Potts, the stationmaster," he said proudly.

"Thank you, Percy. You have a lovely little station here. You must be very proud of it."

Percy puffed out his chest and seemed to grow another inch. "Thank you, very much indeed, Vicar," he said, beaming.

"Now Percy, let me give a hand there, my wife seems to have packed our entire worldly goods into that case."

Percy accepted Andrew's offer with gratitude, and together they manhandled the huge trunk onto the trolley.

"Hellfire-and-Brimstone-Baxter." Dr Bill was still spluttering with laughter, as Andrew approached them.

"Oh dear, what has my darling wife been saying now? Has she put her foot in it already? Poor old Baxter." Andrew looked reproachfully at his wife.

"It's alright, Andrew. They thought it was funny," Annie smiled with delight.

"Well, I could not have described that dreadful man better than your wife did, Andrew." Bernard laughed. "And it was very kind of you to help Percy. Now let's get you both back to the vicarage. There's a very impatient welcoming committee waiting for you."

There was little conversation on the way back to the vicarage. Both Andrew and Annie Wellbeloved were gazing around them in such sheer delight as the lovely old village revealed itself that Bernard was content just to watch their faces. The welcoming committee, Polly, Bessie, Aggie, and Ernie were standing by the vicarage and nudged each other in excitement as the traps carrying the newcomers came into view at the bottom of the lane. One look at the delighted look on Annie's face and the gentle smile and friendly wave from their new vicar assured them that this young vicar was not going to be another Rev. Baxter.

ANDREW AND ANNIE WELLBELOVED

That evening, when the last of the visitors had departed the vicarage, Annie and Andrew stood on the bridge in the soft twilight, watching the reflection of the moon on the river and listening to sounds of the countryside around them.

It had been a wonderful evening of warm greetings, good food, laughter, and meeting new friends. There had been a suggestion that the bell ringing could begin again soon, and Andrew had confessed that he himself was a bell-ringer. Then, little Grace Dove ventured to ask about restarting the Sunday School, and Annie's enthusiasm for this was received with delight. It was late evening when Bernard, seeing Annie trying to hide a yawn, said firmly, "No more visitors tonight, Andrew. We must leave you and Annie to settle in now."

Now, as they stood and looked across the river to the twinkling lights of the village, Annie grasped her husband's arm. "Andrew, I feel as if we have stumbled into paradise."

"I know what you mean. These people love their church so much, and it seems as if they have missed their vicar more than the bishops were aware. I think Ernie Brown has accepted us, despite telling me what a wonderful old man the previous resident vicar was. Thank goodness you got on so well with Bessie. I wouldn't want to get on the wrong side of her. I must admit I did worry about how we would be received."

Annie linked her arm through her husband's. "I know you were a little sad to leave St Mark's, Andrew, but I just could not wait to get away from London, and now we are here in Shorehill, I don't think I ever want to leave."

Earlier that day, on a crowded Victoria Station, Andrew Well-beloved and the perspiring porter had trouble keeping up with Annie, weaving her way through the milling crowd with one hand holding firmly onto her hat as she eagerly looked up at the departure board.

"Here we are, Andrew, Platform 7, departing in ten minutes. Come along. Let's get our luggage loaded," she chivvied the perspiring porter.

"Annie, you go along and see if you can find an empty carriage for us darling, and I will give this poor chap a hand." Andrew urged.

Once the luggage was loaded and Andrew had tipped the porter, he found Annie a few carriages down, hanging out of the window and waving wildly. "Here Andrew, quickly, this one is nice and empty."

When the last of the carriage doors had been slammed shut, the porter waved his flag, and with an ear-piercing shriek and great burst of steam, the train chugged out of the station, rapidly gathering speed as it left behind the coal yards, factories, workshops, and smog of London town. Before long, they were puffing their way through tall trees, grazing cattle, and fields of swaying yellow corn. Annie opened the window and took a deep breath, her eyes shining with anticipation and excitement. She grabbed his hand and laughed out loud as the train rattled and swayed over an iron bridge, and she pointed to a silver ribbon of water far below the thick steel girders.

"Look Andrew, quickly, look how far down the river is. Darling this is so exciting!"

Andrew watched her in amusement and again was struck by his wife's sheer joy of life, and he laid his head back contentedly and allowed his thoughts to drift. St. Mark's was deep within the miserable, sprawling streets of East London. St Mark's, in Lime House, was a forbidding, cavernous seventeenth-century church soaring above a maze of grim, narrow-terraced houses, and within, the sounds and smells of the polluted River Thames.

Soon after, Andrew had suffered another bout of pneumonia, the second within a short period of time, the bishop had decided that the ever-growing parish of St Mark's was too much for the dedicated, hardworking young vicar. Taking him to one side, he told him firmly that he had done a sterling job in his time at St. Mark's, but it was time for a change, and advised that Andrew should consider a more rural parish and suggested St Dominic's in Shorehill. "It's a small, rural parish, Andrew, but the village is delightful, and of course, there are various hamlets that come within the parish. It's a mixed community of millworkers and farmers. The mill owner and the church warden, Bernard Maycroft, is a wonderful fellow who has suffered a dreadful tragedy. His younger brother, sister-in-law, and her family were lost when Titanic was lost, and Bernard appealed to me again recently. They are in desperate need of a resident vicar, as Bernard put it, 'St Dominic's is the heart of our village.' Talk it over with Annie, and let me know as soon as possible, old chap."

When Andrew broached the subject, Annie Wellbeloved did not hesitate. For months, she had been concerned about Andrew's health and his stubborn refusal to work fewer hours. "Of course, we must go, Andrew. There is no question about it. This is a village that needs us, and we need St Dominic's."

The next day, she sent a grateful letter of thanks and acceptance to the House of Bishops and began packing.

The first morning in the old vicarage, Annie Wellbeloved woke and blinked in the brightness of the emerging day. She rubbed her eyes and turned to look at the empty space in the bed next to her. Andrew had gone, his pyjamas neatly folded on his pillow, and she remembered that he had an early morning meeting at the church with Bernard Maycroft and Ernie Brown, the verger. A drifting breeze blew through the open bedroom window, lifting the flimsy curtains and carrying with it the faint scent of lavender and the promise of another fine day. The river, running at top level after a sudden storm, sparkled in the sunlight as the low mist dissolved in the warmth of the early sun. Outside the window, high in the branches of a vast chestnut tree, a couple of magpies chattered crossly, and small birds, searching for insects, flitted in and out of the thickly twisted wisteria that scrambled across the flint wall.

Annie jumped out of bed, and finding her robe at the bottom of the crumpled bed, she slipped it on, wrapped it tightly around her slender frame, and ran, barefoot, over to the sun-faded window seat. Gazing around her in delight, she leant out of the window to breathe in the sweet morning air and looked in wonder as iridescent dragonflies darted and hovered above the river as it bubbled through trailing branches on its way to the weir. A loud rustling in the branches above her head made her jump. Her sudden appearance had alarmed the squabbling magpies, and they abandoned their quarrel and swooped away, an indignant blur of black and white against the pale blue sky. A loaded hay wagon, pulled by a pair of giant shires, trundled slowly over the bridge, and in the distance, on the other side of the river, she could see school children gathering in the playground. A bell jangled, which silenced the chattering children, and in the hush that followed, she became aware of the faint rise and fall of voices coming from downstairs.

Still lost in her pleasant daydream, Annie yawned contentedly and turned to look at the clock on the bedside table, and her eyes widened as she realised that it was already past eight o'clock. "Bother," she said crossly, no time for the lovely, long bath she had promised herself, and reluctantly abandoning the idea, she grabbed some clothes from the wardrobe and hurried into the bathroom to dress.

When they had arrived the day before, Bessie had proudly taken Andrew and Annie on a tour around the vicarage. Annie had been almost speechless with delight. There were three bedrooms tucked under the eaves, and the two front bedrooms had little window seats that looked out across the river toward the village. The polished brass bedsteads gleamed, and the high feather beds were covered in pretty patchwork quilts. The pillows piled at the top of each bed were each covered in crisp white linen pillowcases.

Pretty voile drapes framing the windows moved softly in the light breeze. The fireplace in the largest bedroom was piled high with fresh-cut logs. An old pine wardrobe leant a little crookedly by one wall, and there was a dressing table and tallboy against the opposite wall. Sitting on either side of the enormous feather bed were two bedside tables with small vases filled with sprigs of lavender. "Plenty of space for all your things, Mrs Wellbeloved," Bessie had announced with a certain satisfaction, waving her arms around the room.

"Bessie, this is so lovely. What a wonderful welcome. Thank you for making everything so perfect."

"Yes, thank you indeed," Andrew had added.

"Haven't finished yet, sir," and with a flourish, Bessie had opened a connecting door to reveal a small bathroom, fitted with a toilet, a little hand basin with a mirror above, and a pretty claw-foot bath. Annie gasped,

"Oh, Andrew, look, a proper bathroom. How wonderful"

"Yes, and plenty of running hot water, Mrs Wellbeloved," Bessie said, holding her head high with pride and pointing to a copper geyser on the wall near the bath. "It only takes about ten minutes to heat the water. It's a mite noisy though."

Now, Annie hovered in the bathroom gazing longingly at the bath. She shook her head regretfully and filled the wash basin with water, promising herself a leisurely bath before she went to bed. She washed quickly, cleaned her teeth, brushed her hair until it shone, and ran downstairs, a little nervous, but excited to begin this wonderful new life. The voices were coming from the kitchen, and she knocked shyly, opened the door, and peered in. Bessie and Aggie were seated at an enormous old table sipping their tea and chatting. A big teapot covered in a bright red-and-yellow striped tea cosy sat in the middle of the table, and there was a tantalising smell of hot buttered toast.

Annie ventured further into the room. "Good morning, ladies. I simply cannot remember the last time I had such a wonderful sleep. What must you both think of me, but it's so peaceful, I just slept on." She smiled sat down at the table next to Aggie, who beamed at her.

"Never mind that, madam, you both looked exhausted last night. Needed a good night's sleep, I would imagine. Now then, a nice cup of tea before breakfast." Bessie got up briskly and fetched another cup and saucer and set in on the table in front of Annie.

"Thank you, Bessie," said Annie gratefully and smiled at Aggie. "But please, both of you, you must call me Annie, or Ann, but certainly not Mrs Wellbeloved."

Bessie looked a little doubtful, but replied, "Well, if you are sure? Annie, the vicar said to tell you that he has gone to meet Mr Bernard at the church. Ever so excited he was and said for you to join him when you are ready. First things first though. What you would like for dinner tonight? I shall be off to the shops when I have done your breakfast."

"My goodness Bessie, I had no idea that you cook for us as well."

"Well, I only do four nights a week, and I get the shopping in for the rest of the week, but I am always available should you need me."

"Bessie, that sounds wonderful, and whatever you have planned for dinner is fine. Andrew and I are not fussy eaters."

Aggie, who had been listening in silence, relaxed as Bessie gave Annie one of her rare smiles. Somehow, Annie, in a very short time, had endeared herself to the prickly little housekeeper.

"I'll do some bacon and eggs for breakfast then, and Aggie can show you round the rest of the vicarage, can't you Aggie?"

Aggie heaved herself to her feet, "Come along, Annie, come and inspect your new home. We can start in the hall." Aggie had no problem calling the friendly young woman by her first name. There was a mischievous liveliness in Annie's brown eyes, and her mouth seemed to tremble with the promise of a smile.

The old vicarage was not a large house, rather it sprawled comfortably at the side of Old Mill Lane, and the windows glinted benignly over the river to the village beyond. The rear garden, encompassing a small orchard, was a lovely wilderness of lilac, buddleia, wild honeysuckle, and roses with a little gate that led directly to into the churchyard. On a polished table near the massive front door, a tall vase was filled with deep-red roses, and their evocative scent mingling with the smell of beeswax filled the old panelled hallway. Dust motes danced in the sunbeams streaming through a window halfway up the old oak staircase, warming the sun-faded wood floor.

"What beautiful roses," Annie gently touched a velvet petal.

"They are Grace Peabody's pride and joy. You met her last night, she is our postmistress. We will begin with the dining room," said Aggie, and apologised as she opened the door. "It's a bit chilly in here. Being on this side of the house, the trees don't let much sunlight in. The old vicar liked to use it for parish meetings, though."

Annie didn't reply, but made mental note that the parish meetings, and any other meetings, could be held around the big table in the warm kitchen.

"Sitting Room next." Aggie opened the heavily-carved wooden doors with a flourish and stood back to watch Annie's reaction.

The elegant sitting room ran almost the full width of the house. At the far end of the room, French doors led out to an orangery filled with fragrant climbing plants, roses, jasmine, and tall, creamy lilies. The walls were painted in the palest of primrose yellow, and the picture rail and dado rail were picked out in periwinkle blue. In the centre of the soaring ceiling, a cut-glass chandelier shimmered in the breeze from the open door. Two deep, heavily-buttoned red velvet sofas sat either side of a welcoming inglenook fireplace filled with apple logs. In the alcoves, the tall bookshelves were crammed with books of every size and colour.

"Oh Aggie, what a beautiful room. Everything about it is perfect, and just look at that wonderful garden." Annie walked slowly across the polished parquet floor. "I can see the church bell tower through the trees."

"And you can hear them," Aggie chuckled.

Spotting a narrow door in the wall almost hidden by the bookcase, Annie was intrigued. "Where does that door go to?"

"Now that would be to the vicar's study. Such a nice little room, I always think." Aggie replied, opening the door.

Annie peered over her shoulder and felt a rush of pleasure. The room was far from little, a single door led out into the garden and there was a deep picture window with a clear view across the trees to

St Dominic's. More bookshelves were lined against the walls, and a little iron fireplace was tucked away in the corner of the room. A rolled-top walnut desk sat under the window, and several rather worn squashy armchairs were scattered haphazardly around the room.

"Oh, Aggie, Andrew will love this room. A study, all for his own. He used to have to write his sermons in his tiny bedroom."

Aggie put her arm through Annie's. "Well you are here now, my dear, and you are both as welcome as the flowers in May. You have no idea how much our village has needed our own vicar, especially after we lost Mr Henry and Miss Estelle."

Annie was sorely tempted to ask more, but Aggie sniffed, shook her head, and cleared her throat.

"No good dwelling, as our Bessie says. Let's get back to the kitchen before Bessie scolds."

Once again seated at the table with an enticing plate of crispy bacon and golden eggs in front of her, Annie looked around the enormous kitchen with satisfaction. The front windows faced out onto Old Mill Lane, and a door at the side led out to the scullery and the larder. The scullery had a side door for deliveries, a flagstone floor, and a deep sink for washing the laundry. Standing next to the sink was the mangle and on the other side a deep larder with marble shelves.

In the centre of the kitchen, a weathered farmhouse table was surrounded by a variety of mismatched chairs, and this was where Annie was seated. The huge, black kitchen range, where Bessie was busy frying eggs, gleamed, as did the copper pots hanging from hooks above. Bessie turned and pointed to the scullery. "The larder is in there, Annie, it's nice and cold in the scullery. When you have finished your breakfast, go and have a look."

The larder door had two meshed windows, and when Annie opened the door and peered inside, the cool, dark interior, she was lost for words.

The marble shelves were crammed with trays of large brown eggs, cold cuts of meat, a bacon hock, pork pies, apple pies, and hanging from a large hook in the ceiling was an enormous breaded ham. The rush baskets on the floor were filled with vegetables, beetroots, tomatoes, and salads.

Suddenly, it was all too much for her, and she turned back to look at their expectant faces. "How wonderfully welcome you have made us both." Annie's voice trembled, and she was barely able to contain the hot tears. "But I promise you that Andrew is a wonderful vicar and a friend, and with your help, I shall be the best vicar's wife. I will put my heart and soul into Shorehill."

"There now, don't you go upsetting yourself," Bessie said briskly. "I am sure you will both be very happy with us. You come and sit with Aggie, here, she will tell you why we have needed our very own vicar more than ever this year. Help yourself to more eggs, there's plenty."

Bessie untied her apron and took a large, straw shopping basket from the larder.

"The fish van will be down by Willy Dales's shop, and I'll get you and the vicar some nice cod fillets for supper, and some of Willy's sausages for breakfast." The side door banged, and she was gone.

Annie, still ravenously hungry, helped herself to more eggs, all the while listening in disbelief as Aggie told her about Henry, Estelle, and the Grieves-Croft family being lost on the Titanic.

"We still cannot believe that it really happened, all those lost souls, and Polly, our poor girl, no wonder she can't speak about what happened. She was the only one saved out of the whole party. But we thank God that we still have young Master James."

"Oh, Aggie, how awful, but I just wonder how poor Mr Maycroft has stayed so strong. So, then none of the family survived apart from Polly?"

"Just our Polly. Mr Bernard, well, he must stay strong because of young James, Henry and Estelle's boy. And of course, there are some young Berkshire cousins, and being such a dear man, he is helping with them as well. Master James is at Eton now, but the cousins are being cared for by their nannies and the rest of the staff who are wonderful. But now you and the vicar are here, and we can have a proper service in St Dominic's for Henry and Estelle. Master James and Mr Bernard refused to have it held anywhere else."

Annie poured herself another cup of tea. "It's too shocking to think about. An entire family just gone, and Polly doesn't have any idea what happened to them?"

"No, and Mr Bernard has said we must never ask her. She was that devoted to the mistress. I've known that girl all my life, and I can't get her to talk, and I doubt she ever will, but she's changed, has Polly, and who wouldn't?" Aggie's voice was heavy with sadness. Annie placed a gentle hand on the housekeeper's arm and changed the subject.

"Andrew went to Eton as well, you know, but he doesn't say too much about his time there. I think he was a lot happier at University."

"Does it run in the family then, is his father a vicar?" Aggie was curious.

Annie burst out laughing. "Oh, my goodness no. My esteemed father-in-law, Lord Horatio Wellbeloved, is a very successful businessman. He and Lady Mary, my mother-in-law, have a house in Belgravia and a villa somewhere in the south of France. I am afraid that Andrew's parents do not approve of me, or the fact that Andrew chose to be a vicar. We don't see a great deal of them. Andrew goes to see them once a year, but I haven't seen them for a few years. It is sad, as I only have an elderly aunt and Andrew is an only child."

"Well that is a shame then," said Aggie stoutly. "I am sure that once you settle into Shorehill, you will think of us as your family."

Andrew and Annie Wellbeloved had been in the vicarage a mere ten days when Polly wrote to James:

"My dearest James, the new vicar and his wife, they said to call them Andrew and Annie, have settled in very well, and in just a short time, they have turned us all upside down; such energy, boundless love and faith. They have taken to our village, James; I gather they have come from a dreadful place in the East End of London. St Dominic's is looking wonderful again, full of fresh flowers, and our new vicar gives such wonderful sermons, even the children sit still. Old Ned is back playing the organ as badly as he did before, and we have the beginnings of a choir. Sunday school has begun again, and there are even plans for a Christmas fair. I hesitate to ask, but your Uncle Bernard

has asked whether you would mind if our memorial service was held in the middle of October. He is worried that it is too soon for us, but he will be writing to you himself anyway. So now, my dear boy, it's Friday evening, and soon Manners will be here to take me to Grieves-Manor to see our precious Sadie and Rupert. They ask for you constantly, and so look forward to your visits. Rupert will not be separated from Bear, Nanny Ryan tells me.

Devoted love always

Your Polly.

P.S Annie told me that Andrew Wellbeloved went to Eton.

But Bernard didn't write to James. On an impulse, he telephoned Eton College and asked to speak with him. "I would like to meet James for tea and discuss the memorial service we are planning for his parents in our local church."

The House Master readily agreed. "Why of course, Mr Maycroft. I am glad to have the opportunity to speak with you. As a matter of fact, I was about to write to you."

Bernard felt his heart quicken. "What's wrong. Is James in trouble?"

"Not at all, Mr Maycroft." The Master hastened to reassure him. "It is only that there had been some concern about James since the death of his parents. James began to spend a lot of time alone in his room and had withdrawn from all social activities, which he was very enthusiastic about before. He has, however, befriended a new boy, Alain Trouve, and we have noticed that the friendship seems to be bringing James out of his shell. Now, James has put in to join our Rifle Corp, and I thought, as you are his legal guardian, I ought to keep you informed. I gather he has not mentioned this to you?"

"No, indeed," replied Bernard faintly. "James never mentioned this at all, although I cannot imagine on what grounds I could object. James is a sensible boy, very mature for his years, I think."

"Indeed. I do agree that James will be an asset to the Corp. Just one other thing before I send for James. We have allowed a good number of weekend leaves for James to visit his cousins. The training in the

Corp will take up some weekends, which will curtail his home visits. I don't feel that this is a bad thing; James needs to settle again in his House. Please allow James to tell you himself about the Rifle Corp."

"I am very grateful for the support that everyone at Eton has given James, and certainly he says he is very happy in his House. Master, please accept my heartfelt thanks for your understanding, and I agree that James need to settle down again. Of course, I will wait for James to tell me his plans."

Bernard's conversation with James was brief. "Good to speak to you, Uncle Bernard. You're coming to visit, I hear. If you're coming by train, I can walk across and meet you on the bridge?"

"James, good hear you too. Yes, I am planning to come on Sunday afternoon. I thought I would stay overnight at Grieves Manor on Saturday to see the children and your Uncle Clarence. There are some things I need to discuss with Clarence."

"I received a letter from Polly about the new vicar at St Dominic's," James hesitated. "Did you want to speak about the memorial service now that we are able to have it in St. Dominic's?"

James's voice trembled slightly, and Bernard felt his heart wrench.

"Yes, dear boy, the new vicar is a kindly fellow, and I think he understands perfectly what we require. I wanted to have a chat rather than write to you as it would seem to be the right time to move forward with the memorial service for Henry and Estelle. I should be arriving in Windsor on the two-thirty. Will that suit you?"

"Of course, I look forward to seeing you on Sunday then, Uncle, please give my love to everyone."

The train from South Ascot arrived at Windsor and Eton Riverside Station at precisely two-thirty, and Bernard took a leisurely stroll down to the lovely old Windsor Bridge. The river was busy; several steamboats crowded with noisy tourists and holiday makers churned their way upriver.

A pair of racing row boats passed under the bridge, both coxswains urging their team forward, and by the river bank, a family of swans drifted majestically and serenely around enjoying the admirations of onlookers. It was a blustery day; the sky was heavy with rain clouds, and Bernard pulled his great coat around him. He was gazing down at the river, lost in thought when he heard his nephew's voice.

"Uncle," and there was James striding toward him, holding firmly onto his top hat, the long, black Eton coat flapping in the wind behind him.

Bernard hesitated, wanting to run and hug the boy, but instead he held out his hand, and James grasped it warmly.

"Good to see you, sir."

"And you, James, my boy, and you." Bernard leant back and looked at his nephew. In a few short months, James had grown, the pinstriped trousers were short of his ankles, and when James had reached out to shake his hand, he was eye-to-eye with his Uncle.

"My word, James, you have grown so much. We shall have to get you some more trousers, I think."

James looked down ruefully. "Yes, and I need new cricket whites as well." Looking sideways to gauge his uncle's reaction, he added casually, "By the way, I have joined the Rifle Corp, Uncle, so I shall require another uniform, I'm afraid."

Bernard was equally casual. "Have you, by Jove! That sounds jolly exciting, you will have to tell me all about it over tea."

James visibly relaxed. "So, no objections then, about the Rifle Corp, I mean."

"None, James, if that is what you want to do. Tea now, I think."

"The tea rooms on the corner of Thames Street have especially good high teas, Uncle, and you look as if you could do with a hot drink."

They walked as they talked, and several other Eton boys passed them, all immaculately presented in their Eton uniform, and as they neared, they touched the rim of their top hats respectfully and called a greeting to James.

The low-ceilinged, eleventh-century tea room was crowded with visitors and locals enjoying the famous high teas, but the waitress, nodding a greeting to James, hurried them over to a table by the window where an elderly couple were about to leave.

"I take it you are a regular visitor here then, James," Bernard teased and thanked the waitress.

"Whenever we can, Uncle," James agreed.

The sandwiches, cakes, and crumpets were indeed delicious, and the conversation was light as they relaxed and enjoyed the food. They chatted about Sadie and Rupert, the nannies, and the on-going legal work which hopefully Clarence was dealing with on his many trips to the London solicitors. They discussed the Rev. Andrew Wellbeloved, and Annie his wife, and how they had brought new life into the village. There was a gap in the conversation, and Bernard hesitated before saying something that had been on his mind for a long time.

"James, you know, I never really knew how unhappy you were at Barrow Hill, and without bringing up old grievances, you knew that I was never in favour of you going there with the twins."

James winced. "It was pretty dreadful, Uncle, and that is why I was dreading Eton so much," he said candidly, looking at Bernard with those clear, green eyes, so like Estelle's that Bernard's heart thumped painfully in his chest.

"But you are happy at Eton, are you not, because if you are not, then as your guardian, I can make changes." Bernard urged.

"Uncle, as much as I miss you and Polly, I simply could not bear to live all the time at Riverside. I am so sorry, and I feel the same about Grieves Manor. Please forgive me, but I am settled now at Eton, and I really hope that I can go on to Oxford, if I am good enough, of course."

"Don't apologise, James. I am just glad that you are happier here than you were at Barrow, although I must admit that I was worried about the 'fagging' at Eton. One hears such dreadful tales."

James laughed easily. "It turns out that I am rather a good debater and, oddly enough, not a bad bowler either, so I have got away lightly. But honestly, it is not bad at all, and I am in a good House with a decent set of chums, and most of them are in the Rifle Corp already."

Bernard nodded, thankful that his fears were unfounded, but sad that Estelle's beloved son only felt truly at home at Eton.

James leant across the table. "I have been thinking about the memorial for Mother and Father and came up with an idea," he hesitated. "I hope it's alright with you, Uncle. I thought that perhaps could we use Mummy's butterfly bronze as the memorial to them instead of the angel. Of course, that is, if it is not too late change things, but I think Mumma would really like that."

Bernard looked down at the boy's bent head and the long fingers clasped tightly together in tight fists. His bony young wrists jutted out from his coat sleeve, and Bernard felt a surge of love for his beloved nephew. "James, what a tremendous idea, and you are right. Estelle would love to think of her precious bronze being admired every day instead of being hidden away. We could arrange for our new vicar to bless it after the service. What do you think?"

James nodded wordlessly, and Bernard pretended not to see the single tear escape his downcast eyes and drip onto the snowy tablecloth. Bernard cleared his throat before broaching the subject that he had been dreading to mention. "There is just one more thing, James, dear boy, and I assure you that I will understand perfectly if you refuse. Foxy, of course, will come to the memorial service, but would you object to Perry coming with him?"

James lifted his head, and this time his eyes were clouded. "Of course not, Uncle. After all, Perry loved my father; it would not be fair to forbid him to come."

"Thank you, James, I think that is very good of you. Andrew suggested Sunday the 13th of October for the service and the blessing. I thought perhaps Manners could collect you and, of course, anyone else from Grieves Manor will be welcome. I had a word with Mary Ryan about Rupert and Sadie and perhaps old Nanny Florrie, but she thought it would be too upsetting for poor little Sadie, and Rupert is too young. Nanny Florrie, sadly, is too unwell."

James nodded, and simply replied, "Thank you for arranging it, Uncle."

James had previously avoided any discussion regarding the memorial service apart from insisting that it should be held in St. Dominic's. But from this conversation with his nephew, it was clear that James had been thinking about it, and his suggestion to use the little bronze sculpture as a memorial to Estelle and Henry had raised Bernard's fervent hope that he was coming to terms with the loss of his parents.

On his return to Riverside, Bernard took Polly to one side. "Polly, I have been able to speak with James about the memorial service, and he agrees, the middle Sunday in October would perhaps be the best time. James would like Estelle's butterfly bronze as Estelle and Henry's memorial. Polly, everyone will understand if you feel that you cannot attend, especially James."

"I have spoken with Mary Ryan, and she has said that she will stay at Grieves Manner with Nanny Florrie, Sadie, and Rupert. Perhaps you would prefer to go and stay at Grieves Manor for a few days?"

Polly swallowed hard. "Thank you, Bernard. Yes, I think I should like to be with Sadie and Rupert."

Bernard nodded, "Of course, my dear, that is settled then," he replied gently.

After a miserable and cool summer with days of constant rain, early October, though cold and bright, was a welcome change from the constant drizzle that had dogged the summer months. On the morning of the memorial service, there was a light ground frost, but it was dry, and the low mist covering the cropped fields drifted away as the sun climbed higher in a cloudless sky. The village awoke to the sombre tolling of the bells of St Dominic's, and as the time of the service drew near, a steady stream of people crossed the old bridge. Farmers, farm workers, and shopkeepers, the school children led by a softly weeping Miss Dove, and mill workers, led sombrely and proudly by Cedric, and many others from the outlying hamlets all made their way to the church.

Bernard had received word that Foxy and several of Henry's London friends would attend. "I have not heard from Perry," Foxy admitted, "But he does know what time the service is."

"Thank you, Foxy," Bernard replied with a sense of relief. Perhaps Perry would not attend after all.

Mick Carey had made guest rooms available at the Hop Vine, and Bernard ensured that refreshments would be served to all following the service. St Dominic's was filled to capacity, and those that couldn't get inside stood outside in the autumn sunshine.

At Bernard's request, Andrew Wellbeloved kept the memorial service simple, but in its very simplicity, it was all the more poignant. James stood rigidly between Clarence and Bernard, his head held high as he stared straight ahead. When Andrew, in a warm, gentle voice, spoke of Estelle as James's beloved mother, Bernard felt a shudder run through the boy, but still he held his composure and his head erect. Bessie and Ernest Brown stood in the front pew also, and between them, they supported a distraught Aggie.

When Andrew Wellbeloved's deep baritone led the choir in the last hymn, "I will lift up mine eyes," the combined voices of the congregation inside and outside the church rang out across the river and soared over the fields.

After the short service, the congregation, led by James and Bernard, filed out into the soft sunshine and gathered around the beautiful little filigree enclosure. Andrew made the sign of the cross, and gently placing his hands on *Estelle with Butterflies,* set now on the marble plinth, he prayed for the repose of the souls of Henry and Estelle Maycroft.

It was only then that James collapsed against Bernard. Annie stepped forward, and together they held the sobbing boy close, gently leading him away, back to Riverside.

The sun was low in the sky when Bernard left an exhausted James fast asleep in his bedroom, watched over by the kindly Clarence and a hovering Aggie. He felt lost and empty, hollow with grief. It was the finality of the memorial service that brought home to him that he would never again hear Estelle's laughter, or hear her footsteps as she ran through the house, calling to him, or Polly, or James. His heart twisted in pain, his head was pounding, and he did not want to be in the house, but neither did he want to be with people. Without stopping to get a hat or coat, he hurried into the kitchen where Tip and Aggie were talking quietly.

"I am going for a walk now, Aggie. Please keep an eye on James. I won't be long." He left without waiting for a reply.

The churchyard looked empty and desolate, although he could see that the church door was half open. Fading sunlight flickered through the falling leaves, and the mossy ground around the graves was littered with acorns and chestnuts. Autumn had moved in quickly, and already he could smell the wood smoke from the nearby cottages, and he breathed in deeply, feeling the fresh air clear his fuzzy head.

At first, he did not see the solitary figure standing motionless in the shadow of the cherry tree. The man was tall, hatless, a long black cloak slung casually across his thin shoulders. He stood perfectly still, staring fixedly at the engraving on the memorial stone. His head was bowed low, and his bony hands were clasped together over the top of a gold-tipped cane.

Bernard frowned, and hesitatingly lifted his hand, partly in greeting and partly to shield his eyes against the glare of the low sun. There was something about the man that seemed strangely familiar, and Bernard walked toward him. It was as if the man had sensed his approach, because he raised his head, and as he grew closer, Bernard found himself staring directly into the coal-black eyes of Peregrine Porter.

But this was not the suave, handsome, and confident man-about-town that Bernard remembered. This man was gaunt, almost skeletal, his face etched with deep lines, and his hair, once so black, had sweeping wings of pure white.

For a split-second, Perry held his gaze without a flicker of expression in his dark eyes, then he swivelled around, his cloak swirling out behind him, and he was gone, swinging his cane as he strode swiftly across the churchyard. Bernard stood transfixed until the tall figure was lost from view and jumped when he felt a hand touch him lightly on his shoulder.

"Bernard, old chap, sorry I startled you. Are you alright? I wondered how young James was?"

Bernard swung around. "Foxy, my God, was that Perry? I almost didn't recognise him. Has the poor chap been ill? Why did he rush away?"

Foxy shook his head sadly. "No, not ill, Bernard, well not physically, but Perry was totally grief-stricken when Henry died. He took it very hard and just went to pieces for a while, and I am afraid that he is still drinking far too much."

Bernard shook his head. "What a shame. That poor fellow. I had absolutely no idea. I just didn't realise how much he thought of Henry, although of course, I know that all Henry's friends love and miss him."

Foxy looked at Bernard with eyes filled with sadness. "Bernard, Perry didn't just love Henry. Perry was in love with Henry and had been for years. I thought for sure that you knew. All that business at Eton all those years ago, when Henry was forced to stand down, and then how badly Perry behaved when Henry married Estelle." Foxy's voice trailed off at the look of disbelief and confusion on Bernard's face. "Bernard, old chap, I am so very sorry. I honestly thought that you knew. I must go after Perry; I am sure you understand. Give James my love, and please do take care of yourself."

After a restless night of confusing, tangled dreams, Bernard eventually dozed off in the early hours of the morning but was woken from his uneasy sleep by the sound of a door being carefully closed. He lay for a while and listened, but hearing nothing else, he reached for his dressing gown and padded barefoot over to the window.

In the weak light of early morning, he saw James walking purposely down the garden path before disappearing under the apple trees at the far end of the garden. Bernard dressed quickly and made his way down to the kitchen, stopping briefly to glance inside the dining room. The table was undisturbed, still laid out for breakfast. Aggie, looking pale and tired, appeared behind him.

"Master James has gone down to the Folly, Mr Bernard. I heard him tell Tip that he was going back to school today." Aggie sniffed and brushed a hand across her eyes. "That cannot be right, Mr Bernard. The poor lad is not ready to go back to school."

"He said he didn't want any breakfast. He wasn't hungry. I am so worried about him, Mr Bernard. It's just too much to bear for a lad of his age." Her ample chins wobbled, and the tears rolled down her cheeks.

Bernard put his arm around her. "Now Aggie, don't you worry.

You just lay a couple of places at the kitchen table. I will go and have a chat with him, and then we will eat our breakfast in your nice, warm kitchen."

Aggie gulped. "I'll do that, Mr Bernard. I just wish that Polly was here with him. He needs our Polly now."

"Polly will be back soon, Aggie. The service would have been too much for her, we both know that."

Bernard found James standing on the riverbank, gazing down into the sun-dappled water, his hands thrust deeply into his trouser pockets. "James, old chap, are you all right?" His nephew turned a pale but composed face to his uncle.

"Did I wake you, Uncle? I am sorry. I could not sleep."

Bernard laid a gentle hand on his nephew's thin shoulder. "Not really, James, I was just dozing. I must admit that I did not have a very good night's sleep either and I could really eat some breakfast now. Would you keep me company, dear boy?"

James took a deep breath. "Of course. But after breakfast, I need to pack and get ready to go back to Eton, today if possible." He stared anxiously at Bernard, silently pleading for his beloved Uncle's understanding.

Bernard nodded sadly. "James, if that is what you want, then of course I understand. Let us have our breakfast, and perhaps we could contact Manners to come and collect you."

James shook his head. "No, I would rather go on the train, Uncle, please. I am perfectly all right, I assure you, and I will ring you as soon as I arrive back."

Bernard looked at James's set face. " Of course, James. I will accompany you as far as Windsor, however, as I need to speak with Clarence. But do promise me that you will call when you are back at Eton."

"Yes, sir, I promise," said James gratefully.

Bernard understood that the staff at Grieves Manor, despite their grief, would be worried about their jobs, and he was unsure whether Lord Grieves-Croft's solicitors were coming closer to settling the estate.

Clarence Grieves-Croft was a perfectly charming, but unworldly, man and seemed utterly bemused by what had happened. A confirmed elderly bachelor, he confessed to Bernard that he found Rupert's exuberance disruptive and Sadie's barely-concealed grief made him uncomfortable.

"Couldn't cope without you and Polly, old boy. I would be in a fine mess, and of course, the Brents and the nannies have been so kind and helpful, but I really need to be back in France as soon as possible," he was apologetic and clearly anxious.

"I know what will happen," Mrs Brent said to her husband. "We will all be given our marching orders, that's what will happen. Mr Clarence won't want to stay here for much longer. He'll go back to France as soon as the will is all settled. Whatever will happen to those children, I wonder?"

"Things won't be settled that quickly, even if Mr Clarence goes back to France. But don't fret about the children. They still have us and Mary and don't forget Polly. She is devoted to them. Mr Bernard will make sure they are all looked after. We just have to carry on as best we can." Brent reassured his wife with a certainty that he was far from feeling.

At the end of October, little St Dominic's was overflowing for Andrew's first Harvest Festival Service. Andrew and Annie were once again astounded at the generosity of the villagers. The weather was fine enough for the traditional Harvest Festival feast to be held in Lower Meadow. The tables and chairs were dragged out from the village hall, and the tables soon laden with hams and chickens, stuffed marrows and steaming beetroots, mounds of potatoes and hot meat pies. Pat O'Donnell loaded his hay wagon with barrels of homemade cider which he sold for a penny a jug, and Mick Carey provided lemonade for the children.

When it was time to go home, and as the moon rose over the harvested fields, Andrew said a prayer of thanks to God for a bountiful harvest. With Bernard standing next to him, he asked the people of Shorehill to join with their neighbours and pray for the souls lost on the Titanic, and for the survivors, ending with a special prayer for the Maycroft and Grieves-Croft families.

Bernard Maycroft held tightly onto Polly, as she stood stiffly by his side, knowing that he would be eternally grateful to the bishops for sending the Wellbeloveds to Shorehill at a time when the grieving village were sorely in need of such a strong and compassionate man of God.

If Bernard had found solace and comfort in his growing friendship with Andrew, then Polly also had found a good friend in Annie Wellbeloved, and like Bernard, she was a frequent visitor to the warm and welcoming old vicarage. Over the months since her return, Polly had quietly and efficiently taken over the running of Riverside with the support of the ever-loyal Aggie. Bernard made no objection to any changes in the house but, even with Polly's gentle encouragement, he refused to allow any work to Estelle's garden.

"Just make sure that the Folly is cared for, Polly. Matthew can take care of the gardens, but Estelle's garden is to be left alone," and on this matter, Bernard remained strangely resolute.

The weeks slipped by, and Estelle's lovely gardens became lost to the brambles and the weeds as they greedily took over. The pretty French garden furniture that Estelle and Henry had brought back from their honeymoon, so much admired by their guests, was locked away in the stables. One early winter morning, wandering aimlessly around the garden after breakfast, Polly paused under an arbour of tangled honeysuckle and rose hips and looked around sadly. The garden urns that had once overflowed with brilliant red geraniums and sweet lavender were empty now with just strands of dead ivy.

A stone mermaid perched at the side of the dried-up waterfall was pitted and freckled with lichen, and her fanned tail drooped sadly into a green and stagnant pond, a pond that was once filled with darting goldfish and delicate, waxy water lilies. Polly walked over and pulled strands of stubborn bindweed away from the mermaid's smug, stone face. A slight, almost secret smile hovered around the mermaid's mouth, and Polly could hear Estelle's voice as the statue was unpacked and her peals of laughter that had rang out across the garden.

"Polly," she had called. "Oh, Polly, do come and look at this mermaid. She's not very pretty, but my goodness she is looking rather pleased with herself, isn't she?"

Tip, as was his early morning custom, was exercising Captain around the yard, and saw Polly standing with her hand resting on the stone mermaid. He sighed and shook his head. "Sad times, Captain," he said, patting the stallion's enormous rump. "I'll wager you are missing your Master, too," and led him back into the warm stables.

When Tip went into the kitchen at dinner time, he said, "I saw Polly in the garden earlier. Is our girl all right, Aggie?"

"I wish I knew," Aggie sighed. "But I'm not as worried about her as I was before the vicar and his wife arrived. She spends a lot of time at the vicarage with Annie Wellbeloved, and I think it has done her good. But she still goes off to Berkshire every other week, and I don't know why. That great house must feel so empty now. There is just that girl cousin, Sadie, and I think the boy is still there, and of course the servants. Polly says that the nanny stayed to take care of the little boy, and Sadie is very delicate. Mr Bernard said that Master James will not be able to spend so much time at the house because he doesn't get weekend leave any more. There's enough staff at Grieves Manor to take care of everything, so why she has to go rushing off there so often, I do not know."

"Maybe she just wants to fill her time up, Aggie. After all, she was always with Miss Estelle or Master James. Perhaps being with the young'uns down there helps her. Has she ever said anything at all about that night, you know, when Titanic went down?"

"Not a word. I said to Mr Bernard, it's almost as if she's wiped it from her mind. He said good job, too, but I'm not so sure. I know one thing though, Tip. I'll be glad when this year is out and over and done with."

CHRISTMAS 1912 - ALAIN TROUVE

A few weeks before Christmas, Annie Wellbeloved tentatively approached Polly about the Christmas party for the children.

"Polly, I wonder, should we cancel the children's Christmas party this year? Ernie told Andrew that it is a Maycroft tradition, but under the circumstances..." Annie hesitated.

Polly shook her head firmly. "No, Annie, Mr Bernard has said that there is no question of cancelling the party. It must go ahead, just as usual. The children love it so, and all the usual festivities must go ahead as well. Miss Estelle loved Christmas. She and Master James even used to decorate the Folly with paper chains and holly, and we used to sing carols down there on Christmas Eve, even if it was freezing. We should get started on the arrangements soon, Annie. Aggie and Bessie have been nagging me as well. Come to tea next Saturday afternoon. Mr Bernard is going down to Grieves Manor for the weekend. James wants to go Christmas shopping for the children."

That Saturday, Andrew was locked in his study working on the Sunday sermon. Bessie had gone shopping with Aggie, promising to be back in time to meet Annie at Riverside in the afternoon. Annie Wellbeloved was restless. The weather for most of December had been miserable, heavy, low clouds with drizzling mist and dank dark days that seemed to drift into night-time. "It's too early to go to Riverside," Annie mused, looking gloomily out of the window. "But I could go across to Lovett's and pick up some wool for Andrews's socks and go on to Riverside from there." The idea of chatting with the ever-happy Lovett sisters cheered her up and, pushing her feet into her boots and grabbing a coat from the hallstand, she called goodbye to Andrew and set off.

She had barely crossed the bridge when it began to rain in earnest, icy, driving rods of rain that bounced off the river and stung her face. Annie pulled her coat over her head and cutting short her planned visit to the Lovett's, she set off in the direction of Riverside, running under the dripping trees and jumping over the puddles. Breathless but exhilarated, she dashed through the rusting old gates and along the drive. Taking the steps two at a time, she huddled in the doorway and lifted the heavy old door knocker and banged down hard, twice, three times. The sound echoed around the hallway, and Annie waited and knocked again. There were no familiar sounds from the stable yard, no clatter of hooves on the cobbles, or Tip's tuneless whistle. Riverside appeared to be deserted. Pulling her now-sodden coat back over her head, she ran back down the steps, around to the back of the house, and through the kitchen yard.

The kitchen door was closed, and she cupped her hands over her eyes and peered through the streaming window. Polly had her back to the window and was standing at the sink, washing up. Annie rapped hard on the window, and Polly turned around, waved a greeting, and ran over to open the kitchen door. "Annie, you poor thing, you are wet through. Come in and sit down by the stove."

Annie shrugged out of the wet coat and shook it, sending a shower of rain drops in the air.

"Here," said Polly. "Give it to me and take your boots off." Polly stood Annie's muddy boots on an old newspaper by the stove and hung the wet coat up behind the kitchen door.

"Sorry I'm early, Polly," Annie said breathlessly. "But I was so bored at home, I was going to get some wool, but it started to rain so heavily, I just came on here."

"Never mind," said Polly briskly. "I'm on my own today as well. It's the kitchen maid's half day, Tip has taken Pepper and Captain to the smithy, and he stays for ages gossiping with Jacob. Aggie and Bessie have gone on the train to Sevenoaks, but they shouldn't be long; Tip is picking them up from the four-thirty. I'll make us a nice cup of tea while we wait." Polly busied herself at the stove, and Annie sat back and looked out of the kitchen window, blurred with rain.

"The garden must have been so lovely at one time, Polly," she observed idly.

Polly put the cups and saucers on the table and took some biscuits from the tin, put them on a plate, and set it down in front of Annie. "Blanche Dove's best shortbread," she said, and sat down. "It was beautiful. This part of the garden was Miss Estelle's. She had such wonderful ideas, everyone talked about the gardens. Once, they were featured in a London Magazine, and my goodness, the parties they used to have here, almost every weekend. Well, that was until Master James started school at Barrow Hill. He was a boarder, you see, and after that, well, Miss Estelle, she sort of lost interest in the garden. Just went back to Grieves Manor whenever she could so she could be closer to Master James when he came home at the weekend."

"But why doesn't anyone take care of the garden now?" Annie was curious.

Polly shook her head sadly, "Nobody took much care of the gardens after the old master and mistress died. The gardeners just cut the grass and kept it tidy. That was long before I started to work here. But when Miss Estelle arrived, everything changed. She and Mr Bernard used to sit in the library for hours, planning where to put her statues and urns that she brought back from Italy and France. They would go through magazines searching for the most exotic plants they could find. It was wonderful."

Polly looked out of the window, seemingly lost in her memories. "Mr Henry wasn't interested in the gardens, only for parties for his friends. He wasn't happy to stay at Riverside for long, as he always wanted to be in London or off to the races or the clubs. Miss Estelle never complained and went along with anything that made Mr Henry happy, but when James was born, she stayed home more and more, and never wanted to leave him. Mr Henry said she spent too much time at Riverside, and she should go back to London with him."

She smiled wryly. "But of course, when the gardens appeared as a feature in *Country Life* and everyone was talking about Riverside, Mr Henry suddenly took an interest and began inviting his London friends down for weekends, and the parties went on all through the summer. But Miss Estelle and James, they were forever down at the Folly, paddling in the river, and sometimes on warm nights, they would sleep there, tucked up together, nice and cosy. Miss Estelle taught young James about the insects and the birds, and he could name the wildflowers in the meadows when he was really little. We were so proud of him. Then, when he was old enough, Blanche Dove came to the house to tutor him, and they got on so well, you could hear them laughing together in the nursery. They were such happy times." Polly's tone was wistful.

Annie listened intently without interrupting.

"Then, one weekend, out of the blue, Mr Henry said that James was too old to be schooled at home, and it was time to join his cousins boarding at Barrow Hill. That caused an almighty upset, I can tell you, and Miss Estelle was heartbroken, but Mr Henry insisted that it would be good for him and would not listen to anyone, not even Mr Bernard. That friend of Mr Henry's, Peregrine, Miss Estelle said it was his fault, he told Henry that James should be sent away. Peregrine used to scare me."

Polly shivered, seeing Peregrine's black-hooded eyes and the cruel, sardonic smile and slow wink he gave her whenever he caught her glance.

Annie, who could contain herself no longer, asked curiously.

"So, Polly, if Bernard and Estelle spent so much time on the gardens, why wouldn't Bernard want the gardens to be kept in the way that he and Estelle designed them?"

"We just don't know," Polly admitted. "It's almost as if he wants the gardens to remain exactly as she left them. Jacob Brown made some lovely new gates for Riverside. Miss Estelle designed them, but they are hidden away in the stables. Mr Bernard won't have the gates put up, because they were delivered while we were in France, and Miss Estelle never saw them."

It was the first reference to the fateful trip to France that Polly had ever made to anyone, and Annie held her breath. It seemed that now that Polly had broken her silence, she was eager to carry on talking, and she continued, her voice low.

"Mr Bernard was devoted to my mistress. She changed his life when she married Mr Henry and they came to Riverside. I think that Mr Bernard must have been lonely before Miss Estelle arrived, and I do believe now that she has gone, his heart is broken. The evening before we left for France, I remember watching them from the bedroom window whilst I was packing. Mr Bernard and Miss Estelle, they were talking together and walking arm-in-arm around the garden. Mr Bernard told me later that Miss Estelle had asked him to help her to redesign the garden when she came back from New York. She felt that she had neglected the garden whilst James was at Barrow Hill, but now he was a boarder at Eton, she said she could spend more time at Riverside. That is what Mr Bernard told me, and now he won't let anyone else do any work in her gardens, although he allows Tip and Matthew to take care of the Folly. Miss Estelle loved that little Folly so much. It was their special place, you see, her and James."

Polly gazed at the rain streaming down the kitchen window.

Annie stood up and put her arms around Polly. "Come, Polly, we won't speak of this anymore. I'll make more tea, and we can take it up to the library and make a list of what we need for the party."

Bessie and Aggie returned from their shopping trip, dripping with rain and laden with bags of shopping, to find Polly and Annie chatting comfortably by the fire in the library. For the remainder of the afternoon, the four friends shared ideas on how best to entertain a school full of excited children.

Later that night at dinner, Polly discussed with Bernard the ideas the ladies had decided on for the children's party.

"Thank you so much for organizing the party, Polly. Sadie and

Rupert will enjoy it. I am sure spending Christmas at Riverside would be better for them this year rather than staying at Grieves Manor."

"An excellent idea, Bernard," Mary Ryan had replied gratefully, when Bernard had suggested that they should come to Shorehill for Christmas. "You have your obligations to the village, and it will be far better for Sadie and Rupert to be away from this house for a while. There are too many memories of last Christmas, and now with so many of the rooms locked up, it's a very sad house. Nobody wants to be here, especially at Christmas. The Brents have already asked if they can have Christmas off, but said, of course, they will stay if needs be."

Bernard wrote to James, and his reply took Bernard by surprise. As he read it, his heart dropped:

Dear Uncle, I am glad that it is all settled. Rupert and Sadie will love Christmas at Riverside. I have some rather exciting news to tell you too. Do you remember my chum Alain Trouve? Alain and his father have invited me on a skiing holiday in Chamonix in the New Year. Alain's aunt has a chalet near Mont Blanc, and they ski there every year. Alain's father, Comte Trouve, is writing to you with the travel arrangements. Of course, I do need your permission, Uncle, but I would rather like to go. I do hope that everyone at Riverside is well.

With love, as ever James.

Bernard stared at the letter and sank wearily into his battered old chair by the fire in the library. Of course, he would give his permission, and he was glad that James sounded so excited, but there was a nagging feeling that James was drifting further and further away from them. It was apparent to Bernard that James would prefer to be anywhere rather than at Riverside, or indeed, Grieves Manor, and who could blame him, he thought sadly.

Polly found him slumped in his chair gazing moodily into the fire. "Bernard, it's freezing in here. The fire has gone right down."

She leant down and took some logs from the basket and threw

them into the grate. When Bernard did not reply, she turned to him and saw the letter lying crumpled on the side table, "Is that from James? How is he?"

"James is well, but Polly, read what he says about Christmas," Bernard replied gloomily.

Polly read the letter in silence, smoothed out the creases, and placed it back on the table. "Well, at least James will be here for Christmas, Bernard," and added, "You should allow him go to France with his friend."

"I know," Bernard replied sadly. "But I feel as if we are losing him, too, Polly. Surely you can see that he would rather be at Eton with his friends than be with any of us."

"I know, and for a while I thought he was avoiding coming to Riverside because I reminded him of what happened."

Bernard looked at her in horror, but before he could say anything, Polly hurried on.

"But now I don't think that at all. He's not avoiding any of us, Bernard. It is just easier for him not to be where there are memories, and there are so many of them here and at Grieves Manor. Let him go, Bernard, because I know he will come back to us in the end. We must just be patient."

Bernard sighed. "Of course. I would not dream of stopping him. It sounds like a wonderful trip, but I do hope you're right, Polly. I pray, in time, that our boy comes back to us."

Polly picked up the letter and read it again. "Who is Alain Trouve? I don't think that James has ever mentioned him."

"Alain Trouve is in the same House as James, The Trimbralls. I met him once. He's a funny little chap, half French. I believe his mother is dead, and the father is in the Diplomatic Corp. Well, I suppose I shall just have to wait for the Comte's letter, which, no doubt, is on its way." Bernard replied a little disagreeably.

The "funny little chap" that Bernard referred to was Alain Trouve, and he had arrived at Eton halfway through James's first term. The House Master introduced him after supper one evening,

"Gentlemen, Mr Trouve will be joining The Trimbralls, and I would like you to welcome him."

The boys stood up and clapped politely, murmuring, "Welcome, Trouve."

Alain Trouve, thin and wiry, was at least a head and shoulder shorter than most of the boys. His jet-black hair flopped across his pale face, and beneath his fringe, his black eyes danced with merriment as he gave a short bow. "Good evening, and thank you gentlemen," he replied with a heavy French accent and a sardonic grin.

The boys sat down.

"Not you, Maycroft," the Master said. "Trouve is in the room next to yours. Pop him along to Dame and then show him his room. There's a good chap."

Normally, James would have resented being picked out, but there was something about the cool confidence of the strange boy that he found intriguing. "Why do you have to see Dame first?" he asked curiously.

"Dodgy chest," the boy replied and punched his chest with the side of his fist as if to demonstrate. "Just out of hospital, so I missed the beginning of term. I have to go to Dame to make sure I am fit and well, which I am of course, although I would be grateful if you could slow down a bit," and he grinned at James.

James's long strides had taken them quickly through the corridors, and now he stopped and could clearly hear the boy wheezing. "Sorry, Trouve. You should have said, but we are here now," and he rapped sharply on the door in front of them.

If it hadn't been for Alain Trouve's many talents, he may have easily had a much harder time settling into the close-knit House than he did. Apart from being a gifted mimic, he could also sketch cartoons of the Masters at lightning speed, and the likenesses were remarkable.

The French boy was also a gifted scholar, and handled each subject with ease, and his ability to laugh at himself and his constant illnesses, combined with his willingness to help the slower students, soon made him a popular member of The Trimbralls. He did, however, form a close friendship with James Maycroft, drawn as he was to the tall, quiet, reserved boy who could hold his own in heated debates and excelled on the cricket pitch.

It was inevitable that sooner or later, one of the Trouve cartoons would fall into the hands of one of the Masters, and one did, of course. The cartoons were not in any way malicious, but they were cleverly executed with just an emphasis on the Master in question's more prominent features, a slightly longer nose, exaggerated ears, tufty hair around a bald pate, long chin, or bulging eyes.

Most of the Masters, of course, had a favourite saying or quote, so each cartoon had a balloon coming from his mouth with wicked variations on the words. If a Master turned from the blackboard to find a group of boys sitting close to Trouve rocking with silent mirth, then he would simply hold out his hand to Trouve, who would stand up and hand over the sketch with a polite bow.

It would have been difficult to find a great deal of fault with the sketches, as they were brilliantly drawn, and soon there was a collection of *Trouves* in the staff room, each new one affording the staff great amusement.

When the somewhat rotund Latin Master was heard to remark, "The little blighter hasn't done one of me, just let me catch him," there was a splutter of laughter from the History Master, who took his pipe from his mouth and said, "Billings, pop out and look in the gatehouse. The porter has had a rather excellent caricature of you pinned to his wall for a couple of weeks."

When James had returned to Eton after the Titanic sinking, his house mates were quietly sympathetic, some openly expressing their sorrow, whilst others were unable to express their sympathy with the right words. The House Master accepted that James needed time alone to grieve and try and come to terms with the loss of his family and would have worried more about his desire for isolation had it not been for the irrepressible Alain Trouve.

There were times when the House Master popped his head around James's bedroom door to find both boys engrossed in a game of chess or arguing fiercely on the merits of various famous cricketers. When James awoke in the night calling out in a panic that he could only describe later as sinking into a black hole, inevitably, Trouve would be with him, shaking him awake.

"Sorry, Trouve, did I wake you with my yelling again? Bloody nightmares are a nuisance."

"And I thought I woke you with my bloody coughing, Maycroft," would come the dry reply.

Sometimes, James wandered off on his own, seeking some quiet away from the hubbub in the House. Alain Trouve knew where to find him. James could be found sitting dreamily on the bank at Barnes Pool, watching the brown trout darting in and out of the reeds.

"It reminds me of Riverside and the Folly," James explained.

"Take me to Riverside, and I will draw it for you, Maycroft," Alain replied simply.

The opportunity for Alain to visit Riverside came sooner than either boy could have realised.

When the letter from Comte Trouve arrived at Riverside in a heavily embossed envelope, stamped by the French Embassy, it contained precise details of the travel arrangements to Chamonix. Bernard opened it with a heavy heart. The formal letter, typed with precision, was signed at the bottom, "Comte Trouve," and would have appeared stiff and cold, had it not been for the note that the Comte had written after his signature:

"Dear Mr Maycroft, I would like to express my gratitude to you for permitting James to accompany Alain to Chamonix. Regretfully, due to official commitments, I am unable to spend Christmas with my son, but I will be free to accompany them both to Chamonix to stay with my sister. Rest assured that James will be well-looked after, and I am sure he will enjoy learning to ski. Alain is an excellent skier and will tutor James well."

Sincerely Yours

Comte. L Trouve.

After dinner that evening, Bernard was enjoying his pipe by the fire in the library when Polly came in to say goodnight. "The letter from Alain's father arrived, Polly," and he pointed the stem of his pipe at the mantelpiece, "It's behind the clock. Read what it says; there is rather a nice note at the end, and it has made me feel better about James going off to France."

Polly reached up and took the envelope. "From the French Embassy," she said with raised brows and settled down on the window seat to read it. When she finished, she gazed out of the window, then turned to Bernard. "Might you think about asking James if his friend would like to spend Christmas here with us, Bernard? The boy sounds lonely."

"I was thinking the very same thing," Bernard admitted.

Polly jumped up. "Good, then I shall write to James straight away. If he says Alain wants to come, we will have a full house," she said with a great deal of satisfaction and counted on her fingers. "Let me see now. There's Nanny Ryan, Rupert and Sadie, Ernie and Bessie, Andrew and Annie, James and Alain, you and me, and Tip, of course. That's not too many, and Annie and I will help Aggie in the kitchen," and with a happy nod to Bernard, she hurried from the room.

James replied almost immediately:

"Dear Polly, thank you and Uncle Bernard. Alain says he would love to spend Christmas with us at Riverside and says to thank you for the invitation."

What in fact Alain had said was, "Maycroft, you have saved my bacon. I was going to have to spend Christmas with my Aunt Drippy."

James snorted with laughter. "That's not her real name, Trouve. It can't be."

"No, it's not. She's an old spinster, somehow related to my late Ma. She lives in this ghastly old house in Richmond. It's always freezing cold because she is too mean to light the fires." Alain pulled a face.

"Perhaps she can't afford the coal, poor thing, but why Drippy? You still haven't said."

Alain shook his head, "Oh, she can afford to buy coal for the whole of London if she so wished. She is as rich as Croesus. She's just mean, and because the house is so cold all the time, even in summer, her nose is always dripping, hence Aunt Drippy." He smirked. "But she's the only relative I have in England, so Father had to ask Aunt Drippy if I could stay with her for Christmas. So, thank you Maycroft, your invitation is gratefully accepted, and tell your Uncle that he has saved a chap from a soulless Christmas dinner of cold lamb chops, boiled potatoes, and hard Brussels sprouts."

The invitation for Christmas at Riverside elicited another letter from Comte Trouve, thanking Bernard profusely for his hospitality and confirming that he would collect both boys for the skiing trip from Riverside after the Christmas holiday.

Bernard made a call to Grieves Manor a few days later, Brent answered. "Brent, good day to you, I wonder if I could speak with Mary, just to make the final arrangements for Christmas. What are your plans for the holiday?"

"Good day, Mr Maycroft, well as you know, Mr Grieves-Croft is going back to France soon, so we will close the house up and spend Christmas with Mrs Brent's mother. We are quite looking forward to it, I must say, " he hesitated. "I wonder, Mr Maycroft, whether you could find room for Manners at Riverside. The other staff have families locally, but Manners has no family." Brent hurried on before Bernard could reply, "We would ask him to stay at Mrs Brent's mother's, but her cottage is so small."

Bernard interrupted him, "Of course Manners can stay with us, Brent. After all, it makes sense if he is driving everyone here anyway. There's plenty of room in Tip's place above the stables."

"That's a great relief, sir. Mrs Brent will be so pleased. I'll fetch Mary for you."

The House Master of The Trimbralls called Bernard the very next day. "Mr Maycroft, I just wanted to thank you for taking young Trouve for the Christmas. Comte Trouve is eternally grateful. The boy suffers from asthma and has had several bad attacks this term, so staying with his aunt was not going to be ideal. I will fetch James for you now and you can confirm your travel arrangements."

There was a light tone to James's voice when he picked up the phone, "Uncle, jolly good. I was hoping you would ring. I take it Manners will be bringing all of us next week?"

"Yes, James. It's all arranged with Nanny Ryan, and she says that Rupert and Sadie are very excited. How is Alain?"

"Alain is very excited as well, Uncle, but just one more thing. Sadie wrote and said to ask would you please not dress the Christmas tree until we get there."

Bernard laughed. "We would not dream of it, James. Part of the fun at Christmas is dressing the tree."

In truth, until recently, Bernard had thought that James would prefer a quiet Christmas and had not therefore made any arrangements to decorate the house. So, happy now at the change of plans, he instructed a delighted Polly to speak to Tip about a tree. "Tell him to get the biggest he can find and put it in the usual place in the hall. We are going to have a proper Christmas after all, Polly."

When on Thursday before Christmas, the Daimler, with Manners at the wheel, rolled to a halt on the drive at Riverside. There was a brief respite from the rain that had lashed down since early morning., but the wind was howling through the village, tossing the willows on the river into frenzy and bending the branches of the tall trees around Riverside. This did not deter the excited passengers, and they tumbled out of the car to be hurried inside the gaily decorated and warm hallway. There was a confusion of kisses and loving hugs, and amidst this Alain, diminutive next to an ever-growing lanky James, gazed around him, smiling with delight. Rupert, still holding tightly onto Sadie's hand, was dancing up and down with excitement and pointing to the massive, unadorned Christmas tree that stretched high up into the stairwell.

Alain, remembering his manners, held his hand out to Bernard, and gave a stiff little bow, but the wide smile never left his face. "Again, my thanks, Mr Maycroft. I am sure that James has told you that I have been saved from a dreadful fate."

Bernard chuckled, immediately taking a liking to the engaging young boy. "Well, we are very pleased that you are spending Christmas with us, Alain," and turning to Polly, who was still hugging James, "Polly, if you will show everyone to their rooms, I shall assist Tip and Manners with the luggage."

Sadie, on the journey from Berkshire, had almost overcome her shyness with Alain and had been persuaded to leave Mary Ryan's side, and one by one, the guests made their way to their rooms. Manners was hurried away by Tip. "A nice big whisky for you, my lad," he said after helping Manners with the luggage.

When Bernard came back into the hall, he was greeted with hoots of laughter coming from the drawing room. Alain was sprawled out on the floor in front of the fire, sketching rapidly. Rupert, watching every pen stroke, was sitting next to him, wide-eyed and silent for once. Polly and Sadie were looking over Alain's shoulder, convulsed with giggles. Alain made to get up when he saw Bernard in the doorway, but Bernard shook his head. "Carry on, Alain, but what have you done to the girls? I don't think that I have ever seen Rupert sitting so quietly."

"Alain is drawing his Aunt Drippy," gigged Sadie, all shyness forgotten. "Please come and look, Uncle Bernard. It is so funny."

Alain had sketched an impossibly tall lady, with enormous feet sitting at a tiny dining room table on which sat a plate with two small lamb chops, a mound of mashed potatoes, and three sprouts. In one large hand she held a fork whilst the other clasped an oversized handkerchief against her long red nose.

Alain looked up at Bernard innocently, "I am not being unkind, sir. Really, it really is a very good likeness of Auntie," but try as he might, he could not disguise the merriment dancing in his black eyes.

Bernard laughed. "You have a very unusual talent, young man."

When in darker times, Polly looked back at that Christmas of 1912, she did so in wonder and gratitude to the little French boy who, with his irrepressible love of life and people, lifted their spirits at the end of a year of immeasurable sadness grief and loss.

During his stay in Shorehill that Christmas, Alain Trouve

endeared himself to almost everyone he met, making friends instantly as he darted through the village, sketching rapidly. At the end of his visit, it seemed that almost everyone in the village were proud owners of a Trouve sketch or cartoon.

On Christmas day, Alain presented James with a sketch of the Folly, precise in every detail, the doors slightly open, giving a glimpse of the interior. There was Estelle's chaise longue and at the side, *Estelle with Butterflies,* and on the table, a vase filled with sunflowers. James received it with barely concealed tears, and Alain turned away.

To Bernard, he presented another sketch of Estelle's bronze. It had been lovingly drawn, with every curl defined, even the entwined daisy chain around the tiny head. He had captured perfectly the smile of an innocent child. Rather than place her on the memorial marble, Alain had drawn *Estelle with Butterflies* amidst a green field of a million daisies. Bernard was touched beyond words and vowed to have it framed. He placed next to the window seat in the library, where he could gaze on it every day.

Sadie, Alain had drawn as a tiny fairy, light as dandelion fluff floating on a pink cloud in a clear blue sky. Rupert, he drew, sweetly asleep in his striped pyjamas with Bear on his pillow and a Christmas stocking on the end of his bed.

He drew the innocent-faced school children, open-mouthed singing in St Dominic's on Christmas Eve, and rather wickedly depicted Miss Dove as a little angel hovering above the children with a baton poised above her head.

Alain pestered Bessie daily. "You are not going to draw me, young man, so be off with you now." Bessie told him firmly, but even then, he drew a sketch of Bessie with a fearsome grimace on her face chasing him out of the vicarage kitchen with a tea towel. This reduced Ernie to helpless laughter, and he refused to hand it over to Bessie but pinned it on the wall in his shed and locked the door.

Tallow, the drayman, nodded, and after studying a sketch of his beloved Shires standing serene and magnificent in the shallows by the bridge, smiled briefly at the boy. "Not bad at all," he allowed, and Alain knew that it was high praise indeed from the taciturn old man.

He drew the Ancients, puffing on their old pipes, hunched over on the bench by the river, bony knees pressed together, gummy smiles on their old, lined faces. Much to Andrew's delight, he drew the Revered Andrew standing in the pulpit, hands pressed together in prayer with a saintly halo above his head. When Alain drew a smiling Aggie on a garden swing with Tip as a tiny leprechaun sitting on her lap, it was Tip's turn to chase the laughing boy around the stable yard.

But the sketch he did at the request of Mick Carey, the landlord of the Hop Vine, caused the most merriment in the village. Finding Alain, sitting on the bridge one afternoon busily sketching Blanche Dove cleaning her windows, Mick took him to one side and related the story of Constable Charlie Briggs's unfortunate encounter on the bridge with Jacky Dales and the terrible Brown twins. Mick was able to give a fair description of the constable, and Alain had already sketched the boys in question.

Constable Briggs was not a great favourite of Mick's. The overweight constable was always ready to point out any tiny infringement of the law to Mick, but nevertheless expected to able to sup free pints of stout whenever he was off-duty and passing through the village.

Alain, having heard the story, could scarcely believe his luck at being handed the perfect comedy sketch and set to work, his fingers moving lightly and rapidly across the paper.

When a broadly-grinning James and an innocent-faced Alain delivered the finished sketches to Mick, the landlord was speechless with delight, for there were two sketches, and Alain had captured the incident as if he had witnessed it himself. The first sketch depicted an enormously fat policeman on a miniscule bicycle approaching the humpbacked bridge. He was bent over the handlebars, his fat face blood-red beneath the tiny helmet that was perched on the top of his wispy hair, and every button on his uniform was strained to bursting point.

In the second sketch, the constable was flat on his back with two fat legs waving in the air and the upturned bicycle beside him. The unmistakable faces of the twins, Toby and Theo Brown and little Jacky Dales peered grinning over the side of the bridge, and to add insult to injury, Alain had drawn Blanche Dove outside her cottage, convulsed with laughter.

Mick could hardly contain himself, and within a few days, both sketches had been framed and hung above the bar, much to the amusement of locals and visitors. Charlie Briggs, on his next visit to the Hop Vine, nearly choked on the free pint of stout that Mick innocently handed to him, and he thundered out after one gulp, muttering angrily under his breath.

1913

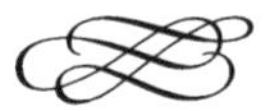

Early in the New Year of 1913, on a bitterly cold day of biting wind and snow flurries, Comte Trouve arrived in Shorehill to collect James and Alain for their skiing trip to Chamonix. The Comte was unexpectedly tall and thin with a stern air that softened when he spoke about his son. He shook Bernard's hand and said in faultless English, "Mr Maycroft, I cannot thank you and James enough for your hospitality to Alain. I do hope he has behaved himself; he can be rather exuberant."

Bernard, in all honesty, was able to reply, "It has been a real pleasure to have Alain stay with us. I think we were all rather dreading Christmas, but Alain has been a true breath of fresh air, and I will be eternally grateful to him for his friendship and loyalty to James during the last dreadful year."

The Comte's dark eyes, so like Alain's, were filled with compassion, but he replied simply, "This friendship with James has been good for my son too. Alain rarely forms an attachment with any boy, or group of boys. Because of his health, he is often away from school, but his friendship with James is different, which is why I thought the visit to Chamonix would be appropriate."

The men were sitting in the library waiting for James and Alain to say their goodbye to Sadie and Rupert, and the Comte went on. "Alain goes to Chamonix twice a year to stay with his aunt. A friend of mine, an eminent Professor of Medicine, lives across the border in Switzerland, and he comes to see how Alain is progressing whenever he can. The mountain air is good for Alain, but he gets bored staying with my sister, and sometimes makes quite a fuss about going, so you see, when Alain asked if he could bring James along, I was very grateful," his tone was apologetic. "Does that seem selfish of me, Mr Maycroft?"

"Not at all, Count. Initially, I was grateful that you allowed Alain to stay for a similar reason. Alain has been a very welcome distraction for all of us, I can assure you."

"Of that, I am sure," agreed the Comte with wry smile.

It had taken many months for Clarence Grieves-Croft and the London solicitors to begin to unravel the complicated legal matters that had arisen following Lord Grieves-Croft's sudden death, complications made worse because George Grieves-Croft, his son and heir, had died alongside him. At the end of February, after nearly a year, matters were still far from settled, and the solicitors gloomily predicted that it could take many more months before probate was finally granted. Added to which, Lady Grieves-Croft had owned several London properties in Blackheath, inherited from her father. The solicitors confirmed they had not even begun to investigate these properties, and Clarence was anxious to return to his home in France.

Clarence invited Bernard to Grieves Manor to discuss what to do under the circumstances, and he was quite emphatic. "I think we should close the main house, Bernard. It's far too big, and only a few rooms are used now. I cannot stay on and run the household. I must be getting back to my own house, and then, of course, there is the question of Sadie and Rupert," he sighed heavily.

Bernard was hesitant. "Of course, Clarence, I do understand. It's a very difficult situation. Well, if you must go back to France, I suppose the children could come and live here at Riverside until something is settled. That's if they want to, of course," he added hurriedly.

It was Mary Ryan who came up with a simple and sensible solution that would not cause too much disruption to Sadie and Rupert. It would solve the immediate problem, and Clarence could return to France.

Estelle's and Sadie's old Nanny Florrie had died in the winter of 1912. Since her retirement, she had lived comfortably in Oak Lodge, looked after by the staff in the main house. Oak Lodge, sitting on the edge of the estate, was within walking distance of Hope Village. It had four large bedrooms, and two bathrooms, a pleasant sitting room, and a large kitchen and scullery, and a single stable block with accommodation above.

"We all knew that things had to change," admitted Mary to Clarence and Bernard. "I was just walking down the lane to the village, and the gate was open to Oak Lodge, and I thought, why we don't move Rupert and Sadie in there? I could stay and look after them, and James could come and stay. There's plenty of room, and it's such a pretty house."

"But you couldn't manage that on your own, Mary, and anyway, Grieves Manor cannot be left unattended. What about the rest of the staff?" Bernard protested.

"Well, obviously, most of the staff will have to find other work, but Brent and Mrs Brent could stay and live above the stables. Mrs Brent has said she could take over as cook, and Brent, of course, could be a caretaker for Grieves Manor, until things are settled, that is."

Bernard had written to James:

"Let me know what you think of the idea, dear boy, but it would solve a problem. Your Uncle Clarence is very eager to return home now, and it would mean that Nanny Ryan can stay with Sadie and Rupert, and you will have a place to stay during the holidays. Will Alain be spending Easter with us at Riverside, as Mary will be bringing Sadie and Rupert to visit?

. . .

But the winter had not been kind to Alain Trouve, and James had replied:

"Trouve has been in and out of the sanatorium with another of his ghastly chest infections, Uncle, so his father is packing him off to Chamonix until the summer. I will come home for Easter, of course. I think Oak Lodge would be perfect for all of us.

Love to all. James."

As Easter and the anniversary of the loss of the Titanic approached, Bernard was mindful of both Polly and James's feelings about the memorial service to be held at St. Dominic's, and after some discussion with Andrew Wellbeloved, decided that just a simple mention of Henry and Estelle Maycroft at the Easter service would be sufficient.

When Andrew relayed the conversation to his wife, Anne nodded. "I am so glad. What a very kind man Bernard is. Polly said that she was dreading the memorial service, and James had written to her to say that he was too, but James did not want to upset his Uncle, although Polly said that he would understand."

The weather at Easter was unexpectedly warm for late March, and Rupert, settling quickly at Riverside, enjoyed the Easter egg hunt with the local school children after Grace Dove had taken the shy little boy under her wing.

On Easter Monday, Polly suggested taking a picnic down to the Folly, and when Sadie took Rupert off for a walk by the river, James said casually, "Uncle, my House Master has suggested that I take a short leave for a few weeks in April."

Bernard nodded. "I know, James. The headmaster called me to say that it had been discussed. It is very thoughtful of them. What would you like to do? Have you made any plans?"

"Not really plans, but I have had an idea. I thought perhaps we could go to the farmhouse in Dawlish for two weeks or so. Nanny

Ryan knows the farmhouse so well, and I am sure that Sadie and Rupert would love to go, and Polly could help out."

He looked at Polly, "I think I would like that, James," she said quietly.

"Well then, that sounds like an excellent idea, James, and if it's all right with everyone, I would like to come along as well," said Bernard decisively.

Oddly enough, James was to remember that hastily planned holiday in the long, low whitewashed farmhouse nestling in the Devon countryside as one of the happiest times of his life. It was a totally carefree few weeks, without planned mealtimes or bedtimes. It was sleeping in the tiny, beamed bedrooms with their tilted floors, it was breakfast in bed, it was snuggling down by a roaring fire and listening to Bernard reading from the big book of fairy tales that Nanny Ryan always carried with her. It was flying a kite on the hills with a helplessly giggling Rupert hanging onto the string. It was a laughing Polly chasing Sadie through the spiky marram grass on the beach. It was running across the ridged sand and shivering as the tiny waves rippled across bare toes, and it was evening walks just with Polly, his arm tucked through hers, not talking but remembering, because James could only do this with Polly.

April 14th dawned, fair and breezy, and whilst no mention was made of the Titanic, there was a sense of melancholy at the breakfast table. Rupert had woken early and eaten his breakfast before the others had woken and was now under the table with his toy train and the ever-present Bear.

"I think," said Mary Ryan firmly, "That we need to blow the cobwebs away." She looked out of the window at the fluffy clouds scudding across the high pale sky. "The weather looks fit, so we should wrap up warm and take a picnic down to the beach and collect some driftwood for the fire."

Sadie's eyes lit up, and she nodded eagerly. "I love the beach, and we could collect shells as well."

"We will take your bucket and spade, Rupert, and find some crabs for Polly." James leant down and peered under the table. "Polly's scared of crabs." he whispered. Rupert's eyes widened with delight and scrambled out and flung himself at James. He looked solemnly at Polly. "Don't be scared of crabs, Polly, I will look after you," and added, "Is it a very special picnic, James? Cos I think it's a very special picnic, so can Bear come too, please?"

There was a moment of stillness, and James looked steadily at Bernard before hugging the little boy close. "You are right, Rupert. It's a very special picnic, and of course, Bear must come, and it's very kind of you to take care of Polly."

Bernard looked at his young nephew with love and gratitude and wondered again at his maturity and bravery. "It is indeed, Rupert; it is indeed the most special picnic."

Polly smiled brightly. "Thank you, Rupert, I will try not be scared. I know that you and Bear will take care of me," and under the table she clenched her hands together until they hurt.

That evening, after an exhausted and wind-tousled Rupert was tucked into bed after falling asleep over his boiled egg, James and Sadie sat down at the table to a game of snakes and ladders. Polly, who had her tea with Rupert, declared herself to be exhausted, and when she did not come down after putting Rupert to bed, Mary crept up and found her fast asleep cuddling the small boy. Gently tucking covers over the two of them, she closed the door softly and went back downstairs where Bernard stood by the kitchen sink peeling potatoes.

"Oh good, you've started. I'll get the pasties ready," she said, taking an apron from behind the kitchen door and wrapping it around her waist. Bernard looked up.

"Where is Polly?"

"Fast asleep and tucked up next to Rupert. Polly adores that little rascal," Mary replied, smiling, as she placed four golden pasties on a tray and popped them into the oven.

"She certainly does, and who wouldn't? He is a delightful child, very lovable," agreed Bernard. "You know, that was a very good idea, Mary, the picnic on the beach. The children have had a wonderful day, as did I." He turned and looked over his shoulder at James and Sadie seated at the table. Their two heads were pressed close together,

James's soft curls and Sadie's flaxen plaits, and they were bickering quietly over whose turn it was to throw the dice. Mary was quiet, and she leant on the sink and gazed out of the kitchen window and across the fields.

"I am glad they enjoyed it, and it's hard to believe that it has been a whole year since I have scolded my twins about their mischief and teasing," and the tears ran unchecked down her cheeks. "I miss them all so much, you know, Bernard. I can't wait to move out of the big house. I see the twins everywhere I go, in the nursery and the schoolroom." Her shoulders were shaking.

"You have been so strong, Mary, that sometimes I forget what you have lost as well. I am so sorry." Bernard looked distressed.

"Oh, I'm alright, Bernard, just a silly moment, and I thank the Lord every day of my life for Rupert, Sadie, and James." Mary sniffed and rubbed her face with her apron. "Enough of that now, let's get those potatoes on to boil."

After dinner, when James and Sadie had trailed sleepily up to bed, Bernard and Mary settled down by the fire, Mary to her knitting, and Bernard to his pipe and newspaper. Outside, an owl hooted, and a gust of wind whistled down the chimney. Bernard, who had been staring into the fire with the paper still folded up on his lap, remarked.

"Mary, I've been thinking about Sadie moving into Oak Lodge. Does she know about her mother and what happened at Oak Lodge?"

"Sadie knows a little, not everything of course, but Lady Rose always spoke to her about her mother, and Sadie has always understood that Grace was very sick." Mary stopped knitting and laid it on her lap. "Of course, old Florrie told me the whole story, so I did worry about Sadie living at Oak Lodge, but she has taken everything in her stride. Rupert will be starting at the village school after Christmas, and Sadie has her little job helping out with the infants, so I'm not worried about too many changes for Rupert." She chuckled. "Although I shouldn't worry about that little scallywag. He's more like the twins than James."

"Do you know, I still find it very puzzling that Rupert's mother has never tried to find out where he is. Is he truly a Grieves-Croft?"

Mary had picked up her knitting again, and her tone was brisk, "Of course, he is. Young Delfie had some kind of breakdown when Nigel Grieves-Croft was killed, and Miss Estelle has looked after Rupert almost from birth, and that's why he came to live with the family. Why do you ask?"

"No reason, really," Bernard replied. "It's only that Rupert has brown eyes, even though he bears a remarkable likeness to James as he gets older. James and all of the others have those wonderful green eyes, just like Estelle and Lady Rose, even those red-headed twins of George and Jenny."

As Bernard said their names, suddenly could see them again quite clearly, seated around the table at Riverside for that last dinner, and he was overwhelmed with sadness. "I can see them so clearly, you know, Mary, but I can't speak of them with Polly or James, and there are times when I want to so much. There are questions that I want to ask Polly but dare not." He stared into the crackling fire and sighed. "You know, Mary, at first I thought that it was all a mistake and that they had all got on to a lifeboat after all, and we would hear that that they were safe in New York. But then as the weeks went on, I knew that they were gone forever, and still I can't quite believe it."

Mary, who had been listening in silence, nodded.

"I dream of them sometimes, you know, Bernard, and even when I am awake, I think I hear them all around the house. Jenny scolding the boys and then laughing with them, gentle George with his big laugh, and Lord Archie and Lady Rose, wandering around the gardens together just like sweethearts. I try to keep them, hold onto them, but they fade away, and then all I can see is that terrible night, and I pray to God that they were all together and pray that the twins were not scared."

Mary was openly crying now. "Then I think about silly little Belle, and I bet old Dottie never left Lady Rose's side. I talk to Mrs Brent whenever I can, but Brent is like Polly and James; he does not want to speak about them. You can just see that he is heartbroken. He was devoted to the whole family but had a real soft spot for Miss Estelle." Mary gulped back more sobs.

"And Sadie, how is little Sadie now?" Bernard was gentle.

"When it first happened, there was no consoling her, the poor little mite sobbed day and night," replied Mary sadly. "We called the doctor, and he gave her something to sleep, but she just cried and cried that she wanted everyone to come back. She sleeps in the twins' nursery, you know, made us move her bed to where the boys' cots used to be. They were so close, those three, she was like a little mother to her precious twins. Of course, she is devoted to James and Rupert, but she misses those boys so much."

Bernard got up, walked over to the dresser, took down two glasses, and poured two generous measures of brandy from the decanter, sat back down, and handed one to Mary.

"You know, Bernard, sometimes I want to speak about them all, say their names out loud, but I have to be so careful not to upset Sadie. Rupert never asks now, of course he remembers very little, thank goodness, and sometimes I wish I did not remember everything so clearly. I simply cannot accept that they are not coming back. I keep thinking that my boys are at school and will be home soon when James comes home. I keep looking behind him, waiting for them."

Bernard stood with his back to the fire and took a large gulp of brandy. "I can still see Estelle dancing in the garden and picking flowers to put in the Folly. Sometimes I can see her with James on the terrace trying to catch the butterfly shadows."

"And Henry," prompted Mary. "What about Henry? He was such a handsome man."

"Of course, Henry, but Henry spent so little time at Riverside. I don't believe he ever considered Riverside his home, and to this day I don't know why." Bernard stared into the flames, lost in thought, and they sat in silence for a while.

"Do you know when Sadie began sleeping and eating properly again?" Mary said suddenly. "It was when that strange little French friend of James came to stay. When he heard how close Sadie had been to the twins and how upset she was, he drew a picture of them for her. Of course, the lad had seen the twins at Eton, and his drawing looked so like them, that Sadie laughed out loud, and she could even tell them apart."

Mary smiled then. "Walter, you see, well his ears stuck out more than William's, and that little French boy, he had spotted it straight away. He drew this picture of the twins punting down the river laughing and being chased by the House Master running along the bank waving a cane at them. James said it really did happen, the twins skipped a lesson and took the punt for a dare. But that boy, he made it look so funny, and Sadie pinned it on the wall in the nursery and touches it every day."

"Ah, so our Sadie has a *Trouve* as well," said Bernard. "I thank my stars for that boy, Mary, I really do. James has a true friend in that boy."

Each lost in their haunting memories, Mary and Bernard did not see or hear Polly sitting on the top stair in the darkened hall with her arms clasped around her thin body rocking to and fro, shuddering in helpless, dry-eyed grief.

On the train back to Shorehill, James looked at Polly, who was reading a sleepy Rupert one of his favourite stories, and said, "Polly, if you want, we could all do this again next year at the same time, and perhaps Alain could come with us."

Polly smiled, and there was a light in her eyes. "I would love that, James. Alain would have such fun, doing his lovely drawings of us all on the beach."

Alain Trouve never returned to Eton that summer, although his health had improved slowly in the clear clean air of the Alps. Comte Trouve wrote to Bernard, "Sadly, Alain will not be returning to England for a while. At least not at until his doctor says he is well enough. Alain, of course, is most distressed and misses Eton and James most dreadfully, and so rather prematurely, I have promised that if he ceases from making my poor sister's life unbearable, I would ask you whether James could once again visit us in Chamonix after Christmas."

. . .

"My dear Comte, "Of course I will give my permission for James to visit Chamonix again in the New Year. James so enjoyed his last holiday with you, and I feel that he has benefitted greatly from his friendship with your delightful and talented son. Please extend the family's very best wishes to Alain and thank him for the delightful sketches he sends to Sadie and Rupert. Nanny Ryan tells me that the postman is eagerly awaited these days.

With my very best wishes, Bernard Maycroft"

In 1913, in Great Britain, there were continuous periods of deep domestic turmoil which dominated the news. The Trade Union Act was passed, and union membership was growing rapidly. The suffragette movement became more and more militant, and the damage to both private and public property lost the women a great deal of public sympathy. On June 4th, Emily Davison dashed out in front of the King's horse at the Derby as a protest against the treatment metered out to their leader, Emily Pankhurst, only to die a few days later. In Ireland, the Ulster Volunteer Force was set up, and the Home Rule movement continued to campaign for self- government.

All this unrest in England gave rise to long and heated arguments in the debating societies at Eton, and none more so than in The Trimbralls. James, who was considered to be a knowledgeable and articulate opponent, entered into all of them with great enthusiasm. So, although he missed his mischievous and entertaining friend, he was finding life at Eton during this period so thought-provoking that, to a degree, it occasionally dulled the deep ache of loss that he lived with daily.

In the late autumn of 1913, Clarence Grieves-Croft fulfilled his wish to return to France and left England after a long and protracted meeting with Lord Grieves-Croft's London solicitors. They agreed with the suggestion that Grieves-Manor should be closed, on the condition that nothing in the house would be disposed of until the grant of probate, and that included all the deceased's personal items. Several clerks were dispatched to prepare an inventory of the entire contents of Grieves Manor and of the houses in Blackheath owned by Lady Grieves-Croft.

The apartment in Paris was closed, as there was some uncertainty about the legal ownership, and the Dawlish farmhouse had been placed in trust for James. Oak Lodge would be ready for occupation early in the New Year once the decorators had finished and the house had been thoroughly cleaned, and so once again, Mary Ryan gathered up her charges and travelled to Shorehill to spend Christmas with Bernard and Polly at Riverside.

It was certainly a quieter Christmas without Alain, and there was real concern for him in the village when Bernard explained that the boy had been unwell. Alain had, without a doubt, endeared himself to all who met him, and James was showered with messages for his friend at the Christmas Party. James departed with Comte Trouve for Chamonix two days after the New Year, and Mary Ryan, together with Sadie and Rupert, left to return to Berkshire.

"If we are to move into Oak Lodge next week, then we must go home and decide what we can take from the house. Mr Clarence said we can take any furniture we need from Grieves Manor. I am sorry it's such a short visit, but there is so much to do. I am glad to be leaving the big house, I must say," Mary Ryan was apologetic.

"Then you must take Polly with you. She would be happy to help, I am sure. At least she can help you with the children."

But when Bernard suggested it to Polly, she was unhappy about leaving him so soon after James had gone.

"My dear, I think that Sadie and Rupert need you more than I do now," he hesitated and looked into the cool, grey eyes of the young woman who had been Estelle's lady's maid and her dearest friend. "Mary will need your support when they close the house up, and Mrs Brent wanted to do it before James came back home."

"Then, of course, I will help, if you are sure that you will be alright. I shall come home once they have settled into the Lodge."

"Please don't worry yourself Polly. Don't forget I have Andrew for company, and Aggie will no doubt spoil me." More so these days, Bernard sought Andrew's company, and whilst he enjoyed the vicar's dry wit, together with his unshakable faith in God and his fellow man, he found also that Andrew shared his concern about the growing unrest in Europe.

There had been many times recently when Bernard had tucked his pipe in his pocket, folded a newspaper under his arm, and had wandered over to the Vicarage. Weather permitting, the pair would stroll together around the village, occasionally stopping in at the Hop Vine. Initially, the locals had been a little surprised to find the new vicar leisurely enjoying a pint of ale with Bernard, but finding him both humorous and approachable, they soon relaxed in his company, and as his popularity grew, so did his congregation.

1914

In early January, the beautiful gates to Grieves Manor were locked, the empty stables closed and bolted, and the rowing boats upturned and placed on the lakeside. The lovely arched windows which once reflected the rays of so many fiery sunsets were now dark and shuttered. When Bernard had tentatively offered his assistance in closing the house up, Mary Ryan was grateful.

"That is so kind, Bernard, but I think we must leave it for the Brents to organise. I believe they think that it's their last duty to Lord Archie and Lady Rose, and of course, they know the house so well."

She was right, and Brent organised the shutting down of Grieves Manor like a military operation, and he began as soon as the small family moved into Oak Lodge, working tirelessly, grim-faced until it was completed to his satisfaction.

The East Wing, where George, Jenny, and the twins had lived, had been closed soon after the Titanic disaster. Mary Ryan, feeling that part of her duty should be to clear the school room and the nursery, approached Brent, who agreed that it was only right that she should. So, choosing a bright sunny day, she left Sadie in charge of Rupert and made her way across to the Manor. When Polly offered to help, Mary had shaken her head firmly. "I am sure I will be alright. I just need to collect some things for Rupert, and I suppose I want to say goodbye. We had such happy times, you know, old Florrie and I in our own little top-floor kingdom with our babies."

But when Mary opened the door of the nursery, she was overwhelmed by a sudden crushing sense of sadness, and she felt her head spin. She hung onto the door to steady herself before walking across the room on shaking legs. She sank down gratefully into Florrie's old rocking chair by the window and closed her eyes. It was here that she had heard for the first time the tragic story of Sadie's mother, Grace.

Mary waited for her heart to stop racing, and in the quiet of the old house, the memories of her time with the children drifted back to her; vivid memories of her red-headed twins rollicking through the rooms, causing chaos wherever they went.

Their little cots were still in the nursery, the wall by Walter's cot scraped and dented where he banged his cup against the wall shouting to be lifted out. William, the peaceful twin, would be sitting in his cot, sucking his thumb and watching with interest as his twin was roundly scolded for waking him up.

Mary could see them sitting in the school room. There was Walter, his red, tufty hair sticking up, kicking his feet against the chair, twirling his pencil in the air, longing to be out in the sunshine, his arithmetic paper in front of him untouched. William, hair still smoothed down after his morning wash, bent over, chewing the end of his pencil and frowning as he carefully wrote down the answers to his sums.

On the sunlit hall landing, when the prisms of light danced down from the atrium above, she remembered how the twins loved to chase the rainbow reflections, reaching up with chubby hands and giggling as the light played through their fingers. Then the memories faded, and the realisation that her twins were gone forever engulfed her, and awash with grief, she covered her face with her hands and sobbed in raw anguish.

That was where a worried Polly found her, hunched in the chair sobbing. She ran over. "Oh, Mary, Mary please, please don't cry."

Mary shook her head, her face still buried in her hands. "I have just realised, Polly. I will never kiss them again, I won't smooth down that wonderful hair and watch them grow into tall, strong beautiful men."

She dropped her hands and turned a tear-drenched face to Polly. "I won't dance at their wedding or hold their lovely red-headed children in my arms. I dreamt of being nanny to their children and prayed that they would have twins." Her grief turned to sudden anger, and she banged her fists on the arms of the chair. "Why did they take them, tell me, why did they take my boys on that damned, damned ship? It was cursed, Polly. I want to know what happened to my boys. Tell me. I want to know where they are!" she shouted.

Crouching down on the floor by the chair, Polly, white-faced and shaking, wordlessly shook her head, tears streaming down her face. "I can't think of it, Mary. I don't know where they are. I don't know where any of them are," she whispered brokenly.

Mary reached down and put her arms around Polly. "Polly, I am sorry, my dear. I am so very sorry. I know you can't tell me what happened. I am just so angry; I didn't mean to upset you. I loved them so much, and this is so final, you see, closing their old nursery, moving of all their things out." She took a deep breath, reached inside her apron, took out her handkerchief, and wiped her eyes.

Then she stood up shakily, and when she spoke, it was the strong, calm Mary Ryan again. "Come now, my dear. This won't do at all, will it? There is far too much still to be done. We can't leave it all for dear Mr and Mrs Brent, can we? You can help me to pack up some of their toys and books for Rupert. We must not forget to take Alain's drawing of the twins down from the wall. He did it for Sadie, you know."

Polly nodded and said with a shaky smile, "James said that Alain had a crush on Sadie, although Alain would never admit it to anyone. Sadie is very beautiful; I think most of the boys in Shorehill are a little in love with her, too. They are always hanging around Riverside in the holidays hoping to catch a glimpse of her."

A few hours later, in the dwindling light of the late afternoon, with a wheelbarrow loaded full of books and toys, Polly and Mary headed off across the gardens in the direction of Oak Lodge.

"Polly, you can say no if you don't want to, but shall I ask Mrs

Brent if you could close up Estelle's rooms? I know that she wants to do Lady Rose's rooms, but I wondered, should I ask her for you? What do you think?"

Polly hesitated, and then nodded. "Thank you, Mary. I think I would like to do that. I would like to look around one more time."

It was a grim, grey afternoon when Polly collected the keys to Estelle's rooms from Mrs Brent. Sudden, sharp bursts of icy rain and sleet rattled the window frames, and the house felt cold and suddenly hostile, as if it resented being abandoned by its people. The Brents were clearing the kitchen, the only warm room in the house now, and Polly shivered as she ran lightly up the stairs to Estelle's bedroom.

Hesitating for only a second, she slipped the key into the lock, turned the door handle, and walked slowly inside. Even though the shutters had not yet been closed, the room was dark and chilly, the lowering sky outside was black and threatening. Polly walked slowly across the thick carpet, and as she breathed in the perfumed air, she felt Estelle's presence all around her. The bedroom looked almost exactly as she and Estelle had left it on that April morning nearly two years ago.

Then the room had been filled with spring sunshine, a variety of partly-packed valises and hat boxes in the dressing room, and Estelle's bed scattered with clothes. Estelle had been determined to be excited. "Polly, dear, please don't forget my grey fur. I'm only taking that one, Pa said he would buy me one in New York. Now then, let me see, which perfume should I take, or should I take all of them? What do you think, Polly?" and she had chattered on without waiting for a reply, her voice brittle and hard. She had picked up a perfume bottle, an exquisite Faberge purple-and-gold teardrop-shaped flacon with "Mon Cherie" etched in gold across the front. "Only this one, I think; it is so pretty, and anyway, I shall buy some others in New York," she had said airily as she took the stopper from the bottle and dabbed generous amounts of the expensive French perfume on her wrists. "And I shall buy Gabilla's latest perfume for you, Polly."

Polly could hear that low, husky voice almost as if Estelle were standing next to her, and she shivered. The beautiful glass dressing table was thick with dust, and Estelle's heavy silver-backed hairbrushes still lay as she had left them. "Madam," Polly could hear her own voice now, "Shall I pack these hairbrushes?"

Estelle's voice had been cold and disdainful. "Oh no. I don't want to take those ones, Polly." and she had picked one up and stared at the monogrammed initials. "EM," she said aloud, laying them back carelessly on the dressing table. "Estelle Maycroft. They were a wedding present from Henry, you know."

"Yes, I know, madam, so if you are not taking those hairbrushes which ones would you like me to pack?"

"I'll take the ones that Ma and Pa bought me for my twenty-first birthday, they are far nicer, the ones with EGC on the back, please, Polly."

Polly, her thoughts lost deep in the past, was standing with her hands resting on the dressing table staring at the brushes, and she did not hear Mrs Brent open the door. "Are you alright, Polly? It's getting very late; we were getting worried about you." There was a look of anxiety on the housekeeper's lined features.

"Thank you, Mrs Brent. I am alright. I was just wondering if I may take something to remember her by," and she reached out and touched the nearest hairbrush.

Mrs Brent looked worried. " I don't think you can take anything, girlie. Those solicitors have lists of everything. Did you want one of Miss Estelle's hairbrushes?"

"No, not a brush, just her comb," and Polly picked up a thin, silver-and-tortoiseshell comb, and Mrs Brent could see a few strands of red curls caught in the teeth.

"And this, if I may, Mrs Brent?" Polly pointed to a sheer, silk peignoir that Estelle had carelessly flung across the back of an armchair.

"Then take both, Polly," replied Mrs Brent impulsively. "I am sure that they won't be missed, and anyway, from what Mr Bernard says, these rooms could be locked up for a very long time."

"I will then, thank you," said Polly, and she gently picked up the soft, pink silk-and-lace gown, and held it close, breathing in the unmistakable scent of "Mon Cheri." With a gulping sob, Polly thrust the keys at Mrs Brent, and clutching the robe, she fled from the room, vowing never to return to Grieves Manor.

Polly was to return to Grieves Manor, but never in her wildest dreams could she have imagined the circumstances that would bring her back to the lovely old Manor house.

Following the move to Oak Lodge, Mary Ryan wrote to Bernard:

"My dear Bernard,

Our little family has settled in rather well after all the upset of closing the big house, and Oak Lodge is perfectly delightful. Rupert is enjoying school, because, of course, he sees Sadie in school almost every day. Mrs Brent is an absolute treasure, as my culinary abilities are very limited. Brent, of course, spends his time checking the grounds around Grieves Manor, and naturally, he is a most diligent caretaker, and I do think he finds it a comfort to be still in charge of the house. James, dear boy, still writes several times a week to Sadie and Rupert, and we have very amusing letters from young Alain in France. Polly tells me all is well at Riverside, and that you are very busy at the mill with lots of new orders. Do please try and find some time to visit when the weather is more agreeable. Poor Sadie has another cold. We are hoping to visit Dawlish again this year, and sincerely hope that you will be able to accompany us.

With the very best of wishes,

Yours most sincerely, Mary Ryan.

"Dear me, the grubby kisses and fingerprints at the bottom here are from Rupert."

As the second anniversary of the sinking of Titanic approached, Bernard consulted James about returning to Dawlish. James had seemed reluctant:

. . .

"Rather a lot going on at college, Uncle, and I don't feel that I can ask for a long leave, but of course I will be home for Easter."

Bernard was disappointed, but then Sadie, who had had been unwell with a succession of coughs and colds on and off throughout the winter, came down with chicken pox, followed by Rupert, and so the trip to Dawlish was abandoned. Sadie and Rupert were confined to Oak Lodge throughout Easter, and James spent just a week at Riverdale before returning to Eton.

In early June, Bernard received a letter from James:

"Alain has invited me to spend some of the summer break with him and his father in their apartment in Paris. Comte Trouve says he has plans for us to visit the Opera de Paris, the Louvre, and I would love to see the Galleries Lafayette, but of course, once again with your permission, Uncle. Comte Trouve will write to you soon, as they are planning to travel on the last week in July. The best news of all is that Alain is hoping that he can return to Eton with me in September."

Bernard responded immediately:

"Dear James, I am delighted that you have a chance to visit Paris in this exciting season, La Belle Epoche. I understand, and, of course, you must go. As you say, wonderful news that Alain may be returning to Eton. I am sure that he has been sorely missed. I shall look forward to hearing from Comte Trouve."

But then on June 29th, 1914, the British newspapers reported the assassination in Sarajevo of Archduke Franz Ferdinand and his wife,

Sophie. Comte Trouve wrote to Bernard to say that he had cancelled the planned trip to Paris:

"We are living in very worrying times, my dear Bernard. The mood in France is one of great unrest, and sad to say, there is excitement at the prospect of a war. Alain has been speaking with James, and in truth, I cannot consider returning Alain to Eton until matters have settled down."

After dinner on the evening of July 24th, Bernard, after a long day in London, was unable to settle. Polly had remarked at how little he had eaten. "I am fine, Polly. I had rather a large lunch in the city, and I think it has spoiled my dinner. I think I need a spot of fresh air." He smiled kindly at her, and with a well-thumbed Daily Telegraph tucked under his arm, he wandered out onto the terrace and slumped down into his old chair.

It had been rather an indifferent summer's day in what had been so far a blazing summer. The sky was still cloudy, and the air was cool and refreshing. Reaching into his jacket, he took out his pipe, and puffing thoughtfully, he looked down at the folded newspaper on his lap. A robin sang sweetly in a tree nearby, and Bernard could hear the clatter of pots and dishes from the kitchen and Aggie, roundly scolding the scullery maid. The mill workers had long since gone home, the tramp of their boots and low murmurs of conversation could be heard over the garden wall as they finished their shift at 6:00 p.m. It was just as it should be, a normal summer's evening, but try as he might, Bernard could not quell the sense of unease that had troubled him since his morning meeting with his bank manager and solicitor in London.

When the invitation to lunch in the city had come from two old school pals, Bernard had guessed that it was to be more than just a friendly lunch. Arriving that morning and sitting in a stuffy office in the Bank of England, high above Princess Street, he looked at his friends' grim faces, and his heart sank, his worst fears realised.

In the hour that followed, Bernard sat mostly in silence and listened but knowing without being told that Austria's ultimatum to Serbia had set Europe on a war footing. Arty Grey, the bank manager, shuffled some papers on his desk and looked across at his friends.

"It's already started in Europe, you know, panic since Austria's ultimatum," he announced bleakly, running his hands through his hair. "Heavy selling on the European stock markets because investors are selling in a rush for gold, serious disruption in the stock exchanges, and some of the continental banks have simply closed their doors."

There was a strained silence. Charlie Farrow, senior partner in a large law firm in the city, looked shaken. "I've heard rumours, Arty. Everyone has, of course, but what's going to happen here? How is this going it affect us?"

Arty shrugged. "Depends. Interest rate rises first, and nobody will want paper money. We have to prevent a rush on gold and panic selling here as well. Between you and me, there is an emergency meeting in the bank tonight with some senior members from the Treasury. I will know more after that and will let you know, if I can."

There was a silence as both men digested what Arty had said. "Sorry, my friends, but the feeling in the Cabinet is that rather than accept the terms of the ultimatum, Serbia will turn to Russia, and of course, Austria will have Germany's backing," Arty added heavily, as he stood up and pushed his chair back. He looked pale and tired. "Well, at least let me buy you both some lunch, if I haven't already spoiled your appetite. I rather think that it's going to be a long day." He shrugged his coat on and reached for his hat. "We are not prepared for this, you know; everything has centred on the Ulster crisis for so long." his voice tailed off, and Bernard and Charlie exchanged worried looks as they followed him out the door.

Once outside and into the clamour of Threadneedle Street, Arty seemed to cheer up, and placing his top hat jauntily on his head, he gave it a tap. "I've booked lunch at Sweetings, if that's alright with you both." Flinging his arms across the shoulders of his old friends, Arty strode purposely forward, calling out greetings to passing acquaintances.

Charlie relaxed and shot a relieved smile at Bernie, but Arty was known for being calm and level-headed, and to see him so disturbed had shocked them both.

Bernard, convinced that he would not be able eat a thing, found after all that he could not resist Sweetings' famed fish pie, followed by a generous serving of apple pie and custard. The atmosphere in the famous restaurant was jovial, and so, despite the gloomy meeting at the bank, the three old friends found plenty to talk about other than the prospect of war.

But on reflection, sitting in an empty carriage on the 3:30 from Victoria to Shorehill, Bernard wondered if they had unconsciously avoided speaking about the implications to Great Britain. Arty, like himself, had never found time to marry, but Charlie Farrow had two boys at University, and Bernard felt a cold shudder run down his back as he thought of James at Eton, seeing in his mind's eye the slender figure of his nephew in uniform. Fighting a growing sense of panic, he chided himself. James was far too young to enlist, and anyway, there may not be a war that involved Great Britain.

As the train left the teeming capital and chugged through an England of undulating green hills and fields of golden corn, an England unchanged for hundreds of years, Bernard's head fell forward, and he drifted into a troubled doze. When the train ground to a halt in Shorehill's sleepy station, Bernard woke with a start, blinked, and looked around him. Home already, and he grabbed his hat and brief case and stepped down into the warm sunshine. There was no sign of Percy Potts, and Bernard was glad. He was in no mood for polite conversation, and old Percy had a habit of repeating himself these days. Bernard walked swiftly out of the station, down the slope, and into the lane, carefully averting his eyes as he passed the station house in case old Mrs Potts was sitting at the window and called him in for a chat. Bernard was more shaken than he cared to admit as he considered the possibility that by tomorrow morning, the country could be one step closer to war. He did not hear the birdsong, or see the tangled hawthorn in full bloom, nor did he hear the happy shouts of children playing in the woods, enjoying the freedom of the beginning of the summer holidays.

That morning, on the way to the station, he had called into the vicarage to see Andrew. "It's not looking good, Bernard, is it?" Andrew had the newspapers spread out in front of him on the kitchen table.

"No, I'm afraid not, but I will get a better idea of what's happening from Arty."

"Look, if it's not too much trouble, could you come in on your way home? The parish council are meeting here later to sort out the Bank Holiday fete, Ernie in charge of course." Andrew smiled.

Bernard nodded. "Yes, of course I will, but I agree, the news is not good, and we should be prepared for bad news, Andrew."

As he reached the bottom of the lane, Bernard remembered his promise to call into the vicarage. The front garden gate was open, and as he walked up the path, he could hear the murmur of voices coming from the back garden. He knocked loudly on the door and was stooping down to take an appreciative sniff at the deep-red roses, when the door suddenly opened.

"Welcome, Bernard," said Annie, laughing at his surprised face. "Andrew said you might call in on your way home," she explained. "He guessed that you would come in on the 3:30, and anyway, I saw you walking down the lane. You look tired, you poor thing. Just go on through to the garden and find a seat. Andrew is out there with Ernie and some of the parish council, chatting about the fete. I'll go and help Bessie with the tea and sandwiches, and then I'll come and join you."

"Thank you my dear, and by the way, your garden is looking beautiful,"

Annie leant forward gave him a brief hug, "Thank you, Bernard, although some of it is down to Polly's hard work." As Annie watched the slim figure head through the hall toward the open garden door, she was suddenly filled with compassion. "Stay for supper, Bernard," she called out on an impulse.

He turned and gave her a tired smile and shook his head. "No, thank you, Annie, so kind, but I've had a wonderful lunch, and it's possible that James is coming home for the Bank Holiday after all."

Annie looked after him thoughtfully before turning back into the kitchen. Bessie was busily slicing a large tomato into quarters before placing them on a plate next to wafer-thin rounds of cucumber. "Bessie," said Annie. "When Aggie came in this morning, did she say whether young James was expected back for the Bank Holiday?

Bessie paused and turned, the knife still in her hand, "Well, I think she did say that Mr Bernard was expecting him back for the fete. Why do you ask?"

"I just wondered because I asked Bernard to stay for supper, and he said that he was expecting James home," observed Annie. "Well, I hope he does come home. Bernard could do with some cheering up. He looks worn out after his trip to London."

Bessie put the tomatoes to one side, wiped her hands on her apron, and taking a fresh loaf from the bread bin, sliced it slowly it into even slices. "Annie, you don't think there will be a war, do you?" I read the paper this morning, and it's all about a war with Germany." Bessie's voice wobbled, and her eyes filled with tears. "I'm thinking about my sisters' boys, you see. She got four, and all old enough for the army."

Annie shook her head. "I just don't know, Bess. I really hope not; it may be alright after all. We just have to hope and pray."

Bessie began stacking a platter with the sandwiches. "If the vicar is going up to London for the Regatta, perhaps he can find out a bit more from Lord Wellbeloved," she asked hopefully.

"I don't know whether he is going to the Regatta, Bess," Annie replied honestly. "Andrew still hasn't made up his mind, although I am sure his parents will be expecting him." She stood back and ran her eyes over the plates stacked with food and said briskly, "No more talk of war now. You can take the sandwiches, and I will take the cakes. The plates are already on the table, and I'll put the kettles on to boil."

Annie filled two large kettles with water, placed them on the stove, and gazed out of the kitchen window at the garden, a riot of roses and lavender, but she was not seeing the lovely garden, she was worrying why James had cancelled his trip to Paris so suddenly.

Bernie made his way across the grass and raised his hand in greeting at the group of people seated around a table in the shade of a large apple tree. Andrew stood and beckoned him over to the empty chair next to him.

"Just in time, Bernard, here comes Bessie with the food, and tea is on the way. Will you be staying over for supper? There's plenty, and it's your favourite, Bessie's shepherd pie."

Bernard rubbed his hands tiredly across his face.

"No, I won't tonight, thank you, Andrew. There has been a change of plans. James is not going to Paris after all, so we are expecting him at Riverside. The summer term has ended early for the older boys in the Officer Training Corps, so they can spend more time with their families."

There was a short silence, and Bernie looked at the people grouped around the table and felt a rush of affection at the concerned faces turned toward him. He knew how much they all cared for James. They had watched him grow, some had seen him play in the village with their sons, shop in the village with his lovely young mother, and mourned with broken hearts at the loss of his family.

Opposite him, the large figure of Grace Peabody, the postmistress, perched on a chair that was far too small for her ample bottom, shifted around uncomfortably, but catching his eye, she nodded shyly and smiled her sweet smile.

Ernie Brown, the verger, who was busily swatting at a cloud of midges just above his head, stopped what he was doing. "James coming home! Well, it'll be good to see the young fella again."

There was little Grace Dove, who had included James in the school plays and activities even though Henry had insisted that James was not to attend the village school. Grace's mother, Blanche, a clever, sweet lady who had tutored and loved James through his tender years, was now smiling gently at him. There was big Pat O'Donnell, one of his tenant farmers, who had persuaded the nervous little boy to ride on the back of his giant shires, and Dr Bill, who had nursed James through a severe bout of measles and was always there when Estelle called him out for trivial ailments, understanding the nervousness of a first-time mother.

"Will James be home in time for the fete?" Blanche Dove smiled at him as she handed Bernard a plate of sandwiches.

"Yes, we are expecting James at any time." Bernard said, and his tone was measured. "In view of the current situation in Europe, James won't be going to Paris with Alain, and so we will have him home for longer than usual."

The implications of what Bernard had said was not lost on anyone sitting in the garden on that lovely summer afternoon. Andrew, looking at Bernard's drawn face, placed a gentle hand on his shoulder, knowing exactly what was going through his friend's mind. If there was going to be a war, then young James may miss it, but if it were not over quickly, then he, as an Eton boy, would be in the thick of it.

Andrew shuddered, recalling his days at Eton. Everything about an English public school did not just physically train a boy for war, they were also mentally trained to aspire for heroism and find immortality in a heroic death with unquestioning loyalty to their Alma Mater and country. Dr Bill, also a public-school boy, was remembering, with a degree of affection, his Alma Mater in the remote Scottish Highlands, where the emphasis was more on sport and personal achievement.

It was early evening when Bernard arrived back at Riverside, and an eager Polly was waiting for him.

"James called, term has finished early, and so he is going to spend a few days at Oak Lodge, and then Manners will bring him here on Friday. Did you know that Manners stayed on after the house was closed? Mary said that Manners was too much in love with the car to leave it, so he is living above the stables and helps Mr Brent out around the grounds."

Bernard smiled at the excitement and the light in Polly's eyes. "Well, that is excellent news indeed, Polly. We shall have James with us for longer now."

But Bernard's heart was heavy. For days, he had read with growing dismay the headlines, "Crisis on the Stock Exchange," and "Anxiety in the City," "The War Cloud in Europe," and then Asquith's statement that the situation was one of extreme gravity. Arty Grey had called him late one evening. "It is as I thought, Bernard. We have had a day of panic here in the city, and we have been besieged by customers wanting to change up their paper money into gold. The foreign market has collapsed, of course. I will keep you updated, old friend, but measures are afoot."

As Arty Grey had predicted, the Bank of England, facing the unthinkable, a total collapse of the British financial system, raised the bank rate to four percent. They raised it again to eight percent at 10:15 on the same day, and The London Stock Exchange closed for the first time since 1773. On August 1st, the bank rate rose to a record high of ten percent.

Friday, July the 31st, had been another fine, warm summer's day when James arrived back at Riverside in the late afternoon. Polly ran down the steps to greet him, and he caught her in a giant hug and swung her round. "Hello, my Poll. Sadie and Rupert send you their love. I must say, I really liked Oak Lodge. My little bedroom is right up at the top of the house, and all you can see out of the window is apple trees. Nanny Ryan says to tell you that they are all very happy there."

James was in a state of high excitement as he shook Bernard's hand. "Uncle, have you heard, it's all begun, you know. Hi, Tip," he said to the groom as he appeared from side of the house. "Have you heard Tip? It looks like war now."

"Well, I do hope not, Master James," Tip replied gloomily, as he began to help Manners to unload the car, "I bloody hope not."

Bernard interrupted hastily, "Come now, James. It's not our war yet, so let us hope that common sense prevails. There is still time."

But James wasn't listening, and taking Polly's hand, he ran lightly up the steps and into the house. Bernard followed slowly, knowing that James was right. Great Britain was on the brink of war with Germany, but James was home now, and the most animated Bernard had seen him in many months. He shrugged away the feeling of despondency and determined that nothing was going to blight James's homecoming.

The next morning, when Bernard went in search of James, he found his nephew in the dining room poring over the newspaper, "Good morning, Uncle, have you read this," and he pointed to the headline, "The War Crisis in Europe." "Russia has mobilized, and Germany has declared martial law. I should be ready to get back to Eton. The Master said we could be recalled if war broke out."

Bernard was horrified. "James, even if we did enter into this war, you could not enlist, you are not old enough," and his voice was sharp with fear.

"I know that, Uncle, but the chaps in the Officer Training Corp are seventeen, and they will enlist, and, of course, I have a duty to join if the war continues. This is why we need extra training." To Bernard's dismay and anger, he saw that his young nephew's face was alight with excitement.

"James, not a word of this nonsense to Polly, I forbid it. It will break her heart." James nodded impatiently, but Bernard knew that his warning had fallen on deaf ears. Hearing footsteps approaching, he quickly changed the subject just as Polly came into the dining room.

"I was wondering, James," he said smoothly, "Have you heard anything from young Trouve recently?"

James had received letters from Switzerland, and it was clear from the tone of the letters that both Alain and his father had little doubt that Great Britain would be drawn into the war, but sensing his uncle's anxiety, he shook his head. "Not for a while, Uncle."

"I see. Well, I hope all is well with Alain and Comte Trouve. By the way, James, I have invited Andrew and Annie to join us for dinner this evening."

The evening was warm when they sat down at the heavily laden table. The dining room doors were open, and the evening air was heavy with the scent of honeysuckle and jasmine. On such an evening, the prospect of a war seemed impossible to contemplate, and as an unspoken agreement, any reference to the worsening situation in Europe was carefully avoided. Bernard listened with pleasure as James entertained them with amusing stories of his Eton life and the heated discussions held in-House. James seemed eager to hear of Andrew's experience at Eton.

"I believe you spent some time at Eton, sir. Did you enjoy it?"

"My time at Eton was not as happy as yours, I fear, old chap," Andrew replied ruefully. "But I am delighted that you have settled in so well. I have heard that Trimbralls is an excellent house to be in. I occasionally see some of the old boys at the Henley Regatta. My parents are keen for me to go again this year. It's a great social event for them, and I am under considerable pressure from my father to attend."

Andrew pulled a face, and Annie laughed.

"Do you and Annie not enjoy the Regatta?" Bernard was curious. "It looks rather good fun, all those punts on the water, especially if the weather is good."

Polly, who knew of the disagreement between Annie and her wealthy in-laws, said quickly, "Shall we sit out on the terrace for a while after dinner? It's a lovely evening; I do hope it lasts until the weekend for the fete." Annie gave her a grateful smile, and the talk automatically turned to the eagerly-awaited annual Bank Holiday Village Fete.

Later that evening, Bernard and Andrew strolled down by the river in the soft dusk, and Bernard voiced his fears to Andrew. "I could not say too much at dinner, Andrew. I don't want to alarm Polly, but it seems to me that the wretched regime at Eton has bred a generation of war-hungry boys. I must say that I am shocked that James seems to have been caught up in this craziness. Do you know, he now he wants to cut short his holiday and go back for additional training in the event the older boys enlist?" and there was real despair in Bernard's voice.

Andrew placed his hand on the older man's shoulder, and his voice was gentle. "Bernard, we will go to war you know, because Germany will invade Belgium. It's all gone too far now, and the only thing that we can do is pray for a short war. I have made up my mind to visit my parents this weekend. The situation between my parents and Annie has been difficult for some time, so I will go alone."

"I am sorry to hear that, Andrew." Bernard was surprised, knowing little of the animosity between Annie and the Wellbeloveds.

"I will leave for London after morning service tomorrow and return as soon as possible after the Regatta. I could have a word with James before I go, if you think it will do any good, of course. I know that whilst I loathed Eton, James does seem to flourish there."

Bernard shook his head sadly

"No, but thank you, Andrew. I should be happy because James was so utterly miserable at Barrow Hill. Henry would be delighted that James is settled at Eton."

AUGUST BANK HOLIDAY 1914

It was Sunday, August 2nd, and in time-honoured tradition, just before the morning service, the bells of St Dominic's pealed out their joyous message across the villages and farms. The sun shone down from a clear blue sky, and the villagers, eagerly looking forward to the August Bank Holiday, streamed into their church for the blessings. The ancient little church was, as usual, full to bursting. The Reverend Andrew Wellbeloved stood in the pulpit and looked down on his congregation. The sun streamed through the ancient, stained-glass windows down onto their bent heads, and soon, the organ pipes would wheeze into life to accompany the soaring voices of the village choir, praising their Lord with the timeless hymns that their forefathers had sung before them.

Few amongst them dreamt that it was to be the last time that they would hear the bells again for four long years, but the war drums sounding in Europe were coming closer to the shores of Great Britain, and at the end of the Bank Holiday weekend, the bells in churches and cathedrals all over the country would be stilled and silent. History and the face of Europe would change forever.

When the last of the congregation had streamed out of the church and into the bright sunshine, Andrew took Ernie Brown to one side.

"I am going to London see my parents, Ernie. Please keep an eye on everything for me. Annie and Bernard will be around as usual for the fete. I will be back as soon as I can on Monday evening."

"Don't you worry about anything, Vicar. Me and my Bessie will take care of things," replied Ernie, puffed out with importance. "Everything is organised for the fete, but it is a shame you will miss it this year."

Annie handed Andrew his battered old suitcase, which he had insisted was adequate for his short stay with his parents.

"Please, dearest Andrew, do not let your parents irritate you. Enjoy the Regatta and stay safe. Is Tip taking you to the station?"

"No, my dear. I prefer to walk. Everyone is gathering on the meadow to help put the tents up. I will be back on Monday, I promise."

"Then I shall go and help Bessie in the kitchen. She has a mountain of cakes to bake before tomorrow."

Annie gave him a quick hug and pushed him gently out of the door. "Now, go. Everything will be fine," and she closed the door firmly behind him.

Andrew walked slowly up the lane toward the station. He could hear the shouts of laughter coming from the meadow and the high voices of excited children, and he paused just once to look at the shimmering river and at the rambling old vicarage. A sea of blue wisteria covered the flinted walls, and Andrew was sure he could still smell the sweet smell of lavender and roses. Outside the station house, Percy Potts, round and red-faced, and in full uniform despite the hot weather, was busily sweeping a few dead leaves away from the door. There was a delicious smell of roast beef wafting out from an open window in the station house.

Hearing Andrew's footsteps, Percy straightened up, leant his broom against the wall, and touched his cap. "For the London train, Vicar?"

"Yes, Percy, I am going to visit my parents for a few days."

"Thought so. Well it's on time, as usual," Percy announced proudly. He looked over his shoulder and lowered his voice to a whisper.

"What about all this going on in France, then Vicar? I hope that young friend of James is safe. I took a bit of a liking to the lad."

Andrew looked at him curiously. "Why are you whispering, Percy?"

"Sorry, Vicar, but all this talk of war really upsets Mother, so I try not to tell her too much, you see."

"Quite right, Percy, but it is a very worrying situation. I am sure that Comte Trouve will ensure that Alain is safe. I think the entire village was taken with that entertaining young man."

It was not until Andrew had boarded the train and settled in his seat that he suddenly remembered that old Mrs Potts was almost completely deaf and could not hear a thing unless she had her ear trumpet, which was always invariably lost somewhere in the station house. His mood lightened, and he laughed out loud.

LORD AND LADY HORATIO WELLBELOVED

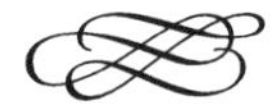

It was late afternoon when the taxi dropped Andrew off at Chester Square in Belgravia. The square was quiet and deserted, many families having departed to their country homes for the Bank Holiday. The long terraces of white stucco Georgian houses, grouped around a gated garden square of flowering cherry trees and exotic shrubs, basked in the late afternoon sun. Only the very affluent and titled could afford to own a property in this exclusive part of London, and Andrew's parents owned the largest house on the south-east corner of Chester Square.

Lord Horatio Wellbeloved was a highly successful industrialist, and the family home was ruled over by Andrew's mother, the gimlet-eyed Lady Mary, who was reputed to be one of the finest hostesses in London. It was considered a rare honour to be included on the guest list for one of the Wellbeloved's famous dinner parties, attended by socialites, high ranking politicians, and government officials.

Andrew walked slowly across the square and paused to look up at his childhood home with an air of detachment. The wisteria-covered vicarage by the river that he had left that morning was certainly a far cry from the imposing three-story house that he was looking up at now, immaculately elegant in the serenely quiet square. The spearheaded, ebony-black railings running the length of the terrace contrasted dramatically with the pristine white houses. The same elaborate railings enclosed the first-floor balconies, and on the polished, black door, the snarling lion's-head brass doorknocker gleamed in the sun. Perfectly clipped bay trees in terracotta pots stood like sentries on either side of the marble steps, and stone urns of brilliant red geraniums lined the steps down to the basement.

As he drew closer to the house, Andrew could hear low voices drifting down from the balcony, snatches of a conversation, then a bark of laughter from his father. Taking a deep breath, he placed a determined foot on the first step, and grasping his small suitcase firmly in one hand, he resolutely mounted the steps. There was no need to grasp the lion's-head knocker because, as he reached the top step, the front door swung open, and Andrew found himself looking into the dour face of Roberts, the butler.

For a split-second they looked at each other. "Roberts! Good afternoon to you. Obviously, you have been expecting me. Were you waiting behind the door?"

Roberts inclined his head. "Good afternoon, sir," he replied coldly, ignoring Andrew's jibe, and reached out to take the small, rather battered suitcase that Annie had packed so carefully that morning. "Shall I have this taken up to your room? Lord and Lady Wellbeloved are waiting in the middle drawing room."

"No, thank you, Roberts," Andrew replied curtly and stepped inside hall. "I'm perfectly capable of carrying my suitcase to my bedroom."

Roberts inclined his head slightly, raised his eyebrows, and sniffed through his long, thin nose. "This way then, sir," and he led the way across the vast, circular, lily-scented entrance hall to the middle drawing room.

Andrew gritted his teeth and resisted a schoolboy urge to shove the pompous butler hard in the middle of his back, but instead enquired politely, "And is all well with you, Roberts?"

The butler hesitated and, without turning, replied smoothly. "Very well, thank you, sir."

Roberts stopped outside the closed doors, coughed discreetly, rapped smartly, and waited.

The familiar, deep voice boomed from within. "Come!"

The butler turned, and with a slight nod to Andrew, he swept the door open onto an enormous, sunny room with pale grey walls and soaring ceilings edged with deeply moulded cornices. On the far side of the room, leaded glass French doors opened out onto the front balcony. The doors were opened out wide to the afternoon sun, and just a whisper of air moved through the room, stirring the multi-tiered crystal chandelier hanging on thin gold chains from the centre ceiling rose. The shimmering crystals, catching the sun beams, cast glittering patterns across the walls, and instantly, Andrew was reminded of the lovely terrace at Riverside. On the high mantle above a magnificent, black marble fireplace, an exquisite Ormolu clock struck five o'clock. Andrew paused in the doorway and took a deep breath before stepping inside.

Lord Horatio Wellbeloved, a heavily-built, dark-haired man, was seated in a high-backed leather armchair with an open newspaper on his lap and swirling a large brandy glass in his hand. Lady Mary Wellbeloved was draped elegantly across a pale green chaise longue which had been placed just beside the open doors. Her eyes were closed, and she was fluttering a lace handkerchief in front of her face.

"Mr Andrew, my lord," Roberts announced stiffly.

Lord Wellbeloved looked across to his son. "Andrew," he said heartily, and folding the paper carefully, he placed that and the brandy glass on a side table, before standing up and walking toward Andrew. "Up for the Regatta after all then, very good, hoped you would come, but your mother thought you might not. Now, what would you like to drink?"

Andrew shook his father's outstretched hand. "Good afternoon, sir. A small whisky, if I may." He looked across to his mother and bowed slightly, "Hallo Mother."

Mary Wellbeloved opened her eyes and sat up. "Oh, thank you Roberts," she called across to the butler who was still waiting in the doorway. Roberts inclined his head, backed out of the room, and closed the door softly.

Lady Mary Wellbeloved turned a pale face towards her son. "Andrew, how lovely. Do come and see me. I would get up, but I really am too hot to move," and waving a thin pale hand, she beckoned him over.

"How are you, Mother? You are looking well," he replied formally and walked across to where his mother was now sitting up, her legs crossed elegantly in front of her.

Mary Wellbeloved's smile faltered as her son walked toward her. Her eyes narrowed, and she gave a sigh of exasperation. "Darling, really, do you have to wear that wretched dog collar all the time, and why are you carrying your suitcase? Roberts should have had it taken up to your room."

"Mother, I am a minister, and I came straight from Morning Service, which is why I still have my collar on, and yes, Roberts did offer to take my case, and I refused. I can take my case up when I go." Andrew bent to kiss his mother's long, manicured hand.

"Been goading Roberts again, have you, Andrew?" said his father jovially, handing him a heavy-cut glass tumbler half full of whiskey. "You know the old boy has no sense of humour."

"It is not that Roberts lacks a sense of humour, Father, the man is simply rude. In case either of you have forgotten, he does not like me, or my wife for that matter. Oh, and before you ask, Annie is very well." Andrew's voice was low and controlled.

There followed an uncomfortable silence, and Andrew caught the fleeting glance that passed between his parents at the mention of his wife's name. Andrew waited, preparing to be admonished, as a remark like that about the faithful Roberts would normally have brought a sharp response from one of his parents, but to his surprise none came.

"Ah yes, good. So glad Annie is well. Shame that she couldn't make it this time. Take no notice of old Roberts, a bit set in his ways you know." Lord Horatio cleared his throat.

Mary Wellbeloved raised a carefully plucked eyebrow and patted a spot on the chaise longue next to her. "Don't be testy, dear boy. It's tiresome, and anyway, it is far too hot to get cross. Sit down here next to me for a while before we change for dinner. Tell me now what's happening in that little village of yours."

Her tone was patronizing, and Andrew felt a stab of irritation. "Oh, you know, Mother, country life rarely changes, but of course, the news in Europe is worrying, and like the rest of the country, we are waiting to find out whether we will get involved in this war."

Andrew looked questioningly across to his father, who was now positioned in front of the fireplace. "And what do you think, Andrew?" asked Lord Wellbeloved slowly. "How do you think the government will deal with the German aggression?"

Andrew looked down at the golden liquid in his glass. "For whatever it is worth, Father, I hope and pray that we can be saved from a war with Germany. If the newspapers are to be believed, then we are virtually at war already, unless you know differently?"

Horatio Wellbeloved placed his glass on the mantelpiece and took a fat cigar from his top pocket. Still without speaking, he snipped the end, put it between his lips, lit it, and puffed a fragrant cloud into the air. He looked across at his son through narrowed eyes.

"Well, Father, do you know any different, or are you not prepared to discuss it with me?"

Lord Wellbeloved took the cigar from his mouth and rolled it thoughtfully between his fingers before replying. "Andrew," he said heavily, "I know that you are totally against war, but Asquith is running out of time, and I have to say patience. Edward Grey and Lloyd George have been trying for days to get an assurance from Berlin that they will not annex Belgium, and personally, I don't think that we will get that assurance. You know as well as I do that if Germany enters Belgium's territory, under the Treaty of London, we have guaranteed to protect Belgium's neutrality. Edward Grey has made it clear to the German foreign minister that this country cannot and will not run away from its obligations."

Andrew, with a sinking heart, listened in silence.

"There is something else that will be announced tomorrow," his father continued. "The Bank of England must stop this run on gold. There has been a Cabinet meeting today, and it has been decided to extend the Bank Holiday period for the rest of the week and re-open the banks on Friday. This will buy some time to pass emergency legislation to cope with war conditions should we go to war with Germany. We need stability now, not panic. I know this is not what you want to hear, Andrew, but personally I cannot see a way out of this. Edward Grey is said to be addressing the Commons tomorrow, so I suppose we shall have to wait and hope."

There was a short silence as Andrew digested this information, but hearing the finality in his father's voice, his heart sank further, although, in truth, it only confirmed his worst fears.

"Thank you, Father," he said bleakly and turned to face his mother. "Under the circumstances, and I am sure that you will understand, Mother, I will leave for Shorehill immediately after the Regatta. I must be with my parishioners and Annie of course, should the worst happen."

Lady Mary, who had been silent during the exchange between father and son, now glared at her husband. "Horatio, we really don't know for certain what will happen," she said sharply. "I am sure that our German friends will not want to go to war with Great Britain. However, we shall not talk of it any more tonight, and certainly not at dinner, I forbid it."

Lady Mary turned an expressionless face toward her son. "It would be rather a shame if you did leave early, Andrew, especially as I have booked a table at Claridge's for dinner tomorrow night after the Regatta. Please do reconsider and don't disappoint."

Without waiting for a response, she stood up gracefully and looked across to her husband. "Horatio, I will rest before dressing for dinner. Cook has prepared a special meal for Andrew, and she would be most upset if we were late sitting down. I will send Roberts in for your suitcase, Andrew."

She held up an imperious hand as if to ward off any protest from Andrew. Lord Wellbeloved raised his eyebrows at his son, and with a glimmer of a smile said, "We shall see you at dinner then, my boy," and taking his wife's arm, they left the room.

Andrew stood for a moment, looking after them. Then, not wishing to confront Roberts again, who would undoubtedly obey his mother without question, Andrew took his glass and walked out onto the balcony.

The air was warm, a blackbird scolded high in the trees, and in the distance, church bells were tolling for evensong. On the surface, it appeared to be a perfectly peaceful summer's evening, but as he recalled his father's warning, he shivered, and in his mind's eye, he could see the rolling black clouds of war engulfing the country. An irrational urge to abandon his visit swept over him, and he made a silent resolution that, come what may, he would return to Shorehill the following day, and nothing or nobody would prevent him.

Horatio and Mary Wellbeloved were both only children themselves, and selfish in the extreme. It was a mutual decision arrived at before they got married, that there would be no children from their union. So, when, after two years of marriage, to their utter dismay, Mary found out that she was pregnant, with military precision, she had set about making arrangements to have the child taken care of in a way that would not interrupt their lives.

Mary Wellbeloved found the whole business of being pregnant repugnant, and after her fourth month, she retired to the house and refused to be seen in public. As the pregnancy progressed and her body swelled, her temper grew shorter, and Lord Horatio stayed in his office for as long as he dared. A month before Andrew was due, a suitable and discreet wet nurse and permanent nanny were employed. One afternoon shortly before Andrew was born, Mary Wellbeloved was impatiently flicking through the Court News when she spotted a short item that made her sit up. For the first time in weeks, a smile crossed her face and her eyes sparkled.

When her husband returned that evening, he found his wife in a state of high excitement. "Horatio, look read this," she commanded and stabbed a finger at a ringed item in the Court News. There were court rumours abounding that Queen Victoria was planning a visit to the French Riviera close to the Wellbeloved's villa in Menton. "We shall go to France as soon as the child is born," Mary declared with a smile of satisfaction.

"And we shall stay for the entire season, my love, and you will have plenty of time to recover before returning to London," Horatio promised.

In a private London nursing home, Andrew, politely and conveniently was born on time and without fuss. He was immediately handed over to the waiting nanny. After a few days rest, when she refused all visitors but her husband, Mary Wellbeloved kissed her infant son distractedly on the head, bade the nanny, "Take care of the dear boy," and allowed herself to be tenderly wrapped in furs and led out to the waiting car.

Lord Wellbeloved peered into the cradle at the infant's clear, blue eyes and growled. "Good, good, yes, well then, the boy will be well taken care, of my dear, don't fuss. He's far too young to miss us," and so they departed.

Whilst Andrew was travelling back to London in the arms of his besotted nanny, Mary Wellbeloved was being whisked away by her husband to Portsmouth and then by private yacht across the channel, to France, with little or no thought given to the child they had left behind. If, at any time during the summer months, after lingering on the beaches and relaxing with friends, Mary Wellbeloved grew a little wistful, Horatio would present her with a new piece of jewellery or indulge her fascination at the casino tables, until she sparkled again and entertained his influential friends.

Andrew had seen very little of his parents in the early years, and he had grown up watching their lives from a distance. Watched over and loved by a doting nanny and all of the house staff, Andrew was a serene, well behaved, biddable child, but so prone to chest infections that he had been considered too delicate to attend school, so it was decided that he should be tutored at home.

The entire basement of the Belgravia house was converted into a sunny school room, and a few close friends with boys of a similar age sent their children to be tutored privately with Andrew. The tutor that his father employed was a kindly young man who disliked Lord

Wellbeloved intensely. However, he recognised Andrew's obvious need for companionship and found the boy's eagerness to learn engaging. Thus, the school room became a haven for Andrew.

Lord Wellbeloved, in addition to enjoying a great deal of success as a wealthy industrialist, was also heavily involved in local government and had many friends in Parliament and the House of Lords. He also spent a great deal of time at the House and was a valued and respected member and speaker at many private clubs. Lady Wellbeloved, a perfect foil for her ambitious husband, played bridge and tennis, attended tea parties, and was the perfect hostess to her husband, faultlessly gracious and elegant, with no ambition other than to entertain and be entertained.

On the odd occasion Lady Mary visited the school room, sometimes staying for tea with Andrew before waving him an airy kiss and drifting back upstairs, Nanny was heard to remark, "Wonder of wonders, her Ladyship remembered she had a son, and her conscience smote her."

At Christmas and on birthdays, as a special treat, his parents took Andrew out to dinner at The Ritz. Andrew, awkward and nervous around his father, invariably fell ill during the meal and was more than often sent home in a carriage whilst his parents stayed to finish their meal.

Andrew always knew from the thunderous expression on his father's face that he would be virtually banished to the school room until such time that his father had forgotten the incident. Quite content with his own company and his books, Andrew did not consider this as any kind of punishment, as the school room was his home. At the tender age of thirteen, true to custom, Andrew was packed off to board at Eton College, leaving behind a tearful nanny and a concerned tutor, but not a tearful mother. As he had expected, Andrew hated every moment of life at Eton, and because, for the first few years, he spent a lot of time in the sick room under the House Dame's watchful eye, he made very few friends.

In a rare moment of concern, and aware that his quiet, reserved son could be the perfect target for the popular initiation ceremonies that were part of Eton tradition on entry, Horatio Wellbeloved had a discreet word with the headmaster. Recognising the authoritative and powerful man he was dealing with, the headmaster agreed to keep a watchful eye out for the boy. As a result, Andrew was teased unmercifully, called a baby and a sissy by his housemates, and although he managed to escape the humiliating new-boy ceremonies, he did not manage to escape the endless goading and certainly not the odd fist that slyly came his way.

Over the years, he grew tall, and favoured his fair-haired blue-eyed mother, and bore no resemblance to his burly, dark-haired father, for which Andrew was eternally grateful. He had come to realise, that whilst his mother was highly bred, vacuous, and vain, with little idea of the world outside her circle of wealthy, haughty, likeminded friends, his father was an arrogant, self-opinionated man nursing an overwhelming ambition to enter the world of politics. Money and power were his father's gods, whereas, Andrew had discovered from an early age that he wanted to serve a different God, a fact that he kept well-hidden from his parents, knowing well enough that his father would attempt to groom him into politics. The truth emerged when he gained a place at Christ Church at Oxford University and chose to enter the Faculty of Theology and Religion to study Philosophy and Theology.

Lord Wellbeloved was furious after discovering that his son, rather than joining the family business or going into politics, fully intended to enter the church when he graduated. Andrew, finding himself surrounded by likeminded individuals, thrived at Oxford. He never missed a lecture or class, and he excelled in the one-to-one tutorials. Preferring to lodge in the Halls, he rarely saw his parents. His asthma attacks became less frequent, and he grew in confidence.

After obtaining a First-Class Degree in Theology, Andrew reluctantly sent out an invitation to his parents to attend his graduation. Lord Horatio, puffed with importance, arrived in a chauffeur-driven Rolls-Royce accompanied by Lady Mary, suitably attired in the latest fashion.

Andrew, watching his father strolling among the Oxford dignitaries, puffing a large cigar, and boasting about his business acumen was more than ever convinced that his choice in life was the right one. So, despite coercion, bribery, and downright bullying from his ambitious parent, Andrew, confident now in his faith, continued his chosen path, and at the age of twenty-three, became curate to an elderly vicar at St Mark's in Limehouse.

There he stayed until, until four years later, the exhausted vicar retired, and Andrew was ordained as the vicar. During those years, he distanced himself from his parents and their lifestyle, visiting only as a duty, every visit ending acrimoniously in bitterness and recriminations for not "making more of himself after all of the opportunities he had been given."

St Mark's was a poor parish, close to the docks, and the cloying mist from the river choked the miserable, narrow streets. Little terraced houses, sometimes housing families of ten or more, were squeezed among canals, railway lines, timber yards, coal yards, factories, and workshops. Limehouse was polluted, disease-ridden, and overcrowded, and full of public houses, beer shops, and dance halls.

Andrew's chosen path proved to be very hard. The hours were unforgiving, and his duties were sometimes heart-breaking and often unrewarding. Infant deaths were high, and the people endured grinding poverty, but slowly and surely, Andrew, with the help of some charities, was reaching out to them. Sunday services became better attended, and with his determined dedication, more and more children could attend school.

Andrew arranged a Sunday school, and he persuaded the local school master to help him to form a choir. The baptisms increased, and gradually people began drifting back to St Mark's. Andrew realized that he needed help, and so he appealed to his bishop, and help came in the form of a young curate, an eager-faced Yorkshire lad, David Baker, who was full of zeal, vigour, and good intentions. Andrew was delighted to have David and his jolly young wife to share the burden of the parish, and the many and varied responsibilities that came with a poor and overcrowded part of London. Young Peggy Baker took over the Sunday school classes and through her enthusiasm and happy nature, managed to recruit a small army of volunteers to help at St Mark's, arranging flowers and cleaning.

Andrew's living accommodation was a narrow Victorian villa next to St Mark's, presided over by the housekeeper, a disapproving elderly spinster lady whose cooking was hit and miss, on occasion barely-edible, and always grudgingly served. When she heard about the curate and his wife arriving, the widow had grumbled loudly about stretching the housekeeping even though she had a generous stipend from the church.

When after a few months, Peggy went over the household accounts and realised that provisions were disappearing out of the back door on a regular basis, Andrew wasted no time in dismissing the outraged housekeeper and decided that once David and Peggy had settled in, he would look for other lodgings. With the bishop's permission, the house was given over to the young couple, and Andrew moved into a room in Lady Grace Villas in Pitt Street, an area away from the damp and mist of the river. Lady Grace Villas was run by Mrs Regan, a genteel middle-aged widow who, finding herself in straightened circumstances after her husband's untimely death and needing an income, looked thoughtfully at the three empty bedrooms, and decided that the sensible option was to let the rooms out. Not only would she have an income, but company as well.

The very next day, a large notice appeared in the sitting room window. "Rooms to Let," and within a few weeks, Mrs Regan had tenants for two rooms. The front bedroom was let out to a retired school master who played the piano and the other to a retired governess of indeterminate years.

Andrew heard from a neighbour of Mrs Regan that there was a room available at Lady Grace Villas, and he wasted no time in making his way around to Pitt Street to introduce himself. When Mrs Regan bustled to the door, duster in hand, she found herself looking up at a tall young man in a clerical collar with fair hair, blue eyes, and a wide smile, who announced that he was the vicar of St Mark's and enquiring about the room to let. Disconcerted, she bobbed a greeting and ushered him inside a hall which smelt of polish and mothballs combined with a faint but delicious aroma of roasting lamb.

Andrew, seeing her confusion, gently explained the situation at the church house and went on to assure her that all his parish meetings would be held in the church house with his curate. He explained that he just wanted a quiet, clean room for himself, and Lady Grace Villas looked perfect for him. The little landlady swelled with pride, and puffed her way upstairs, assuring Andrew that that the top room was the best room, and the quietest part of the house. When they reached the top of the house, the landlady flung open the door and stood back to let Andrew in. He walked over to the window and looked out across the rooftops to the spire of St Mark's, gazed around the simply-furnished bedroom and narrow bed with snow-white sheets, and smiled with delight.

Mrs Regan explained that for an extra shilling a week on top of the rent, she would provide a cooked breakfast and an evening meal. Remembering the mouth-watering smell of roast coming from the kitchen, Andrew readily agreed to the arrangement. Mrs Regan was overjoyed, for there could be nothing more respectable than having the local vicar as a paying guest, and the deal was struck.

Andrew moved in the next day and never regretted his decision. After long days working in his parish, he looked forward to going back to Lady Grace Villas, assured always of a substantial meal, a clean warm room, and good company. The retired governess had a pleasant singing voice, and some jolly evenings were spent around the piano. The schoolmaster playing the piano, the governess singing, and the contended little landlady sitting by the window knitting and tapping her foot in time to the music.

The next few years slipped by, and Andrew remained in Lady Grace Villas, forming an excellent relationship with the other lodgers and with Mrs Regan. Mrs Regan's friends and neighbours watched in amusement as the volatile little Irishwoman took the young vicar under her wing, making sure that he ate a good breakfast before he left the house. If he was not home at supper time, Andrew would find carefully-wrapped sandwiches and a flask of strong tea waiting for him in the kitchen. His clothes were laundered and ironed and placed on his bed, his socks neatly darned, and his shoes buffed and polished.

One soft summer evening in July 1909, Andrew was rushing up the steps, late again for dinner, when the sound of a girl's angry voice floated up from the basement and stopped him in his tracks. "Blast and blast again, where is that wretched key?"

Intrigued, Andrew hesitated on the top step, and holding onto the handrail, he leant over to look down into the basement. "Excuse me, miss, but may I be of assistance?"

At the sound of his voice, a figure emerged from under the steps. A slightly built young girl with bobbing brown hair turned to look up at him, cupping her hands over her eyes against the bright sunlight. "Not unless you have a key to this door, and I doubt that you have," the girl retorted crossly.

"Perfectly true, I'm afraid, but I may be able to help," Andrew replied and ran back down the steps and into the basement, taking care to avoid a small stack of brown paper parcels on the bottom step.

The girl was fumbling around in a large black handbag. "I was so sure that I had the key in this bag."

Andrew smiled. "As I said, I do not have a key, I'm afraid, but I do live upstairs, and I am sure my landlady will have a spare key. After all, it's her basement."

The girl looked up. "I know that. Mrs Regan is my auntie." She frowned, then her hands flew to her mouth, and her eyes widened in horror when she spotted Andrew's collar. "Oh, my lord, you're Auntie's vicar aren't you? Did you hear me swear? Oh no, and I just said, 'my Lord.' I am so sorry," she spluttered, still holding her hands up her mouth in an attempt to stifle her laughter.

Andrew looked on in amusement waiting for her giggles to subside. The girl, making an effort to compose herself, cleared her throat, and still with a small smile playing around her mouth, held a small hand out. "How do you do," she smiled prettily. "I am Annie Regan."

"How do you do, and yes, I am indeed 'Mrs Regan's vicar,' but you may call me Andrew, and I am sure that the Lord will forgive you for taking his name in vain, because I certainly will," and he took her outstretched hand, and shook it gently.

"Well, thank goodness for that. Auntie would never forgive me if I upset you. You do know that you are the apple of her eye, don't you?"

Without waiting for a reply, she rushed on. "When Auntie gave me the key, she said to take care as it was the only one that she had. I do the mending for her, you see, and when I finish it, I just leave it in the basement rather than knocking on the front door. Auntie loves a chatter, you see, and sometimes I'm too busy to stay and chat. Does that sound awful? But I do love her, she has been so sweet to me." She paused for breath, then her face lit up. "I've just remembered. I think I left the key inside on the window ledge when I collected the mending last night."

Andrew watched her in fascination, a slight figure with a strong face, intelligent eyes, a rather long nose, and a wide, mobile, upturned mouth.

He was suddenly aware that she had stopped talking and was observing him, her head on one side.

"You do know that you are staring at me," she teased.

Andrew flushed and was about to stammer an apology when they heard a familiar Irish voice from above the stairs.

"I know someone is down there. I can hear you, come out whoever you are."

"Auntie, it's only me, Annie," the girl shouted and walked out from under the steps.

Her aunt was leaning over the top railing, brandishing a large broom above her head.

"Sorry, Mrs Regan, did we startle you?" Andrew called up apologetically, "I was just trying to help Annie to find her key."

Mrs Regan was taken aback at the sight of them, and then her face broke into a huge smile, and she put the broom down hastily. "Well goodness me, Vicar, what on Earth are you doing down there? Come on up. Annie is always losing that key, aren't you dear? Why didn't you just come and knock on the door?"

"We were just about to, Auntie," Annie replied with a grin and whispered aside to Andrew. "I'm not always losing the key; I just forget where I put it. May I call you Andrew?"

"Please do. No matter how many times I ask your aunt to call me Andrew, she always goes back to calling me vicar."

"Right, Andrew it is then," and grabbing a couple of the parcels, she bound lightly back up the steps. Andrew, picking up the remaining brown bags, followed her to the open front door where Mrs Regan was waiting. Ushering them into the hall, she scolded her unrepentant niece. "Fancy asking the vicar to carry the linen, Annie."

"Really, it's no bother, I am glad to help," Andrew assured her and placed the parcels into her outstretched arms.

"Stay for dinner now you're here Annie. We don't see nearly enough of you," said her aunt firmly. Annie grinned and raised her eyebrows at Andrew. "Yes, Auntie, that will be nice, thank you very much."

This made Andrew strangely happy, as he found to his surprise that he wanted to get to know this unusual girl a lot better. During the meal, Andrew learnt that Annie, until six months ago, had lived with her mother above their wool shop in Blackheath. When her mother died, Annie could not afford the rent on the little shop and had moved to Limehouse to stay with a friend of Mrs Regan.

The friend was a seamstress and ran a little business from her home at the end of Pitt Street and was teaching Annie the trade as a favour to Mrs Regan. Andrew simply could not take his eyes off this fascinating girl with an outrageous sense of fun. Once, when she looked over to him and caught his eye, she had given him a cheeky wink, and then smirked when he flushed and dropped his head.

To cover his confusion, he said, "How is it that we haven't met before today, Annie?"

"Oh, that's easy. I normally come during the day and leave the mending in the basement."

Andrew found himself blurting out. "I have got to go back to St Mark's this evening to lay out the hymn sheets for choir practice, would you like to walk with me?"

In June 1910, days after Annie's twenty-first birthday, at St Mark's parish church in Limehouse, Annie Regan and Andrew Wellbeloved had married. Reverend David Baker conducted the marriage ceremony, and Mrs Regan provided a substantial wedding breakfast afterwards at Lady Grace Villas. All in all, there were twenty-five guests. Lord Horatio and Lady Mary Wellbeloved sent their regrets. They were travelling in Europe and were unable to attend the wedding but hoped to be able to arrange a dinner party on their return and introduce their new daughter-in-law to their friends.

Annie moved into Lady Grace Villas with Andrew until 1912, when the wonderful summons from the bishop came to take up the post as resident vicar in Shorehill Village. Annie had met her parents-in-law twice before Andrew took up his post in Shorehill, once when they met for afternoon tea at the Savoy, followed by the disastrous dinner party at the family home in Belgravia.

Now, here he was he was back in his parent's home, not wanting to be here, but comforted at the thought of his return to Shorehill and Annie. Andrew gulped down the last of the whisky and turned back to the drawing room. His suitcase was no longer where he had left it by the side of the chaise longue, and he smiled grimly to himself, knowing that the surly butler would have arranged for it to be taken to his bedroom just as Lady Wellbeloved had ordered.

The thought of dinner and an evening with his parents nearly tempted him to pour another small shot of whisky, but he decided against it and consoled himself with the thought that at least it would just be the three of them sitting down and none of his father's awful friends and their braying wives. After a respectable time, he would feign tiredness and go up to his room. Closing the balcony doors, Andrew selected a newspaper from the sideboard and made his way out into the deserted hall. It was strangely quiet for such a large house, just the faint sound of laughter drifting up from the kitchen below. Andrew crossed the wide hallway and paused at the bottom of the majestic sweeping staircase, suddenly recalling his mother's instructions from long ago.

"Andrew, straight back, please, and ascend the stairs with dignity. Do not run and bound. You are not a goat."

"Here we go then, Mother," he said softly to himself with a grin, and taking a deep breath, he raced up the stairs, his long legs taking two at a time until he reached the top hallway. He was bent over, hands on his knees, catching his breath and smiling in pure satisfaction when he heard the distinctive click of a door closing close by.

Andrew grimaced. He was not in the mood to have another conversation with his parents and stood for a moment undecided whether to go back downstairs or hurry to his bedroom. He was still standing there when a little maid came scurrying toward him carrying a mound of clean towels on her outstretched arms. She was humming tunelessly, almost hidden behind the towels, and jumped when she saw Andrew standing at the top of the stairs.

"Oh, my lord. I am sorry, sir. I did not see you standing there," she smiled nervously.

Andrew smiled and stood aside to let her pass. He watched in amusement as she tripped lightly down the stairs, her brown hair bobbing under her white cap, and he was overcome with a rush of longing to see his Annie's cap of smooth, brown hair. "Only dinner this evening to get through, and Henley tomorrow, and I can escape." Andrew comforted himself with that thought.

Andrew's old bedroom was at the far end of the upper hall, and when he opened the door, he could see that the little maid had been making the room ready. The battered old suitcase was unpacked and placed at the bottom of his wardrobe. His pyjamas and dressing gown had been laid out on the bed, and in the adjoining bathroom, his toiletries had been neatly arranged on a shelf below the wall mirror. The wardrobe door was open, and he grimaced as he spotted his dinner suit, the black trousers with a perfect crease, and a neat triangle of white handkerchief folded in the top pocket of the jacket. An obviously new, pristine-white shirt swung from the next hanger, and below on the shoe rack, a pair of black shoes had been polished to a glass sheen. On the bedside table, the maid had laid out a variety of neckties.

Out of curiosity, he opened another wardrobe and shook his head at the selection of casual jackets and trousers hanging there. On the shelf below, sat a neat stack of carefully folded jumpers and shirts. It was obvious that his mother had expected him to stay for more than a day or two and was determined that he would not appear to her friends as a country vicar. But what was also patently obvious was that Mary Wellbeloved had not anticipated that her daughter-in-law would accompany Andrew.

Annie had never considered accompanying Andrew to the annual Windsor and Eton Amateur Regatta. She had no desire to spend any time with her in-laws, who by their icy demeanour on the two occasions when they had met, made it perfectly plain that they did not approve of the union. No attempt was made by either of them to hide the fact that they were deeply disappointed with the match, and neither Andrew nor Annie missed the veiled comments and pointed remarks that, "Andrew could have done well had he chosen differently."

When Andrew challenged his father on a remark about his "life choice," Lord Wellbeloved had feigned surprise and protested. "Of course, I am referring to your choice of career, the church instead of politics." On Annie's insistence, Andrew reluctantly left the matter there, his hurt and anger seemingly lost on his parents.

Shortly after their marriage, and during a particularly-tense dinner at the family home in Chester Square, things had come to a head. It was obvious that the invitation to dinner had been an attempt to persuade Andrew to abandon his country parish and come back to London to further his advancement in the Church. Annie, outraged, had hotly defended Andrew, and emphasised the important work he was doing in Shorehill, but she had been virtually ignored. Holding her hand up imperiously to prevent Annie from speaking further, his mother smoothly listed on elegantly-painted fingers, all the advantages that could come his way if he would just meet with the bishop and discuss the option of taking over an affluent London parish.

The very last straw came, however, when halfway through the dinner, Roberts glided into the dining room with the wine decanter, and after slyly flicking his eyes over Annie's empty glass, he sailed imperiously to the head of the table to replenish Andrew and Lord Wellbeloved's glasses before making his way toward the door.

Incredulous, and scarcely believing what she had just seen, Annie took a deep breath to calm her rising temper, stopped eating, and placed her knife and fork neatly on her plate and cleared her throat. Opposite her, Lady Mary carried on eating, but despite her bent head, Annie knew that her mother-in-law was watching her closely.

Andrew looked up and catching his wife's furious glare in the direction of her empty wine glass, took in the situation immediately. He broke off the conversation with his father and called out sharply to the butler's retreating back. "Roberts, my wife's wine glass is empty."

Roberts had paused in the doorway, then slowly turned and made his way back into the room and over to the table. "Sir," he said, eyebrows raised.

"I said," said Andrew, his voice low with suppressed fury, "My wife's wine glass is empty. Please refill it immediately."

There was a short silence as Roberts moved over and silently refilled Annie's wine glass.

Lady Wellbeloved looked up at the butler's expressionless face. "Thank you, Roberts," she said coolly, and waited until the butler had left the room then she looked across at Andrew and sighed.

"Goodness me, Andrew. There was absolutely no need to shout at the man. Obviously Roberts could not see that Annie's glass was empty," and shooting a contemptuous smile across the table, addressed Annie, "Was your glass hidden by the fruit bowl dear, or perhaps by your napkin?"

Annie caught in her mother-in-law's icy stare, did not trust herself to speak.

The meal was finished in controlled silence, and Andrew, tightly angry, thanked his parents and made their excuses to leave. At the front door, Roberts stood with the footman holding out their coats. Roberts moved to place Annie's stole around her shoulders, but Andrew snatched it from the butler's outstretched arm and laid it gently around his shaking wife, holding her to him closely.

Lord Wellbeloved shook his son's hand, careful not to meet his eyes, and placed a stiff kiss on Annie's cheek. Lady Wellbeloved leant toward her daughter-in-law, kissed the air near Annie's face and said, "Goodbye, my dear. Make sure Andrew brings you back soon."

She turned to her son. "Darling, so lovely to see you. Don't leave it so long next time, and please think carefully about what your Father said about the vacancy at Westminster. After all, we are only thinking of you and your future."

Andrew nodded. "I'm sure you are, Mother," he said drily. "Goodbye, thank you again for dinner," and still holding his wife tightly, they made their way down the steps and into the street without once looking back.

In silence, both too upset to speak, they hailed a passing cab to Victoria Station. Once inside, Andrew turned to look into Annie's tear-filled eyes. "That was unforgivable of my parents, my darling," he said, his voice shaking. "That will never, ever happen again. I promise you."

"No, it won't, Andrew. They will never forgive me for marrying you, and if they cannot show me the respect that I deserve, then I will never see them again, but you have a duty to them, and I will never interfere with that."

However, by the time they were settled on the train and speeding toward home, Annie had regained her irrepressible sense of fun, and they were soon giggling together at the pompous butler's discomfort when Andrew had called him back into the dining room.

Annie was true to her word, and whenever a rare invitation arrived at the vicarage from Lady Mary to attend "A little luncheon with friends," or "A trip to the Theatre," or "Just a little supper," Annie had politely declined, replying briefly that as the vicar's wife, she had several parish duties to attend to, and she was sure that they would understand.

Occasionally, persuaded by Annie, Andrew had made the odd trip to Belgravia to visit his parents, staying only for the day, and he was always ready with a reason not to stay overnight.

And now, here he was, standing in his boyhood bedroom, looking out of the window onto the leafy square below, wondering what news tomorrow would bring. He missed Annie and her gentle wisdom, and as he recalled the events and the consequences of that last dinner, he wondered whether his parents ever regretted their treatment of his lovely wife and wished that they had behaved differently. He checked his watch. It was six o'clock, dinner would be at eight as usual. Two long hours, then, he sighed. The conversation with his father had unsettled him. It was obvious that Lord Wellbeloved knew more than he was saying and was preparing for war, even if his mother wasn't.

The Daily Telegraph lay on his bed where he had thrown it, folded at the page that his father had been reading, and there was no mistaking the message that screamed up at him. "Special Sunday War Edition."

Suddenly the room felt airless. The sun was still hot through the open window, and the whisky had made his mouth dry. There was a pitcher of water on the bedside table, and he poured a tumbler full, gulping it down thirstily, but even the water was warm, and he could feel the first nag of a headache, a dull ache over his left eye. He felt sweaty and breathless as he fought down a rising sense of panic. Controlling his trembling fingers, he sat on the side of the bed, unbuttoned his collar, and loosened his shirt, taking a deep breath at the same time. It had been years since he had had one of these attacks, and Annie's voice came back to him. "Move around, Andrew. Go for a walk; just keep telling yourself that this will pass."

One thing was for sure, he had to get out of this room. Perhaps he could just walk around the square, but then someone might see him, and he would have to make conversation. Out of the blue, an image of his old school room swam into his head. The school room in the basement, his old school room, the only place in the whole house that as a small boy, he had felt safe and loved.

The panic subsided, and he opened the bedroom door and stepped out onto the deserted landing. Closing the door quietly behind him, he moved quickly and silently down the stairs and into the hall, praying that the door to the basement would not be locked.

It wasn't. The key was in the door, and it turned smoothly in the lock. He stood for a while, adjusting his eyes to dim coolness, a few steps down, and he was standing at the school room door. The door was slightly ajar, and he reached out a tentative hand and pushed it open. Immediately, he was assailed with the familiar, comforting smell of chalk and linseed oil. A quick glance told him that little had changed. The blackboard was wiped clean now with just a faint shadow of old chalk marks. The walls were still hung with the posters he remembered so well. This one, the history of ancient civilisations, curling away from the wall, then the coloured map of the world which he had, as a boy looked on in wonder when his tutor tapped the map with his cane, pointing out the names of far-off continents. There was his old favourite, the lurid dinosaur poster of pre-historic creatures, their monstrous teeth dripping with blood. How he had loved this room, and he could still remember where everything was kept. A shelf with strips of modelling clay neatly arranged in colours and separated with tissue paper. Next to the clay, the long, thin mysterious boxes of pencils, and he could remember the thrill of receiving a smooth new pencil with a red rubber end and a shiny new red exercise book.

Andrew could recall quite clearly the kindly young tutor sitting at his desk on the raised dais by the blackboard, chalk dust on his waistcoat, spectacles perched on the end of his nose, marking pencil poised, as he blinked short-sightedly at the boy's books.

The desks were still placed in a neat line facing the blackboard. Andrew's desk had always been the middle one, and he stood in front of it now and ran his fingers slowly over the initials carved on the lid and smiled. A wobbly "A" joined up with an even wobblier "W."

His tutor had gently chastised him, warning that if Lord Wellbeloved saw it, Andrew would be punished. But he knew, as Andrew did, that his father never visited the school room, and so the tutor contented himself by issuing Andrew as punishment, a hundred lines, "I must not damage school property."

He opened the desk lid. The inside smelt musty and stale. He touched a dusty corner where, once, an age ago, he had hidden the sticky buns that Cook saved him, and the forbidden barley sugar from Nanny's penny bag. There was a well-thumbed Boys Own Annual, and several blunt pencils, the brass ends flattened and chewed through. He closed the lid and sat on the top of the desk.

The sunlight filtering through a high window was warm on his face, and he closed his eyes, allowing the familiar smell of the school room to take him back to his boyhood, then the dreaded Eton, Oxford, and his first parish, St Mark's, and seeing Annie for the first time on that magical summer evening.

Now, a dream come true, a country parish of his own with Annie by his side. "Come on, Andrew," he told himself firmly. "If there is going to be a war, there is work to be done, and this time tomorrow, you will be back in Shorehill, come what may." He glanced around his old school room one more time, then closed the door firmly and made his way back up the steps.

Roberts was lingering around in the hall, seemingly adjusting flowers on the hall table and glanced sideways as Andrew emerged through the basement door. "Ah, Mr Andrew. I wondered why the basement door was open. Would you like me to lock it for you? Lady Mary said to remind you that dinner is at eight."

Andrew looked at the butler coldly, turned the key in the lock and without replying, bounded up the stairs to his bedroom. "Loathsome man," he muttered under his breath.

During dinner, despite Lady Mary's best efforts to keep the conversation away from the subject of war, it inevitably drifted back to whether Germany would respect little Belgium's neutrality and the consequences for Great Britain if they didn't. Matters were not helped, when much to his wife's intense disproval, Lord Horatio insisted on taking a number of telephone calls throughout the rest of the evening, and at just after ten o'clock, she kissed Andrew briefly, glared furiously at her husband, and swept out of the room.

"Andrew, my dear, I will see you in the morning. I do believe that the weather will hold for Henley. I have left some suitable clothes in your bedroom; we must be there by eleven o'clock."

"Thank you, Mother. Good night."

"Well," Andrew turned to his father who, oblivious of his wife's snub, was chewing thoughtfully on his cigar, "What were the telephone calls that were so important?"

"Germany has invaded Luxembourg and has demanded free passage through Belgium. King Albert and his ministers have refused, claiming that it would be in breach of Belgium's neutrality and independence." His father's response was brutally blunt, and Andrew slumped back in his chair.

"Well, that's that then," he said bleakly. "So, what happens now?"

Horatio Wellbeloved shrugged his shoulders and gave a short bark of laughter. "Well, your mother's plans for a meal at Claridge's will have to be cancelled. Most of the cooks and waiters are either German or French reservists, and they are already gathering at Charing Cross to try and catch a boat train home. Oh, and Keir Hardie is holding a peace rally in Trafalgar Square, for all the good that will do. The Cabinet have been assembled at 10 Downing Street this morning, and again this evening, and I understand the German Ambassador was present at the morning meeting."

Andrew had not taken his eyes off his father's face whilst he was speaking, and he knew that Horatio was telling the truth. Lord Wellbeloved ground his cigar out into the ashtray, flung the last of his drink down his throat, and stood up.

"And now, Andrew, I have to go and break the news to your mother that she will not be hosting tea at Claridge's tomorrow. I will see you at breakfast, my boy."

When Andrew came down to breakfast the next morning, suitably attired in his new clothes, he looked to his mother. "Good morning, Mother. I hope you slept well. Do I pass muster this morning?"

Lady Mary was picking distractedly at the small amount of food on her plate, and she looked up and smiled tightly. "I did not sleep well at all, Andrew, as I am sure you did not. You are very pale this morning."

Andrew had suffered a night of vivid dreams and had woken up violently several times during the night. He helped himself to toast and kippers and a pot of coffee. "I am fine, Mother. Where is Father?"

"Your father is taking breakfast in his study where he has been since five o'clock this morning when he arose to answer the telephone. I hope your father did not wake you. You do look very nice, my dear. Did you find your hat and cane?"

Andrew looked at his Mother's set face and felt a stab of pity. "Yes, I did, Mother. Would you mind if I joined Father?"

Lady Mary shook her head and signalled to the maid to clear the breakfast things. "Andrew, the car will be around at ten o'clock. Please ensure that you and your father are ready."

Andrew gathered the morning papers from the hall table and made his way to his father's study. The study door was slightly open. Andrew knocked and pushed the door open wider. Lord Horatio was seated at a vast desk. The table lamp was on, and Andrew was not sure if his father was sleeping. He walked further into the room, and hearing his footsteps, Horatio swung round in his chair to greet him. Andrew could see that the breakfast tray on the desk in front of him was untouched. Lord Horatio's face was grey and weary, and he rubbed his eyes.

"Good morning, Andrew." He did not bother with pleasantries but went on, "I was just coming to find your mother, but you can save me the trouble. I am going straight to the House this morning, so please let her know that I will be unable to accompany you to Windsor."

At ten o'clock, when Andrew came downstairs with Lady Mary, they found that Lord Horatio had already left the house. Roberts was standing by the entrance door. "The car is ready, madam."

"Thank you, Roberts. Come along, Andrew," she said grimly.

Jimmy the chauffeur opened the car door and touched his hat respectfully, "Good morning, your Ladyship. Good morning, Mr Andrew. The traffic may be heavy today," he said apologetically.

The car weaved slowly through the morning sunshine toward Windsor, and Jimmy was right, the London Streets were crammed with cars and carriages. Union Jacks hung from posts above the shops and here and there through the open car windows they could hear bursts of the national anthem being sung. A strange fever, more than just a Bank Holiday mood, seemed to have gripped the people of London, and there was an air of subdued excitement.

"Are you alright, Mother?" enquired Andrew, looking at his mother's tense jawline.

"Perfectly well, thank you, Andrew. I have a little headache, but I am sure the fresh air will help." She leant her head back and closed her eyes, clearly not in the mood for further conversation.

There was a crumpled newspaper on the seat next to Andrew, and he glanced through it. Canterbury Cricket Week had opened as usual, he read with disinterest, and the Telegraph's theatre programme listed "Kismet" playing at The Globe Theatre, and Carman playing at the Prince of Wales. Life as normal, it would appear, but the inside pages of the Telegraph told of the stark reality of what was really happening on this glorious summer's day. "France on the Brink of War," "Mobilisation of the German Army," and "North Sea sealed by the British Navy." Andrew shuddered, folded the paper, and placed it back on the seat.

"It's not looking good, sir, is it?" Jimmy caught Andrew's eye in the rear-view mirror.

Andrew shook his head. "No, Jimmy, I am very much afraid that, unless a miracle happens, we could find ourselves at war with Germany."

"Not today, Andrew, please. Let us have one day without any more of this ridiculous talk of war. I absolutely forbid it." Lady Mary's voice was sharp.

"I am sorry, Mother. I thought you were asleep, and you are right, we should enjoy the day."

Andrew was not deceived by his mother's apparent denial of the very real prospect of war. He suspected that up until last night, she had refused to believe that anything untoward could happen to her closeted and privileged world, and he felt nothing but pity for her.

Despite the gathering war clouds, the Regatta was proving to be as popular as ever, and the roads were crammed with carriages and cars, but Jimmy drove smoothly to a private area by Brocas Meadows. The meadows were crowded with happy and excited parents and visitors making their way to the riverbank. Lady Mary's mood improved visibly, and she opened her parasol and looked around at the beautifully decorated marquees. She waved her parasol in the direction of the largest marquee, adorned with fluttering union jacks and lettered bunting.

"There, Andrew, there is my group on the riverbank. Do you see them?"

Mary Wellbeloved picked her way lightly across the grass toward the marquee, and a cry went up: "Mary! Over here, my dear, over here! What a beautifully fine day we have, and so well attended." A large, handsome woman in an enormous colourful pyramid of a hat sailed toward them. "Andrew, dear boy, what a treat," she gushed, looking past him over his shoulder. "Where is your father? Where are you hiding the handsome old devil?"

"Mrs Ash-Bowan, how delightful to see you again," Andrew replied politely.

"Horatio sends deep apologies, Edna, but he has been held up on business, however, he hopes to join us later," Lady Mary interrupted smoothly.

The other woman looked shrewdly first at Andrew then at his mother. "No matter, no matter. Come and sit down and let us see what wonderful food you have for us. We already have some delicious hampers, and of course, we have champagne."

As the loud chorus of voices greeted his mother, Andrew leant forward and said quietly, "I'm going for a walk along the river, Mother."

"Don't be long then, darling." His mother's voice was high and light, but she gave him a barely perceptible shake of her head.

Andrew thrust his hands grimly into his trouser pockets and strolled across to the far side of the Brocas, where the grounds rose in a gentle slope and the clamour of the crowd grew fainter. There were just a few people around, sitting quietly on the grass. It was too far from the river to see the races, and he sat down on the warm grass and looked down across the crowded meadow.

Both sides of the riverbank and the punts on the river were packed with chattering, excited spectators, and there were straw boaters, bow ties, and colourful parasols as far as the eye could see. It was quieter up here away from the noise, and he lay back thankfully with his hands behind his head. High up in the clear-blue sky, a kestrel hovered and circled slowly before drifting away, and Andrew could hear his faint cry above the hubbub below. He was tired and dispirited, but the sun on his face slowly relaxed him, and he stretched luxuriously before drifting into a light doze. He dreamt of Shorehill and the clear, sweet river that ran through the village. The voices he heard were not the shrill voices of the privileged crowd below him, but the laughter of the village children, the warm voices of his friends, and the lilt of Annie's voice as she chatted to Bessie. When he woke an hour later, he felt refreshed, clear headed, and calm, and he knew with conviction that it was time to go home. He would not spend one more night in London.

A great shout came from down below, and he could see a line of boats racing to Firework Island, signalling the end of the Regatta, and he made his way down to the marquee. Normally, his mother would stay and enjoy the rest of the afternoon with her friends, but smiling her excuses, she asked Andrew to summon the chauffeur. "Something must have delayed Horatio. We should get back and see what has held him up," she explained charmingly to her protesting friends.

On their way back to the car, barely concealing her anger, she said, "Not only did your father fail to make an appearance, Andrew, but I had to lie and make an excuse for your rudeness when you did not come for the luncheon. The chairman toasted the king, and it was rather jolly. Your absence was noted, and I explained that you were troubled with a headache."

"Then you should not have lied on my behalf, Mother. I am sure that I was not missed," Andrew replied evenly.

On the way back to Chester Square, Lady Mary, despite her brittle gaiety throughout the day, said very little, other than to comment with barely-contained bitterness, "I simply cannot understand why on Earth I had to cancel my dinner at Claridge's this evening. Father says that the waiters and cooks are trying to go back to France. It is most unfair; everyone was so disappointed, and Cecil Ash-Bowan said that it a disgrace. All this commotion is a grand fuss over nothing. His mother has had the most dreadful trouble in Paris. The restaurants will not let you dine unless you can pay in gold or silver." Lady Mary fanned herself with a lace handkerchief. "And another thing, did you see those wretched suffragette women, Andrew, trying to push their disgusting paper on us? Cecil soon told them what for," she pursed her lips in a grim smile.

Andrew gritted his teeth but remained silent, and when he looked up and caught the chauffeur's eye, he grimaced and smiled an apology.

Chester Square was still and quiet as the car purred to a halt outside his parent's house. Andrew jumped out and opened the door for his mother. The chauffeur opened the boot, removed the empty hamper, and handed it to the parlour maid, who was waiting at the top of the basement steps.

"Thank you, Jimmy," Andrew smiled at the chauffeur. "You have a family, I believe?"

The chauffeur touched his cap and nodded. "I do indeed, sir. Five boys and two girls, and now I am told that I am soon to become a grandfather."

"That is wonderful news, Jimmy, congratulations. God bless your family, and I will pray for you all."

Mary Wellbeloved, who was waiting at the bottom of the steps, raised her eyebrows and tapped her foot impatiently. She turned to look at Andrew and opened her mouth to speak, but her son quelled her with a look.

The chauffeur beamed at Andrew. "Thank you, Mr Andrew, and God bless you and your wife."

"Thank you, Jimmy. I will be sure to convey your best wishes to my wife. Would you please wait here for me? I shall collect my case, and then you can take me back to the station if you will. Come, Mother," and Andrew held out his arm to his mother, who took it silently.

Once inside the cool hallway, the ever-present Roberts was hovering in attendance. Mary Wellbeloved handed the butler her gloves and parasol. "Andrew, I understand that you will not be joining us at dinner this evening?"

"No, Mother. I explained when I arrived that I planned to go home after the Regatta."

His mother nodded; her face expressionless. "Then please find your father and let him know that I have a headache and I am going to rest in my bedroom. Roberts, please arrange to have some cold lemonade sent up and make sure that I am not disturbed."

Andrew leant forward and kissed her cold cheek. "I shall say goodbye now then, Mother."

"Goodbye, Andrew."

Andrew watched as straight-backed and elegant Mary Wellbeloved made her way up the staircase. He shook his head, sighed, and went in search of his father. Roberts, without even a glance at Andrew, glided silently across the hall in the direction of the kitchen.

Horatio Wellbeloved was not in his study. He was sitting in the drawing room, staring out of the window, an unlit cigar clenched between his teeth.

"Father, I am sorry to disturb you, but mother says to tell you that she has a headache and has gone to her rooms."

Lord Wellbeloved nodded wearily. "And you my boy, you are off home now, I expect."

"I am, Father. I have said goodbye to Mother. I should go and pack if I am to catch the eight-thirty train. Jimmy is taking me to the station." Andrew paused in the doorway. "What happened at the House, can you say?"

Horatio Wellbeloved paused before replying. "The king has ordered that the army reserves are to be called up on permanent service. Grey made an excellent speech. He has assured the French ambassador that France would have the support of the Royal Navy should the Germans attack. Germany now have until midnight to respond to our ultimatum to respect Belgium's neutrality."

"And if Germany refuses and invades Belgium?"

"Then Andrew, Great Britain will be at war with Germany."

Horatio stood up and walked over to where Andrew was standing immobile in the doorway. In an uncharacteristic gesture, he placed both hands on his son's shoulders. "Take care, Andrew, travel safely, my dear boy, and please give Annie my very best wishes. I will, of course, call the vicarage when there is further news."

"Thank you, Father. I shall, and may God bless you both and keep you safe," Andrew replied bleakly and left the room.

He had no need to pack his suitcase. It had been neatly packed and placed in the centre of the bed. He gave a grim smile, little doubting that Roberts, who seemed to know everything that went on in this house, had anticipated his departure. He paused just once outside his mother's bedroom, touched the door with his fingertips, and whispered the same blessing that he had given his father, "May God bless you, Mother."

On the way back from the Regatta, Andrew had seen the tension and anger on the faces of the men milling around the packed streets.

Suddenly, he could not wait to be away from the city, and when he heard Roberts close the front door firmly behind him, he ran down the steps, and without a backward glance, jumped thankfully into the waiting car. As Andrew left London on that balmy summer evening, the British Embassy in Berlin and the German Embassy in London were under attack from angry mobs, and the Central London Recruiting Depot was swarming with reservists and volunteers.

AUGUST 3RD, 1914

In Shorehill, the Bank Holiday Monday fete had been a great success. The sun had shone from a cloudless sky, and the village was full of visitors arriving in pony traps, dog carts, by train, and buses. By midday, the sun was high in a hot, pale sky, and Lower Meadow was packed with happy people enjoying the displays of plants, flowers, vegetables, and fruit. There was ginger beer, home-made cakes, toffee apples, and donkey rides for the children and a large and noisy beer tent for the men.

Much to the hilarity of the villagers, James and Bernard gamely entered the sack race, falling down several times and then taking part in the fiercely fought tug of war with a neighbouring village. Polly and Annie took it in turns to man the coconut shy, and Annie, standing in for Andrew, did her best not be intimidated by the gimlet-eyed contestants as she awarded the prizes for the best roses at the flower show.

At the end of a near perfect day, the sun warmed, and weary visitors reluctantly left the fields and the riverside to make their way to the buses and trains that would take them home. Few, if any, gave a thought to the deadly menace that was gathering speed and moving relentlessly across the channel to the shores of Great Britain.

James, delighted to be back with Billy Hunter and the blacksmith's twins, had laughed aloud when they good-naturedly teased him about his posh-boy accent. But then, how loudly they cheered when James won the meadow race and when he pulled as hard as any man in the "tug of war." Strolling home through the soft dusk, Polly was laughing with Bernard and describing Bessie's outrage at losing the best cake competition to the Lovett sisters, when James, who had been walking a little ahead of them, suddenly stopped.

He turned to face Bernard and Polly. "Uncle, it has been a wonderful day, but I would like to return to Eton tonight. Most of my chums will be going back tonight. Some had refused to go home for the weekend until they knew what was happening." He looked pleadingly at his Uncle and added simply, "I should be there too, you see."

Bernard looked into the boy's troubled eyes, knowing in his heart of hearts that to try and persuade James to stay would be fruitless. "James, my dear boy, of course I understand, and we are thankful that we had you at home for the fete."

Polly, who had been standing quietly listening, bit her lip and looked away quickly to hide her ready tears.

James put his arm around her. "Don't be sad, Polly. I am only going back a few days early."

"Pay no mind to me, James; I am always sad when you go back anyway. Let's get back to the house, and I will help you to pack. You know you always make such a dreadful mess of it." James grinned at her gratefully, and Polly caught her breath, seeing Estelle's mischievous sparkle once again in those clear, green eyes.

"Lots to do then, James," Bernard said briskly. "Supper first. You must eat before you leave, Aggie will insist."

After supper, as Polly was folding each garment carefully before placing it in the open trunk, she suggested casually, "James, why not wait until tomorrow morning, or wait at least until Andrew gets back from London? The news may not be so bad after all."

James closed his trunk firmly and moved around the bed to give her a hug. "Dearest Poll, if it is not bad news, then I shall get another short leave very soon. Try not to worry, and if I hear anything from Alain, I will let you know."

Heaving his trunk onto the floor, he dragged it out of the bedroom and bumped it down the stairs. Polly smoothed the bed cover, plumped up the pillows, and glanced briefly around the bedroom before following James downstairs.

In the kitchen, Aggie was angrily pounding dough on the floury table. "Is that right Polly? Tip says Master James is leaving tonight. Why is that, I'd like to know? Why is Master James leaving so soon, he has only just arrived, and Tip thinks that we are going to have a war with Germany. Is that why Master James is going back to Eton so soon?" Aggie spoke quickly, furiously stretching and kneading the dough, careless of the flour she was scattering across kitchen floor.

Polly shook her head. "Aggie, James has to get back Eton. If there is to be a war, James said that he has friends who will enlist, and he wants to say goodbye to them," and she frowned at Tip, who was attempting to slide out of the kitchen door.

"I only said to Aggie that there is a chance that we could go to war with Germany," he said sheepishly. "It is what everyone is saying in all the papers."

Polly raised her eyebrows. "Honestly, Tip, at the moment, it is all talk and gossip, no matter what the papers say, and now you have worried Aggie."

Aggie pointed a floury finger at James's battered tuck box standing by the kitchen door. "Master James's food is all packed and ready to go, Polly. I packed it in a hurry, so goodness knows if I have left anything out."

"Thank you, Aggie," Polly said gratefully. "Tip, have you seen Mr Bernard? James is waiting in the hall, and he needs to get to the station if he is to catch the train."

"Mr Bernard said that he would not be long. He said to get the trunk loaded up and wait for him. I'll pop out now and get Pepper into the trap."

James came back into the kitchen and looked around anxiously. "Where is Uncle, Polly? He is not in the library."

"He won't be far away, James," Polly replied soothingly. "Now say goodbye to Aggie.

James walked around the table and caught Aggie up in an enormous hug. "Dear Aggie, please don't be cross, because you do look awfully cross, you know," he teased.

Aggie shook her head and pushed him away gently. "Now look at you, your nice coat all covered in flour. Go on, Master James, off you go and take care of yourself." she scolded.

"I hope you haven't forgotten to put plenty of your apple pie in my tuck box, Aggie. The fellows do so look forward to my tuck." James hoisted the overloaded tuck basket up in his arms and followed Polly out of the kitchen door.

In the stable yard, Pepper was clearly excited at the prospect of an outing and was pawing the ground impatiently. When the little piebald spotted James and Polly walking across the yard, she tossed her head and snorted. "Steady up girl," Tip said, holding her rein tightly. James rubbed her velvet nose gently "What a treat, eh, Pepper? Just when you thought you had been stalled for the night."

There was a loud whinny from the end stall. "Now I suppose I shall have to give old Captain a turn around the yard when I get back. Listen to him in there," Tip grumbled. "The old boy does not like to be left out. Come along then, young James, give me a hand up with this trunk."

After the luggage was safely strapped on the trap, and there was still no sign of Bernard, James was getting fidgety. "Where on Earth is Uncle? I don't want to miss that train."

"He won't be far away, James, and we still have plenty of time," Polly replied calmly. "He may have walked across to the church. We shall go and find him."

Tip watched them go, the boy now as tall as Polly. "I'll wait out front," he called, and flicking the reigns, he trotted the impatient pony out of the yard.

On this fragrant summer evening, whilst the world trembled on the brink of war, in the quiet churchyard, Bernard Maycroft stood in silent prayer, resting gentle hands on the bronze statue of the girl child. High above his bent head, the soft, warm breeze barely moved the rustling leaves, but still a few spiralled down slowly to settle on the marble plinth. He stared at them, stark green on the cold, white marble, and he bent to pick one up and rest it on his open palm. The leaf was summer green, not yet tinged with autumn gold, and Bernard shook his head. "It's too soon. It's far too soon, but still they fall," he said brokenly as the leaf floated down to the ground. Standing by the low wall at the edge of the graveyard, Polly and James watched him. Out of the shade of the trees, the evening sun was still strong, and Polly brushed a few damp strands of hair away from her face, at the same time wiping away the tears that trickled slowly down her cheeks. James, head bent, shuffled his feet, uneasy and helpless to comfort her. He wanted to call out to his uncle, but the words would not come. Bernard looked up and saw them standing, watching, and he raised a hand in an awkward half-wave. With gentle fingers he lovingly traced the tight curls on the little bronze head one more time, and then he left the enclosure, closed the gate softly, and walked toward them. Bernard reached out and rested an arm across his nephew's bony, young shoulders. "Come along then, James. You have a train to catch."

When it was time for the final goodbye, Polly watched them go and waited until she could no longer hear Pepper's little hooves on the cobbles, then walked slowly back into the kitchen. "Are you alright Poll? Don't fret. Master James will be home again soon. Come and have some supper with me and Bessie." Aggie put a comforting arm around Polly's shoulder.

Polly shook her head. "I am alright, Aggie. I am going to tidy James's room, then I think I will walk over and see Annie. Bernard said that he would call into the vicarage after dropping James at the station and wait for Andrew to come home."

Aggie sighed, and unable to bear the sudden veil of sadness that seemed to have returned to Riverside, shrugged herself into her old coat, rammed her big black hat on her head, locked the kitchen door, and hurried out to Ernie and Bessie's cottage.

High up in her bedroom, Polly opened the window seat, reached in, and pulled out a roll of paper and a cardboard box. She carried them across to her bed and gently unrolled the paper and smoothed out her precious drawing. It was a charcoal sketch of a star-studded winter sky and a full moon above a bank of snow-tipped bare branches. Framed in the window, with heads together, and looking up at the night sky, the artist had drawn two figures. It was of a woman and a small, curly-haired boy kneeling on a window seat. In the bottom, right-hand corner, Alain Trouve had written, "Moonstruck." The drawing had been Alain's special gift to Polly after she told him that when James was little, they used to sit on the window seat and talk to the Man in the Moon.

Polly stared at the drawing for a long time, then laid it tenderly to one side. She lifted the lid of the box, took out a sheer silk peignoir, and held it up against her face as if to breathe in the very essence of its lost owner. Next, she lifted out James's christening shawl, then a silver and tortoiseshell comb. Finally, tucked safely in a corner and wrapped in a soft, damask cloth and still emitted the delicate fragrance of "Mon Cheri," a beautiful glass perfume bottle. Finally, she took out two envelopes: one filled with postcards, tickets, and menus from the Titanic. The other envelope, she opened carefully and shook the contents onto the bed. Four tiny purple sweets delicately shaped like Parma Violets and a handful of mother-of-pearl chips from the casino at Le Touquet. She touched each one in turn, then reached for her precious notebook and read again the last entry written by Estelle.

"Tell me what to do, Estelle. What should I do?" Polly whispered. But there was no answer for Polly, and with shaking hands, she gently replaced her treasures and closed the box.

After seeing James settled on his journey back to Eton, Bernard went back to where Tip was waiting for him. "Take Pepper home, Tip. I am going to the vicarage. It's a nice evening, so I will walk."

With a heavy heart, he strolled through the soft night, and it seemed to him that the evening birdsong was sweeter, there was music in the rush of the river, and the stars glimpsed through the canopy of trees appeared brighter and clearer.

Annie greeted him with a welcoming smile. "Bernard, my dear, do come in."

"I am unsettled, my dear Annie. May I gain refuge with you until Andrew returns? James was eager to return to Eton, and I have just put him on the train."

Annie grasped his arm and drew him in. "Then you shall join us for supper. Bessie has left a cold chicken and some lettuce and tomatoes from her allotment. Andrew will be so pleased to see you."

In Berkshire, in Oak Lodge, Mary Ryan closed the story book, tucked the covers over a drowsy Rupert, and kissed him gently on the forehead. "Goodnight, Rupert. Goodnight Bear," she whispered. Across the hall, Sadie's door was closed, and Mary listened outside for a while. Sadie had been troublesome at night recently, not wanting to go to bed and calling out in the night, but all was quiet now, and Mary Ryan made her way downstairs to write letters to James and to Bernard.

Mrs Brent was laying the table ready for the morning breakfast, and Brent, unable to settle, was walking around the grounds of Grieves Manor. It was a beautiful evening, and the setting sun was reflected in the still, dark waters of the lake. He paused by the old boathouse and looked back across the lawns at Grieves Manor. Was it only two short years ago that the family were all there, Lord Archie, Lady Rose, George, Jenny, and the twins and the maids, Dottie and little Belle? On a summer evening such as this, the doors would have been flung open, and there would be lights, laughter, and music echoing around the lovely gardens. Filled with sadness, Brent turned away from the silent house and walked back in the direction of Oak Lodge.

Through the trees, Brent could see a light at the top of the house, and he paused to look up. It was coming from Sadie's bedroom, and she was leaning out of the window as still as a statue, just staring out across the tops of the trees. There was something odd about her stillness, and Brent shivered and hurried inside.

"That girl is not right," Brent had confided to his wife recently. "She wanders around talking to herself when she thinks nobody is around and laughs as well, a funny secret laugh, and when she looks at you with those strange eyes, well, it fair gives me the willies, I can tell you."

Mrs Brent sighed. "Poor little thing. She seemed to be doing so well, but I have noticed a few little things lately. I did have a word with Mary Ryan and told her I was worried. Rupert seems a little scared of her sometimes. Sadie can be very sharp with him. Mary promised to keep an eye on her, and Mary is very good with her."

On that same summer evening, in a tiny, terraced house in Chislehurst, Joe McBride, packed and ready to join his ship at Scapa Flow, stood looking down at the neatly-tied cardboard box sitting on his narrow bed. The name scrawled on the box read, "Polly Dawes." Inside the box, a soft grey fur coat was wrapped in layers of tissue paper. Joe took a clean sheet from the linen cupboard, wrapped it twice around the box, and slid it under the bed as far as it would go. Then, slinging his kit bag over his shoulder, he ran down the stairs to say a final goodbye to his tearful aunt.

When the nine-thirty train from London puffed its way into Shorehill Station, Andrew was the only passenger to alight. Percy, as usual, was waiting on the platform. "Good evening, Vicar," Percy touched his cap.

"Good evening, Percy. Did the fete go well?"

"Yes, Vicar, a great success. Mother won a prize for her scones. I had to put a drop of whisky in her cocoa to calm her down; she was that excited."

"Well, that is good news. I expect Annie will tell me all about it, but now I bid you good night."

Andrew gave Percy a distracted smile and hurried out of the station. Percy wandered back to the station house. "Vicar don't seem himself, Mother," he said and received a gentle snore in reply from the old lady slumped in an armchair by the fireside.

Before Andrew could put his key in the lock, the door of the vicarage flew open, and Annie greeted him with a delighted smile.

Andrew gathered her into his arms and gave her a fierce hug. "Annie, it is so wonderful to be home at last."

Annie drew away and looked at him closely. "Darling Andrew, oh my poor dear, you do look exhausted. Was it that dreadful?"

"Yes, indeed it was, but it is not just the parents, Annie. Nothing has changed much there." He forced a laugh, but his face was grim. "The news from London is not good."

Annie's heart missed a beat. "Bernard is here, and so is Polly. James went back to Eton tonight, all a little unexpected, and it has rather upset Bernard. James insisted on going back, and Bernard said that there was not a chance of changing his mind, even though Polly asked him to wait until you returned from London."

"Well, of course he's gone back. After all, he is an Eton boy, and I expect they all went rushing back at the prospect of war. They will be like lambs to the slaughter, Annie." Andrew fought to keep the anger out of his voice.

"Hush. Don't let Bernard hear you say that, Andrew. Come and sit down. I have saved you some supper."

The look on Andrew's face when he followed Annie into the kitchen told Bernard everything that he needed to know. Andrew greeted Bernard and Polly with a tired smile and a shake of his head. "We must be prepared for the worst, I am afraid. Father is at the House and has promised to call when he has news. Bernard, Annie says that James has gone back to Eton?"

Bernard nodded. "Yes, he says that some of his house chums will be old enough to be given a commission, and he wants to be there for the goodbye ceremony."

There was a silence, and Andrew pushed his barely-touched food to one side. "I am sorry, my dear. I have lost my appetite. You know, Bernard, as I left London there were already crowds of men rushing to recruit."

Bernard rubbed weary hands across his face. "I know, and we should be prepared for the news to break tomorrow. There are many from the village who will enlist; my men from the mill and from the farms."

Horatio Wellbeloved rang at twelve-thirty. "We are at war with Germany, Andrew," he said bleakly. "London has gone mad; thousands and thousands are outside the palace singing the national anthem and shouting for the king. It has begun."

"Thank you, Father, give my love to Mother." Andrew put his arm around Annie, who was standing next to him, and looked at his friends. "We are now at war with Germany. God help us all."

It was in the early hours of the morning when Bernard and Polly finally left the vicarage to walk back to Riverside. Before they left, they agreed that Andrew would put a notice in the post office suggesting a general meeting in the Hop Vine at six that evening.

At seven o'clock the same morning, summoned by a grim-faced Tip, William Hunter and several of the mill managers were gathered around the kitchen at Riverside. Bernard looked at the men gathered in front of him, and his message was brief.

"As you all know, we are now at war with Germany. Andrew Wellbeloved has suggested that we meet in the Hop Vine at six this evening. Everybody is anxious, I know, but until we have more news, we should carry on as normal. I would be grateful if you could let as many people know about the meeting tonight as possible. Grace Peabody has posted a notice in the post office. Thank you, gentlemen."

Aggie, who had been clattering around the kitchen, sniffing loudly, began serving breakfast to the silent men, but Bernard refused breakfast, and guessing that the telephone lines would be busy, he went into the library to call James.

"Uncle. What news! So sorry, but I must be quick, everyone wants to call home. Lots of my chums are leaving, and there is to be a grand parade of the Officer's Training Corp. It's all very exciting here." James's voice was wistful, and Bernard knew with sad certainty that James was wishing that he was old enough to join them.

James ended with a rush. "Uncle, be sure to give my love to everyone at home, especially to Polly and to everyone at Oak Lodge in case I do not get time to call. Tell Rupert to take good care of Bear. Let me know if you hear anything from Alain or the Comte. I'm not sure what leave I will get now, but I will let you know. Bye, Uncle." Bernard was standing and staring out of the library window when Polly put her head around the door.

"Was that James? Did you manage to get through to Eton?" she asked eagerly.

Bernard nodded. "It was, Polly. I am so sorry, he had to be quick, all of the boys wanted to call home, but he sent you his love."

Before Polly could reply, the telephone rang again.

"Bernard, thank goodness. I have been trying to call you," Mary Ryan was clearly upset, and her normally calm voice wobbled,

"Brent has just brought the morning papers in. So, it is happening. I mean, we are really at war with Germany. Sadie saw the paper before I did, and the poor child is so upset. Where is James? Is he with you, Bernard? He is too young to enlist. I told Sadie he was. I am right, aren't I?"

"Mary, my dear, I was about to call you. James returned to Eton a little earlier than planned. He wanted to get back in time for the service for the older boys who will of course be enlisting. As you quite rightly say, James is far too young, so please tell Sadie not to worry. I have just spoken with James, and he is well. I will be calling Comte Trouve again this morning to see what I can find out about Alain."

A sudden thought struck Bernard. In all the turmoil, he had completely forgotten about Clarence Grieves-Croft. "Mary, have you heard from Clarence?"

"No, I have heard nothing at all, Bernard. Should I try and call him?"

"No, don't worry. I will call him, although I suspect, like a lot of other people, he will be trying to arrange a passage back to England. Mary, would you like to bring Sadie and Rupert to Riverside?"

"That is kind of you Bernard, but perhaps we should stay here. Rupert is settled in school, which is the best place for him, and I will tell Sadie that James and Alain are safe and well. Please let me know if you hear from Clarence and the Count. Tell Polly that the children are fine, and we look forward to seeing her. I know she will be worrying."

Just as Bernard had predicted, Clarence Grieves-Croft was already on his way back to England, regretfully leaving his hilltop villa high above La Touquet. The loyal and tearful staff had been paid generously and dispatched back to their families. It had broken his heart to leave his home and friends, but Clarence's one consolation was that his beloved hounds would be safe in the care of his manservant Etienne and his wife Martha.

Later that morning, after Bernard had made several more unsuccessful calls to Chamonix, he managed to get a connection, and the telephone was eventually answered by the Comte himself. "Count, I am so pleased to hear your voice. James says that he has not heard from Alain for a while, and we are all so are worried about you both."

"Bernard, my friend, we are well, thank you. Alain is staying with some family friends in Berne, as I have been recalled to Paris. It is good that you stand with us, my friend, although there was never had any doubt that you would. A truly terrible turn of events for all of us, and I am fearful for our beloved France. I trust everyone is well. How is James? Alain is anxious to know."

"We are all well, Count, and James has gone back to Eton for the autumn half. Everyone will be delighted that you and Alain are safe. I know that it will be difficult, but please try and keep in touch with us and give Alain our love and say that his sketches still cause great amusement with his friends in the village."

"I will do my best, dear friend, and ask your wonderful village to pray for us."

There was a click and then silence, and Bernard, filled with a heavy feeling of dread, replaced the receiver.

At six o'clock that evening, the Hop Vine was full of people, some talking quietly in groups, some calling out loudly to arriving friends. Others gathered outside, and there was an air of subdued excitement as Bernard and Andrew edged their way inside. Percy, who had seen them arrive, held up his hands to hush the chatter, and shouted, "Vicar and Mr Bernard are here now, everyone," and puffed out with importance, he shuffled into a space next to Ernie Brown, who frowned at him. "No need to shout, Percy. You're not in the station now." There was a ripple of laughter, then an expectant hush.

Andrew looked around the crowded bar, recognizing most of the faces in front of him. Farmer Pat O'Donnell, Bridget, his wife, and their four sons, Brin O'Donnell, Ernie Brown, and his cousin, Jacob Brown, and next to Jacob, his friend and neighbour Willy Dales. There was William Hunter, Dorothy, and their boy, Billy, and many others, some from his congregation and others not.

Polly, Bessie, Annie, and Aggie were seated by the back door with Jacob's sixteen-year-old twins, Toby and Theo, whose faces were alight with excitement. Little Jacky Dales, their faithful companion, was, as always, seated next to them and some younger boys shuffling and giggling, scarcely believing their luck that they were inside the Hop Vine. Blanche and Grace Dove were sitting with Grace Peabody. The Ancients, the old men of the village, were at their usual table, supping their beer and watching the goings-on with interest.

Bernard walked across to the bar and spoke quietly to Mick Carey. Mick, looking at Andrew's pale, tense face, measured a shot of brandy and handed it to him. "Warms the throat nicely, Andrew," he smiled.

Andrew nodded gratefully and took a deep breath. "Good friends and neighbours, I do not have to tell you all that we are now at war with Germany. I know that it is very worrying for you all because we do not know what will happen next. Mr Maycroft and I feel that we should have a place in the village where we can all meet and keep in touch and help our neighbours and friends. We must take care of the older people who live alone, because there will be food shortages for some, so we all need to help each other. I did think of the village hall, but my wife tells me that it is far too small and damp."

This was greeted with quiet laughter.

"Polly had the idea that the old barn in Lower Meadow could be a good meeting place. It is large enough and close to the village. The roof needs some work, and there are other things that will have to be done before we can use it, but Pat and Brin have offered to carry out the repairs."

There was a round of polite applause, and Pat ducked his head shyly.

Andrew carried on. "I can see that it will be a great comfort to meet up with our friends and neighbours in these uncertain times. It will be something for the village to focus on, I am sure that you will agree, and once the repairs are completed, the barn will be somewhere safe for the younger children to play as well as the older ones. I am sure that Pat and Brin would welcome any help, so that we could have the barn ready as soon as possible."

When Andrew had finished speaking, the offers of help came in thick and fast and it was agreed that the eager work force of volunteers should meet at the barn the following day. Slowly, people began to make their way home. The Brown twins and Jacky Dales ran ahead to slip under the bridge with some tobacco stolen from Jacob's pouch and hoped that the war would not end before they were old enough to enlist. Mick Ryan, with a heavy heart, wiped the bar down and stacked the chairs, whilst Bridget O'Donnell, walking home with a silent husband, was gripped by a nameless terror when she thought of her two eldest sons.

An exhausted and travel-weary Clarence Grieves-Croft arrived back to a chaotic Charing Cross Station, packed with French and German families waiting on the Boat Train platform anxious to return home. Before he left his pink villa in the hills above Le Touquet, Clarence had the foresight to book rooms in the Charing Cross Hotel, and now, catching the eye of a harassed porter, he offered him a generous tip to take his trunk into the hotel lobby. The hotel, as anticipated, was teeming with anxious travellers, those who had left Europe in haste, and others unable to secure a passage back across the channel. Without waiting to find a porter, Clarence took his key from the besieged desk clerk and manhandled his trunk to the lift. Thankfully, his room on the first floor was close by the lift, and he wearily dragged the trunk through the door. Clarence collapsed onto the bed, and too tired to reflect on the next step of his journey, he fell into a deep slumber.

At Riverside, Bernard paced restlessly around the library. Polly and Aggie had gone back to the vicarage with Annie and Bessie. He glanced at the clock on the mantelpiece, nearly nine o'clock, and knocking the remainder of his pipe embers into the fireplace, he made his way quietly out into the dark, silent hall. He shrugged a coat across his shoulders, unlocked the heavy front door, and slipped out into the cool darkness. It was a breezy night with thin, racing black clouds, and there was a smell of approaching autumn. Pulling his coat collar up around his neck, he thrust his hands deep inside his coat pocket and strode quickly away from the house. The churchyard was quiet, but there was a light in the church porch, and he pushed the old door open and breathed in deeply.

Everything about this little church was so dear and familiar to him, the waxy smell from the brightly burning candles, the earthen altar vases on their pedestals, now filled with crimson and gold chrysanthemums from Ernie Brown's garden. At Easter, the old vases would be tumbling over with the soft colours of spring, and in the summer the church would be filled with the heavenly scent from the roses and lavender from Grace Peabody's little garden.

Bernard walked slowly up the flagstone aisle, stopping at the heavily carved, dark wood rood screen. He looked through at the sacristy and altar, and the pew where long ago, he had stood as a choir boy. By his feet, embedded in the flagstone floor, the brass plaques recorded the births and deaths of his ancestors. There was the pulpit where generations of clergy had sought to save the souls of the congregation. Left open on the rosewood lectern, was a battered old Bible with a frayed cover and yellowing pages, and mounted on a carved stone pillar, the hymn-holder displayed the numbers of the hymns to be sung at the morning service.

Above him, high in the old oak beams, he could hear the faintest of rustles, a shifting sound, and he smiled. For as long as anyone could remember, kestrels had nested in the old church and bell tower. Bernard could remember his father frowning a warning to an excited young Henry, when, in the middle of a long, rambling sermon by the resident vicar, Henry had pointed a finger upwards and in a high childish whisper, said, "Bernie, quick look. There are angels in the roof."

For hundreds of years, everything in this hallowed old church had remained the same. But beyond the sanctuary of his beloved St Dominic's, the world was spiralling out of control, hurtling toward death and destruction, and suddenly Bernard felt an urge to be back at Riverside, back in the warmth and safety of his home, and he tugged on the heavy door and hurried outside.

In the short time he had been inside the church, a strengthening wind had chased away the clouds, and the moon shone down from a starry sky, but there was one more thing he had to do before he went home. Bernard walked through the filigree enclosure, stood underneath the cherry tree, and laid tender hands on Estelle's child bronze. It was cold now, much colder, and Bernard shivered. An unknown and terrifying world awaited them all tomorrow, and he knelt on the sweet-smelling chamomile grass and prayed. "Take care of our boy, Estelle. Watch over him and protect him. Keep him safe."

As Bernard walked through the whispering darkness of the churchyard, the drums of war were thundering their unstoppable way across the English Channel to Great Britain.

THE END

ABOUT THE AUTHOR

M S Talbot is a Kent based Estate Agent who has always been fascinated in the period homes that she valued and loves to explore the histories of the families who have lived in them. The location of the book is based on a combination of the many lovely Kent villages she has visited over the years. She has always had a deep love of books and is an avid reader.

ALSO BY M S TALBOT

Watch for the next two books in the series:

Spirits of the River

Polly's Diary

Printed in Poland
by Amazon Fulfillment
Poland Sp. z o.o., Wrocław